The Magic of Time

~~~

By

Patricia Grace Joyce

February 15, 2013
For Ron ~
Thank you for your continued
love & support! May all
of your dreams come true...
with Love & Light,
Trisha
xo

The Magic of Time

~~~

By

Patricia Grace Joyce

Countinghouse Press, Inc.
Bloomfield Hills, Michigan

The Magic of Time: ISBN 978-0-9786191-4-5 Hardcover,
ISBN 978-0-9786191-6-9 Trade paperback.

Cover design by Sans Serif, Saline, Michigan.
Printed by Color House Graphics, Grand Rapids, Michigan.
Published by Countinghouse Press, Inc., 6632 Telegraph Road, Bloomfield Hills, MI 48301. Phone 248.642.7191.
Email: nuhuguenot@aol.com; web: www.countinghousepress.com

This is a work of fiction. All persons and names are fictional, as are most places. Any resemblance to actual persons, living or dead, is entirely coincidental. Where real places are mentioned, they are used in a fictional context, and events described as occurring in those places did not actually occur.

Dedication

For My Parents,

Sadie Grace Joyce and John William Joyce *(Deceased 4/19/2007)*. I am eternally grateful for your unconditional love, support and encouragement. Like the rays of a lighthouse beacon, you have taught me to trust and to have faith, guiding me to navigate the ever changing seas of life. With the magic of time, all will be well. There is nothing to fear when you listen to your heart

Acknowledgments

My sincere gratitude goes to my agent, Diane S. Nine at Nine Speakers, Inc. Thank you for always believing in me, and for your continued time, efforts and persistence on my behalf. You have taught me so much about the world of publishing. To my publisher, Leonard Charla and Elizabeth DuMouchelle at Countinghouse Press, Inc. Thank you for your support, guidance and for taking a chance on me as a first-book author.

To my attorney, Darin M. Frank at DMF Law, and his law partner Jill Varon, and legal assistant, Blanca Andrade. Thank you for your friendship, support, generosity, time, and legal advice.

With love and appreciation to my wonderful family. Your wisdom, unconditional love, continued guidance and support have truly been a Godsend...Sadie Grace Joyce, Hon. Kathleen Coffey, Joseph Coffey, Sr., Jacqueline Coffey, Joe Coffey, Patricia Coffey, Michael J. Joyce, Martha Olsen Joyce, Shannon Joyce, Katie Joyce, John and Lynne Joyce, Mike Joyce, Jennifer Joyce, Mary Jo and Vinny Cavaliere, Karen Joyce and Marco Franchini, Sharon Tuttle, Annie Tuttle, Elizabeth Tuttle, Brian Lawrence, Michael Lawrence, Kevin O'Brien, Michele and Peter Farnung, Jack Farnung, Birkly Farnung and John Cola.

Wit love and gratitude to my loved ones who have returned to their Spiritual home. May your loving light continue to embrace us . . .Giuseppe Aluia (Deceased 4/30/1966), Grazia Aluia (Deceased 6/20/1980), Joseph Aluia (Deceased 10/1/1981), Josephine Nina Aluia (Deceased 11/11/2010), Claire D. Cola (Deceased 3/11/2010), Anna Griffin (Deceased 2/1970), Maurice J. Griffin (Deceased 4/1/1961), Elizabeth K. Joyce (Deceased 12/28/1977), John William Joyce (Deceased 4/19/2007), William Joyce (Deceased 10/9/1947), Sandra Lawrence (Deceased

3/20/2001), Joseph R. Lawrence (Deceased 5/23/2002), and Vivian E. Lawrence (Deceased 7/10/1999).

With gratitude to Dennis L. Wood, M.D., *F.A.C.S (Deceased 12/21/2006)* Cedars-Sinai Medical Center in Los Angeles, California; who encouraged me to follow my passion. Your skillful care, guidance, love and compassion were not only admirable, but exceptional.

With sincere appreciation to the entire medical community at Cedars-Sinai Medical Center in Los Angeles, California; especially Peter J. Julien, M.D., Lyle D. Kurtz, M.D., Sabrina O. Falkner, M.D (Snellville, GA), Mae M. Ushigome, M.D. and Alan S. Zaentz, M.D. Thank you for all that you did for me and continue to do for so many.

Special thanks to Harold A. Lancer, M.D., F.A.A.D and his staff. Your friendship, generosity, sense of humor, encouragement and medical expertise have given me the self-confidence to move forward again on my life path.

With sincere gratitude and appreciation to Dr. Brian L. Weiss and Dr. Adrian Finkelstein, for your contributions of research, studies and writing involving past lives and the process of past life regression.

Additional thanks to my aunt Josephine Nina Aluia *(Deceased 11/11/2010)*. Not only did you teach me to play an awesome game of rummy, but, I can still hear your words of encouragement, "Never give up!"

To the residents, staff, administration and volunteers at Detroit Baptist Manor, Farmington Hills, Michigan, especially Liz Akins, Nejla (Nancy) Atiyeh, Vincent Bailey, Gail Baker, Kathie Baker, Theresa Bellamy, Theresa Biendit, Fatou Ceesay, Mimi Chen,

Nikeshia Daffin, James Darby, Cynthia Donahoo, Elizabeth Goleski, Katie Goleski, Ryan Goleski, Kendra Graham, Keisa Hampton, Michelle Hanson, Lorraine Hayden, Melanie Hibbard, Marilyn Hollis, Jyothi Joseph, Tyiana King, Bonnie Leeberman, Calvin Lyons, Joan Matheson, Oliver Mensah, Steve Minisci, Rajesh Mohindra, Sandi Nickel, Awuraama Oppon, LaShonda Phillips, Vidya Ramurthy, Catherine Richards, Ruth Reuter, Sherri Shaul, Jackie Sherbrook, Tyler Slone, Flo Smith, Diane Tolasky, Jean Turner, Shannon Turner and Adrian Williams. Through your dedication, love and kindness, you have taught me to count my many blessings.

To William F. Rabaut, Esq., Detective Terry Antrikin, Fr. Brian Chabala, Chiarina (Rina) Tonon, Mary Jane Borich and David Bowlin...your love, compassion, humor and guidance in assisting me and Josephine N. Aluia were truly a blessing.

To the entire medical community at Henry Ford Hospice and Henry Ford West Bloomfield Hospital, West Bloomfield, Michigan. Thank you for all that you did for me and Josephine N. Aluia, especially Rashid Alsabeh, M.D., Monika Grewal, M.D., Lynne C. Johannessen, M.D, Vera Khasileva, M.D., Nabil Khoury, M.D., Jane King, R.N., Siri Levi, M.D., Jenny Minor, R.N., Zafarullah Muhammad, M.D., Reyne Nowicki, R.N. and Alkesha Rogers, R.N.

To my "Dream Team" in Savannah, Georgia...Amy Bradley, Mark Bradley, Esq., Paul Bradley, M.D., Barbara Sutker-Rubin (Charleston, West Virginia) and Thomas R. Herndon, Esq. Your love, guidance, humor, advice, support and encouraging words helped me to heal.

Additional special thanks go to the intuits, metaphysical healers, psychics, spirit messengers, sensitives, light workers, earth-angels, mentors, and astrologers who have provided loving insight, communication and guidance to me through Spirit...Bill Attride, Andrea Blake, Karen Bruce, Victoria Bruce, Barbara Droke *(Deceased),* Gus Estrada, John Farahi, Teresa Gamage, Doree Glaser, Betty Greenberg *(Deceased),* Faith Griffin, Soledad Haren, Marcia Holtzman, Serena Hua, Elizabeth Joyce, Fay Koliai, Elyce Larsen, Arthur Lawrence, Lauren Liebowitz, Heidi Mahoney, Patricia McLaine, Iman Mohamed, Vicki Monroe, Sr. Sheila O'Friel, Roberta Stillman Parry, Brenda Jiron Prince, Judy Pugatch, Kathleen Robinson, Linda Salvin, Angela Siuta, Victoria St. Cyr, Leigh Stewart, Geraldine Whitney, Claire C. Matthews (Deceased 2/25/1986), Margaret W. O'Friel, Paul G. O'Friel (Deceased 7/28/2007), Julie Orr, John Orr (Deceased 9/15/2012), Susan G. Schaefer, Esq., Annie Pinatelli Winkleman (Deceased 6/29/2010), and Cathy Carrasco-Zanini *(Deceased 10/26/2011).*

Last, but not least, I am grateful for my amazing friends. You are truly earth-angels, standing by me in life with support, love, laughter, encouraging words...and always a good bottle of wine!

Thank you all. This book would not have been possible without your presence in my life.

Patricia Grace Joyce
Los Angeles, CA
September, 2012

Preface

Life takes us down many paths, a journey with signs along the way that ultimately reveal our true personal destiny. That is, if only we take notice and choose to observe and listen to the signals and cues along the way. Each and every one of us has an inner voice. Some often refer to this voice as intuition, a higher power, a spiritual guide, a gut instinct, an energy or simply just a knowing deep within our hearts and souls...a feeling or sensation that seems to speak to us and guides us to realize our true purpose, ultimately leading to the discovery of personal fulfillment on our path in this lifetime.

Ever since I can remember being a small child, my intuition has been a source of valuable insight in my life. At a very early age, I had the ability to hear, feel and observe certain signs and cues; a source of information that was revealed to me by a little voice within...a gut instinct within my heart and soul. Some of this information came to me through a simple "knowing" and oftentimes in revelations through exceptionally lucid dreams.

Of course, as a child I was confused and frightened by many of the things that did occur in my dreams and during waking hours...the appearance of spirits in my room at night, the vivid nightmares, the sleepwalking, blinking of lights and numerous other instances that most parents would simply regard as a child's overactive imagination. I always sensed that I was different from other children. Extremely independent and drawn to the creative arts, I preferred an "unconventional" approach to doing things. Let's just say that I never colored within the lines! Fortunately, I grew up within a large family with five other siblings and two dedicated parents who were nurturing, warm, compassionate, and supportive loving souls.

Yet, as we attempt to live our human existence on earth, personal crises occur in our lives every day. Tragedy and suffering are always a part of life. These situations intimidate, confuse and often distract us along our life path. However, through personal experience, I have come to the realization that it is in these times of disorientation that an individual has the greatest opportunity to transform their life and grow through learned lessons. But, one must also remember they do have a choice as to how they respond in these situations and this will ultimately affect their transformation.

This transformation, if focused upon surmounting the obstacles, can positively affect the individual as well as his/her loved ones. It is in one's darkest hour that a person must confront their issues and push to move forward in life... to evolve and discover their true life path.

Of course you may be thinking that this is easier said than done. How often has each of us experienced losses in life? This varies by individual. Yet, if we have faith, trust and listen to our heart–our little voice within, our continued efforts will guide us to find our strength and our personal power to push forward again within our lives.

My own personal crises in life were to become the primary motivators and essence for my writing this book. Among numerous others, these crises included a dysfunctional nine-year marriage, an arduous separation and divorce, eventually leading to my being diagnosed with breast cancer.

In 1991 my unraveling marriage ultimately fell apart. After my divorce in 1993, I chose to move cross-country from Savannah, Georgia to Los Angeles, California in an effort to put the pieces of my heart and my life back together again...to start my life over again, and to find some solace and peace of mind living by the sea.

Trying to make some sense of a difficult, failed marriage, I yearned to discover who I really was deep down inside. Yet, as time passed, I found myself still stuck within my emotional pain and grief and not moving forward six-years after the divorce was final.

My creative spirit and passion felt as if they had died along with my marriage. I no longer painted. I stopped working with my clay. I no longer wrote my poetry and song lyrics. I stopped taking photographs. Sometimes I could not find it within me to even listen to music. It merely brought back too many difficult memories. Emotionally, I felt as if I was dying a slow death. I even stopped writing. In truth, I felt as if my heart and soul had passed-on and died. To deal with my emotional pain, I chose to avoid it. It was easier for me to simply not discuss it in detail with anyone…to pretend it never happened.

In reality, my greatest fear was to open myself emotionally again. I avoided getting close emotionally in my relationships. I intentionally made the decision to place my work first, hiding behind it, like a veil to overcome my uneasiness and discomfort in social situations. To avoid finding true intimacy and to avoid learning to trust again, I was always working–day and night, seven days a week.

Well, this can only go on for so long until the body and mind need to heal. I ignored my intuition–all the cues, signals, symptoms or clues that my body was in distress in any way, shape or form. I just kept working and avoiding my pain, making myself and my life more and more out of synch with the natural order of the Universe. Every time my despair chose to rear its ugly little head, I chose to push my emotional pain deeper within.

On Saturday, February 27, 1999 I had a sudden awakening or more commonly known and referred to as "a huge wake-up call" when I had a conversation with a girlfriend, Linda Salvin. Linda is a gifted metaphysical healer, medical intuit and a psychic. Over the years while I lived in Los Angeles, we had become friends. I have always been drawn and attracted to "unusual" individuals in my life and likewise, they seem to be drawn to somehow finding me.

With both of us juggling busy schedules, Linda and I would try to get together to see a movie, have dinner or merely just to talk as girlfriends. February 27, 1999 was one of those days when we met and sipped a cup of coffee in her living room to catch up on news and share some time together. I clearly remember that Saturday afternoon as we spoke to each other. Linda suddenly interrupted our conversation by telling me that she felt there was something wrong with me.

I remarked jokingly, "Yes, you're not telling me anything new. I already know there is a lot wrong with me."

At that point, she repeated her statement more emphatically and said, "I am serious. I feel and sense darkness somewhere within the frontal left upper-side of your body." Well, now I was getting a bit more concerned and Linda further remarked that she wanted me to go for a medical check-up. After nearly two weeks of hesitation, I finally scheduled a medical examination at Cedars-Sinai Medical Center in Los Angeles.

Although unaware at that time, this was the beginning of what was later to manifest as a total transformation of my life. I was suddenly thrown into the medical world as a patient and diagnosed with breast cancer in my left breast. My life was dramatically altered and ever since then, evolved into an entirely different way of life because of this experience...far different from that which I could ever have imagined!

Today, I am blessed and grateful to be able to say that I am a breast cancer survivor. My personal experience with breast cancer was such a powerfully enlightening and positive involvement with my doctors and the medical community at Cedars-Sinai Medical Center, that I was compelled to write this book as a way to give something of myself back to the medical community and to the Universe...to say thank you from my heart and soul for all that was done for me by my parents, family, friends, doctors and medical staff. I am elated and fortunate to be able to state that I have been cancer-free since May 14, 1999 when my surgeon, Dr. Dennis L. Wood, successfully removed my breast cancer and truly gave me another chance at life.

Over the passing years I have learned how to listen once again to my inner voice, my intuition... to listen to my heart. I have learned to find my harmony and balance once again–to acknowledge and accept my true feelings and emotions. I have learned to express my inner truths and feelings, creatively and passionately with love and compassion for others through my writing, my artwork and the way I choose to live my life. Everyday is a miracle as I move forward creatively and joyously again on my life path. I have at last found a true direction and purpose, traveling on my life journey.

Believe in yourself and trust the inner voice. If I can do this, surely you can as well! Listen to your inner voice and follow your heart. It will always speak the truth! Step-by-step, moment-to-moment you will begin to move forward. Eventually you too, will take that final giant leap to cross over the chasm of despair and grief. When you find this balance and harmony, life at last will be filled with more joy, compassion and love.

Oh, ever so carefully we tread on this path. Sometimes we take two steps forward and three steps backwards. And, oftentimes we even just choose to pause and rest by the side of our own path–to take a deep breath and collect ourselves a bit. Yet, truly the greatest glory on this path is when we are moving steadily forward in search of our life purpose–with open eyes, open ears, open mind and most importantly with an open heart and soul.

Trust and continue to have faith along your own personal path. That little inner voice inside your heart and soul will lead you in the correct direction to your ultimate highest good. All is possible in life–for all that you hold to be true and real, will one day manifest and present itself to you. Believe this, and you will one day see the light, leading the way to your true personal path; embracing and surrounding you within its warmth, joy and love–this compassionate and loving light of life

-PGJ

One

The full moon glows so very bright
As high seas rage with all their might
The shadows dance upon this night
And, spirits whisper of my plight

Drifting, waxing, floating freely
Searching for what is meant to be
The soul does lives eternally
A winding path towards Destiny

It has been said the soul never dies, reincarnating on earth to experience another lifetime, and quite possibly even multiple lifetimes. I have always had my doubts, yet tonight I could not help but wonder if a past life might at last hold the key to my identity, unlocking the mysteries of my haunting dreams. It was not death that I feared, but the thought of embracing love is what truly sent me running.

The growing darkness of this warm and sultry summer's night softly caressed me as I listened to the echo of my black-patent stiletto heels clicking rhythmically upon the downtown Los Angeles pavement. My mind wavered back-and-forth in the drifting breeze as I walked briskly from the parking structure along South Grand Avenue towards the exquisite shimmering contemporary architecture of The Walt Disney Concert Hall. Although my playing was far from the level of a novice, with every attempt tonight, I felt myself failing to maintain a required and necessary degree of concentration upon my music. My mind was roaming far and wide from the piano concerto that I would be performing shortly, but rather, it veered in the direction of my psychoanalyst, Dr. Christopher Alexander.

I felt as if this past week's therapy session was somehow different, more significant. At that time, the doctor advised me to set aside at least three hours for my upcoming appointment. I agreed to what seemed like a reasonable request at the time, but inexplicably, tonight I was having second thoughts.

Reaching the concert hall, I entered a back door and made my way into a private dressing room. Removing my turquoise Pashmina shawl, I suddenly felt numb all over, my eyes staring blindly into voided space. I stood before the brightly lit mirror. In all honesty I was stupefied. Call it a bad case of nerves, yet I knew in my heart that I was making excuses for what I was really feeling. Was I falling in love? My thoughts remained tortured…conflicted.

All of a sudden, the silence within my tiny dressing room was rudely interrupted by a loud knocking at my door. Before I could respond or speak, the door flew open.

"Hey, Gorgeous! It's your night and you're going to play like an angel," the male voice said with a smile. I turned around from my reflection in the mirror. The Conductor's eyes panned seductively up-and-down my low-cut little black cocktail dress, undressing me until getting lost within the cleavage of my full, creamy white breasts.

"I'll just be a few minutes," I replied, abruptly turning back around to face the mirror again, as I struggled to pin my brunette curls into a French twist. "I'll meet you on stage," I continued, speaking in a tone of disdain. I could hear him mumble, as if cussing under his breath, and then the door abruptly closed behind me. I peered deeply into the mirror. Alone, I stood in a whirlwind of reflection, unable to focus on anything, but my uncertainty. As a concert pianist, I often wondered that if I did not have my music to comfort me, I'd surely go insane. My weekly therapy sessions with Dr. Alexander had endured for over nine months with no signs of a viable resolution in sight. I could not sleep at night.

When I finally did fall asleep, the dreams I experienced were disturbing—images reminiscent of a different time and place, strange voices softly whispering to my soul. I found this all rather frightening.

With a final long look at my reflection, I hurriedly touched-up my makeup, applied another coat of mascara to my black lashes and gently placed a shimmering pink gloss upon my full, plump lips. I paused, then turned around to exit as my hand trembled, pulling on the doorknob. Entering into the dimly-lit backstage hallway which led to the bustling stage wings, tonight seemed odd, somehow very different from my previous performances. My increasing insecurity led me to contemplate that perhaps, I was even slowly losing my mind.

Approaching the stage wings, I could hear the audience stirring. Anxiously awaiting my introduction, I observed the Conductor move towards the curtain and the bright lights, until quite unexpectedly he hesitated…turning around to softly whisper into my ear.

"Stop avoiding me, Graziella. You know how I feel about you."

An icy shiver ran up my spine. Cringing, I tried to maintain my composure as the Conductor arrogantly made his way into the luminescent spotlight. The roar of the crowd was exhilarating as I glared angrily in the Conductor's direction. I often wondered why this pathetic man continued to pursue me, when I made every effort to ignore his countless advances.

"Ladies and gentlemen, it gives me tremendous pleasure to have this honor of presenting to you this evening, the internationally renowned pianist…Graziella Fortuna," he said with feigned eloquence. Loud applause once again filled the concert hall as I advanced across the polished light-oak stage floor. The pit of my stomach fluttered as my mind continued to prey upon thoughts of only Dr. Alexander. You see, ever since our first meeting, the doctor was special…as if I had always known him. Here I stood tonight taking my bow before the audience, simply trying to make some sense of all of this. I remained hopeful of understanding, hopeful of one day forgetting a horrific recurring nightmare…a tall, thin, light-haired, light-skinned gentleman wearing clothes from another place and time. Chasing me, the man nears closer and closer. There is a cage within his hand that contains two large black-colored birds…ravens. Although this in itself is most perplexing, with each reverie the gentleman's face becomes more and more apparent, slowly morphing into a horrid visage of disfigured flesh. Approaching the exquisite black grand piano, I could hear the doctor's recent words still reverberating within my head.

"I believe your dreams allude to a past lifetime, and I'm even willing to consider that hypnosis might facilitate, shedding some light upon what has happened to you that it might help to explain why you continue to run from your heart."

Swiftly my consciousness returned to the concert hall as the Conductor tapped furiously upon the podium. With a surly smile upon his face, he stared glaringly into my eyes, and then turned to face the audience.

"This evening Graziella will be playing Beethoven's Moonlight Sonata in C Sharp, op. 27/2. Another cold shiver ran up my spine as I rested my fingers upon the bone-white piano keys. It was absolutely imperative that I now focused my full attention upon the task at hand. I paused and breathed deeply, trying to relax. As I commenced playing, my passion ascended…dancing carefree within me with every euphonious note. The moment was magical, as if the music softly caressed me…that was, until my eyes intermittently drifted, gazing outward upon the sea of faces filling the concert hall.

My body instinctively tensed, my fingers froze, stumbling as I played. The Conductor looked at me with disgust, befuddled with regards to what was actually occurring. All I could do was gawk at a man seated in the center, second row. "My God!" I murmured. I wondered if he could truly be the man in the dream.

His penetrating gaze and grossly disfigured face sent me reeling in fear. I stopped playing, but I knew that I had to finish the piece. I had to give it another go…at least to save face. The audience stirred as I sat dejected upon the stool. Had I finally encountered my nemesis?

Without any notice, the man in the audience stood upright and defiantly gazed into my eyes. Abruptly, I too, arose from the piano, gathering my music sheets. I exited the spotlight. Running off-stage, I could only think of one thing. I knew that I had to get out of there. I knew that *he* was coming to get me as my panic grew to be overwhelming. Hurdling my way down the dimly-lit corridor, I eventually reached my dressing room. I quickly grabbed my shawl and purse. Continuing my departure down the darkened back-corridor, I brushed past two stagehands, briskly shoving aside a security guard to finally exit the concert hall through a backstage door.

The pounding of my heart reverberated as I ran towards the parking structure, my body surging forward like a flooding street through this warm summer's night. Again, I could hear the tapping of my black-patent stilettos upon the concrete sidewalk. My lungs felt as if they would explode as I gasped for air, wheezing with every precarious step. Nearly breathless, I reached for my cell phone and speed-dialed a number.

"Damn it! I can't even get a signal. I've got to see you tonight," I mumbled into the phone. Reaching the car, I searched for my keys, at last unlocking and opening the door of the silver Audi TT convertible. My body crumbled upon the soft black-leather seat as I burst into tears, pressing my forehead against the steering-wheel.

It was at that moment when my attention was quite unexpectedly drawn to a small white envelope secured upon the car windshield. Curious, I lowered the convertible top, then the windows. Reaching around the windshield, my left arm strained as my fingers grappled with the paper envelope. Strangely, it was blank on the exterior with no name, or address. I observed its delicate texture…a fine white parchment. My fingers fumbled with the wax seal, opening the small parcel until a playing card suddenly fell into my lap…the Queen of Hearts. I picked up the card and held it closer to my eyes, studying the image with great detail. A parchment enclosure was also evident as my fingers searched further into the envelope. Quickly, I unfolded the document as my eyes apprehensively perused the sepia-colored writing.

"God help me!" I whispered, staring in confusion at the parchment as I read the anonymous message.

"Graziella, you can run, but cannot hide. You're the Queen of my heart."

I felt my face flush with fear as my eyes suddenly welled with tears. Shifting the car in reverse, then into first and with a rapid jerk into second gear, I haphazardly made my exit into the bright lights and bustling sounds of downtown Los Angeles. Swiftly transitioning into third gear, I realized little reassurance approaching South Grand Avenue as I careened onto the I-10 freeway. Desperately, I fought back the tears, trying to remain in control. With cell phone in hand, I made the call again, at last connecting as I listened intrepidly to the monotonous ringing. My ear was glued to the phone as I impatiently awaited his compassionate voice.

"You have reached Dr. Christopher Alexander. Please leave me a message and I will return your call as soon as possible. If this is an emergency, please page me at (310) 555-1111. Thank you."

The voice-mail beeped into recording mode as I strained to speak.

"Where are you? I need you," I shouted anxiously into the phone. Quickly, I disconnected the call and frantically redialed. The phone rang twice, when suddenly a voice sounded on the line.

"Hello?"

"Thank God, you're there! I have to see you tonight, or I'll surely die!"

"Who is this?"

"It's Graziella…Graziella Fortuna."

"Oh, I'm sorry. I didn't recognize your voice," he said as I distinctly heard a woman's voice in the background.

"Hang up!" the woman's voice shouted.

"You sound upset," he continued as his voice grew louder.

"What's the matter?"

"I can't think straight. I'm so confused. Can we meet?"

"Tonight?"

"It's really important," I pleaded.

"What is it?" he remarked as again I heard the woman's voice in the background.

"Who the hell is it this time?" the woman cried out.

"Hold on a second," he said to me, as he paused from our conversation. "For God sakes, Rachel…It's one of my patients. I can explain."

"Sure, you can explain! What am I? Chopped Liver? Why the fuck can't you ever finish anything you start?" the woman retorted angrily in the background.

"I'm sorry. I have company tonight," he said, whispering sheepishly into the phone.

"Please," I begged. "I cannot be alone tonight."

"Relax. You'll be fine, Graziella."

"But, I'm *not* fine. I must see you."

Whispering into the phone again, he remarked, "Tonight's just not a good time."

"You're my doctor. Who else can I turn to?"

Again, speaking under his breath, he hurriedly replied, "Okay. Okay. I'll see what I can do. Meet me at my office at the beach house in Malibu. I'm in the Hollywood Hills. Give me an hour." The phone suddenly made a clicking noise as the buzzing sound of the dead line filled my ear. Arriving at Dr. Alexander's darkened Malibu home, I realized it would be a while before he would join me. As I exited my car, I initially sought relief taking off my stilettos, followed by the removal of my pantyhose. The beach front was a stone's throw away as I tip-toed in my bare feet around to the front of the magnificent contemporary glass home. Reaching the beach, my sore feet were soothed by the playful shifting white sand and cool ocean water between my toes. The sound of classical music filled the air, softly playing from the direction of a neighboring home as the dancing ocean waves rushed onto the shore. I positioned myself nestled comfortably upon a sand dune as I gazed upward into the night sky. Passing the time, I was lost in thought, staring at the full moon as it glistened upon the turbulent waters. In awe of the moon's brilliant glow amongst the luminous stars, my eyes were led to one of the most radiant orbs. I made a wish.

"Send me the love of my life…someone who is compassionate, loving and true…someone who brings magic to my heart and soul."

The approaching seductive hum of Dr. Alexander's black Ferrari suddenly filled the night air as I stood up to return towards the house. Reaching the driveway, the blinding car headlights glared into my eyes. Frozen like a timid deer, I stood motionless as the sound of the car radio played loudly in the background.

"Hello Graziella. Sorry it took me so long," he said reaching out to take me by the hand as he dismounted this Italian Stallion.

"I'm so grateful you could meet with me," I said. Looking upward into the starlit sky, he took me by the hand, drawing my body closer to his.

8

"This is going to be a magnificent night for us," he whispered softly as he stared into my eyes.

Growing anxious, I wondered about his comment, since the events of the night had been everything, but, magnificent thus far.

"Come this way. I've missed you, darling," he continued affectionately, placing a kiss upon my forehead.

I stopped in my tracks, fearful for a moment of the doctor's intentions as I suddenly pulled away from him. Resisting his advances, my heart was racing as I breathed deeply in anticipation of his reaction. I wanted to flee.

"I'm sorry. It's okay," he said reassuringly as he motioned for me to enter into the house. Like a wounded animal, he backed off, releasing my hand.

"I'm just happy to see you. Let's go inside. We have a lot to discuss," he continued.

Shyly, I lowered my head, my eyes focused downward at the polished white marble walkway, until I heard the door unlock as we stood beneath the dimly-lit glow of the front porch's light. Together we entered into the contemporary foyer as the doctor turned on an entry light, leading us into the ultra modern glass living room with a 180 degree view of the majestic Pacific Ocean. "Please make yourself comfortable. I'll be with you in a moment," he said as he opened a closet door to retrieve three white candles.

"Shall I meet you in your office?"

"We'll be fine in the living room. Please…sit down." Dimming the living room lights, Dr. Alexander positioned the candles upon a long gray-slate cocktail table, and then carefully struck a match to light each of the three candles.

"I feel like I'm falling to pieces," I said as I sat upon a plush white leather sofa.

"You look whole to me," he said with a glimmer in his eye. I sensed he was trying to make light of my statement, attempting to elicit some humor into our conversation.

9

"Are you a stand up comic too?" I remarked with a smile.

"How about a glass of wine before we get to talking? Do you like Cabernet or Merlot?" he inquired, grinning back at me with hopes of winning my trust again and cutting through the thick wall of tension that still hung heavily within the room.

"Wine? Oh, I probably shouldn't."

"It might relax you."

"I'm not so sure," I replied as I watched him open a bottle, and then pour the cerise-colored vintage into two large elegant bulbous crystal glasses.

"Try this," he said handing me a glass. "I think you'll like it. It's a '99 Opus One…smooth, full-bodied with a hint of oak and vanilla. It's one of my favorites."

Positioning himself next to me upon the sumptuous leather couch, he leaned forward with his glass-in-hand. "Let's make a toast. Here's to new beginnings for you, Graziella."

"Yes, new beginnings, and here's to closing the door on the past."

The delicate sound of the crystal glass rims clicking filled the air within the soft candlelight.

"Salute."

"Salute," I replied, taking a sip from my glass as I smiled approvingly of his selection." It's nice of you to see me, tonight. I hope your company understood."

Swirling the prized vintage within his large crystal glass, the doctor gazed for a moment into my eyes." It really was not a problem. Your phone call had me quite concerned."

"I have to talk to you about something…about," I hesitated, trying to speak.
"You're safe now, please go on."

Taking another sip of wine, I continued, "It's that recurring dream. You know…the one with that ghastly gentleman. In the dream his face is grotesquely scarred as he carries the cage

10

containing two enormous black ravens. However, tonight I am almost certain that he was even in the audience."

"At your performance?"

"I have no doubt that it was he."

"Are you absolutely certain?"

"Umm…yes. Of course, it must have been he, but no sooner had I locked my sights upon him, he seemed to vanish into thin air."

"Did you get a good look at his face?"

"God…no! I could barely even play my piece. It was as if my fingers froze upon the keys. Just like in my dreams, his face was appalling."

"What happened next?" he inquired, placing the crystal glass to his lips.

"It was all so eerie as if a dream, but I swear he was the man. You must believe me. He was real. Strangely, all of a sudden he smiled at me and stood upright, staring defiantly into my eyes."

"What did you do?"

"What could I do? I felt helpless as I watched his face. It was horrifying. The situation seemed to even worsen with his sudden departure from the concert hall."

"Where do you suppose he went?" the doctor inquired.

"I'm really not sure, and I wasn't going to hang around to find out. I had to get the hell out of there!"

"You left the stage?"

Humiliated and consumed with embarrassment, I rocked to-and-fro upon the white couch, now holding my head between my hands.

"I panicked. I'm sure you'll read about it in tomorrow's LA Times. The critics are certain to have a field day with this. Do you believe me? Have I lost my mind, doctor?"

"Graziella, what's most important is that *you* believe the incident tonight was real. That's all that actually matters right now."

"I do…I really do!"

"So, you think that he followed you?"

"It's very likely. I even discovered a strange note when I returned to my car."

"From him?"

"Who else could it be? Oddly, there was a playing card with it too…the Queen of Hearts." I retrieved the envelope from my purse.

"Here it is. What do you think?" I continued, giving the thin parcel to the doctor.

As he took the envelope from my hand, Dr. Alexander suddenly grew quiet perusing the document and the playing card.

"I guess I may have over-reacted," I continued nervously.

"Strangely, I feel as if, not only is someone following me in my dreams, but in real life too!"

As he swallowed another long sip of wine, the doctor stared intently at the message and the playing card. Without further comment, he returned the enclosures into the envelope, discreetly placing it within his pant pocket.

"Calm down. What are you really running from?" he continued. "I'm afraid, so frightened of many things. I'm confused." Again, I felt my face flush with warmth to a bright pink.

"In our toast you mentioned, *closing the door on the past.* There's something I have wanted you to experience in our therapy sessions together," he said as he looked intently into my eyes.

"About my past?" I inquired. My interest was fully piqued by the doctor's comment. I sat upright, repositioning myself upon the couch as I awaited his words.

12

"Please listen and keep an open mind. If you recall, I briefly talked about this in our last session, but I'm wondering if tonight..."

"Is this another one of those shrink head-games?"

"There's no time for games. I have a serious proposition to make to you," he pleaded.

I was growing more and more uncomfortable with each passing second. "Proposition?" I wondered what he was up to.

"What kind of proposition?"

He spoke of a unique approach to therapy that only a tolerant individual like me would possibly consider...a process called Past Life Regression.

"Do you recall my briefly speaking of this? Although I was planning to explain the procedure in our next session, tonight seems the perfect time to discuss this further," he continued. I had never been hypnotized before. Sure, I had read a lot about the phenomena of Past Life Regression in books and magazines, yet by no means had I ever considered going under hypnosis myself.

"I really have my doubts," I said rolling my eyes with reservation.

"So, you're closed to the idea?"

I told Dr. Alexander that I didn't believe I could have ever lived a past life.

"Hear me out," he continued. "Life is a matter of choices, Graziella."

"What are you saying?" I inquired, puzzled by his statement.

"Every choice in life manifests one or more consequences, offering opportunities to learn life lessons." I nodded my head, at last understanding his point of view.

"Yes, and I've made some truly bad choices, doctor."

"We all have. I don't know of one human being who hasn't. Life's a journey."

"And, what a trip it has been!" I said, chuckling under my breath. The doctor told me that he chose to believe we all have experienced past lives, whereby the soul evolves to a higher level of awareness.

"In every lifetime we make conscious choices as individuals to either live our lives with love, compassion and tolerance, or to choose fear, hatred and contempt. Sometimes people, like yourself get stuck in life…besieged by their fears."

"How do you know all of this?" I inquired, twitching my nose with uncertainty. He took a sip of his wine before answering my question, then paused and looked into my eyes again.

"There are Higher Powers that speak to the soul. It's just that some of us are more open to listening to these voices than others."

I couldn't help from laughing aloud. "So, doctor…you hear voices?"

"I realize this all must sound very odd to you, but these voices are more like an inner knowing that speaks to the soul."

"Really?" I inquired, beginning to find this all marvelously interesting as I took another sip from my wine glass and repositioned myself upon the couch.

"For starters…in a Past Life Regression, I'll hypnotize you, taking your soul into a deep trance. Your soul will travel back into another lifetime, and that's when this really gets fascinating."

"I'm not so sure about this. It sounds weird and scary."

"I'll be with you every step of the way," he said as he reached for my hand, placing it gently within his. "I promise." Dr. Alexander told me that I would have nothing to fear, that he would even tape record our session together. This way, when I awakened from trance, I would be able to hear what actually occurred during the Past Life Regression.

"Can I think about this? When would you want to start?"

14

"Tonight, of course, and when you awaken from the experience, we'll both have an even greater awareness of the present lifetime."

"But," I said, hesitating as he continued to explain.

The doctor told me that through the experience of Past Life Regression, I would attain more insight, a deeper knowledge of why I do the things that are part of my behavior today and why I even react in a certain manner to individuals and situations.

"Ideally, Graziella, we may even determine why you run from your heart. All of this will be possible because the soul truly does live forever."

Again, I felt my face become increasingly flushed with warmth as I sensed that the doctor hit the nail correctly on the head with this statement.

"You know me better than I know myself," I said. "What can I expect? From your professional experience, give me the best and worst case scenarios of this Past Life Regression process that you speak of."

The doctor believed that by undergoing hypnosis in this regression, I would certainly feel more positive regarding my conflicting emotions of love VS fear. He told me that in some cases, individuals not only experienced an internal transformation, but even a physical change.

"Like what?" I inquired.

"Such as a variation in eye color, or the appearance of a birthmark; only minor alterations. There's nothing to be frightened of."

"And, the worst case?"

"The worst case scenario would be…you might not be able to go fully into trance," he continued. "Or, your soul may haphazardly skip from one past life to another, without any parallel or relevance to your current life."

I was startled at the doctor's comment as I sat erect upon the couch. "Do you actually believe that I have lived more than one past life?"

Dr. Alexander told me that he believed we had known each other from several past lives...that the soul reincarnates in similar soul groupings. "In each lifetime," he continued, "The soul chooses to play a different role, walking in different shoes, so to speak, and quite amazingly, it's possible for the soul to have lived in another lifetime as the opposite sex and even as a different race."

"Will this process actually work?"

He told me that he was absolutely convinced this would be perfect for my situation, since traditional therapy had not seemed to play a significant role in resolving my issues. "Shall we give it a try?" he continued. "To say the least, we're bound to find some answers to your underlying fears.

"You always have a way of making things sound so much better," I replied, swirling the wine around-and-around within my glass.

"Well...what's your choice, Graziella?"

"I guess so, but how far back into time will I go? And, will my soul return safely to the present lifetime?"

"Your subconscious will determine which lifetime you will regress into. That's totally within your power. Once you are in trance, your soul will navigate your journey and what you will actually speak of. My role will be one as a facilitator to monitor you during the process. Hopefully, there will be no interruptions, that is, unless I need further clarification on a specific issue, or if I believe the safety to your present physical state is compromised.

"Will I be in any danger?"

"Not if the regression is conducted properly. That's why I'm here. If there are any complications, I'll remove you from that particular past life situation by taking you forward into a different

16

phase of the very same life. You have nothing to fear. All will be well." The effects of the wine, Dr. Alexander's soothing voice, his genuine compassion and charm appeared to be the winning combination.

"Okay. My choice is yes!"

"My pager is off and I'll turn on the tape recorder. We'll begin if you are ready?"

"I guess I am about as ready as I will ever be."

"Graziella, you won't regret your choice. Now, lie back in a reclining position."

"I can only hope that you're correct," I answered, extending my legs upon the sofa.

I swallowed hard, as my head rested upon a pillow. My heart was racing, and I wondered if Dr. Alexander could hear it too. I stared at him, still doubtful if anything positive would actually come of our session together on this night, however, I must confess that I would be in absolute denial if I failed to reveal that I was somewhat attracted to Dr. Alexander – in the physical sense of the word and even more. I liked everything about him—his large blue eyes, his thick blond locks of hair framing his angular face, his voice, his strong muscular physique. Most of all, it was his compassion that drew me closer to him with each office visit. He really did care about me - about my feelings, about calming my anxiety, and I knew he was attracted to me as well.

Of course, I found myself putting on the brakes. This attraction scared me beyond any obvious comprehension. Tonight, I could only surmise that for the sake of professionalism, the doctor–patient relationship, Dr. Alexander understood my terror, respectfully choosing not to fully address this inexplicable magnetism between us.

"I'll begin by playing a CD…something soft and ethereal," he instructed. "It will relax you as I go through the process of bringing your mind and body into trance. I want you to simply

17

breathe slowly. Focus on a beautiful scene and try to imagine yourself at peace. Find a place of tranquility, a center of balance within the images painted in your mind. As I count backwards, every number spoken aloud will facilitate your passage, taking your soul deeper and deeper under hypnosis. Relax, focus and listen to the music. Together, let's explore this inner journey to another place and time. Ninety-nine, ninety-eight, ninety-seven, ninety-six, ninety-five, ninety-four, ninety-three..."

Closing my eyes, I stared blankly into inner space. I lay still, breathing deeply and listening to the rhythmic timbre of my breath. The soothing melodic music expedited my passage into this hypnotic state of consciousness as the doctor's steady, soothing, methodical voice continued counting aloud—eighty, seventy-nine, seventy-eight, seventy-seven, seventy-six..." Little-by little, every muscle in my body relaxed as I let go of my inhibitions one-by-one, gradually entering into trance.

In what seemed like merely a matter of seconds, my thoughts were carried to an echelon of nothingness. For a moment only the darkness of shifting shadows surrounded me. I was anxious until a small white speck of light appeared in front of my mind's eye. I felt weightless and followed the light as it grew larger in size and brilliance with every step of my approach. I could feel my entire being, floating closer as if drawn effortlessly to a magnet in a whirlwind—surrounded by a vivid spectrum of swirling colors, sounds and images. My soul's journey into the past had indeed...commenced.

Two

Blowing in the winter's breeze
Drifting thoughts and memories
In the darkness spirits speak
Whispers echoing my plea

Full moon dancing on the sea
Crisp, cool air surrounding me
Visions of my destiny
Leading to a new journey

The dead of winter enfolded me on this fourth day of February, 1811. My carriage had departed London five days prior, traversing the southerly land route across the snow-blanketed English countryside, and today journeyed toward the west coastal village of Boscastle. I was returning to my ancestral home in the region of Cornwall along the Cornish cliffs, uncertain of my future...uncertain of more than I could ever envision at this time. The weather was inclement, alternating between rain and snow as I persisted in rubbing my thinly-gloved hands together, hopeful of easing the bone-chilling numbness within my bluing fingertips. The coach advanced sluggishly, crossing over the precarious River Tamar, a natural border uniting the western regions of Devon and Cornwall – a river rumored that even Satan would have second thoughts about navigating.

It was the time of the Ton, the High Regency period in England when life was flamboyant, decadent, opulent and lush - a glimpse into an era that resonated the essence of only living for the moment, purely for immediate pleasure and gratification.— My life had been focused upon the expression of an affluent lifestyle, high society, attending the infamous Prince Regent's Regal Balls at Buckingham Palace in London, satisfying primal needs and the endless search for true love, lust and sexual gratification.

I reminisced on the past, thinking about the city of London on the night of fifteen November, 1810. Over the course of the past three months I had come to discover myself stuck, wallowing within the mire of a tragic dilemma. How could it be, that only I could explain my circumstances and account for my actions on that unfortunate autumn night? Surely, someone would at last come forward, vindicating me of any wrong doing or crime. A series of unforgettable images rapidly flashed before my mind's eye. My husband, Lord Kendall Worthington had mysteriously disappeared, failing to surface as a member of the living, or the deceased. Although the London leading investigator, Constable Nigel Gordon, declared this a matter of a missing person case, I remained the primary focus in the scope of the investigation. Other than the grotesque blood-smeared walls within my bedroom chamber, there was no physical evidence, a weapon or more importantly…a body to illuminate Kendall's fate.

The only substantiation of the events on that night was solely my recollection, a matter that rested squarely upon my tiny shoulders, a nightmarish memory that I now feared would always remain a part of me – a part of my soul. So many unanswered, puzzling questions still existed and overshadowed the investigation. I had searched high-and-low for clues, longing to make some sense of my quandary.

Was it Divine intervention? Had the Higher Powers interceded on my behalf? Perhaps the spirit world had successfully swayed the Constable, whispering sweet mercies into his ear? Quite unexpectedly, I had been granted a temporary reprieve to depart London - to journey within the borders of England until further information surfaced for evaluation.

This pause in my life came none too soon. My bones were frail, my mind and body listless. I was drained mentally, emotionally, spiritually and physically. My senses had become deadened, anticipating news with each passing day, hopeful of discovering an explanation of my husband's providence.

Regretfully, my nine-year marriage to Kendall had produced no children, no heirs to the prosperous Thornwood Estate in Boscastle, nor for that matter had the Worthington Estate in Westminster, London produced its birthright heir to carry-on the Worthington family name and tradition.

Somehow, I sensed these past years would merely dwindle to a tragic memory of what once was a loveless marriage. With so much uncertainty, I felt unstable, as if my foundation was crumbling under the wake of each passing day. Many changes were occurring, and all so unpredictably. Quite shockingly, in my present state of affairs I now found myself displaced, living a life in solitude.

At times I envisioned the Higher Powers had forsaken me. I had prayed to the souls of the deceased – the spirit world, imploring their blessings, but now I prayed they would grant me the strength to make decisions for the correct reasons, not out of revenge. I felt as if Divine guidance had abandoned me. Or, perhaps the truth of the matter was that I had neglected the Divine.

I reposed my head upon the lush brocade carriage cushion, closing my eyes. My imagination ran wild from moment-to-moment, dreaming of a return to life as I had always longed for it to be, an existence filled with understanding, sensitivity and unconditional love from a compassionate man.

As the stately horse-drawn carriage approached the westerly coast, I inhaled the scent of the damp and salty sea air, lingering in the clutches of this night. My eyes searched the horizon for the once familiar contour of the mystical Cornish cliffs. I had departed London in such a flurry, desperately seeking some sense of peace. Traveling in the company of my chaperone, Madam

21

Marcella Lumiere, and my two personal attendants, the French sisters Caron and Josephina La Tour, I felt as if there would be no end to this journey.

Throughout our many years together, Madam Marcella was a father figure, a disciplinarian utilizing compassionate guidance, and rearing me since the young age of seven. An obese, round-faced, gray-haired woman who stood as tall as she was wide, Marcella was well-mannered at the age of sixty years, but exuded eccentricity within her every bone. You see, Madam Marcella was gifted mystically. Although she shared this rare and unique ability with her three younger sisters, Madam Clara, Madam Lindsey and Madam Victoria, there was an amazing distinction that set Marcella apart from her siblings. Since birth, Marcella's hands bore a unique physical deformity…each hand possessing six fingers, and said to be the sign of a true healer.

The Lumiere sisters had established quite the reputation in London, as well as along the English coastal region of North Cornwall, and more specifically within the Atlantic coastal village of Boscastle. They were unusual, oftentimes bizarre—each characteristically odd in addition to having various distinct physical features, yet of most significance was the sisters' unusual ability to see, hear and sense the past, present and even into the future.

Through personal contact and interaction, many devotees professed the sisters' skills as mystics. Some even proclaimed the Lumiere sisters had special powers, endowed truly from the Divine, from the Higher Powers. The sisters were able to see into time as clairvoyants, sense the unknown as clairsentients and hear messages from the spirit world as clairaudients. They were recognized as healers and herbalists, yet discretely referred to as gifted, possessed, otherworldly, odd, different and even supernatural. In other words, the Lumiere sisters possessed the phenomenal metaphysical healing powers of the *craft,* commonly known as Sorcerers, who were involved with the ominous realm of witchcraft.

Over the years, word of their unique gifts and healing abilities had grown widespread. The sisters were notorious amongst the English nobility, the wealthy aristocracy in London and Brighton. King George III and his son, the Prince Regent, were both intimate with the sisters' mysticism, seeking assistance for the King's mental problems. The sisters' prophecies were profoundly accurate, affirming that the King would be declared incurably insane. In fact, at our present time of England's war with France, even the French nobility and aristocracy of Paris had clandestinely sought the intervention of the Higher Powers, partaking in rites and rituals in search of healing and guidance to bring forth a desired result, or event. It was often rumored that Napoleon consulted privately in seclusion with the sisters at Thornwood Estate, just prior to waging war with England. To one-and-all, the Lumiere sisters were commonly referred to as the Mystic Women by the sea.

I too, had become *one* with the craft. All my life I was aware of my uniqueness, and ever since my birth, life proved to be rather unconventional. It had been said by the sisters that I was born with a fleshy veil attached to my face, a thinly porous and translucent skin membrane that left the doctors mystified, however, it was not until two days after my birth, that one skillful London surgeon, Dr. Bertram Alexis, was at last able to successfully cut the delicate veiled tissue, detaching it to reveal my unscathed porcelain face. To this day, all that remained as physical proof of this phenomenon was a small scar upon my forehead and beneath my chin.

In my youth, the sisters shared with me their gifted powers to see, hear and feel the past, present and into the future…and they had taught me well. My mystical powers, however, steadily dwindled during the years of my discontent…the nine arduous years of marriage to Kendall. During this phase, my husband adamantly insisted that I refrain from practicing any of the magic. When I would be so bold to attempt to use my powers, Kendall sought swift and unforgiving retribution upon me with his physical wrath. Within this period of separation from the sisters, I noticed my powers had become increasingly dulled and lessened to near extinction.

I often wondered, however, what I would have done in my youth without the sisters' guidance and insight. With the benevolence of the Higher Powers, I now prayed that the return of the Lumiere sisters in my life again, would help to unearth the answers to my questions. Over the years I had never taken for granted my good fortune, receiving the comfort of their words – advising, teaching and guiding me in the magical ways of the spirit world.

Impatiently looking about the interior coach, my thoughts returned to the carriage journey. It became more than obvious that Caron and Josephina had also grown uneasy as they squirmed upon the brocade cushion, tapping their feet restlessly upon the wooden carriage floor. My attendants often reminded me of myself, now a passing memory of my youthful innocence. Josephina was the elder sister at the age of sixteen, fair-skinned with rich green eyes and a head of full blonde curls which she wore like a hat, bouncing in step with her cheerfulness. Caron was fifteen years, incessantly delightful with an eternal smile upon her face; however, she was very much the opposite of Josephina in coloration. Her dark-skinned complexion, cocoa-brown hair and deep-brown eyes often led me to wonder how they could possibly be blood sisters. Throughout the years, Caron and Josephina had remained devoted, loyal and trustworthy—always at my beck and call.

The coach moved slowly, yet steadfastly towards the village of Boscastle as the sound of the horses' hoofs hitting the frigid winter ground, returned my thoughts to bygone days. I recollected images of the past with a sudden flashback to the Constable's interrogation of the mysterious night in question, fifteen November 1810.

Several of the local London authorities, including our renowned investigator, Constable Nigel Gordon, had queried me on various occasions about this perplexing case. The Constable was a grossly short, rotund and portly man, at the age of four-and-sixty. His beady dark eyes were like pieces of raw coal, symmetrically positioned upon his fleshy round face. A halo of thinning salt and pepper hair flew wildly in all directions about his head. With a pair of tin-wired spectacles perched awkwardly upon his bulbous veined nose, I observed his scraggly mustache and beard displaying evidence of his most recent meal. His stressed, mis-buttoned shirt beckoned a thorough washing as I repulsively perused the tattooed trail of past meals marked randomly upon the now dulling linen. This slovenly, disheveled appearance evoked the notion that he seemed more suitable as a street sweeper, than as the leading criminal investigator of London.

The Constable's enormous belly jiggled with his every movement, overwhelming his mid-section and protruding well beyond the confines and limits of his weary, taut belt. He relentlessly persisted, however, with an impressive interrogation, hopeful that I might shed more insight on the case. Of most importance, was the determination of my whereabouts that autumn night.

I remember giving my sworn testimony to Constable Gordon during the interrogation. I told him everything that occurred, at least everything that I could recall.

"Before you proceed, I must have you take an oath…to swear to tell the truth. Put your right hand here. That's it. Place it upon this bible," he commanded. I followed his instructions, lifting my trembling hand, positioning it upon the massive, onyx-colored, leather-bound book which sat squarely upon the weathered oak examination table.

"By the powers of God, state your name."

"Lady Grace Worthington," I said, gazing directly into the pitch-black cavernous depths of his shifting spectacled eyes.

"Do you swear to speak only of the truth and nothing, but the truth, in this matter regarding your missing husband, Lord Kendall Worthington?"

"Yes," I replied, nodding my head emphatically.

"Begin with your story."

I was restless, my body squirming nervously from side-to-side upon the large wooden straight-backed chair. Disturbingly aware of what seemed like the chair crying aloud, I could hear its high-pitched voice, creaking when I shifted my weight. My foot was anxiously tapping the floor. I hesitated. At last, summoning the fortitude to open my mouth and speak, I inhaled and took a deep breath to begin my testimony.

I recollected that Kendall and I had been arguing on that night. Once again, we had a difference of opinion. "Let me begin by saying that discord was rather common in our marriage. On the night of fifteen November, Kendall had been drinking."

I told the Constable that this was nothing out of the ordinary. Throughout our marriage Kendall had lived in a stupor, inebriated more often than not. In fact, in all honesty it had even become difficult for me to sometimes differentiate between when it was *more often* than *not*. Two stiff glasses of gin upon rising, a full-blooded glass of claret midday with several tankards of ale at nightfall, all became part of his drunken constitution.

"On the night in question, Kendall came home late to the Worthington Estate house in London, and was returning from the St. James, a prominent gentleman's club along the Thames riverfront."

26

"Yes, I'm familiar with the St. James," the Constable said. "At approximately what time do you believe that your husband arrived at the estate house?"

I remembered hearing the bells tolling from the Cathedral that night. "It was just past the eleventh hour," I replied. I recalled how Kendall startled me. Upon entering the bedroom chambers, he grabbed my head from behind. His breath reeked of pipe tobacco and whiskey as he forcibly tried to kiss my lips, pulling me towards him, my long hair knotted firmly in his grasp. With his body pressing against mine, my legs bowed as I shuddered, pinned within the corner of our small bedroom chamber. Kendall raised his voice and shouted. His behavior was hideous. Like a raving lunatic, he demanded, "Strip, you wretched harlot."

"Is this really the truth?" the Constable asked.

"Unfortunately, I'm afraid so."

I recanted the events of that night to Constable Gordon, explaining how Kendall was abusive, swinging his arms about, as he physically advanced toward me with his imposing figure. I proved no match for him when engaged in any conflict, especially physical confrontation. I resisted his assaulting embrace. Lunging forward with the full weight of his body, he wrestled me onto the bed.

"Why didn't you leave?" the Constable queried.

"I tried, but with his large frame pressed against me, his body caged me like an animal. His hands pawed at me, awkwardly groping at my breasts." Remembering the events of that night brought to mind that I could even actually smell the omnipresent musky scent of his arousal.

I observed the Constable writing hurriedly, scribbling notes upon his large pad of paper. Looking up from time-to-time, he focused rather oddly upon my bosom as opposed to my face. Though I found this all rather peculiar, I attempted to ignore his rather strange behavior and resumed my testimony.

I told him how my husband strangled me to near death on that night. With one hand securely holding my hair within his fist, the other tore my undergarments from beneath me, cutting the flesh of my inner thigh with this forced action. I spat in his face, resisting his advances, and in doing so, Kendall threw a forceful blow to my jaw with his fist. His hands now encircled my neck as he squeezed fiercely, his long tapered fingers wrapped about my collar like the twisted roots of a tall oak. My head grew light as I gasped frantically for a breath of air. I remembered hearing his laughter when he gazed downward as I could only imagine my face turning a cool pallid white. In a daze, the full weight of his body forcefully pressed upon me. I could barely breathe, unable to speak or gesture for his remorse. What I could only surmise as his hands growing weary, Kendall at last removed them from my neck, quickly positioning a pillow cushion over my nose and mouth. I lay listless.

Coughing, I gagged on my very own saliva. My lungs ached, feeling as if they would implode. I searched for a breath of air, gasping aloud. Unexpectedly, Kendall spitefully rolled my body over and demanded that I get on all fours. Tearing my silk dress into tatters, he removed it from my body, clawing deeply at my back with his soil-encrusted fingernails. My lungs wheezed as I remembered screaming in pain, but it was hopeless. There was nothing more that I could do to resist. As he knelt, lunging to-and-fro, with a burst of excitement, he climaxed, excavating his buried treasure hidden deep between my rigid thighs. Again, I screamed from the pain.

"Where were the servants?"

"Asleep in their quarters," I replied, sensing the Constable becoming more and more flustered as he listened to my testimony.

That night I felt sensations of both tremendous fear and rage. The very memory, once again brought pangs of nausea, yet I knew

28

that the story had to be fully told for the Constable to understand the truth, the horror of my ordeal. I told him that my neck and throat ached, my legs were sore; burning from the pain as Kendall repeatedly violated me in our marital bed. The putrid sweat from his overbearing body smelled rancid, his breath and drool still reeking of alcohol and tobacco. We lay amongst the stained linens, in a mire of bodily fluids, including my very own blood.

Oddly, the Constable smiled, hastily scribbling additional notes upon his writing pad. I stared at him, finding his behavior all rather shocking and disgusting for a man of the law. His piercing gaze shifted once again upon my breasts, only adding insult to injury. I felt increasingly uncomfortable as my body quaked with revulsion. My skin crawled just looking at him, and I even wondered if he was actually listening to my words. To state that the Constable's behavior was inappropriate, would be a gross understatement on my part. What was he *really* writing in that pad?

"Did you resist your husband's advances?" he inquired. "Or, perhaps your true intentions were to invite the pleasure of this rendezvous?"

I was puzzled by the Constable's question. *Pleasure?* Was I not making myself perfectly lucid? How could he even begin to imagine that I would enjoy this ordeal? For, in my mind, I absolutely knew what had occurred - my nearly suffocating to death by strangulation. I clearly remembered struggling, wrestling with my husband upon our bed. My body still bore evidence of my plight. I showed the Constable proof, the purple and blue bruises marked upon my face, neck and arms.

That night of fifteen November, I only wanted to become invisible. The room had begun to swirl about as I succumbed to Kendall's arousal, lost in his passionate lust, disillusioned by the dissonant cacophony of his moaning ecstasy.

Eyeing me with shameless pleasure, the Constable's gaze remained captivated by my cleavage. My face flushed warmly to a bright pink as I watched him staring boldly. I wanted to tell him how uncomfortable he made me feel. I wanted to tell him exactly what a vulgar prig I thought him to be, but I bit my tongue, refraining from speaking. Sitting in silence, my anger and humiliation continued to build, raging throughout what seemed like every bone in my body.

"Continue, Lady Worthington. I must know every last detail." I told him that I could hear Kendall breathing hard, moaning with pleasure as his body fell upon me, like a dead man. Slowly, I eased out from underneath, purging him from within me. I struggled, at last rolling his weight off of me. Wiping his dripping semen from my burning crotch and thighs, my entire body rattled with vengeance. I loathed him - now, more than ever.

With my head held down, I paused in silence, hopeful that the Constable would finally show some mercy and dismiss me to return home.

"Surely this is not the end of your story?" he ranted. With veiled disappointment, I sighed, taking a deep breath and continued my testimony.

"When I was finally free from Kendall's grasp, I gathered my scattered clothing."

I explained that my husband reached out with his hand, catching my leg. He grabbed onto my ankle. I tripped, falling to the floor. Again, I grappled with him, barely freeing myself—biting his arm. I remembered leaving an impression of my teeth as I gnawed in desperation, cutting his flesh. Eyeing my black-velvet cloak hanging at the bedroom chamber entry, I raced toward the door, stepping into the shadows of the darkened hallway. I heard Kendall shout and yell my name, and then…there was only silence.

"This is your story?"

"Yes, but…Kendall fell."

"What did you say?" he inquired.

30

"I think that he fell," I said, looking at the Constable directly in his eyes.

"You *think* he fell?"

I told the Constable that I heard a loud noise coming from within the bedroom chamber suite. Slamming the chamber door behind me, I never looked back. Swiftly, I donned my clothing, scurrying down the main staircase, and ran into the darkness of the night. My legs wobbled from the pain, but I still ran as fast as I could.

"That was the last I saw of this ghastly husband of mine."

"It seems you've remembered more of the scenario than I would have ever expected, but perhaps this husband of yours did not truly fall?"

"I don't understand your question."

"You claimed that you *think he fell* and that *you never looked back*, yet how could you be certain that he actually *did* fall?"

There was never a doubt in my mind that Kendall was drunk, fumbling and disoriented as he staggered about the room. "I'm most certain that he must have fallen." Again, the Constable's lusting eyes caressed me in his gaze.

"There's really no proof. That is…unless, perhaps there was a witness? Are you certain that you were alone on that night? Might there have been a domestic of sorts, a servant or butler lurking unknowingly in the veiled shadows of your chambers, observing you in this ecstasy of passion?"

"That's absurd," I shouted in a rage as I arose from my chair.

"Be still, Lady Worthington. I'm trying to simply make some sense of all this."

"Well," I continued, hesitating to collect my composure.

"How could there have been another amongst us?"

"Surely, someone had to have seen, or heard something that night?" he queried.

"Would not this individual have stepped forward and assisted me? I was nearly *strangled to death*, Constable Gordon."

"So you claim."

Now I had truly grown weary of the Constable and his questioning. I could only pray that Divine intervention, the Higher Powers, would expedite my overdue departure. I could not bear a moment longer to even be in his presence. As far as I was concerned, the Constable was merely an arrogant rogue, claiming to serve justice, professing to honor the law.

"It's quite obvious we don't see eye-to-eye on this matter," he continued. "Do you have anything left to say for yourself?"

Before I could give my answer, he added, "Where were you going in such haste, so scantily clothed on that night? Didn't you fear for your safety departing the estate house, Lady Worthington?"

"I knew if I could just reach my destination to see the Bishop, all would be well."

"The Bishop? What does he have to do with this?"

"I can explain."

I told the Constable I was astounded that I had escaped from Kendall. Like a raging river, I surged along the cobblestone roadside, following the lights in the distance toward Westminster, searching for the Cathedral and Lambeth Palace. "This is where the Bishop Samuel Bartholomew resides."

"Did you always make a habit of paying visits with the clergy at this late hour?"

I told him it was purely a visit to seek the Bishop's Divine spiritual guidance. Bishop Samuel Bartholomew was distinguished —a devout man of the cloth, a man of The Church of England, a man of God. The attractive clergyman was at his prime in his mid-fifties with a trim, muscular physique. A hint of gray tastefully accented his sandy blonde curls. His penetrating green eyes sparkled like the shimmer on a wind-blown field of clover.

Education, kindness and social adeptness were some of his finer qualities, serving only to enhance his immense popularity and charm amongst the parishioners of Westminster Abbey, most notably amongst the female sector of the parish.

The Constable sighed, "Of course, you must be aware of the rumors of danger posed by the grave robbers roaming about the city streets by night and sleeping by day? Unfortunately, I fear there is more truth to these claims, than not. These resurrection men would have been all too pleased to have stumbled upon you that inclement night. Lady Worthington, evils lurk and thrive within our grand city of London. More specifically, there are those who would even go as far as murder—to maliciously take the precious life of another, merely to make a profit from the sale of a corpse to the medical community. These desperate rogues are none too particular. I gather your young flesh would have brought a tidy sum to these ruffians upon delivery to a surgeon's dissection table."

The grim vision of fleeing that night from Worthington Estate was overbearing. That cold, damp night engulfed me like a fog, reeking of the city's dankness and the Thames' horrific stench. My mind had only been focused on my freedom, finding safety within the arms of the Bishop. A chill ran down my spine as I thought about the ills that might have befallen me. As much as I hated to admit it, Constable Gordon was absolutely right. There was enormous profit in the underworld business of securing fresh bodies for anatomical research. Although surgeons in the medical community would surely be prosecuted for actively engaging in this practice themselves, it was common knowledge these resurrection men were a welcome blessing, enabling medical research. Fresh cadavers were necessary on a daily basis for fine tuning surgical skills and for instructing medical students. With the medical schools back in full session, that dismal November night would have proved most opportune, however, these grave robbers wouldn't have thought twice about killing to render their nightly quota.

"Lady Worthington, I suspect that you must have had other reasons to seek the Bishop at this ungodly hour? Have you forgotten that you're under oath?"

"Not at all, sir."

"Was the Bishop at the Cathedral?"

"No, I journeyed across the Thames in search of him at his residence at Lambeth Palace."

"His residence?'

"Yes."

"Did you finally meet with him?"

"Well, not actually."

"What do you mean? Did you, or did you not meet with the Bishop?"

"To my dismay, Bishop Bartholomew and I were unable to meet at his residence. He simply was not available to receive me that night at his home."

"So, you returned to Worthington Estate?"

"Regretfully, my only choice was to return to the Cathedral."

"Let me rephrase my question. When did you finally return to the estate house?"

"I waited until the light of daybreak."

Constable Gordon raised his eyebrows, mumbling something under his breath. "Daybreak?"

I nodded my head, avoiding his gaze, hopeful of an end to this nerve-racking questioning.

"Yes, sir."

"What about the night Watchmen? Do you recall on that night, passing any of these enforcers of the law while traveling on foot?" he inquired.

"No, sir."

"I know of at least three watch posts that you must have encountered while en route to the riverfront," he argued.

"My statement remains," I insisted. "I did not have occasion to cross paths with one, two, nor anyone nearly resembling a Watchman."

"What did you do all night within the Cathedral, Lady Worthington?"

"I prayed to the Higher Powers."

The Constable shook his head from side-to-side, mumbling,

"Higher Powers?"

By the expression upon his face I could only infer he was confused beyond belief. Of course, there was still so much information, yet to uncover. During the interrogation, it had become as plain as the aloof, sophisticated nose upon my porcelain face that the Constable had increasing doubt concerning my story. With the hope of ascertaining more evidence, he planned to interrogate the Bishop in the future. At this point in the investigation, it was obvious Constable Nigel Gordon wasn't barren of clues, yet there was something still lacking—pertinent information to fully unlock the door to Kendall's fate.

From what I could only gather as the intervention of blessed souls whispering their pleas from beyond the veil, the Constable's sole recourse for the moment was to finally release me from his unrelenting questioning, and fortuitously I was set free.

Patricia Grace Joyce   *The Magic of Time*

.

Three

A full moon hangs within the sky
Observing life as time goes by;
And, gazing upward mesmerized
The stars shine brightly in my eyes

The universe unfolds its gifts
To all who hear the voice of change
A motion to go forward again
In times surreal with strife and pain

As the carriage approached the steep jagged cliffs that precariously hugged the coastline, my thoughts alternated, drifting from the present into the past, then floating back again, like the chilling gusts of salty coastal air. The rain was transforming from a dewy mist into a crystalline light snow, falling as if a glazed sugar-coating upon all that it touched. In the distance, I searched for some familiar form or recognizable light, a point of reference to determine the remaining journey time. The coach rounded a wide bend, initiating the long uphill climb to the top of the seaside cliffs. Eventually my traveling companions and I would finally reach the blackened iron gates of Thornwood Estate.

My imagination was spinning as I envisioned the large white-stone estate house situated upon a massive bluff, facing westward toward the sea. I sensed there would be many changes forthcoming in the days ahead with my relocation to Boscastle, bringing the world of the mystical and bizarre even closer to my doorstep.

To be a part of Thornwood Estate was truly an uncommon experience. A life of benevolence, elegance and luxury behind the main entry black estate gates was the only perception that the public was privy to, but within daily life at Thornwood Estate, the reality was far more complex and perplexing. It was as if a lace veil had been draped to shield and protect the unconventional essence of a world of eccentricity, mysticism and the macabre. In fact, life within Thornwood Estate bordered at times on the precarious razor sharp edge of the surreal.

The spirit world at Thornwood Estate was continually weaving its webbed influence around those who dared to set foot upon these sacred grounds. The ninety-room, white-pillared estate house had been in my family for over two centuries. As the sole heir and only surviving Thornwood descendant, my inheritance legally became the property of the Worthington family with my marriage to Kendall. Within this matrimonial bond, an increased economic value of more than twenty-fold was endowed upon him. Kendall was certainly guaranteed an upper crust lifestyle.

According to the English laws of marital inheritance, should my husband eventually be found dead, my ancestral home would legally be awarded to his ruthless brother, the lone surviving Worthington relation, Lord Russell Worthington.

I could only shudder as this consideration crossed my mind, an idea that was irritating to my serenity and inner peace. Although Kendall and Russell were fraternal twins, they had never shared a loving bond. I had knowledge, information well beyond the obvious concerning Russell, for at the virginal age of seventeen, I had somehow involved myself in a brief intimate affair with this man, merely a few months prior to my introduction to his brother. To say my relationship with Russell was devoted would be far from the truth. It was grossly fickle.

I have never forgotten an appalling incident that occurred along the Boscastle waterfront one foggy spring evening. Russell nearly lost his life dealing with a boisterous gang of pirates who often frequented the array of sordid drinking establishments along the docks. He was trading with these smugglers. Though warned to stay as far away as possible, he found himself increasingly intrigued by their cargo of contraband. With each new day, Russell could not stop conversing about the riches that lay waiting in port. The lure of power—an abundance of fine Italian silk, African spices, Chinese porcelain, French wines, perfumes and Spanish gold were as enticing as aphrodisiacs, difficult for even the most pious of mortals to resist.

Unfortunately for Lord Russell, it was a smuggling deal that would go terribly awry, leaving him maimed and grotesquely scarred for life. Not only was his handsome face repeatedly slashed and sliced from chin to ear, his thumbs were brutally hacked off from both hands.

It had been rumored this was the mark of the legendary pirate, Captain Ian Cutter. I knew for a fact, however, that it was more than merely hearsay. It was absolutely all Cutter's doing. It had been alluded to in passing gossip amongst the tavern clientele that the Captain had eyes for me, yet I had actually sensed the attraction weeks before our first encounter. My impressions were all confirmed from the very first moment I laid my eyes upon this princely man. Of course, I initially wanted to believe that our meeting was purely coincidental as I milled without a care amongst the village folk that April afternoon. I was in the company of my chaperone, Madam Marcella, strolling in the midst of a bustling marketplace along High Street. The sights and sounds of the vendors peddling their wares filled the air. Purple cabbages, lime-colored beans, claret-red plums, safflower-yellow corn, an array of toasted grains and multicolored herbs danced spryly before me as the vendors bartered within the market square. I hurriedly made my way through the crowd to Millicent's Millenary shop on a mission in search of a new spring bonnet, but who could ever have imagined on that fated day, I'd come away from Boscastle with more than just a new fashion accessory?

There he stood before me. Both of us stopped dead in our tracks, as if frozen in time.

Of course, Marcella and the sisters adamantly disapproved of my new friendship with this disarming character. The Captain's company demanded the utmost of secrecy. The more time we clandestinely shared under each other's spell, the more enamored we became. From that first day forward, I now realized that I could never have imagined how this man would influence my existence for better and for worse in the years to come.

With both Russell and Ian vying for my affections at that time, my life became rather baffling. It's true that on occasion I found myself content to be solely in the presence of Lord Russell. Still, oftentimes on ensuing nights I would find myself inexplicably drawn into the company of the alluring sea captain.

Over time, I concluded that Russell's discovery of the Captain's intimacies with me constituted part of the reason this trading deal had gone so terribly awry. From that day forward, Russell had never been the same. His disfigured face and hands bore the price of his greed, and I believed this maiming was the ultimate price he paid for my eventual indifference to him, resulting in my unrequited love.

Within days after the marring, however, the whereabouts of Cutter became a mystery. His schooner, *The Destiny* swiftly set sail from Boscastle, without so much as even a farewell kiss from him. To my knowledge, Captain Ian Cutter never returned to Boscastle, or to the port of London, and truthfully my heart has never moved on. As I continued to scan the horizon of my past, I could not deny there had always been chemistry, an attraction, between Russell and me. Whatever the real reasons might have been, it was short lived. How could I ever forget the competition and rivalry between Russell and his twin? If anyone should profit from the disappearance of my husband, wouldn't it seem likely that a jealous brother now had a grander motive to do so? It continued to elude me why the Constable failed to interrogate him. Could it be that he was protecting Russell in some manner? If this were truly the case, then why?

I sat within the solitude of my coach, wondering who truly had plausible motive to warrant Kendall harm, or even to have possibly killed him. Perhaps the Constable actually believed that Kendall's disappearance might be the result of a murder? My inner feeling at this time, however, was that he absolutely thought it could solely involve none other than me.

I pondered the likelihood that the Constable would conclude I had created this entire strangulation scenario as a clever charade, distracting the law in an effort to throw the investigation off course. Might the Constable have actually thought there was an intruder lurking within our chambers on that dreadful night—a hidden pair of eyes that silently observed the horrors, somehow contributing to Kendall's disappearance in the wake of the aftermath? It was true Kendall was not at a loss for enemies. Did the Constable honestly suspect the Bishop? However, who in their right mind, would, or could ever consider a man of the cloth in this suspicious matter?

If Kendall did depart the estate house in search of me on that night in question, perhaps theConstable thought his disappearance might be just an unfortunate circumstance of him being in the wrong place at the wrong time? If this were to have been the case, Kendall could have merely fallen victim to a gang of ruthless ruffians, only out to profit from harvesting a stiff—his dead corpse, however, any corpse would do for lowly scoundrels such as these. Freshly plotted graves were most often the common target for such endeavors. The advantageous slaughter of an inebriated dandy such as my husband would certainly have proven to be fair game for the taking by such lowly thugs. Surely the Constable would never consider that I could be capable of murder.

41

My thoughts were abruptly returned to the journey along the coastal route as the carriage wheels grazed a large tree stump in our path. I sighed, breathing deeply, and my senses were jarred. The crisp, cool winter air filled my lungs with a tingling sensation. I shivered, gazing blindly into the darkness on this icy February night, my mind slowly focused upon the present journey, and returning home to the village of Boscastle. It was the region of North Cornwall where my visions were now adrift. Off to the Cornish cliffs, overlooking the magnificent, healing waters of the Atlantic Sea was where I yearned to be, however, the unsettling bumps and the distracting noises from the elegant black horse-drawn carriage were more than I could endure. Consumed with exhaustion, my eyes closed with the hope of easing my unbearable anxiety on this blustery February night in the year of our Lord, 1811.

"When will we arrive?" I moaned aloud with exhaustion. Marcella stirred reluctantly, awakening from a languid slumber. With squinting eyes, she stared at me from across the darkened carriage interior. Clearing her throat, she responded in her familiar deep, raspy voice.

"Be patient. Look to the West. It's only a matter of time."

I pressed my face closely against the frosty window pane in an effort to discern anything of familiarity along the route.

"Search for the black gates upon the cliffs and breathe in the soothing sea air," she continued.

"Try to refresh yourself. I assure you, it's not much farther. Relax and take deep breaths. The salt air is so invigorating."

The darkness of the night made it difficult for me to see any great distance. A foreboding mist floated about, enhancing the shadows as the carriage traveled onward, crawling up the cliff side of the Cornish coast With my white-gloved hand, I rubbed the condensation from the icy carriage window, pressing my face even closer against the thin glass window pane to scan the horizon.

"Within the darkness of the night, observe the lights all aglow, welcoming you back home again."

I peered intently into the darkness as Marcella continued, "The Cornish cliffs and the Atlantic blue seas are softly calling your name. This is truly where you are meant to be."

"I cannot see anything, but the full moon," I sighed, "I'm exhausted. When will this journey end?"

"Close your eyes and say a prayer. Trust that all of this is happening in your life according to the plan, a Divine plan. The Higher Powers have a role for each and every one of us. Remember, it is indeed, what you agreed to, prior to coming into this life. All of this is the soul's choice to bring forth your destiny."

I fidgeted anxiously, twisting my long locks of chestnut-brown hair around my white-gloved fingers, wondering about this Divine plan that Madam Marcella was speaking of.

"You must have faith," she continued. "Trust, that the individual who you have become today is a cumulative consequence of the various past lives which your soul has lived. The soul is ageless, and has again returned over many lifetimes on earth to partake in fulfilling this Divine plan."

"I only wish that I knew what this plan was," I remarked.

"In due time all will be revealed."

"Easier said than done," I mumbled under my breath. I needed to know these things now, no longer patient to wait incessantly for the answers to come into my life.

The evening's brisk and gusting coastal winds were a constant reminder that the Cornish cliffs awaited nearby. The smell and taste of the salty air was a fragrance of long ago, my only comfort as I listened to the cold rain tapping lightly upon the carriage window. I repositioned my body, wiping the tears from my sallow face. Squirming impatiently within the confines of the darkened abyss of my coach, I grew increasingly nauseated with each passing moment. My bones throbbed with pain from the dampness of the chilling night air. I crossed my arms, supporting my sore breasts as I surrounded myself with several blankets, seeking the added warmth of a rabbit-hair muff to warm my small gloved hands.

The carriage proceeded along its precarious route, and I could neither sleep, nor stay awake from the restless motion.

"I've had just about enough of this," I persisted. "I cannot bear to sit here a moment longer. Please stop!"

The coachmen, John and Michael, slowed the carriage to an abrupt halt. Josephina and Caron escorted me out of the stuffy carriage, and onto the side of the road for a breath of fresh air. To their surprise, I was indeed taken ill for several minutes.

"Let me help you," said Marcella, waving her delicate white French lace kerchief. It was an exquisite, fine specimen that one hoped would never truly serve its intended purpose. "You know how I treasure this one in particular," she continued. "Your mother, the dear Duchess Sarah of Thornwood, gave it to me many years prior to her passing."

"But, Marcella, I feel so ill. Surely, the Higher Powers will show some mercy upon me and spare my young life of this suffering? I am a mere eight-and-twenty years. Can't you do anything for me? Won't you intervene with your magic?"

"Only when the timing is correct will you see the assistance you so desperately seek. I must first have a sign from the spirit world before I may intercede. Certainly, you realize the harm that could be done."

"Of course," I said, instantly recollecting the memory of a situation with a local weaver, Edith Comstock. Over the years, Edith's husband, Archibald, had procured a sordid reputation involving several of the Boscastle village whores. In fact, the rumors and gossip had become so rampant, neighbors couldn't help but wonder why Edith had remained unmoved and

44

disinterested in her husband's soiled laundry. Edith was becoming the laughing stock of the village as she continued to sit silently, spinning and weaving her colored yarns. At last, she succumbed, awakening one morning to find her husband with his cream-stained pantaloons swimming about his ankles, overcome with lusting arousal in the throes of poking a local whore, named Abigail Brighton. Edith sought the aid of the Mystic Women, more specifically Madam Marcella, to cast a spell upon her whore-mongering spouse. Initially Marcella was hesitant, however, warning Edith that she sensed it was not the proper time to work the spell, that in doing so without a full moon, the spell might result in unfortunate consequences, yet Edith raged like a mad woman, insisting that the spell be cast even without the guiding light of the of the full moon. Reluctantly, Marcella acquiesced, working her magic in an attempt to turn Archibald Comstock into a wild boar, all in accordance with his vengeful wife's wishes. Chanting her mystical words of incantation, Marcella held within her hands that very same pair of Archibald's pantaloons, and cast the spell by candlelight within a forest clearing.

Heed this clothing in my hand
Tailored pantaloons of this man
No more enduring one-night stands

Change him into a snorting boar
Fateful stepping upon all fours
Never more to poke this whore

Something, however, went terribly wrong that night, and regrettably Edith was the one who actually transformed into a wild boar before Marcella's eyes, grunting off into the neighboring brush, thereby freeing her husband to impregnate not only Abigail Brighton, but any whore he so desired.

45

"I have a feeling you've forgotten much of the magic since your younger days in Boscastle," Marcella continued. Her words swiftly transported my thoughts to the present. "I sense there are matters of grave concern looming about you," she said as her eyes closely observed my reaction to her comments.

She was absolutely right…again. Of course something was bothering me. I pondered whether, or not I should reveal all of my thoughts in confidence. Due to Marcella's keen senses, however, I imagined that she already was aware of my troublesome woe. Still, part of me could not restrain my agony any longer.

"Since Kendall's inexplicable vanishing nearly three months ago, I have been haunted by the memory," I blurted aloud. "Sometimes I feel as if my life will always be disturbed, like a dark shadow following me. I even wonder if I have unknowingly succumbed to the curse of a ruthless spell."

"The answers are within you," Marcella remarked. "This curse that you refer to is of your own doing, presented to teach you grand lessons in this life. It's all happening as part of the Divine plan, but you have much work to do."

"What are you saying?" I inquired with confusion.

"All I may reveal at this point is that you need to become more aware." Marcella smiled and said, "Now please permit Josephina, Caron and I to assist you into the carriage again. Let's try to make you more comfortable, and continue on our way. The sisters are waiting for us. Hurry, Grace. We must move on."

Slowly, I returned to the darkened clammy interior of my coach and the monotonous journey along the coast commenced once again.

"Go on. I'm listening. Please speak if you should feel up to talking. Share more of your thoughts with me," Marcella continued.

I must admit that I was more than baffled about this, yet I complied with her request. I told her that I often pondered the thought of perhaps no man could ever be worthy of me, nor for that matter, would I ever be worthy of another's affections. Sometimes I even wondered if, perhaps, I might be better off to simply exist without a man in my life, without the complications that a relationship could possibly invite. At the moment, however, all of these thoughts seemed in vain. How could I ever seriously consider another's affections when I was still imprisoned within this miserable bond with Kendall? What were these answers that existed within me? I found this all confusing. If the answers resided within me, why were they so elusive?

As the carriage climbed its way through the coastal night, I reflected upon thoughts of our marriage from its onset. I was hardly an innocent, naive girl of nineteen years. Yet, early on in the relationship, I came to the dismal realization of my inability to bear an heir. I could only conclude that this discovery became Kendall's raison d'être for his adulterous behaviors.

My husband's life had been preoccupied with governmental politics, including the politics of money, women and sex. Additionally, as a charismatic public figure, he was a standing member of Parliament within the House of Lords. There was a certain element of power, prestige and influence, a social acceptance and recognition through association with Lord Kendall Worthington. His material wealth and his position in society posed somewhat of an alluring attraction for most women, enticing to those who chose the path of greed, power and deceit to a man's heart. Although charming, he most definitely had his struggles with adversaries. Self-indulgence, self-importance, arrogance, vanity and his cantankerous behavior were only a small sampling of this man's finer qualities.

Kendall's disappearance had become not only a public intrusion in my life, but an assault on my personal character and privacy.

47

Outrageous accusations and innuendoes from the upper crust of society escalated on a daily basis. All of this resulted in drastic changes within my lifestyle. I now understood that the imagined portrait of my life in London would never be realized. My continuing shock and disbelief of all the issues currently at hand, contributed all the more adversely to my ever weakening alibi on that unforgettable night of fifteen November, 1810.

With these thoughts, I could feel the horses accelerating their pace to a steady gallop along the rocky coastal route. Blanketed by the thickening fog and the coldness of nightfall, the coachmen were fully aware of the hidden treachery that could lay in wait.

Michael and John shouted, "Ehh, Ladies. Hang onto yaw bonnets. 'Tis near the final stretch, slick with mud and ice."

Marcella approved of the change of gait, beaming a radiant smile in my direction. "You see, even the six horses are anxious to return to their country home for a warm and restful night within the stables."

The frigid night air eventually settled into the velvet richness of darkness. The only guiding light was that of the benevolent full moon. The horses periodically slowed their pace, maneuvering to circumvent the dangers of ice, mud and fallen tree limbs amongst the dry, frozen brush that breached the sinuous path. I could hear the gale winds from the coast increasing in force and strength as an occasional downpour of sleeting rain tapped rhythmically upon the coach, in harmony with the pace of the horses.

"Marcella," I said. "Do you believe Kendall may still be alive?"
The only reply was the faint sound of snoring. Marcella and my personal attendants had dozed off to sleep again. For me, however, the reality of the moment was all too interfering, an interruption of my day dreaming fantasies. My husband had simply vanished at the age of five-and-fifty. How and why did one simply evaporate into thin air?

Perhaps in time, the spirit world would bring forth all the answers to me. I believed in the Divine and prayed for their blessing of guidance along my new path. I wanted to trust that the Higher Powers would reveal all that was necessary for me to evolve, all the changes that must now become a part of my new life, including both the benevolent and the evil.

Searching the night skies from the darkness of my coach, my eyes were veiled with ambiguity. Though Kendall was the one who had been missing for nearly three months, the person truly lost at this time was none other than me.

Patricia Grace Joyce   *The Magic of Time*

Four

Whispers I have heard from beyond the veil
A feeling, a thought, an energy all reveal
These are guiding spirits manifested to instill
A sudden awareness, a message to be heeded
Many hear the knocking, but the door remains impeded.

Beyond the veil, beyond the veil
The voices beckon us to listen, be silent and still
A rhythm and a purpose for this and every season
Timing is of the essence. Trust, there is a reason
Beyond the veil

As the horses plodded methodically along their course, the resonance of echoing hoofs could also be heard rapidly approaching in the near distance. I sat upright and listened intently, alerted by the sound of the swiftness of their gait. Quickly I awoke my companions, just as a flurry of chaos engulfed the coach. The carriage wavered as we found ourselves regrettably surrounded by the unwelcome presence of two men racing wildly upon horseback. I braced myself, holding onto the interior door handle as the coach unexpectedly careened off course, sliding into the icy brush.

"What's happening?" I yelled in a panic to Marcella. The carriage swerved abruptly, slipping within the adjacent snow-crusted forest. Caron and Josephina screamed in fright as the arm of a frozen birch tree reached within the interior coach. I now discovered myself with Marcella, thrown upon the carriage floor in a tousled pile.

"Yaw bloody rogues," shouted Michael, as he drew his pistol, cussing at the intrusion of our unwelcome visitors. The carriage came to a sudden halt and I could hear the voices of the highwaymen shouting abrasively with our coachmen. We awkwardly repositioned ourselves upon the seat cushion as the sound of gunfire rang loudly within the tense night air.

"Drop yaw weapons and get yaw selves down," shouted one of the ruffians.

"Do now as we tell yaw, and yaw shan't be harmed," yelled the other rogue.

Again, I heard the exchange of gunfire. "Yaw bastards," Michael shouted. There was a scuffle as the two coachmen jostled about the front end of the coach. From the shattered window, my view was partially obstructed by the frozen tree limb that had comfortably made itself at home amongst us. I observed Michael's body slouching, only to fall with a hard thump upon the frigid brush as John made an effort in coming to his aid. I gasped in horror as Marcella hastily drew the carriage curtains shut. We clung onto one another with hopes the intruders would only take the luggage, yet it seemed ironic this was happening so near to our destination.

"Who are these highwaymen? What do they want?" I whispered.

"Hush. We'll soon find out," said Marcella. "Promise you'll let me do all the talking, should they dare to enter the coach."

In a rage of excitement, the doors to the carriage flew open announcing an unwelcome forceful gust of icy night air. I could see a moonlit sparkle glistening within the darkened eyes of the two masked intruders. One of the highwaymen was muscular, tall and thin, and the other was revoltingly rotund and short. The black-hooded strangers stood within the glowing light of a dimly lit lantern as they rudely shouted into the interior compartment, "Ladies, do as we tell yaw, or yaw shan't live to see the light err' nother day."

My heart was racing, and I could feel every solitary hair standing erect upon my clammy skin. I wanted to scream, but remembered Marcella's words. The rogues demanded our immediate departure from the coach. As we stood in fear, shivering amongst the snow covered brush, I observed the two men securing Michael and John together at the base of a large oak tree. Blood now stained the entire front of Michael's torso. His ashen face grew increasingly morose as he sat motionless—near death. The ruffians moved in our direction, roping our hands tightly behind our backs. Marcella spoke calmly in an effort to negotiate for our safety and release, but they persisted, ignoring her words of mediation.

"Shut yaw mouth, yaw blubbering old hag," cried the stout fellow.

Unfazed by their outburst, Marcella's eyes cleverly focused upon the two as they haphazardly confiscated their booty, making their intentions known. One-by-one they approached each of us, removing anything that appeared to be of monetary value. My attendants shrieked in terror with excruciating pain as the men pulled the pierced earrings from their fleshy earlobes, leaving a trickling trail of blood along the sides of their faces. I cringed as they approached me, bracing for the worse—my hands tightly fastened behind my back. The large-bellied ruffian lightly brushed my cheek with his black-gloved hand and whispered into my ear, "Such a sweet one we have in our sights 'tis night. It'd be a shame to let this lovely go wasted. Get yaw arse on the ground, me wench." I felt an ache within the pit of my stomach as I dropped to my knees in horror.

"Leave her be," shouted the taller rogue.

Under my breath, I sighed with relief at his merciful command, hopeful of escaping whatever wrath his fleshy companion had planned for me. As I knelt upon the frozen earth, I could feel my white gloves abruptly removed from my entwined hands, revealing my diamond wedding ring. The tallest man recklessly yanked the ring from my slender finger. I gasped, observing it now as a dazzling orb of blinding white light within the stranger's gloved fingertips. Chuckling, his body rolled with laughter as he held the ring upward, bathed within the brilliant rays of the full moon.

"This gem will bring a tidy sum," he boasted aloud in a deep, gruff voice.

"Ehh, I'd say so," yelled the squat fellow. "A pretty penny, indeed."

Oddly, in what seemed only the passing of a few moments, I could hear Marcella softly humming a whimsical rhyme as she chanted a verse aloud when suddenly, she released her pudgy hands and held her chubby arms outward into the night air to cast a spell.

Eye of bird, wings of night
Showing what is truly right
Cast a spell upon these thieves
Fly away amongst the trees
One, two, three be off with thee

Instantaneously, the two men stumbled about us in a daze, their eyes rolling backwards within their hooded skulls. It was as if they were drugged or in a drunken stupor. Having difficulty standing erect upon their now wobbling legs, the highwaymen staggered to their knees. Seconds later, they were lying upon the frozen ground, curled-up in balls and moaning in excruciating pain. As their contorted bodies wriggled and squirmed they were remarkably transformed into enormous squawking ravens, blacker than the pitch of coal.

With seemingly little effort Marcella untied our bindings, setting each of us free. After removing the tangled roping, I moved with caution toward the creatures, only to find myself halted by Marcella's fleshy palm, now gripped firmly upon my shoulder as the others scrambled towards the safety of the carriage.

"What are you doing?" Marcella demanded.

"My ring," I cried aloud in desperation.

"Let it go." Reluctantly, I followed her orders. The larger of the two scavengers now grasped the ring within its distinctive orange-yellow beak. Instantly, both birds took off, flying in the direction of the full moon. Obediently, I climbed back within the safety of the coach, still wondering why Marcella had stopped me from retrieving my wedding ring.

From the window, I now observed Marcella employing tremendous effort as she shuffled towards Michael, kneeling patiently next to him. She firmly placed her hands upon his chest, and in doing so, I couldn't help but notice her six fingers. Then, pausing briefly she retrieved a small piece of white parchment from within her cloak pocket. Positioning the paper upon the coachman's motionless chest, Marcella closed her eyes and again chanted aloud.

Light of moon, thorn of rose
Force of life, head-to-toe
Cast a spell from this witch
Heal this coachman in the ditch
Herbs of frankincense and sage
Write his name upon this page

Miraculously, Michael stirred, awakening from death's embrace with absolutely no sign of the bullet injury. Quite remarkably, the wound had completely disappeared. Turning-over the piece of parchment, Madam Marcella slowly arose to her feet and held it upright for all of us to view. The word *Michael* inexplicably appeared written in blood upon the paper.

Josephina, Caron, John and I gasped simultaneously with astonishment, our faces clearly mesmerized by the magic that had occurred before our eyes on this night. Michael sat upright, gradually rising to a standing position as if nothing had occurred...then walked slowly, settling into his full bearings and joined John to survey the damage of the coach I stared in a state of continuous awe as Marcella instructed the coachmen to collect the ruffians' clothing, placing each article so as to create a pile.

With the nod of her head, she spun her rotund body in a circular motion and extended her arms once again, casting another spell.

Puff of white, gray and black
Disappear to leave no track

The clothing vanished into a swirl of smoke, leaving no evidence of any intrusion by the highwaymen.

"These blokes won't be bother'n us again anytime soon," the coachmen mused. "And, fortunately, me ladies, the horses and coach remain unharmed, other than a broken window."

"These miserable souls are no longer of human flesh, doomed forever to roam the earth as winged beasts. May this teach them a lesson. True wealth is not of the material world, but of the richness of the soul. Carry on," said Marcella, as she patted the two ruffians' horses, releasing them so that the coachmen could secure the reins, enabling the horses to piggyback with our carriage.

Sighing with relief as the coach traveled onward, I looked at Marcella with bafflement.

"Who were these men?"

"The Higher Powers are speaking," she replied, "They claim that these rogues were the mark of evil sent to intercept us upon our path. I sense that someone has made a point of letting us know they're quite mindful of your whereabouts. Someone who hides behind a façade or mask is leery of you knowing their true identity." She continued, "From this point forward, you must be extremely cautious, even if need be, taking measures to look over your shoulder."

I gulped and swallowed hard, realizing we had brushed much too close for comfort with ill will, perhaps even near death. "But, who could this person be? And, why would someone dispatch two rogues to take our valuables?"

"I sense this robbery was all contrived, a set-up by whomever had sent these ruffians to find you, yet little did they know the forces that awaited to intercede their fate. Trust. Eventually we'll discover more about the mysterious person who orchestrated this. Sit back and try to rest. We're safe now."

I didn't like the sound of this, as I nervously eyed Marcella and my attendants within the carriage. I persisted, "But, how did you do this?"

"It's really not all my doing, Grace. It's the magic. The Higher Powers are always here for us."

With these words, it seemed imminent as we approached the estate grounds; the days to come would prove more and more revealing, more and more haunting.

We journeyed onward for what seemed an eternity until slowly the carriage came to a halt. I breathed a deep sigh of relief as we finally arrived at Thornwood Estate, hearing the coachmen, John and Michael, yell aloud to the horses. "Whoa! Easy! Whoa! There yaw go. Now we are home safely, sweet ladies. Whoa!"

In the distance, the outlines of three women wearing ivory-colored sheer flowing, ankle-length gowns were set against the defining contrast of the night. With colorful elegant full-length cashmere shawls cloaked about their shoulders, they quickly approached the carriage, advancing from the golden-colored main entry doors of the estate house. The brisk night air was intense, causing their breath to mist as I observed their lips mouthing inaudible words. This vision seemed surreal as I gazed in awe at the contrails of breath dispersing into the night sky. An eerie dankness kissed my dewy skin, reminding me of the past, confirming without a doubt I was once again within the magical realm of the spirit world.

"Good evening and welcome home," exclaimed the sisters. "We've so looked forward to this day. With the blessings of the Higher Powers, our prayers implore that all will be well for you."

I smiled, nodding my head which now felt as heavy as a boulder, soon to roll off my aching shoulders and come crashing down upon the frozen estate grounds. Clara, Victoria and Lindsey rushed to join me and the entire entourage. Surrounding the exterior of the carriage, the sisters anxiously peered within the coach, observing us with lit candles in hand. For a moment I felt as if I was a freak of nature in a traveling side-show, under the gawking scrutiny of its audience, yet perhaps I was acting much too suspicious. The sisters simply had not seen me for the past nine years, and were obviously quite focused upon how I had fared. I breathed a sigh of relief. Finally, for the first time in many years, I could honestly say that I actually felt safe again. At last, I was home.

Clara, a delightful age fifty, was the second eldest of the Lumiere sisters. Her refined physical beauty was classically alluring. Tall and curvaceous, her astounding beauty was further enhanced by her long flaming-red hair, green eyes and hour-glass figure. As the nurturer in the family, she was a teacher of wisdom —honest, compassionate and fair. Her presence, awareness, clarity and energy exuded warmth within the household. While Marcella was definitely the patriarch of Thornwood Estate, Clara was the matriarch. Together they raised me with the sisters, Lindsey and Victoria.

Within this domicile of women, the Lumiere sisters functioned quite competently, managing Thornwood Estate. I was particularly grateful of their financial savoir-faire, since I had been unable to handle the daily assets of the estate due to marital circumstances necessitating my relocation to London.

Throughout the years, these Mystic Women had accrued tremendous affluence, wielding their powerful influence as shamans and energy healers within the Cornish coastal region. With the exception of Lindsey, the sisters were generous and known to be actively involved with humanitarian causes for the betterment of Boscastle. I had granted my consent and full blessings, designating that much of the Thornwood wealth be donated over time throughout the villages of Cornwall, serving to assist those less fortunate souls—the orphans, the homeless, the lepers, the maimed and afflicted, the hungry and the destitute.

"We've had a rough journey," continued Marcella. "The coach was overtaken by the intrusion of two rogues, but now we're safely home and gratefully none the worse for it."

I had always admired Marcella's bravado and devout faith in life, often wondering if I would ever be able to view my life in a positive vein again. For the time being, however, I wasn't feeling *none the worse* from our recent crisis. On the contrary, my memory was troubled by the ordeal we had recently incurred along the roadside.

"The sisters and I had sensed danger for you," Clara said, as she poked her head within the carriage interior. Are you all right?"

"Yes," replied Marcella. "We're quite fine now, just a little shaken up by the intrusion, but everything was under control with a little assistance from the Higher Powers."

"Thank the Divine that you're all safe," said Victoria.

John and Michael smiled and proceeded to fully open the carriage doors, assisting me with my descent as I sighed, "Yes, thank the Divine." I extended my white-gloved hand to both of them, stepping forward from the darkened, musty carriage interior and moving into the radiance of my newfound world at Thornwood Estate.

"We're so joyful to be reunited," Clara said. "I, for one have missed you over these many years."

"You'll always be family to me," I said, making my way from the carriage onto the estate grounds.

"Equally," she remarked.

"How lovely to be home again."

"I feel as if I'm dreaming. Is it really you?" inquired Victoria

"Without a doubt. And, I have missed not only all of you…but the spirits…especially my mother and father, the deceased Duchess Sarah Thornwood and Duke Jonathan Thornwood. They were everything to me," I said.

My parents had lived rather exceptionally, in the sense that they were eccentric and open-minded for the times in which they lived, not only dressing in unconventional clothing, they often upheld radical viewpoints regarding many issues in life.

"My only consolation has been that I've had communication with them from time-to-time," I continued. "Truly, I believe they bring me comforting messages, surrounding me in their loving energy."

"At last, they have safely returned you to your home by the sea," Victoria said.

Lindsey interrupted, "Well, if you communicate with them so often, how could you possibly miss them so much?"

"Hush!" What I really wanted to tell her was that I could see absolutely nothing had changed over the past nine years between her and me, but I was weary tonight, and not in any mood, nor frame of mind to argue.

At forty years of age with long, charcoal-black straight hair and large dark-blue eyes, she was still the same old Lindsey, hardened, abrupt, sleazy and ruthless. In fact, her attire was often mistaken for that of a whore, boldly colorful and scant with an emphasis on exposing her fleshy body. Ruthless by nature, she was vindictive

60

to a fault. When she spoke, her shrill, annoyingly abrasive voice echoed her wrath.

It has been said that time heals all pains. Quite obviously, time had not healed my rift with Lindsey. The wound was still festering. She and I had never seen eye-to-eye, and at times her behavior actually terrified me. She never gave a second thought to crafting an evil spell or cursing a foe. It was winner take all for Lindsey, absolutely no compromises. I pitied the poor soul who fell victim to her spell.

I guess in some strange way I now pitied myself, having to again live in close proximity to Lindsey. Nearly thirteen years ago, the sisters banned her from residing within the Thornwood Estate house, stipulating that her presence would be on an *invitation only* basis. Quite frankly, her wicked magic had taken its toll on all of us, a frightening series of events that motivated the sisters to take drastic action.

In particular, I recalled one ominous episode during the spring. It was a cool March evening and the sun was setting in the western sky, aflame in a glory of fiery pink and orange. That which transpired could only be remedied by a spell, at least that's how I remembered Lindsey justifying her actions. It was a spell that reeked of deception, a cunning act of vengeance.

On that spring evening Lindsey had fed the family cat, Barnacle, his dinner meal of calves liver and chicken gizzards, when suddenly there was an intrusive pounding at the estate door. To our surprise, it was the widow, Charlotte Hillsborough, an attractive well-endowed woman of three-and-thirty who had come knocking. This was a rather bold move, according to Lindsey, for she was disturbed by Charlotte's untimely and unannounced visit. The truth of the matter, however, was that Lindsey envied this woman's ways of persuasion with the gentlemen in Boscastle, for even after her husband's passing, Charlotte had no difficulty finding an audience of interested suitors. Engaging them, however, to stay in her company for more than one night seemed to be a challenge, only perpetuating her desperate actions in an effort to alleviate the pain of her never-ending loneliness.

Now, by no means did Charlotte intend any real harm tapping upon the golden Thornwood Estate doors that evening. She was merely a lonely widow, accustomed to parading about the village without invitation, babbling about anything and to anyone, consumed within her self-serving behavior to occupy her idol hours.

The Lumiere sisters piteously welcomed Charlotte into the drawing room that night, offering her a glass of claret. As the grandfather clock sounded with each passing hour, one glass of wine led to another, then a third until finally after the sixth, the widow Hillsborough was slurring her speech. The now tipsy Charlotte slowly removed herself from the drawing room chaise, intending to return to her coach, only to stumble upon poor Barnacle and crushed him to death.

In a raging furry, Lindsey spun angrily about the room, caressing the limp Barnacle within her arms. Twirling like a funnel cloud, Lindsey raged like a storm. Charlotte only became more dazed and confused, apologizing profusely for the unfortunate incident, but Lindsey would hear no part of it. With her eyes now focused upon the inebriated widow, Lindsey chanted aloud.

As I view this widow stand
I implore the spirits grand
With a motion of my hand

Now there is no turning back
Charlotte shall become a rat
Doomed to perish in my trap

In a matter of seconds, the widow Hillsborough withered, shriveling before our very eyes and morphing into an enormous gray rodent. With penetrating beady black eyes, she gazed hatefully upon Lindsey, biting upon her ankle before scampering off into the darkness of the long estate hallway.

For days, we searched high-and-low within the estate house, hoping to recover Charlotte the rat. Alas, all was in vain until Lindsey beat us at her evil game, stumbling upon the long-tailed creature, only to crush poor Charlotte to death. "What goes around comes around," chanted Lindsey.

From that day forward, Lindsey was expelled from the Thornwood Estate house, permitted only to enter by invitation from the sisters. Lindsey now resided, however, within a spacious guest house upon the property, huddled snuggly between the slate-chiseled cliffs. The guest house faced outward upon the Atlantic. She was now free, to go about her own business, casting her spells in the privacy and seclusion of her clandestine world, the realm of black magic. The sisters and I had at least found some degree of peace, a contentment knowing Lindsey was no longer under foot to disrupt our day-to-day household.

"Perhaps a warm bath would help?" Victoria said. My body quivered as my thoughts raced forward to the present.

With long blonde curls and soft blue eyes, Victoria was the youngest of the sisters at the age of thirty years. Rather plain in her appearance, Victoria dressed conservatively to detract any attention from her frail physique. Born with a deformed leg, she walked with a limp. She and I always had a special fondness for each other, and I knew she understood me the best, for even at this very moment, Victoria realized I was flustered and irritated by Lindsey's thoughtless remark.

I'll have a housemaid draw water for a lovely bath," she continued, "We'll have more time to visit and chat tomorrow."

"That's wonderful. A bath suits me fine." After five long days of travel I would feel more like conversing in the morning. "Now, if you'll be so kind, please pardon my sudden departure. It's not the company, but the hour. Good night. Until tomorrow." Hugging each of the sisters, I ambled onward.

"We absolutely understand," said Clara. "Take this evening to get settled, unpacked and to collect your thoughts."

"With twelve pieces of luggage, I gather you're here for the long term?" Lindsey queried. "If you should need me to work my magic to rid your life of whomever, and whatever, my powers can be rather enlightening for better, or for worse. No one who claims to be united with the craft can hold a candle to my mystical ways."

I rolled my eyes in an effort to put up a brave front and nonchalantly replied, "Oh, yes Lindsey. I'll be sure to let you know." At this time, I believed she was the absolute last person on the face of this earth that I'd seek for spiritual guidance. With courageous disregard, I swung my head and body forward, departing with Caron and Josephina. My weary frame now moved swiftly toward the oversized arched golden-colored entry doors, searching for a moment of calm.

The flurrying wet snowflakes danced upon my warm face, melting into a hundred dewy kisses. A blizzard of emotions raced through me. I was simultaneously anxious, excited and relieved to finally be home again, relishing the thought of resting comfortably on this frigid winter's night.

We advanced into the marble foyer, where an opulent crystal chandelier from the island of Murano, Italy elegantly hung; suspended aglow with thirty-five large white candles. In passing the entry to the drawing room, from the corner of my eye, I caught a glimpse of my black piano.

By candlelight, Josephina, Caron and I climbed the graceful mahogany staircase ascending to the various sleeping chambers. A flood of memories illuminated within my head like the

64

flickering of candlelight reflecting from the crystal chandelier. Since my childhood, I had remained haunted by the tragedy of my parents' untimely death, often wondering if death was ever really a timely matter. The memory of their mysterious fall from atop the Cornish cliffs had never abandoned me. Bordering the western boundary of Thornwood Estate, the rugged sea cliffs extended their reach deep within the Atlantic Sea. The mysterious circumstances of Duchess Sarah and Duke Jonathan still remained an enigma, one that alluded to accidental death, murder and even rumored by the local village folk to have been a passionate double-suicide.

"We've arrived, Lady Grace," said Caron.

Without wasting a minute, I entered into the room, collapsing upon the soothing comfort of my white featherbed as I awaited my bath water, drawn by a housemaid. A fire roared in the massive marble fireplace, warming the entire room. The solid white-colored walls contrasted with the lush floral Oriental carpet which was dusted in soft, feminine colors of pink, silver, white and peach, extending the full length and width of the wooden flooring. This exotic carpet had been a present of adoration from Captain Cutter many years ago, contraband cargo gifted extravagantly upon me as one of his many tokens of affection.

My thoughts returned to Thornwood Estate as I gazed about the bedroom chamber. Removing my black cashmere cloak, I disrobed from the conservatively tailored, black and gray form-fitted traveling clothes. My attire was rather mundane, yet all proper for that of a grieving widow in half-mourning. "I bid these drab clothes a fond farewell. I shall have no use for them here in Boscastle, no need for false appearances any longer."

Although my half-mourning garb might have seemed like a premature display to some, the publicity of my husband's disappearance forewarned that while I was in London, to dress in my usual festive colorful garb would only have focused additional unwelcome attention upon me, opening the door to more burdensome gossip amongst the law, high society and the general public.

With the aid of my attendants, I unfastened my silk and satin under garments, removing my black French silk stockings as Josephina assisted with pinning my locks of hair upon my head. The candlelight danced a thousand dances upon the surrounding walls within the chamber. As I prepared to bathe, I slowly submerged my body into the soothing, warm bath water—firstly my feet, then my long slender legs and eventually my entire torso, until my breasts gently eased into the comforting warmth of the rose-scented waters. I welcomed the sensations of pleasure inviting me to relax. Dismissing Caron and Josephina, I continued to bathe during that hour. At last, I was finally alone.

"Oh, illusions. Why are there so many in my life?" I whispered. My eyes watered with emotion as I stared upon my ringless finger. My thoughts wandered back to the night of fifteen November, enthralled in frenzied passion within the Cathedral. My body tingled with flushed sensations racing throughout my entire being. Laying my head back, I parted my legs. I could feel the heat of arousal racing from my head to my toes. The warm scented bath waters were caressing and seductive, and the motion of the water lapping against my body, rhythmically played between my quivering thighs. With building anticipation, I quickly achieved my intentions, moaning softly in ecstasy, as I envisioned myself in a gentleman's arms. Fantasies clouded my thoughts, dreaming of true love. I sensed that only *he*, could possibly feed the depths of my hunger, and provide the food of my soul that I so lusted and desired at this time. As I continued to bathe, my body remained immersed within the soothing waters, fully aware that the magic of Thornwood Estate was beckoning to merge with my essence once again.

Five

We all have dreams that fill our hearts
Some are clear, yet some are not
But, when I think of you, my dear
My only hopes are that you care

I pray my dreams will soon unfold
Unite together, a love to behold
I know deep in my heart and soul
This love was destined to be so

My eyes blinked as I awakened in the midst of the shadowed night. The cold coastal breeze billowed playfully in-and-out of the sheer-white curtains that hung like a thin veil, gracefully lacing each of the large vertical windows within the bedroom chamber. Disoriented, I laid awake in my bed, motionless. Several minutes passed as I found myself gazing outward into the chamber surroundings, observing the brightness of the moonbeams penetrating within the room. The radiant moonlight caressed my skin, reassuring me that once again I was in the arms of safety at my home in Boscastle. At last, I could breathe with reassurance and less worry, trusting that Kendall would not be storming through these chamber doors.

The cool sea air was invigorating to my senses as I felt it touching lightly upon my cheeks. I tasted its saltiness upon my tongue, wafting sinuously like a ribbon throughout the bedroom space. Simultaneously, the warmth of the roaring fire, softly embraced my entire being as it blazed brightly within the bedroom chamber fireplace.

Gradually my eyes became more focused, adapting to the pretentious furnishings within the suite. Slowly acclimating to this new environment, my mind raced with thought. Such a beautiful night it truly was, a night that I sensed would long be a part of me.

How this moon did speak tonight, whispering softly into my ear, beckoning for me to move closer toward the westward windows facing onto the sea. Slowly, I arose, graciously responding to its call. I could feel every hair upon my skin standing tall as I departed from the comfort of my sumptuous pearl-white featherbed. One of the large glass window panes rested modestly ajar, enabling the icy night air to fully greet me. I approached the window with the intention of bolting it into a secured position. Shivering from the frosty kisses of sea air upon my face, I reached at the foot of my bed for a white woolen blanket to wrap around me.

I listened in solitude to the glorious rhythm of the great Atlantic on this winter's night as I stood before the large windows. The thrashing of the high seas against the rugged slate cliff formations was a welcome symphony to my ears. This was the music of nature, a magnificent sight to behold under the magic of a glowing full moon. The waters were both soothing and at the same time ever so powerful. Indeed, they too seemed to speak to my soul. Looking out upon this majestic ocean, I imagined the sea commencing a conversation and saying, "Stay with me, Grace. Come closer, for I yearn to embrace you. It has been far too long, since you have danced within my arms. How I desire to be as one with you again!"

Time seemed to stand still as I viewed the moon's brilliance, glistening like a diamond upon the open sea. Mesmerized by the sounds of this rhythm of the night, I felt as if I had succumbed into a trance, my eyes now staring blankly beyond the veiled windows and into the voided darkness.

The wind rushed, howling as I listened to its discordant voice. I could hear the haunting wail of the Boscastle blow hole as the low-tide waters surged within its hollowed portal. Without explanation, my attention was drawn to the sighting of a brilliant light upon the distant shore. "What is this?" I whispered, watching the magnificent orb's movement as it advanced at a snail's pace along the shoreline. Squinting, I strained my eyes to discern the hazy image of what appeared to be a dark figure with a lantern in tow. Who could this soul possibly be, combing the beachfront at such a late hour of the night? Attempting to make some sense of this oddity, I could only conclude that it might have been a tin miner, exploring the rocky coastal caves in search of a rich excavation site.

The region of Cornwall was lush and fertile, offering a variety of livelihoods for its inhabitants. Along the coast, the shipping and fishing industry was indeed prolific. Additionally, the inland area provided the bountiful farming of land and livestock—goats, sheep and cattle—as worthy occupations, but the mining of tin ore was the major source of revenue in the Cornwall region, attracting what seemed to be an endless stream of mine workers to its westerly coast.

I curiously observed the figure until the orb's radiant light grew dim, fading into the murky fog of the night. Although puzzled, I had grown weary and returned to my bed. Stilling my thoughts, I nestled beneath the bedcovers. My mind drifted off to sleep once again as the crashing seas composed, playing their soothing music of the night. The rhythmic sounds of the turbulent waters led me into a dream state, the magical realm that so often spoke to me. It was this mystical world that I frequently visited, the spirit world of messages and images from the other side, beyond the veil.

Within my sovereignty of dreams this night, I was led into the presence of many elegantly dressed individuals. Wrought with bewilderment, I searched the myriad of faces, attempting to find a mutual recognition with someone, anyone. The guests appeared to be aristocratic men and women; however, I failed to distinguish any familiarity as I found myself wandering discretely amongst an ebbing sea of strangers.

Who were these people and where was I? Intrigued by the evolving drama surrounding me, I strolled carefree about the room. I could hear the chatter of conversation and the shrill of laughter about me. The music of the night wafted innocently, weaving its spell throughout the ballroom.

As I listened to the melodious sounds about me, I recognized the music of Ludwig Von Beethoven. The orchestra was playing the Moonlight Sonata. How I adored this piece! Observing my surroundings, I viewed myself centered within the midst of what appeared to be an ornate social affair. Its specific nature, however, still remained unclear to me. I thought that perhaps I was at a dinner party. Or, could this possibly have been an elegant wedding gala? Might it even have been the infamous Prince Regent's Ball? All I could gather at this point was that I felt honored and privileged to have been present at such a splendid occasion.

Surveying my situation, my thoughts considered the attending guests. Here I stood as a complete stranger, yet there was an aura of open acceptance floating about me, engaging me in conversation and celebration.

The music was intoxicating. I listened with passion, wanting more and more as I felt my body dancing into the lush velvet hours of the night. Throughout this enchanting affair, I perused the varied assortment of guests, sipping a selection of fine wines and liquors from French crystal stemware. Without a single word spoken, I knew that somehow I was not an outsider amongst them, somehow I belonged. It was a knowing, as if at this very moment every cell in my body—my flesh and bones understood that my physical presence in this room tonight was for a distinct purpose, a grander notion than that of merely engaging in conversation with eloquent guests, sipping exotic spirits. I danced like there was no tomorrow, all the while hoping that the sun would sleep, and forget to awaken the next morning.

I held my head high, poised with balance as an air of nobility surrounded me. My body glided effortlessly, swaying back-and-forth upon my nimble feet, in-step with every rhythm of the orchestra. From the corner of my eye, I viewed the lavish décor swirling about the room, dotted with decadent hanging candle lit crystal chandeliers. Pausing, I stopped to catch my breath and gazed appreciatively at my image within a tremendous gold-leaf mirror. My reflection echoed a translucent, elegantly flowing white, stylish, high-waisted ball gown. The low-cut neckline dramatically revealed the preponderance of my creamy firm bosom, accentuating the bust line with a single strand of snowflake-white colored Roman pearls and matching pearl-drop earrings.

The attending female guests also wore similar fashionable attire, although some were garbed more colorfully in pastel pink, subtle peach, celery green, safflower yellow and indigo blue. The gentlemen guests were clad handsomely in their very finest ballroom apparel of dark evening suits, accented with ivory-white French laced muslin and silk shirts, black and gray tapered pantaloons and swallow-tailed evening jackets. Complimenting colorful silk cummerbunds embraced their waistlines as luscious silk cravats lovingly hugged their necks.

The scent of the finest French perfumes and colognes hung heavily throughout the room as I made my way toward a well-groomed male servant, in search of another glass of champagne to quench my thirst.

Rather unexpectedly, a distinguished, stately gentleman appeared within the crowd. His dark brunette locks of hair, softly framed his elegantly refined face as he moved forward from the depths of the lightness beyond. His skin was the color and texture of fresh cream...pure, flawless and fair. His eyes were large, intriguing and painted a vibrant lapis blue, deeper than the depths of the ocean. I could feel his sights adhered upon my every move as I gazed in his direction, acknowledging his presence with a nod of my head. Smiling at my response, he compassionately gestured with his extended hand for me to approach him.

I blushed shyly, slowly nearing in his direction, cautiously moving towards him. The thought of locating another glass of tempting French wine swiftly abandoned my mind. I was mesmerized, unable to resist his enticing eyes, and immediately drawn to him as if a bee to honey. Removing a silk-white glove, he revealed one of his elegant well-formed hands. The gentleman respectfully bowed.

"Good evening, Madam. I would be honored to have this dance with you."

I was stunned. Who was this? For an instant, I wondered if he was actually speaking to me as I hesitated and looked around for another to respond and advance forward into his awaiting arms. Without giving his request another thought, I replied, "I shall be delighted to dance with you sir." Smiling, I curtsied and welcomed his invitation.

Reaching out to gently grasp my small gloved hand, he pulled me toward him. I found myself sashaying onto the white and gray-veined marble dance floor, lost in an elegant sea of swirling lights, colors, scents and sounds. As we danced, the gentleman softly caressed my delicate face, with his long-tapered fingers lightly brushing against my blushed cheek. He stroked the outline of my full red lips, swiftly pulling me closer in warm embrace. My lungs searched for air, yearning for a deeper breath. I felt my heart racing faster and faster. Listening to its pulsating rhythm, I understood that he sensed my arousal.

I could not fathom ever having experienced a level of contentment as I did this night. Sensations of anticipation and intrigue filled my heart. Although there were hundreds of guests celebrating this evening in our midst, it was as if we were the only two people within the magnificent ballroom, caught within an elegant web of timelessness.

He closed his eyes, kissing my breast and drew me nearer into him, exhibiting a full appreciation of this moment. My wet lips blossomed like a flower, meeting his in a long passionate kiss. I could feel his arousal pressing firmly against me. Adoringly, he stood before me and paused, staring into my eyes. His warm full lips softly caressed mine, engulfing me as his tongue lovingly penetrated into the beckoning depths of my mouth. The beating of my heart pounded, as if it were a drum resonating its rhythm to the music. My entire being was lost in the magic of this attraction as I lusted for more.

"You're a precious gift, a rose without thorns," he said.

Truly something extraordinary was occurring under the glow of this beaming full moon. Our hearts were lost in each other's spell, lost in the magic.

Stirring in my bed, I reluctantly awakened only to find myself surrounded again by the stillness of the darkened suite. I could hear the faint crackle of the waning fire within the chilled bedroom chamber, however, to my surprise the remote sound of enthralling piano music played softly in the distance.

"How peculiar," I whispered, wondering who could possibly be playing my piano at such an early hour. Nonetheless, I had to consider that perhaps I was only imagining the sounds ringing through my ears. As I listened, there was no doubt it was the ethereal music of the Moonlight Sonata wafting from within the first floor drawing room. How could this be? Only my dear father and I had played this instrument. I was puzzled. For a split second, I even believed this was possibly a much welcomed visitation from father's spirit, but I dismissed these thoughts just as quickly, attributing it to my overactive imagination.

It was the predawn hours of another new day. I quickly arose with the intention of investigating, moving closer to the chamber doors. The wintry morning air was frosty and my hands tingled from the cold as I grasped a woolen shawl to drape about my shoulders. Having no sooner moved a few feet in the direction of the doors, the music abruptly halted. The frigid chamber now filled with the nothingness of silence. An emptiness rang loudly.

I thought this all very irregular. Was my mind playing games? As I focused my thoughts, it became more and more apparent that either I was hallucinating, or my yearning to communicate once again with father's spirit was truly the case. In passing years, his loving entity had made many attempts to commune with me, bringing forth messages in my dreams. If this was indeed father, I was more than mildly confused as to what information he desired to convey. Considering this, I slowly recollected the images of my recent lucid dream. Who could this charming dark-haired gentleman possibly have been?

Unable to remember ever having laid eyes upon this intriguing man before, I found my attraction to him rather beguiling. I sensed a familiarity, some sort of knowing him from deep within my heart and soul. I could still smell his lingering cologne, taste his sweet lips, clearly see his alluring gaze, feel his energy and hear his softly spoken words of lust. The very essence of his compassionate soul enfolded me, as the memory of the haunting Moonlight Sonata continued to reverberate within my head. I couldn't help but wonder if perhaps this endearing gentleman could possibly have been a Divine love sent to nurture my heart and soul. "I pray this be my destiny," I whispered.

With these words, I was startled by the interruption of a knocking upon the chamber doors. My body jolted with the shock of the disturbance as I swiftly considered the possibilities at such an early hour of the morning. It was nearly dawn. "Is there no peace for a weary soul?" I murmured. My heart raced, as I

74

imagined that perhaps some dreadful spirit had found its way to my chamber. Did I even dare to open the door? Again, I heard the tapping, but my head filled with images of father. Could it truly be he? Anxiously, I approached the double doors.

"In a minute. Just one moment, if you please," I whispered. With a lit candle in hand, I ventured closer. "Who's there? Who is it? Who's calling on me in these early morning hours? Please speak and make yourself known."

Within the stilled silence, a woman's soft muffled voice replied,

"Grace, it's me, Madam Victoria. Please, open the doors. I can't bear to wait a moment longer."

"Thank the Higher Powers, it's only you." With great relief I moved in the direction of the chamber entryway, only to find the doors secured. I wondered who dared to lock me within the chamber as my elation quickly turned to panic. I struggled futilely to open the massive chamber double doors, pulling with all my womanly might on the interior door handles.

"I can't get out. Where are the keys?"

"Keep calm," she said. Instantly, "click, click, click", the doors gave way as if simply unlocking on their own.

"There we go. Just like old times." Victoria proceeded to effortlessly fling open the doors, entering into the bedroom suite. We hugged, kissing each other, tossing with laughter in celebration as if gleeful children dancing about the room.

"What happened?" I asked.

"There's no need to discuss what simply *is*. It's the magic."

Again, I had forgotten the magic and could only wonder when my powers would at last return to me. As I viewed Victoria, I hesitated before asking her about the piano music that had filled the air this morning, wondering if perhaps it too, was the magic calling out to me.

"Did you hear the music playing?" I inquired.

"Ah yes."

"Was this also the magic?"

"The magic is always with you," she replied.

"How can this be?" I asked, recalling that my powers had deteriorated to a state of nonexistence.

"In time, you will become more aware," she said. Once again, here was the issue of my awareness coming before me.

"Aware of what?"

"Aware of more than you can even dream to envision today," she replied. "The Higher Powers will show you the way, now that you have returned to Thornwood Estate."

With these words, my mind flooded with images from my childhood at the estate house, I despised being confined, controlled or locked up. I was such a free and independent soul. I told Victoria how I remembered the many nights when venturing as a young girl, walking in my sleep throughout this grand estate house. There were so many baffling incidents that occurred at Thornwood Estate. My memory was bubbling, overflowing with haunting visions and conversations, the many antics of these spirits in the night. It was usually during the calm of darkness that these beloved souls would come forth to show their true light. The whispers echoing in the shadows were memories I would never forget. There were so many doors leading to the various wings of the estate house, I would quickly become confused as to which one would lead me back to the safety of my chamber suite within the main estate house.

I had always remembered a particularly strange vision that had its initial onset when I was the young age of eight years. It was during the winter months, the snow falling heavily, and I could hear the crystal flakes tapping gently upon my window pane. I was restless that evening, having difficulty falling asleep. I wandered down the long hallway into Marcella's bedroom suite to awaken her with the hope of receiving a cup of warm milk and one of her mouth-watering fruit filled hot pasties, a Cornish puffed pastry delicacy that melted in one's mouth. Recalling this memory, I could still taste the buttery flaky crust and sugary-sweet ripened fruit preserves. My most favorites were the raspberry, strawberry and blackberry filled pasties.

On that night, Marcella delivered to my bedside, not only one fruit-filled pasty, but a second so that I might have another should I awaken again during the night. In retrospect, I now realized that Marcella's actions were intended to insure her own restful sleep, thereby, her actions of over compensating with generosity so as to keep me content. I ate the first pasty and gulped half of my warm milk, soon to fall fast asleep. During the night, however, I awoke to what felt like the faint touch of a delicate thin hand setting upon my shoulder. Turning-over in my bed, I rubbed the sleep from my eyes in an attempt to focus. To my surprise, there stood a tall beautiful woman with porcelain-white skin and long-flowing black hair. She wore an elegantly draped gown of vibrant chartreuse-green, trimmed in multiple layers of white lace which played against her curvaceous body like the sinuous movement of the River Tamar.

The lovely woman gazed upon me, willing me closer with her large chocolate-brown eyes. I was calmly drawn to her as if we had known each other for many years. As my eyes acclimated to the darkened room, I understood this was none other than my mother's spirit.

That night mother joined me, sitting attentively at my bedside. She brushed my long chestnut-brown hair as I clung to her waist, hopeful she would never leave me.

"You have nothing to fear, for I am always with you," she said.

Grasping the other fruit-filled pasty positioned bedside upon a porcelain plate, I shared it with mother, wanting to eternally prolong her visit. After we consumed the luscious blackberry pasty, she disappeared, her voice echoing that she would return again and again over the many passing years. I so enjoyed our surreptitious parties, for that is what I truly deemed them to be— mother and I secretly playing within my room, eating pasties and drinking milk. Throughout those years, Marcella and the sisters never gave indication of the visitations, always believing that I was the only one eating the pasties, a most logical conclusion after viewing the servants' removal of my empty plate and cup the morning after. Still, to this very day, I had always kept my secret.

"I sense this is just the beginning of a huge transformation for you," Victoria said. Her words brought my thoughts forward into the present. Although I listened wholeheartedly to her language of prophecy, right now I felt as if my life was a distorted blur. My thoughts were spinning around-and-around as if a child's toy top, and I wasn't quite sure where I would be landing. I knew the Higher Powers, however, were already making themselves known to me again. Little-by-little, I sensed their presence. The very essence of their souls was dancing vicariously about me, gently prodding me with messages and wisps of guided insight. I wanted to believe that it truly must have been father this morning, assuring me with the sounds of his soothing piano music that his spirit was once again here with me.

"Grace, you have always been protected by the Higher Powers," she said, as we conversed within the bedroom chamber. "You're such a special soul. Please know that the sisters and I are here to comfort and guide you during this difficult and confusing time. We feel your sorrow."

Victoria and I sat upon the bedside together. I told her that I sensed the road ahead would become quite precarious for me to navigate alone. I had always felt the spirit world's presence more profoundly when I was with the Lumiere sisters, and I believed the sisters were sent by the Higher Powers to assist me in this lifetime.

"Victoria," I continued. "I had a most bewildering dream last night, a dream that seemed so vivid and real, yet very unfamiliar."

"Perhaps we could discuss this reverie in greater detail as we stroll along the coast?" she inquired. "Would you feel up to taking a walk? I realize that your recent journey was not only lengthy, but stressful."

"Of course, you know how I love the sea!"

"Wonderful," she replied. "The magical waters of the Atlantic have long awaited your return." Victoria told me that the Higher Powers would speak in their own special language.

"Open your heart and soul to a new day of expansion and growth. In time, with newfound awareness you will begin to comprehend the changes that have been set into motion. Like the undulating sea, your life will alter."

Six

The years gone by are memories
With thoughts of you still haunting me
And, thinking of the two of us
I wonder was it love or lust?

Chase the rain far away
Tell me that you're here to stay
Bring the sunshine on this day
Let the flowers dance and sway

"Quickly, let's set out on this early morning and listen to the sea," Victoria said. "Tell me more of your dream as we wander along the shore. I'm eager to learn about it. Get cleaned-up and I'll assist you with dressing in warmer attire." She cautioned me to speak softly so as not to awaken the others. "The brisk morning air awaits, leading us in the direction of the coastal path."

I began to dress, donning several layers of wool clothing. My traveling wardrobe of half-mournful colors was a sad reminder of the dreadful possibility that with each passing day, my husband might truly have met a deadly fate. My mind often wondered if Kendall was now purely a soul walking amongst the realm beyond the veil.

Victoria lit two large white candles and enclosed them within small glass lanterns.

"We'll need to look for the church cemetery," I said.

This cemetery, dating from days in Norman times, was located on the westernmost border of Thornwood Estate, adjoining the church property of St. Symphorian's Church and announced the commencement of the coastal path. The church was an ancient structure in cruciform plan, dimly lit with a large central tower.

The adjacent church cemetery was not only rumored to be haunted, I had personal confirmation, memories of lucid visions of the spirits, some kindred souls and others not.

"Hush," she whispered, placing her hand within mine. "Come this way."

We departed the bedroom chamber, slowly journeying downward through the darkened damp and musty inner stairwell. I could smell the mold, the earthy odors that exuded from the moist blackened-slate staircase and the mildewed interior graying stone walls. At the foot of the stairs stood a secured rectangular wooden door, leading us to the westward grounds of the estate house.

I watched in awe as Victoria positioned her hands upon the frigid door handle. With eyes closed, she inhaled deeply and focused upon holding her breath. Slowly releasing the air from within her lungs, her energies merged, becoming as one with that of the physical door. With a slight twist of her wrist, the door handle immediately responded. Suddenly, an open invitation into the snow-covered fairyland beyond awaited us.

"Brilliant," she declared, opening her eyes wide.

We were led onto a snow-drifted flagstone walkway that meandered to the sea. The early morning air was crisp and the snow fell lightly, the tiny wet crystals kissing upon our faces. Carefully navigating our way along the path, the sounds of the illuminating fresh snowfall crunched beneath our feet. Once again, my thoughts were filled with memories from bygone days of my youth.

"This is where the rose gardens thrived in warmer months." My parents had an insatiable passion not only for the sea, but for the wonderful multicolored flowers that flanked the stone pathway. I remembered in particular how the roses were planted in extensive varieties and quantities throughout the multitude of flowering gardens encircling the estate house. To say there were literally

82

thousands of blooms was no exaggeration. The gardeners scrupulously maintained the cherished roses during each passing year. In the spring, summer and autumn, the gardens were magnificently manicured. During the more temperate months, the blissful melodious scents of honeysuckle, jasmine, wisteria and rose could be detected lingering in the early morning air, flowering within the coastal breezes.

Victoria and I continued to follow the flagstone pathway, heavily dusted by the falling snow as it ambled, directing us onward to the sea. I affectionately recollected that my mother had always named the roses after significant people in her life, as I contemplated the different varieties grown within the gardens.

My namesake rose was a well formed flora of opalescent white. Its buds and blossoms were plentiful, with large majestic petals that softly unveiled its allure. I remembered how the scent of this specific rose was heavenly, exuding a sugar-sweet fragrance. Quite remarkably, I began to actually smell the luscious rose-scented aroma wafting in the morning air.

"Do you smell that? It's the roses," I said, staring at Victoria in astonishment. For a moment, I almost even believed I was dreaming.

"Ah, the magic," she replied.

Speechless, I deeply inhaled the essence of the flowers, recollecting memories of creating imaginary stories about the different roses, even speaking to them, giving them human qualities, feelings and emotions. This was all part of my mystical fantasy world. As an only child, I would spend hours in the garden merely conversing with the flowers, and the flowers would in turn, speak to me.

It's true that I lived a protected, somewhat sheltered existence in luxury and elegance, yet I was surely not a lonely soul. As an independent and free spirited child, I was playful, always able to entertain myself, keeping my mind involved with the presence of my imaginary friends. On numerous occasions, I received visits from the spirit world, the dimension existing within present time and space, yet simultaneously beyond the veil. Only those who were accepting of this magical world, were bestowed with the blessings of a glimpse beyond the veil. This other side was an unfolding picture book, illustrated by the spirit realm. Clearly, I was rarely ever bored in my youth.

I recalled an extraordinary incident that had occurred at the age of eleven years. Sitting upon the winding slate flagstone path within the rose gardens, I had grown weary from the summer sun and the salty sea air. Initially, I thought that I may have fallen asleep along the path, swept up within a dream, but after focusing my sights upon the distinguished, eclectically-attired man, standing squarely before me, I understood this was another vision from beyond the veil. I had never quite forgotten his image. The gentleman wore a whimsical oversized top hat of plush black velvet, accented with a gold-colored sash. His elegant black pin-striped apparel, featuring a multicolored silk cravat and checkered-silken vest in vibrant colors of turquoise, apricot and indigo, all flashed the impression of one who was well-heeled. My eyes drifted towards his polished black calf-skin boots. Looking upward into his handsome face, I observed his full head of salt-and-pepper curls, a matching well-manicured moustache with a graying beard, primped along his manly jaw. His large oval eyes reciprocated my gesture, gazing lovingly upon me at his feet. A man of few words, the gentle twinkle in his soft-blue eyes spoke volumes. This was the spirit of father.

My senses were abruptly returned to the present as the stone walkway led us to the entrance of the coastal path along the outskirts of the church cemetery.

"Careful where you step," Victoria said, as her leg limped, and her feet slid, crossing over an icy patch of flagstone.

I remembered how difficult this walkway could be in certain areas. The frozen grasses and neighboring vegetation were lightly covered with the fresh snowfall along the twisting, steep path. Rocks and boulders became more prevalent on our descent, with our every step leading us closer to the majestic Cornish cliff formations.

As we slowly made our descent along the coastal path, I looked behind me towards the ledge of the cliff side. Lindsey's residence stood in the distance, facing outwards upon the sea. Oddly, I observed candlelight glowing from within the bedroom chamber window. I wondered what could have possibly possessed her to awaken at this early hour.

Lindsey, an emotionally imbalanced woman, seemed to thrive quite well on a diet of conflict and drama. There had always been much rivalry and discontent between Lindsey and her younger sister, Victoria. Furthermore, Lindsey had never reserved a place of fondness in her heart for me. Initially, she presented herself as a picture of charming eloquence, yet her pleasing appearance could not have been further from the truth. There was an even darker side to Madam Lindsey, one of manipulation, deceit and control. Verbally blatant and oftentimes tactless, she most definitely had a reputation of being the boldest of the four Lumiere sisters. Lindsey was never known to go out of her way for another, that is, unless the action would potentially serve her interests somewhere down the road. The word 'manipulative' would be an understatement. Controlling and oppressive were kindly modifiers more accurately befitting her manner.

Lindsey's powers leaned heavily into the darker tones of the occult, the world of black magic, as opposed to her choosing the enlightening, spiritual energies of positive white magic. It was no secret that she chose to be quite open with her craft, freely casting spells upon those poor, doomed souls who had the misfortune to cross paths with her evil powers.

On the other hand, Marcella, Clara and Victoria and I had chosen a path of discretion with the magic, this mysticism and healing power. We were all too well aware of the political and social unrest within England at this time, fearful of any misunderstandings and reprisals amongst the Church of England and within the community. The law could be ruthless and unjust at times. The sisters had learned from past situations to pay particular heed to these public displays of retribution, the ultimate persecution of a witch through death by hanging or burning at the stake.

My body shuddered as I recalled the unthinkable—a grotesque spell Lindsey had cast upon an unfaithful lover. I remembered he was a charming man, a visiting French aristocrat, named Monsieur Louis La Pêche. Ah, such disdain Lindsey carried in her heart with the discovery she had been jolted for the enticing delights of another! Not only did Lindsey transform Monsieur La Pêche into a slimy sea bass, setting him loose into the wild sparkling river valley waters of the Valency, she turned his lover into a crawling bloodsucker, gifting the squirmy worm upon a lowly fisherman who fished by day and night along the riverbank. Still, I had never forgotten Lindsey's chilling words, "Now they are truly deserving of one another."

The intense rays of dawning light brought my attention to the increasing gray cloud formations as I looked towards the sky. The radiant beams perforated the darkening clouds in linear patterns, but we continued to make our descent along the coastal path.

"Once again, I'm in need of your gifted insight, Victoria," I said, as we approached the final stretch, leading us onto the pristine shores of the Atlantic.

Since the night of Kendall's disappearance, I had lived in a world of secrecy and isolation, hidden from the public scrutiny of London society. My days and nights had been preoccupied with insidious thoughts of my consuming anguish. I now desired to release this inner landscape of my mind, sharing my world with a trusted soul. At this time, I truly sensed this worthy being was none other than Victoria.

I told Victoria my greatest fear was that the law would eventually find my husband dead. This, in turn, would ultimately send Constable Gordon journeying westward in search of me.

"Certainly, you must be aware that I'm still considered a suspect in Kendall's disappearance?"

"Grace, focus on only positive thoughts at this time." She told me to concentrate on the vision that Kendall would soon be found alive. "Pray and reflect upon your life becoming fuller and more rewarding. I should hope this is what you truly desire? Isn't it?"

Hanging my head, I gazed staring downward upon the frigid snow-drifted flagstone path.

"Sometimes I really don't know what I want."

"But, what if Kendall were to be found alive and well?" she inquired.

"I'm not quite certain that I could ever trust him again," I replied. On occasion, I had even secretly wished that he had passed on, remembering he was often cruel and abusive.

"Am I a wretched soul, praying for the death of my very own husband?"

"With all of the angst you have experienced throughout the passing years in your marriage, I do understand. It's just that, with the focus of the investigation highlighted so intensely in your direction, I must advise you to be shrewd regarding to whom you divulge any information." She told me that even the most innocently intended remark on my part, could play a major role in debilitating my case.

In recent months, I had much time alone to contemplate my situation. I explained to Victoria that my marriage had been like an anchor, pulling me downward, lower-and-lower into the depths of the ocean. For whatever my reasons, I had simply chosen to remain blind in the past to the reality of the situation. My marriage was one grand, glorious illusion of love, harmony and balance.

"Thank the Higher Powers that you are finally awakening from your darkened slumber," she said.

With these words spoken, our footsteps reached the end of the coastal pathway, depositing us onto the open sandy shore. In the distance I could see the Boscastle lighthouse standing tall upon the cliffs, its guiding white light, radiant in the heavy mist. We approached the shoreline walking side-by-side, the sounds of the thrashing seas filling our ears as the grandeur of the waves reflected in our eyes.

Victoria continued, "I'm still puzzled about one matter."

"What might that be?" I inquired.

"If you were so miserable, why did you stay in the marriage for nine years? Why didn't you enlist the assistance of the spirit world? Surely, you must know the Higher Powers are always here for you."

"I believed in the Higher Powers," I replied, "But, Kendall ruthlessly forbade me to ever use my magic again. I was his prisoner, as if a yellow canary confined within a gilded cage."

Now, I grew weary just thinking about the copious amounts of energy I had devoted toward living this charade of a marriage.

"Kendall chose to disrespect and abuse you," Victoria continued, "There will be serious consequences to follow. Trust. The Higher Powers will see to this."

Seven

Be strong, be brave and chart your course
Your life's a lone ship on the sea
Look forward, searching far and wide
Striving to always live your dreams

Search high, look low…never run aground
If fear and doubt should come around
Stay true, knowing love is harmony
Be the captain of your Destiny

Strolling along the shoreline, I paused, taking Victoria by the arm as I looked upon the beckoning waters of the raging Atlantic. On the horizon, the graying skies met the chilled torrid-blue waves, and I could see in the distance, the dramatic image of a solitary sailing vessel, tossing like a cork upon the white-capped open waters.

"A pirate's ship," I said, observing the fragile schooner as it sailed defiantly with few lights aglow.

There was no identifying mast flag billowing in the wintry morning breeze. It took more than guts and sheer determination to safely sail these precarious straits into Boscastle Harbor. It took Divine intervention. I could only wonder if perhaps it was Captain Cutter's ship, *The Destiny*. I had always hoped the Captain would one day make another impromptu appearance within the seaport of Boscastle. It had been over twelve years since our paths had last crossed, twelve long years where he still remained coveted in my heart. No matter how hard I tried, I had never forgotten this man. His affection was like a drug, yet I understood the only way I would ever be free from this attraction, was if the handsome buccaneer had met his ultimate fate on earth, departing from this lifetime. If Ian was still alive, however, I had always prayed the Higher Powers would reunite us one day.

In past years, Henrietta's Ale House was where this pirate had often frequented. The tavern was nestled within the treacherous seaport of Boscastle. To access the establishment also took bravado and courage. It was situated deep within a darkened black hole along the docks, an alley that led to nowhere but a dead end, rumored to be the beginning of hell for some. Henrietta Leach's doors had welcomed an array of questionable characters over the years. Being the peculiar Madam of the Night that she was, her blanched haggard face, ruby-red lips, caking make-up and scantily clothed largesse, merely added to this house of horrors.

Of course, I had only acquired this information second hand, for it was through a past, brief association with Lord Russell that I initially learned of this mire. Additionally, I grew to realize that brevity had its blessings. Russell's insatiable appetite for whores, eventually turned my head around, sending me in the opposite direction, and pointing me toward what I could now only gather had been purely an interim affair with Captain Ian Cutter. After all, I was a lady, and for the very first time in my life at the age of seventeen, this seaman embodied all that I yearned for as a young, naïve woman - love, lust, adventure and passion.

I know it may sound irregular that a lady of my prominence could have ever fallen in love with a charismatic pirate, but the truth of the matter was that even today, my heart had still never ventured to the depths of adoration, as when Ian and I were entwined in the throes of passion. I had always believed us to be soul mates. I now sensed, however, that Ian envisioned a totally different interpretation of our relationship. His unpredicted departure from Boscastle alienated my heart.

Ironically, I found my current circumstances all the more puzzling. As true as my unsavory past affair with Russell was regretful, I had agreed to marry his fraternal twin, Kendall, the following year. With my consent to marry, I must admit, I was desperately hopeful of receiving the nurturing which I so dearly missed from Ian.

As time passed, however, I found that I was trapped, only to find myself enfolded within, yet another deceitful relationship. In retrospect I discovered these twin brothers had so much more in common than they would ever have publicly claimed as truth, for it was becoming more and more apparent to me that my husband proved throughout the years to be just as much of a whore monger as Russell.

During my marriage, I had often reflected upon my circumstances in Boscastle, wondering about my selection of men. What had attracted me to such sordid characters? Whether it was simply a matter of naïveté or poor choices on my part, I was obsessed with winning a man's heart, regardless of the consequences to follow. If love was the issue, however, I certainly had not encountered it amongst Henrietta's clientele. I could only surmise that whatever, and whomever had found their ruffian buttocks planted upon Henrietta's weathered-oak barstools, exchanging intimacies within her soiled leased beds - somehow also risked never awaking to see the light of day.

Victoria and I approached the sea as my thoughts were returned to the alluring ocean waters that lay before me. The irregular chiseled slate of the Cornish cliffside enhanced the sense of excitement and adventure on this winter's morning. Fixating my eyes upon the water, a feeling of light headedness overwhelmed me. Once again, the voice of the magical sea was calling out to me as if to say, "Come closer. Walk with me, side-by-side along my sandy shores. Let me comfort you once again within my arms." However, this time the voice was louder and more direct. The waters of the Atlantic Sea had always spoken to me. Deep within my heart, I now understood the sea was listening, comforting me with the rhythm of its enchanting motion.

As we walked together, I told Victoria that I had often feared, I would not survive within my marriage. I wondered even at times, if I might be insane or near madness.

"You are far from insane," Victoria remarked. "Everything in life occurs for a reason."

"And, just what could this *reason* possibly be?"

"Trust in the Higher Powers," she replied. "We all have choices. Consider choosing to allow the magic to flow into your life again."

Even though my thoughts were running rampant with unanswered questions, I knew that nevertheless, for good or for bad, this was what I had truly chosen for my path in this lifetime. I realized that before a soul entered into a lifetime, it chose a distinct path, agreeing to write a script that would eventually become its very own fates and destinies. I was absolutely certain that my path was not one of a hopeless victim. I definitely came from a position of choice. Victoria was entirely correct. My life was what I had chosen, for whatever the reasons that would unfold in the future.

I also had slowly begun to come to an understanding that Kendall had chosen his path for this life. Somehow I sensed, however, there must have been a grander purpose as to why I was entrapped within an arduous marriage, though, at the present time this seemed to be well beyond my grasp. My current perspective was visibly unable to fully comprehend my plight, yet alone his. I could only pray that one day, my inner truths would speak to me loud and clear.

Victoria reassured me that as time passed, I would discover an awareness of what was necessary in my life—my inner truths would lead me to where, and with whom I needed to be.

Although I was still confused about this awareness in my life, I vowed to communicate with the spirit world, hopeful that I might one day find more clarity. With these thoughts, I could only

92

ponder that quite possibly this world beyond the veil would one day bring me the answers I sought.

Increasing the pace of her steps as we walked together, Victoria said, "It's getting much colder. Let's discuss your recent dream."

"Oddly, my dreams have been more frequent and lucid in the passing weeks," I said.

As I spoke, again we hastened our gait along the beach. I told her that I believed these reveries were intended to provide me with profound messages and warnings from the magical realm beyond the veil.

"Do these spirits ever reveal themselves to you by name? And, are you certain they are blessed souls?"

"Well, their identity is not always clear as to who is communicating."

I explained how I often received a vibration or a feeling. It was more like a sensation, identifying the spirit and conveying information. These spirits were guides, not always appearing as an image, nor did they make a habit of always speaking in audible tones. However, sometimes I actually saw beyond the veil - a face, a name and various images that would appear before my eyes, yet quite often it was a premonition of some event or encounter.

"You have always been extremely intuitive, Grace. I've never doubted your abilities as a witch. I truly mean this in the kindest sense of the word, but I fear that through neglect and misuse over the past years, it appears your powers have grown out of form."

"I understand," I said, with sadness in my voice.

I knew that I was gifted since birth. I had always possessed the magic, but now I needed to discover a way to unleash my powers again. I told Victoria that I wanted the Higher Powers to finally lead me to true love, to my heart's desire. At the moment, that desire was the debonair stranger in my most recent dream.

"Is this regarding your vision of last night?" she inquired.

"Yes, I've experienced none other like it," I said, excitedly.

Expressing my lucid experience in great detail, I relayed all that occurred, revealing the encounter with the handsome dark-haired gentleman, the vivid images of the ballroom and the alluring piano music of Beethoven's Moonlight Sonata still playing within my head. All this and more, now colored the transforming scenery within my mind, now a brilliant visualization of renewal and hope. Victoria told me that love would develop with the proper person and there was nothing that I must actively do. "Once you understand this awareness, love will find you when you least likely expect it, whether that may be with Kendall again, or another. The Higher Powers will see that you are in the right place at the appropriate time. Everything occurs for our highest good."

My eyes looked upon her with more uncertainty. "But, how will I know for certain?"

"Listen to your heart, that little voice within you and pay heed to what it is saying. It is the voice of reason, the voice of truth. The inner voice *never* lies."

Our journey along the coast that morning proved more enlightening than I could ever have imagined. Carefully hoisting up our dresses and petticoats, the cold Atlantic waters playfully rushed and swirled in an effort to wash over our steps. The sea foam collected and pooled in rippled patterns along the shoreline as I felt the increasing cold winds bluster, blowing fiercely against my face and through my hair. The motion of the waves was much stronger and the early morning skies were quickly darkening to a deep charcoal-gray. The sea breeze blew swiftly, nearing gale force, bringing tears to my eyes as the light snow became a mixture of sleeting cold rain, falling upon us.

"I fear another winter storm," remarked Victoria.

"Let's move on and return to the estate house. The skies have darkened with anger."

Cautiously, I kept one eye glued upon the heavens. The amber shore diminished with each step of our retreat. As we neared the base of the coastal path, my booted feet and gloved hands still tingled from the intense bitter cold. Together, we climbed and slowly ascended the cobblestone path along the cliffs, but no sooner had we stepped upon the frigid path, the coastal winter storm greeted us with full onslaught. My legs wavered as I tried to balance myself upon the slippery ice. I could hear the ocean waters raging aloud in the distance. Victoria and I reached for a pine-tree limb, seeking some support along the cliff side. As the winds wailed, I felt the tree bending, and I feared it would give way, releasing us to tumble over the treacherous ledge.

The winds howled, surrounding us with bantering snow and rain. The voice of thunder clapped, rumbling in the distance. We were paralyzed, our eyes fixated upon each other as we struggled at the mercy of the storm's wrath. Through my wet gloves, I could feel my burning fingers becoming numb from the cold as I still clung precariously to the billowing tree limbs.

Lightening flashed its presence, a dark reminder of the cacophony I was presently facing in my life.

"Hang onto me," I said, instructing Victoria to wrap her arms about my waist. "We'll brace each other as we climb the hill." Focused with sheer determination, we slowly advanced forward, yet with every step our footing stumbled, sliding upon the icy glazed cobblestone. I was more worried about Victoria, concerned that her limping leg would interfere with her ascent upon the icy path.

All of a sudden, Victoria shrieked, as I felt her hands leave my side, "Help me! I'm falling…"

"No! Hold onto me," I shouted, watching her body descend hopelessly from atop the stony ledge, spiraling downward in mid-air to greet the angry waters.

"I invoke the Higher Powers to surround you with white light," I yelled aloud as I desperately chanted an incantation.

Sky of black, winds of time
Change direction in my mind
Raise this woman to her feet
Back to safety, now complete
Fast away from raging sea
Bring Victoria back to me.

With these words, I felt the once familiar tingling sensation, now running wildly throughout my body. My skin itched, crawling with every hair standing on end. My spine tensed as a tickling sensation made itself at home within my being. I absolutely understood what was happening as I felt my eyes roll backward within my head. Victoria's body froze in space. Instantaneously, her limp body was engulfed within a ball of radiant light.

However, something was terribly wrong. The glowing orb suddenly spun out-of-control in a counterclockwise motion, swiftly encircling her. Like a rag doll, Victoria violently bounced against the jagged cliffs, her body spiraling downwards into the deadly clutches of the raging Atlantic Sea.

"Victoria!" I shouted, watching her bloodied motionless body descend upon the large rocks, only to become one with the sea. I prayed for mercy and forgiveness from the Higher Powers as my eyes filled with emotion. I had failed to recall my abilities to awaken the magic. At last, I understood what I had lost in the past, might never become a part of my life again. The magic that had once been so much a part of my life in past years, remained far from my grasp.

I was consumed with fear, frantic as tears blurred my eyes. I couldn't contain my sorrow as I rushed past the snow-kissed rose bushes, running up the flagstone path to the main estate house. Victoria's tragic death was all I could think about.

At last, I arrived at the massive estate's golden-colored arched entry, breathless, and struggling to compose myself. Leaning my full weight upon the heavy doors, I attempted to push them open. They gave way, swinging forward, propelling me into the luxurious interior coral-marbled foyer. To my surprise, the butler, Mr. Abernathy, stood in awe before me. Startled, I screamed aloud, gazing upon his handsome face as the droplets of moisture rapidly collected in a puddle, pooling around my weathered calf-skin boots.

Bradford Abernathy was a striking, well-developed man of one-and-forty years. Employed with the Thornwood Estate house for over five-and-twenty years, he took his initial position as a coachman when still just a youth. If ever there was a cure for sore eyes, he was surely the antidote.

"What has become of you? And, where is Madam Victoria?" he queried, with a bewildered look upon his face. I was suddenly speechless, my voice wavering to find the right words as I felt my entire body contort and twist with anguish.

"What is it? Trouble?" he persisted.

I could only nod my head in despair, as I stuttered, "There...there has been a terrible accident."

"Hurry! Come this way," urged Mr. Abernathy as I looked upward to view his now paling face. "I'll request the assistance of Josephina and Caron to dry you off. You'll catch a death of a cold, should you idle about in wet clothing."

"Forget about me," I said. Take me to the sisters." At this moment, I only wished that all of my problems would simply vanish and disappear...like magic. But, my two dear personal attendants quickly appeared...removing my long, saturated coat as they patted the droplets of water from my tortured face.

Mr. Abernathy's face also grew noticeably panicked as we turned around to rush down the corridor. Yet, to my dismay, atop the stairwell now stood Madam Lindsey, leering upon us.

"Of course, I could grant your wishes." Lindsey interrupted. "All it takes is a flaming candle, some herbs and a few drops of essential oils. It's that simple. The power of my incantations, spoken under the radiance of a full moon will bring to you whatever and whomever you so desire. And, at times, even that which you could never imagine in your wildest dreams."

My eyes peered upon her intrepidly. I stood as if frozen in time. Once again, the command of her magic was something I could hardly forget. She was never remiss about fully utilizing her mysticism, as the memory of another spell danced vividly before me. I pitied her one-time beau, Sir Astley Stafford. When Lindsey discovered his infidelity, she nearly destroyed him, however, on this occasion Lindsey managed to conjure an ounce of pity within her stone heart, only dooming him with ill health–leprosy. The very thought of missing an opportunity to exploit the magic was not within her repertoire.

"I fear you could not possibly be of any help," I retorted.

"One day you'll accept my proposition, begging for intervention just like all of the others." Descending the staircase, Lindsey encircled me in the foyer, pacing arrogantly.

She continued, "How could you have ever considered leaving the estate house during a storm? Have you absolutely no sense? Clearly, something is terribly wrong."

"I gather Grace was quite surprised by the sudden onset of this winter tempest," remarked Mr. Abernathy.

"Stay out of this," Lindsey replied, shrugging her shoulders in disapproval.

"People have choices," Mr. Abernathy continued. "Some simply choose to navigate life much differently than you. The sooner you accept this fact, the better off you'll be, in living yours."

With each passing moment, I observed Lindsey growing increasingly irritated as I felt her body brush swiftly against my side. I could feel the bristling tension in the air, deciding it best to leave this discussion alone. Since the magic was not returning to me, the last thing I needed in my life at this time was an irate witch, casting spells upon my nebulous existence.

"You're worthless to me, Grace," she said. "You never were much good for anything. Even your two-timing husband finally awoke to realize that much."

Mr. Abernathy and I proceeded to navigate the long corridor to the parlor as Lindsey's glaring eyes followed us. I found this all rather unnerving. Her stare was chilling and could turn flesh into stone, a look that sent an eerie feeling throughout my entire body. I sensed there would be even more trouble in the days ahead.

Reaching the double drawing room doors, Mr. Abernathy pushed upon them until they swung wide open to reveal the ornate and lavishly decorated chamber interior. Upon two gold brocade sofas, sat Madam Marcella and Madam Clara, feasting on a scrumptious array of what appeared to be tea, scones, raspberry preserves, plum pudding, assorted fresh whole fruit and wild oats. At the moment, however, the last thought on my mind was food. As I stood before them, my stomach grew increasingly nauseous from the wafting aromas.

"Ah, Grace, please come in and join us. I pray you rested well?" inquired Marcella.

"There's plenty of tea and scones. Your favorite...lemon," continued Clara. Approaching the sisters, I could see their faces turn from joy to horror. Startled, the sisters gazed intensely in my direction, but I remained speechless. I believed that unquestionably, they must know of Victoria's plight.

"Thank you, Mr. Abernathy. You may leave," said Marcella. Reluctantly, the handsome butler closed the doors as the sound of his footsteps grew increasingly faint. "There has been trouble," Marcella shouted. "Grace, what has happened?"

"This is urgent. We must convene immediately," Clara insisted.

"Welcome home," Lindsey blurted with disdain in her voice.

"Once again it appears that Grace has some explaining to do!"

Patricia Grace Joyce   *The Magic of Time*

Eight

My thoughts are contained within a cloud
Like a cotton-filled apothecary jar
The rain is storming, raging aloud
Yet, my heart still searches afar

And, I look to the darkened sky
Questioning where to begin
Then I ask myself a simple why
But, all the answers lay hidden within

The drawing room at Thornwood Estate was large and airy with tall rectangular windows aligning the western and northern walls. The patter of the cold and heavy rain, sleeting upon the glass panes, was disturbingly audible to all. As the sisters hovered about me in the elegant, well-appointed room, a fire burned brightly in the coral–veined Italian marble fireplace, bringing a much welcomed warmth and solace to the interior surroundings. In the corner stood a stately black piano, my pride and joy. Under the guided instruction of father, I had played lovingly upon its now yellowing, ivory keys, since the early years of my childhood.

The chaises within the room were fully clad in a plush and ornate floral-brocade of white, black and gold. Enormous oversized gold-leaf mirrors surrounded the grouping, reflecting the unconventionality of the room—a space with only three walls, constructed in a unique triangular design. The drawing room had always been, and still remained, the heart of Thornwood Estate, a place where anything and anyone of importance was entertained; however, a mystery had prevailed throughout the many passing years as to why it had been laboriously fabricated in such an unusual fashion with father's direction and authority.

One-by-one, the Lumiere sisters each took their places around a large circular ebony-colored table, dominating the center of the room. A rose-colored Venetian crystal chandelier was fully aglow with eleven white-tallow candles shimmering brightly above. The onslaught of the winter coastal storm continued to distract me, tapping upon the thin glass panes, audaciously gesturing to take its place within the drawing room.

The sisters anxiously gathered around me, as I awkwardly began my story. I told them everything regarding my horrific encounter with Victoria upon the Cornish cliffs that morning. There was only silence as we all sat in despair, for we were numb with the overwhelming reality surrounding us on this day.

Reluctantly, I moved toward the ebony table. My eyes once again lovingly stroked upon the keys of my piano. Passing thoughts of my recent dream wafted in-and-out of my memory as the tonal clarity of Beethoven's Moonlight Sonata, again played soothingly within my head. At this moment I could only fantasize, anticipating the magnificence of the upcoming days when I would finally play my music again. The sonatas and concertos of Bach, Haydn, Mozart and Beethoven had always been dear to my heart. Recollections of father laced my mind.

My thoughts flashed-back to the surprising sound of piano music that had greeted my ears in the early morning hours just prior to daybreak. Once more, I wondered if it had actually been father's spirit playing. Could this have truly been the magic?

I took my place in the drawing room, sitting next to Marcella and Clara. Garbed tastefully in a fitted black, long-sleeved silk dress with a pastel-pink French lace petticoat, I caught a glimpse of my reflection in the mirror. Discreetly, I admired my brunette curls, coifed stylishly upon my head, yet sadly I must admit that the image I viewed was not what I had anticipated. I appeared

102

worrisome. My complexion was ashen, not the glowing hue of peach I had hoped to envision.

Clara arose from the table, lighting a sprig of dried sage from a flaming white candle atop the center of the circular table, and walked ceremoniously around the perimeter of the drawing room, dispersing its potent aromatic essence. I recalled this was a witch's blessing in preparation to cleanse and remove all unwelcome incarnate spirits from our immediate environs.

Dove of white in radiant flight
Surround us in protecting light
Remove all evil day and night.

The color of white was significantly powerful in that it conveyed all of the blessings and healing mysticism of the Divine. Colored candles, specific wild herbs and fragrant oils were common tools of the craft, assisting a witch to manifest a desired intention when healing with energy and/or casting a spell. These various elements could be used alone, or in conjunction with other substances to create a distinct result. Over the years, the sisters had secretly compiled volumes of formulas containing an assortment of spells and incantations to serve their healing abilities and the craft of sorcery.

"Today we ask all spirits who are not here for our highest good, depart our presence," Clara continued. "We surround ourselves with purity, the white light of blessed souls as we gather to reunite once again with Grace, and to mourn the passing of our sister, Victoria."

Truly, Victoria had been like a sister to me, yet through my tears, I still could not accept the fact that her frail body was now destined to be part of the raging Atlantic Sea.

What shall we do?" I begged, "Is there any way to recover Victoria's body? I feel as if I have only brought despair to each and every one of you."

"Grace," Marcella replied, "This was not of our doing. This was an accident. However, it will be too treacherous for the coachmen or Mr. Abernathy to venture along the rocky coastline in search of Victoria's body. I feel certain we will only jeopardize another's life in this situation. Don't you agree?"

"Very well," I replied with reluctance.

"Well, I most certainly am not going to endanger myself, nor any of you, with retrieving a corpse," Lindsey interrupted.

"Hush, Lindsey!" Clara replied, "Such banter is neither appropriate nor welcome at this time of mourning. In memory of Victoria, let us take this opportunity to focus on the wonderful joys and blessings that she brought forth in this lifetime."

"Grace, have you forgotten that death is only physical?" Marcella inquired. "The soul is eternal and has now returned to its spiritual home, a new beginning, so to speak, for our lovely Victoria."

"As difficult as it may seem at this time," Marcella continued, "I think it is best that we celebrate Victoria's passing, for she would want as much. Death is not something to fear. Trust that Victoria has not gone far. Her soul continues to surround us within her loving embrace, now and forever."

As the sisters each spoke of Victoria's loving and compassionate ways, ironically I began to feel a sense of calmness surround me. . .Almost, I dare say, a state of bliss.

Mr. Abernathy suddenly reappeared, entering the drawing room, and he held a small ivory parchment envelope within his hand as everyone stared with curiosity. As I observed him from my chair, he smiled at me. I wanted to interpret this as a signal of comforting reassurance that all would be well. The voice of doubt prodded me, however, lingering in the back of my mind. Was I fooling myself? Would I ever find that my life would be well?

"A parcel for Lady Grace Worthington," he said, extending his hand towards me.

"Who could be sending me correspondence in Boscastle?" I inquired.

I had only disclosed my whereabouts to a select few. Staring at the envelope within his hand, my first impression evoked the notion that perhaps it was sent from the Constable, but almost instantaneously my thoughts flashed-back to the incident along the roadside involving the masked, hooded highway men. Might this even be news from the illusive stranger who had dispatched those ruffians to intercept us in route to Thornwood Estate? With the thought of this perhaps conveying additional appalling news, I was reluctant to learn of the envelope's contents. My imagination ran wild. What if the Constable had even found Kendall dead and was coming to arrest me, taking me away to my new home behind the gated cell bars of London's harrowing Newgate Prison? I thought this must be it, the end of the road.

"What possibly could this be?" I persisted.

I could only suspect that the news awaiting me would be of a disturbing nature. I even wondered if this sisterly covenant would reveal still, yet another horrendous twist of fate, a manifestation of which I somehow had chosen, to lead me on my path in fulfillment of the Divine plan for my destiny. At the moment, I could only consider one thing. My focus was distracted by the letter. As I sat in awe upon the sofa, my fingers fumbled with the wax seal. My thoughts were laden, filled with the fearful realization that the magic may never return to me.

Listening to the sisters, I determined this meeting was becoming increasingly out of the ordinary with each passing minute. Then again, if my memory served me well, there was nothing ever ordinary about these Mystic Women, nor with residing at Thornwood Estate. While living at the estate house, I had seen and experienced occurrences in past years that would have scared the pantaloons and petticoats off of most mortals.

"Unfortunately," Clara said, "We sense this contains a secret, something of significance which you may not fully be aware of. Surely, I need not remind you, awareness is everything."

My hunches were swiftly proving to be affirmations, but was there no end to this turmoil? It seemed that no sooner had I returned to Boscastle, more rubbish awaited me.

I sensed a queasy countenance traversing my face. Grudgingly, I extended my hand in receipt of the thin rectangular ivory parcel. I wanted to truly give it back to Mr. Abernathy, to close my eyes and avoid this entire matter.

Examining the writing on the envelope, I was hopeful of some apparent mistake, that perhaps it had been erroneously delivered. My eyes rapidly skimmed over the words *Lady Grace Worthington* as my heart fluttered with anticipation. Removing the contents, again I quickly perused the document, a letter written on a crisp piece of fine ivory parchment. The penmanship was elegant and refined, reflecting the use of a quill pen with sepia-colored ink. Clearing my throat, I read the correspondence aloud.

Four February, 1811

Dear Lady Worthington,

I pray this letter shall reach you Godspeed. In recent months I have desired to communicate with you, dare I say—to even make your acquaintance. I'm writing to inform you that your husband has taken a mistress, and I am that fortunate woman.

There is not much point for me to further attempt to conceal this matter, or to prolong your agony, nor mine. I am with child, in my seventh month of pregnancy and will be birthing the first Worthington heir.

I know all about you and the spells that you and your sisters cast. The rituals that you partake in are truly evil. You are nothing more than a 'witch' and I hold you directly responsible for Kendall's disappearance. I pray he may still be alive, that you may have shown at least some mercy with sparing his life.

Furthermore, I am prepared to assist the law and Constable Nigel Gordon in any manner to guarantee Kendall's disappearance may be solved. I assure you, I will go to extreme efforts, ensuring his safe return into my arms again. My demands are simple. I'll take action with the law, should you not agree to pay me a substantial fee for the benefit and support of our newborn child, the rightful heir to the Worthington Estate.
Sincerely,

Madame Lela Pucelle
666 Squires Way – Queensgate, London, England

"This is absolutely outrageous," gasped Marcella as she arose from her chair. "This reeks of extortion, a deliberate attempt to lure you into a trap. How dare this wretched woman plot like a leech, to suck your financial assets! This charade must be stopped, and if I have anything to say, it most definitely will."

I could only gawk blindly at the letter, stunned in a trance of clouded uncertainty as I tightly clutched the parchment within my trembling hand. I felt as if the world was closing-in upon me. My face suddenly flushed with heat. Oddly, what seemed within seconds, my entire body seemed to take on an eerie coldness. Feeling the blood dissipate from my pallid face, I became numb all over. My mind was mystified as I stood up from my cushioned seat and moved forward, taking small steps, one-by-one, approaching the brocade chaise lounge. My legs grew wilted, shaking as I attempted to step forward. I needed to sit down and regain my composure. I needed to try to find some sense of peace in this inexplicable moment. Briefly, I sat upon the soft cushion of the chaise lounge, trying to collect my self-control. Still staring in disbelief at the letter, a state of shock consumed my very being.

"Are you feeling all right?" inquired Clara.

I remained speechless. Now, I only wanted to escape, to leave the room and return to my chambers. In an effort to maneuver my body towards the door, I turned around to walk past the circular ebony table.

"I had no idea, no inclination whatsoever," I gasped aloud in disbelief. "I wish Kendall death!"

My words of despair filled the room as I shrieked, tumbling to the floor. Unfortunately, I could not lessen the initial impact as I felt my body plummeting downward. My head hit upon the side of the massive solid-ebony table leg, exploding with a burst of brilliant crimson, my very own blood splattering in vibrant asymmetrical patterns upon the surrounding carpeting and walls.

I had lost all consciousness. Only the fullness of darkness was surrounding me. Oddly, I felt as if I had abandoned my body. From a bird's perspective, I strangely discovered myself as a nebulous semblance floating in an aura of white light above this scene in the drawing room. I wondered what was happening as I peered through a haze at what looked to be my listless physical body surrounded by the sisters. Was it truly I, strewn upon the drawing room floor with my head lying in a pooling puddle of blood? I was confused. Was this real, or only a dream? What was happening? Could I have been perhaps even dead? But, I wondered how I could have been dead if I was still able to observe, and hear the activity about me? Remarkably, I could see the vague outlines and features of the sisters, enough to determine their identities as the muffled clamor of voices was becoming more audible in the background. For certain, something was dreadfully wrong.

"Quickly! Move her onto the chaise lounge," Clara shouted. "Instruct Mr. Abernathy to summon Dr. Harrington, and gather the servants."

With a white kerchief in hand, I observed Marcella and Clara ardently applying pressure to my forehead, attentively wiping the flowing red river that streamed uncontrollably. Hesitating, Lindsey assisted them with lifting my body and repositioning me comfortably upon the chaise lounge. Two large goose-feather pillows were placed beneath me, propping my head in an upright position in an attempt to deter the river of blood.

Lindsey stooped above me, peering downward with an uncanny smirk upon her face. Halfheartedly, she removed her exquisite lace fan, now fawning over me in a seemingly lame effort to circulate the air. Her laissez-faire attitude toward my well-being only reaffirmed the gaping emotional distance between us.

Mr. Abernathy entered the room with Josephina and Caron, announcing, "Ladies, I've sent the coachmen into the village. I'm certain they'll find Dr. Perry Harrington, even in the midst of this gale force storm."

Out-of-body, I could feel my internal energies now soaring to heights I had never known, or experienced ever before. What was happening to me?

With a blink of an eye, I found myself transported to another place, now fully aware of a gentleman lurking in the distant shadows within the dimming light of a street lantern. He appeared to be well-heeled and of large stature. His hair was light blond in coloration, and from what I could vaguely determine, his complexion was also quite fair. I observed him hastily walking in my direction, rushing along the cobblestone street at a rapid gait, yet still at a far enough distance not to alarm me. As I turned to look again in his direction, however, I was dumbfounded, discovering he was now running towards me–faster–faster–

109

faster. Squinting my eyes, I strained to make recognition, still unable to focus clearly upon his face. I was terrified.

"Grace…Stop!" he cried aloud.

I wondered who this could be. How did he know my name? And, what had bloody possessed this fellow to pursue me? Hastily, I sought shelter as I felt my aura gusting through a tiny alleyway that opened onto a misty riverfront. Could this be the River Thames? The stench from the stagnant waters was horrific as I covered my nose with my hand in an effort to squelch the unsavory odor. My essence traveled along the waterfront as I found myself hovering briefly to pause, looking back in the direction of my pursuer. I wanted to believe this was all a dream, but I knew better. This rogue was hot on my trail, and there was nothing that I could do, but to advance forward at an even quicker pace.

By the appearance of the surrounding building facades, I presumed that I was somewhere within the center of a city, perhaps London, yet remorsefully I was still all alone, albeit this rogue running in chase. I hadn't the foggiest idea as to what this fellow might want of me, nor was I the least bit interested in stopping to find out. I only wanted him to disappear.

He continued to make his approach even more quickly than I had anticipated, when suddenly I turned around, staring in disbelief. The blurred image of his paling face slowly morphed like soft putty into the scarred, grotesque visage of none other than, Lord Russell Worthington.

"You're the Queen of my Heart," he yelled aloud.

"Never! Stay away from me, Russell!" I protested.

I continued floating above the waterfront, sighting what appeared to be an unattended horse-drawn carriage. At last, I thought here's my escape. For an instant I even believed that I might successfully maneuver the vehicle. The ornate black coach, however, was chained securely to a hitching post adjacent to the roadside, the carriage windows draped with a lush golden-brocade fabric, drawn tightly shut.

Surprisingly, from within the coach I detected some activity, hearing voices conversing in a soft whisper. Was this a woman? I paused, pressing my ear intently against the cool thin pane of window glass.

The voice spoke again. "Kiss me," she whispered.

A man replied, "Yes, my love."

I thought that, if only these people might help me, I would be safe, and if only I could summon their assistance, I could evade Russell. I tried to capture their attention by shouting, "Help me! Please!" But, there was no response. Attempting to pound loudly with my fist upon the carriage windows, quite unexpectedly, my hand protruded effortlessly through the glass windowpane, and entered the coach interior. I could not believe my eyes. My body was ethereal, transformed from the physical into that of a vaporous being.

Somewhat confused, I proceeded to press my face against the window pane to render a better view of the occupants, when suddenly my entire head was inside the coach. My eyes yearned to identify the passengers, as I squinted in the darkness. Remarkably, all the while, the man and woman remained oblivious to my presence, as if I did not exist.

Enfolded in each other's arms, my vision was obstructed, but I could hear their voices continuing to increase in volume. Boisterous laughter and playful frolic emanated from within, permeating the air. Then, there was only silence – a deadened space in time.

I persisted, waving my hands and even touching the man and the woman, trying to attract their attention, but to no avail. My heart raced, hopeful they would eventually acknowledge me. More whispering sounded from within until…

"Hush," he murmured.

Instantly, the carriage door flung wide open. I peered anxiously into the hazy darkened interior, attempting again to view the man and woman. In desperation I shouted to them, "I need your help. He's following me! Please..."

The two strangers remained ignorant of my presence, staring through me as if I wasn't even standing before them. Having no sooner uttered my words, I quickly glanced in the direction behind me, in an attempt to calculate how much closer Russell had advanced. Amazingly, and quite to my liking, he had simply vanished. There was no longer any trace that Russell ever loomed behind me, nor was he anywhere within my sights. I thought this entire situation was becoming more bizarre by the moment. I wondered if I had truly wished him away. Quite inexplicably, Russell had disappeared into thin air.

I now stood facing the opened coach door, hopeful the two shadowed strangers would exit the carriage, but I remained puzzled, as they continued to ignore me.

"Please, I am begging you!" I shouted again, attempting to speak in an even louder tone of voice.

From within the darkness, I observed the couple still entwined in a loving embrace. I could barely see their faces until they paused, turning in my direction, as if looking straight through me again. What was happening? Why couldn't they hear or even see me? As each moment passed, it became more and more apparent that my essence was capable of effortlessly defying the laws of physical matter.

Suddenly, the couple briefly refrained from their embrace, and the gentleman turned his head aside, glancing in my direction. With a look of horrendous awe upon my face, I was in sheer disbelief only to discover myself in the company of none other than, the likes of the Worthington Estate African slave, Elijah Foster. There was no doubt in my mind this was he, as I continued to observe his large dark-skinned muscular frame overwhelm his female companion. His full black lips smothered the woman's face with kisses, as his massive black hands searched within her panties for his prize.

However, the identity of his traveling companion remained a mystery. I could scarcely see her face as she reclined hidden within the night shadows, and I could only best describe her as portly, fleshy, well-endowed and most definitely overexposed. As I persisted to scrutinize this tryst, I realized this tart was a scantily clothed woman, to say the least. She was a pregnant whore with her dress raised to the waistline, now fully exposing a swollen belly.

"You're more than one man can handle, my lovely Lela," Elijah remarked, pausing from his lovemaking. "Before we finish tonight, I have much to discuss with you."

At this moment, the strange woman's face appeared fully within the glow of an interior coach lantern. Blurting aloud with laughter, she hissed in glee at his words.

"Why, yes," she said. "Let's begin with the fact we both cannot get enough of each other. Not to mention, we also have so much in common, our desire for abundance and wealth. Kendall and Grace hold the key to our financial success. Death unto both!"

With an odd and curious gaze, I stared, observing this woman even more intently. What did she say? Did I hear her correctly? Horror possessed my essence as her statement finally registered.

I shrieked aloud, "You're the one. You despicable whore!" But, my words fell upon deaf ears.

Spinning within a whirling gust of wind, my essence was swiftly transported back into the drawing room at Thornwood Estate, now keenly aware of the rhythmic tic-toc of the large black-lacquered grandfather clock. I observed the pendulum keeping pace with the house servants as they carried fresh water and linens, and apparently several hours had passed. Marcella was still struggling, futilely applying pressure with her healing hands to stop the bleeding from my forehead.

"Where is the doctor?" Marcella sighed, exasperated from her unsuccessful efforts. "Nearly three hours have elapsed and there's still no sign of him. He is usually so much more dependable than this. What can be the delay? I'm afraid that by the time Dr. Harrington finally does arrive, Grace will have lost much blood. We dare not attempt to move her upstairs to the bedroom chambers."

"Be calm," said Clara, with hopes of bringing forth some measure of serenity to the monotony. "I'm sure the storm has detained him. I sense that your internal energies are scattered at this time. Relax and try to concentrate so as to focus your healing powers. Though the bleeding has slowed, it must be completely ceased, or Grace shall perish."

I observed Marcella's gifted hands, each of her six fingers continuing to administer her medicinal touch upon my temple. As she did so, an iridescent flow of sparkling light now radiated from her fingertips. I could feel the heat of her flesh pressed against my forehead, flecks of luminosity transferring the heat of healing energy into my wound. In only a matter of seconds the bleeding halted. A sigh of relief rang loudly from within the room. "We thank the Higher Powers for their healing energy," she said, as I felt her hand lovingly brush against my cheek.

Gradually the rains turned to sleet and with each passing hour, the temperatures plummeted. Now the snow dominated as the prevailing force of nature. At last, the distant rumble of galloping horses could be heard, as the crystalline snow continued to fall upon the estate grounds. Surveying this polar blanket from the western windows, Lindsey stood guard to alert the household of any impending news. "I believe it's the doctor," she cried aloud, "There appears to be a black carriage with four white horses in the distance!"

114

Mr. Abernathy rushed to the main doors with Lindsey and Clara by his side, greeting the elderly, Dr. Harrington…the Thornwood family physician for over fifty years. The doctor departed from his elegant coach, wearing a black-satin top hat and plush velvet cloak. Shielding his face with an outstretched arm to block the gusting windswept snow, he carried his black-leather medical bag, securely within his white-gloved hand. With his gaze directed downward, his eyes squinted to shun the wet snow, flurrying about his face. Entering the estate house, I could hear him cough, clearing his throat as he moved forward into the glowing candlelight.

"Oh! My God! You're hardly Dr. Harrington. There must be some gross mistake. Where's the doctor?" gasped Clara as she stared dumbfounded at the striking dark-haired gentleman who now stood tall before us.

Patricia Grace Joyce   *The Magic of Time*

Nine

When thoughts speak of lust and love
Our desires create visions from up above
Of Heaven sent gifts on wings of dove
Truly blessings from an Angel's trove

In a passing moment
A sudden glimmer of light
Enlightens our awareness
Two souls merging together this night

"Please pardon me, ladies," replied the attractive stranger. "Dr. Harrington requested that I attend to this matter.

"Who are you?" inquired Lindsey. "And, what are you doing here?"

"I'm Dr. Christophe Alexis, a visiting physician – a surgeon actually. I've journeyed from London to take a brief holiday in Boscastle, staying at the estate home of Dr. Harrington and his lovely wife, Lady Kathleen."

"But, we sent for Dr. Harrington." stated Clara.

"Rest assured, my intentions are not to alarm you."

"Where is Dr. Harrington?" Clara continued, eyeing the stranger with curiosity.

"Unfortunately, he was summoned to the waterfront. There appears to have been an accident, an awful shipwreck occurring early this morning along the cliffs leading into Boscastle Harbor.

"Oh, how terrible! Are there any survivors?" gasped Clara, nearing closer to the doctor.

"None that I am yet aware of."

"What sea captain would ever consider entering the wicked straits of Boscastle during a storm? They must have been a ship of drunkards," said Lindsey. "Such fools. They should have known better, and merely deserve their fate. I have little pity on their souls."

Observing Lindsey with bafflement, the doctor continued, "I can only assume it may have been a pirate schooner. From the account of an eye witness, it appears that the captain and crew were sailing incognito."

My thoughts were clouded, trying to find lucidity within the ongoing chatter about me. I was stunned hearing this news as I drifted in my ethereal state above the ongoing conversation, trying desperately to adhere some relevance to the tragedy of which the doctor was speaking. A disaster – horrific and with no survivors, was the essence of his words now branded into my faded unconsciousness. I wondered if perhaps this ship could be *The Destiny*, even speculated that Captain Ian Cutter had perished.

"Have you any idea as to the vessel's port of origin, or identifying name?" asked Clara.

"It's much too early to determine anything, other than the fact there were numerous casualties. These few eyewitnesses, however, seemed to know of the ship, claiming it may have actually been *The Destiny*. Other than this scant piece of information, there's not much data available at present. The likelihood of recovering any survivors appears dim. No one could have possibly lived through such a disaster. Even I have heard the tales of the unforgiving Cornish cliffs."

With these words, my heart sank, for deep within I sensed it might have truly been Ian's vessel.

Rather than lend a hand with the others at the site of the accident, Dr. Alexis told the sisters that he thought it best to answer the plea of the coachmen.

"The coachmen had such a sense of urgency with their request that I felt compelled to assist. Now let's not delay any longer, wasting more valuable time with my idle discussion. Please show me to the patient, the young woman they call Lady Grace."

Mr. Abernathy and Clara swiftly led the way from the decadent marble foyer. The doctor followed the long candlelit hallway as Lindsey trailed closely by his side, intently observing the handsome physician.

"May I help you carry your bag?" Lindsey insisted. "I am at your beck and call, and please do not hesitate to let me assist you with your every want. I'm very resourceful, experienced in more ways than one."

"Madam, what is your name?" the doctor inquired as he continued to stride briskly down the long corridor.

"Madam Lindsey Lumiere, but you may simply call me Lindsey."

"Well, madam, it's certainly nice to make your acquaintance. If you don't mind, however, I prefer to personally tend to my patients and their needs at this stage, not to say that I doubt you are experienced."

From out-of-body, I observed Dr. Alexis approaching me as I reposed languidly upon the chaise. Marcella continued to dote upon me as the doctor entered into the drawing room. My body showed no movement, other than the small inflection of my chest rising and falling. With a sense of relief, I gathered that I must still be alive as I hovered above the scene, until gradually becoming more adapted to the action taking place about me.

With extended arms, the doctor motioned Marcella to stand back, removing a small brown glass vial from his medical bag.

"So, I see you have brought your own little bag of magic with you, Dr. Alexis," blurted Lindsey.

"Not magic, madam. It's a strong aromatic healing salt that serves to arouse and awaken one's senses." He emptied the contents into the palm of his left hand, pinching within his fingertips a small amount of what appeared to be a pale yellow salt-like powder. As he held the compound under my nose, I began to stir instantaneously. I could feel the floating aura of my essence swirling in circles about the room, suddenly returning at last into my physical being as I awakened from my former state of oblivion.

My eye lids blinked softly as I tried to focus, finding myself peering into a pair of dazzling luminescent eyes, as if basking on an unforgettable deep-blue sea that twinkled brighter than the shimmering waves. Looking upward into the face of this attractive dark-haired stranger, I studied him from my reposed perspective, sensing there was an uncanny recognition between us–an absolute, inexplicable familiarity. I could only wonder if this man was mindful of it as well.

"Where am I? And, who are you? "I inquired, becoming more alert.

"I am Dr. Alexis–Christophe Alexis."

"What happened?" My head throbbed with pain as I attempted to reposition my body in an upright position.

"Can you tell me your name? Do you know where you are?" he inquired as he motioned with his hand for me to refrain from rising.

"Yes, of course. I'm Grace. Lady Grace Worthington, and at this very moment I am in the drawing room."

"Very well," he said.

"But, I was floating above you, high above all of you," I continued. "And, then I was in London, chased by Lord Russell along the River Thames. I came upon a coach. Oddly, the African slave, Elijah was even there too, yet he was not alone. Quite shockingly he was enamored within the embrace of that ungodly whore, Madame Lela Pucelle."

The sisters looked alarmingly at one another as if they absolutely understood the significance of my words, however, Dr. Alexis's face flushed, as he viewed me with peculiarity, clearly baffled by my statement.

"What did you say?" he inquired.

"Marcella gasped, mumbling under her breath, "The magic."

"The magic?" I whispered, staring at Marcella.

"We shall discuss this matter later," she replied in a firm tone of voice. From the look upon her face, I knew better than to push for clarification. My inner feeling, however, was that this could only be absolute confirmation. Was the magic at last making itself known to me, again enfolding me within the powerful arms of its' mystique?

"Very well," the doctor added, with a puzzled look upon his face. "Let's reserve the remainder of this conversation for afterwards. At present, it's paramount that I expeditiously clean and bandage your forehead. You have a serious gash and bruise upon your temple.

Dr. Alexis instructed the sisters to bring him a large deep-sided bowl of hot water and additional unsoiled linens. Meticulously cleansing the flesh and applying a clear salve, he covered the open wound with a piece of white cotton fabric around my forehead, wrapping it with care as if a crown of jewels.

"That looks superb, and fit for a Queen," he said, smiling as he motioned towards Mr. Abernathy and continued speaking, "Now then, Sir. If you please, I shall need a bit of your assistance to guide me as I carry Lady Grace to her chambers."

The doctor carefully lifted me, gently embracing my body. Nuzzled safely within his firm, muscular arms, together we departed the drawing room, his strength supporting my entire body. For some unknown reason, I felt a comforting closeness to this man as if I was instantly melting into his very being.

We ascended the main staircase leading into the bedroom chamber. The sisters followed closely and made preparations to turn down my bed linens, watching keenly as the doctor laid my body atop this feathered nest. A fire roared, glowing intensely within the rose-veined marble fireplace. The scent of birch wood filled the air, as the vibrant red-orange flames brought welcomed warmth to the damp surroundings of my day, having now transpired well into twilight.

"May I request that you leave the room for a short while?" he said, motioning to the sisters. "I shall like to speak with Lady Grace and examine her in privacy. It's so very important that I further evaluate her condition without interruption or distraction. It's vital that we talk."

"Excuse me, doctor," said Clara.

"Yes, madam?"

"I gather you are aware of the necessity to abide by conventions of etiquette, and being that Grace is a refined lady of prominence, I insist that I shall absolutely remain within the chamber suite during this physical exam."

"But, of course. That is quite fine, madam. I only intend on assessing Grace for further injury."

"Precisely," Clara said.

Lindsey interrupted, "Please know that I won't be far. I'm just outside the door, should you need anything, Dr. Alexis. I'm here for you."

"Thank you," he said, gazing in Lindsey's direction. "But, I sense Grace and I will manage quite well without your assistance." The sisters obediently departed from the room, closing the massive double doors to the bedroom suite behind them. Regretfully, the doctor and I were not alone, as Clara sat attentively nearby to oversee this matter. I gazed at him with bewilderment, still baffled, wondering why he seemed so familiar to me.

122

"I want you to breathe deeply and try to relax. How shall I best go about doing this?" he inquired. "Hmmm…would you mind if perhaps, I unbutton your frock to enable you to breathe more freely? Please, just relax. You have absolutely nothing to fear. I assure you, I am only trying to make you more at ease." He continued, "If you should feel the least bit awkward or need me to explain my actions, please stop me. I want to make sure you have not bruised your ribs, or any other part of your body from the fall."

Uncomfortable and nauseated with a throbbing headache, I showed little resistance, openly welcoming the doctor's assistance to proceed with his exam. He meticulously removed my heeled leather shoes, unfastened and removed my silk stockings and unbuttoned my silk dress. Lastly, I could feel his fingertips upon the small of my neck and back. The doctor hesitated before loosening the ties to my white-lace under slip.

"How does that feel?" he inquired.

"Much better," I acquiesced. "But, perhaps you could bring me an additional pillow? My head is still aching with pain."

"Of course," he said, positioning another large goose-feather pillow beneath my brown curls.

Once again I sensed a familiarity with this man. Although, I could not quite pinpoint where I had met the doctor prior, or if I had ever truly met him, I was certain of one thing. Without a doubt, there was an unqualified immediate attraction between us, like the instantaneous sparking of a flame.

As he examined me, I felt his tapered fingers slowly removing my articles of clothing. His gorgeous blue eyes seemed to intentionally avoid my direct gaze as I stared upward at him, mesmerized as if under his spell. I could not help but admire his healthy white teeth and the dark chocolate-brown locks of hair, framing his polished, angular face. During the examination he

123

focused intently upon my body, still avoiding any direct contact with my direct vision.

"Excuse me, Dr. Alexis," I said. "Did you say that your name was Christophe? Christophe Alexis?"

"Yes. Why do you ask?"

"I thought that I may have met you previously, perhaps somewhere in London. You do appear most familiar to me."

"This I sense of you as well," he replied. "I believed the same when my eyes first met upon your face in the drawing room."

"Perhaps we have seen each other merely in passing?" I inquired. "Or, even attending one of the social balls in London?"

"It could very possibly be. I rarely ever forget a face, and I absolutely do enjoy dancing," he said. "Other than a rather extreme headache, how do you feel?" he continued, returning the conversation to his area of comfort–medicine. "Do you have pain or distress? Does your chest ache, or do you have discomfort in your abdomen, your legs or your arms? You took a nasty fall, my dear."

I explained to the doctor that I had been feeling ill with fatigue and nausea during the past few weeks. I also conveyed to him that I had even become ill on my recent journey, and I told him my discomfort was most likely nothing to concern myself with, stating I had been upset with the baffling disappearance of my husband.

"Your husband is missing?" he inquired, pausing from the examination.

"Yes, Kendall strangely vanished three months ago, yet with the news I received today, I fear that he has even taken a mistress."

"A mistress? How awful for you! Go on, please tell me more. I do recall reading something about this case in the London papers."

Before I could speak, the doctor continued with the examination. "Is there any particular pattern to this nausea?" he inquired.

124

"What do you mean?" I asked.

"Do you experience it at a particular time, such as after a meal, or at any certain time of day?"

"Well, I feel rather ill almost every morning when I first arise." I explained to him that on some mornings my distress was more severe than on other occasions, and that sometimes it even lasted all day and night. Lately, I could not eat very much at any time. If I did eat, I found that I simply could not retain my food for very long. I had resorted to sipping hot teas and nibbling on water biscuits throughout each day. This seemed to be the only sustenance agreeing with me.

"How long has this been occurring?" he inquired. "I gather you're well aware one cannot possibly sustain a healthy diet existing only on biscuits and tea?"

"It has been nearly five to six weeks."

"Under normal conditions, I would commonly seek to bleed you for relief, he said. "In your fragile state, however, I sense bleeding would serve only the reverse, most likely further weakening you."

I wanted to believe that my nausea was obviously due to a nervous stomach, as I gave further explanation to the doctor. I told the doctor that I had a great deal on my mind, so much sorrow of recent days regarding my marriage, my missing husband and this clandestine mistress who claimed to be with child–pregnant with Kendall's child.

"I'm sorry to hear this. It's quite evident that you're obviously under much duress at this time. Stress is a terrible thing. It's a difficult matter and can lead to a multitude of so many other conditions and ailments."

"Yes, it's all a terrible matter," I sighed.

"Would you mind if I examined you for a while longer, if we could share a bit more time together?" he inquired.

I looked in Clara's direction, searching for her approval to the doctor's request. Nodding her head, Clara quietly gave her consent for the exam to move forward. I tried not to show my utter delight as I knew this would only arouse her suspicions, but I could not help wonder if Clara already sensed the intense attraction I had with this eloquent man.

"It's so very important that we discuss your condition in detail," he continued. "However, I will need to remove some of your undergarments to further examine you very carefully. It will take a few minutes, if you please. I have a hunch. Let's just say it's an educated guess as to what may be ailing you. Please continue to lay back and relax."

I could hear the sound of Clara rustling in the background as she earnestly moved her chair forward to reposition her vantage point. "Such a thorough exam, doctor," she said. "You should be commended on your bedside manner."

"Thank you, madam. I want to be absolutely certain that Grace has no further signs of injury."

I rested my head comfortably upon the pillow cushions, attempting to calm myself as the doctor removed my undergarments…the white-lace slip and silk corset, with the exception of my flounced lace petticoat. He listened to my heart and lungs, placing his ear upon my substantial breasts.

"I'll need for you to take deep breaths. Slowly, very slowly."

I followed his instructions, yet my eyes remained enamored with him.

"That's fine. Your heart and breathing both sound lucid."
Placing his hands upon my collar bone, I could feel the warmth of his fingertips traveling along the muscles and descending to my shoulders, then leading to my bosom.

"There, that's good," he continued. Carefully observing my body, his hands hesitated before examining me further. "How does this feel?" he inquired as he gently cupped his fingers around my left breast. "Is there any discomfort, any pain or tenderness at all?"

126

I flinched, yet the doctor continued to avoid any direct contact with my eyes as he removed his hand, focused only upon my swollen flesh. "Yes," I replied. "I'm sore." I looked upward again into Dr. Alexis's eyes, yearning for his attention. His eyes nervously shifted, intentionally circumventing mine as he remained preoccupied with performing the physical exam. Placing his hand upon my right breast, he paused.

"Is there something wrong, doctor?"

There was no reply as he positioned his hands upon my rib cage and abdomen, pressing gently against my supple creamy white skin.

"Do you feel anything when I do this? Is there any tenderness in this area?" he asked, pressing the palms of his hands lightly upon my flesh.

"There is some sensitivity."

"I wonder if you have been a bit light-headed on more than just this occasion today. Are you aware that you fainted this morning in the drawing room?"

I told him that I had felt dizzy at times and I wondered if this could all perhaps be a result of my stress.

"How regular have you been with receiving your monthly *visitor* during the cycle of the moon? Do you know what I am referring to?"

"Completely," I replied. "I have entertained this *visitor* every month since the age of fourteen years, that is, until recently. Or, shall I say, I have not had the untimely pleasure of this guest's company since December, or thereabouts."

"Well, Grace," he said, smiling brightly at me. "I may have a fairly accurate diagnosis as to what has been the cause of your physical duress in recent weeks."

At last, with penetrating focus, my eyes finally met Dr. Alexis's large blue eyes. Instantaneously, I now realized where, why and how I had such an overwhelming sense of recognition with this charming man.

"You were the handsome gentleman in my dream last night," I blurted aloud. "I knew that I had met you prior to this day. Yes, that's it! You were with me in my dreams."

He chuckled. "It was all a dream. I believe, however, we've actually met somewhere prior in London," he said, looking at me with awkwardness. "You took a serious fall, resulting in a large contusion upon your forehead. Are you certain that you feel all right?"

"Absolutely," I insisted. "I presume I am about as well as anyone could be, considering what I have been going through." I questioned if the doctor wondered that I may have lost my mind. Was I making any sense to him? I needed for him to understand me, to trust that I was credible, and absolutely sane.

I thought about his comment regarding having possibly met in the past. Since I had resided in London during the past nine years, this too, could have been quite plausible, but deep within my soul, I sensed that our connection was so much more than a casual passing in prior days. The grandeur of my attraction to him was as if we had even been connected within another lifetime. Reposing in my vulnerable position, I continued to stare into his eyes, remaining mystified with the graceful angles of his chiseled face.

"Doctor, are you going to reveal your hunch and tell me the cause of my duress? Could it be that I simply need a compassionate man in my life?"

Dr. Alexis smiled nervously, avoiding my gaze. Distracted from his concentration by my forthright comment, he hesitated and cleared his throat.

"Well, if my diagnosis and calculations prove to be correct, you're going to receive a wonderful gift...a surprise in the latter months of this year, perhaps sometime in late summer." I

128

observed the doctor with incomprehension, feeling my face distort with twisted ambiguity.

"I love surprises! Tell me more," I said, overwhelmed with excitement. "Please, don't prolong the suspense a moment longer."

Ten

An absolute love, a field of spring flowers
Often neglected are tender moments of ours
An embrace, a kiss in these darkest hours
Expressing a truth with passionate power

Listen to your heart and all will be well
Trust in your feelings, time will surely tell
The inner voice will lead you to your highest good
Listen to your heart and all will be well

S uddenly, the double doors to the chamber flew open with the Lumiere sisters pouring forth into the room to join the doctor, Clara and myself. Reaching for my disrobed clothing which lay casually in a pile at the edge of the feather-bed, I attempted to cover my exposed body. Dr. Alexis moved forward, standing before me to provide some sense of privacy, aware of my apparent sensitivity. He took a white woolen blanket from the foot of the bed and draped the soft coverlet atop my bare breasts.

"We sense there is joyful news to share," said Marcella, as the sisters gathered about. "The doctor has a surprise for us. Something about a gift," I said excitedly, directly making eye contact with Dr. Alexis. "But, I know you shall never guess what it is in a thousand years."

"Have you forgotten with whom you are speaking?" remarked Lindsey. "I certainly know all that is about to be revealed. Shall I tell you, perhaps?"

"Lindsey, please let the doctor speak. Go ahead," Marcella said, looking at Dr. Alexis.

"This news involves a child," Lindsey boldly interrupted. "There appears to be discussion of a child between Grace and another. It is a man. Yes, between Grace and...oh my," she hesitated. "I'm really not quite certain of his identity, but in due time, I shall view this with greater clarity."

"What else do you see?" I inquired, now oblivious to my pain as I swiftly repositioned myself upright in bed. I pulled the blanket upwards and tucked it snuggly under my chin. "Do you see Kendall?"

"Why would you ask such a ridiculous question?" Lindsey inquired, with an enormous grin upon her face. "Grace, perhaps you have something further to share with us? Should we have reason to suspect that another handsome gentleman has possibly entangled himself in your precarious web?"

"That's enough, Lindsey!" shouted Clara.

Unable to hide my muddle, I attempted to quickly compose myself. I told Lindsey the reason I wondered if she saw a lucid image of my husband in her vision, was that I feared he may be dead, emphasizing in the same breath, that of course, the only man involved with me would absolutely be only Kendall. "How could you ever insinuate that it could possibly be otherwise?" I retorted.

Always the peace maker, Marcella stepped forward, interrupting the conversation. "Please, Lindsey. The doctor is here in our presence. Let him speak."

With an obvious attempt to change the focus of the discussion, I smiled appreciatively at Marcella and said, "Go on, Dr. Alexis. What is this news of a gift that you want to share with all of us?"

Observing the confusion about the room, the doctor at last made his announcement. "Grace, you're all aglow. I believe you're with child, barely pregnant. I estimate perhaps a month, or two at the very most. Congratulations! You're going to bear forth the gift of a child into this world, an absolutely wonderful soul."

"Isn't this simply marvelous news?" I blurted. Truly, I felt as if I was gagging. My feigned words were lodged awkwardly within my throat, like the log jammed River Tamar in the early spring.

"How delightful!" exclaimed Clara, clapping her hands together in joyous praise.

I sensed my face turn a lighter shade of pale, or rather more the tone of austere porcelain as I listened intently, trying to comprehend what Dr. Alexis was actually saying. I was numb, tongue-tied, astounded beyond disbelief as I attempted to express my assorted emotions. What was happening? Could this be true? How could I have been so unaware? How could I not have known?

"What utterly splendid news," I continued. My haphazardly spoken words still couldn't have been further from the truth. After so many difficult years of marriage, I was now in shocking awe of my situation. I paused in reflection upon this absurdity, since that was what it seemed. For one thing, the reality of my situation posed that it was presently beyond the scope of my imagination to ever envision that I was pregnant with Kendall's child. Perhaps the doctor was mistaken with his calculations, although it seemed highly unlikely this man of science could err in this instance.

My thoughts rushed back in time to that unforgettable night of fifteen November, 1810. I felt my face flush with warmth, turning a bright hue of pink. Oddly, an issue remained very perplexing to me and I was definitely not going to spill the beans at this time. The fact of the matter was, I was overwhelmed by this unexpected news, but I did not dare let on otherwise to the doctor, nor Clara, Marcella and lastly…Lindsey.

I recollected my last intimate encounter with Kendall, disillusioned that I may have actually conceived, impregnated through his numerous acts of abusive unsolicited sex on that dreadful night, however, for the past nine years I had been unable to even conceive a child, never mind the fact of birthing a Worthington heir. My better sense, my inner voice was shouting a much different scenario to me as my thoughts drifted to that same night within Worthington Estate house and at the Cathedral. To my knowledge, no one was even the least bit suspicious, nor had they a clue of the intimacies that had transpired. This was just the way I wanted it to remain, at least for the time being.

Although this dilemma was multifaceted, the truth of the matter was that I had been far from devout in my discordant and abusive marriage to Kendall. In light of this fact, the reality of the moment was still somewhat overwhelming as I became fully aware there was absolutely more than one possibility as to the identity of the father of my child. Now I knew my silence was mandatory. Deep in my heart and soul, I could only pray the father of this child would be none other than he.

The doctor smiled, still observing the three sisters and myself with a look of peculiarity upon his bewildered face. I sensed he was trying to grasp onto some ribbon of logic concerning this conversation. While his efforts appeared strained in comprehending the true gist of the ensuing chatter within the room, I was aware he somehow realized it was not his privilege at this time to view a key piece of missing information. A part of this puzzle was still quite evidently obscure to him.

"Please let me attempt to explain a few matters, Dr. Alexis," I said, in an effort to bring some degree of clarity to the ensuing conversation. I looked directly into his eyes. "My words may sound a bit farfetched. I will do my very best, however, to present what I believe to be some rather unique understandings that exist within our world. You see, my sisters and I have communication with the other side." As the doctor's gaze surveyed me with curiosity, I continued," We are mystics, chosen in this lifetime to fully embody and enable the healing gifts of the Higher Powers on this earth. Do you understand what I'm saying?"

"Well, I believe so," he replied. "I do have some experience in this area."

134

"Oh?" I wondered how he could possibly begin to comprehend, doubting how and where this man of medical science could have ever come to understand what I was speaking of.

"I'm actually quite familiar with what you are referring to, this realm of the spirit world," he continued. "I have even had the opportunity to meet this other world in past years. This is the spirit realm where time and space exists within our own time, yet beyond a veil."

The sisters and I stared at the doctor in awe. It was not that we were immune to this man's special qualities when first making his acquaintance today, however, until this very moment, we did not fully value the depth, fullness and awareness of his soul.

"Who are you?" I inquired, continuing to observe him with bewilderment. "And, how do you account for your knowledge of the Higher Powers and the veil?"

"Please, ladies, I can explain. You see, my background is rather unusual. A convent of nuns with the Church of England in London had initially taken me into their care when I was, but an infant, claiming from what I later learned that I was mysteriously abandoned upon their doorstep shortly after my birth. A unique and gifted metaphysical healer named Madam Martha Alexis and her husband, a renowned surgeon named Dr. Bertram Alexis, adopted me at the young age of six months." He continued,

"Perhaps you have even had occasion to have heard of my parents in years gone by?"

"Indeed," commented Clara, "As mystics and healers, the sisters and I are aware of your mother's gifts, and regrettably of her tragic passing."

"My mother's death was horrific, a burning at the stake two-and-twenty years ago in London," he continued. "Her ways were that of only goodness and compassion, but misunderstood by so many."

"Of course, I remember her well," Clara continued. "She was a beautiful woman, an energy healer, a Divine presence for those who sought her words and blessings of wisdom on this earth. But, such a tragedy, such a loss to us and to this world, yet this is what she chose for her path in this lifetime. Indeed, this is what was destined."

"It brings me great comfort and peace, knowing that she is forever with me in spirit," he continued.

Dr. Alexis told us that he sensed his mother's presence within himself, her guiding rays of light. His mother's passing had taught him to live compassionately, being of service to others. Her selflessness had been an inspiration, encouraging him to also become a healer. The doctor revealed to us that he, however, chose to give of himself as a healer in a more traditional role as that of a physician and surgeon. "For, this is truly the script I have written for myself in this life," he said. "Surely you are aware that the gifts of healing lay within each and every one of us. These energies must firstly be developed to be fully expressed on an array of different levels and through a variety of means. Just as you are able to cure the body, mind and spirit through the healing energy of your mystical powers, I too, restore health through my role as a physician and surgeon."

As the conversation ensued, I quietly took a few moments to reflect upon his insightful words. The doctor appeared to be a sensitive and caring soul. This man was certainly rare, unique, and so very unconventional from the majority of men that I had encountered in my life–a most welcomed change.

Marcella said, "Although it has been several years, I now also remember that your father was the skillful surgeon who assisted us in a most precarious situation. To this day, we are appreciative for his aid in removing a veiled porous membrane from Grace's face when she was a newborn child."

136

"I had no idea this was you, Grace," he said alarmingly as he looked in my direction. "I recall my father mentioning this exceptionally bizarre case of an infant girl who had been born with a grotesque, thin membrane veiling her beautiful face. Had her family not found the appropriate surgeon to skillfully remove the veiled tissue, she would have surely died within the upcoming days...suffocating to death. I'm pleased my father was able to intervene and come to your aid." He continued, "Now look at your radiant beauty! You are like a rose without thorns."

Instantly, I recognized his words. He most definitely was the gentleman in my dream. I wanted to infer this as confirmation. Dr. Alexis could be none other.

"The years seemingly have been good to you as well, doctor," said Clara. "Permit me to elaborate even further in stating that you are quite charismatic."

Dr. Alexis was alluring, a well-proportioned gentleman in his mid-fifties. A humble man, it was no secret to any of us that he was growing increasingly uncomfortable with all of the attention highlighted upon him.

"Hmmm, thank you," he said. "But, I rarely devote any attention to reflecting upon my physical attributes. I have chosen a life of service, a life of serving others. My focus is on assisting my patients to heal, to move forward with their lives, becoming healthy and productive again."

"Such dedication, such a strong selfless purpose in life," Clara said. This is truly exemplary and quite admirable, doctor."

"This is simply who I am, and what I have chosen. This is my path. Medicine is my passion."

Lindsey interrupted, "Dr. Alexis, we all certainly have our passions in life. Some of us, however, merely choose to express these in a different manner." She continued, "Shall we even say some of us respond a bit too passionately? Furthermore, some individuals perhaps even focus this lust–this passion in life upon a personal relationship, maybe even a love interest? Wouldn't you agree with me, doctor?" Lindsey glared at me from across the room as Dr. Alexis hesitated to reply.

"Well," he said, awkwardly gazing about the room. "I suppose some may choose this."

"Surely, a handsome fellow as yourself, must have considerations other than solely medicine as your passion in life?" Before he could elicit a response, Lindsey abruptly continued with what I could only determine was her self-serving banter.

"Perhaps you might invite the notion of passion in the physical sense of the word?" she inquired. "Have you ever considered the notion of envisioning yourself with a fine woman, like me—the lovely, stunningly beautiful, elegant and sensual Lindsey Lumiere?"

"Hush!" exclaimed Clara. "Have you no manners, Lindsey? I'm sure Dr. Alexis has more than his fair share of admirers, more than his share of flirtations from the female sector. In fact I would even venture to state that the handsome doctor must have women professing their devotion and affection–their eternal love. I imagine that a physician such as Dr. Alexis would be wise to become quite cautious and selective as to whom he might permit to enter into the inner circle of his life." Gazing directly at Lindsey, she continued, "There are many woman of lowly character and morals, and if the doctor was unaware, some women could even quite possibly deceive, taking him as a love interest only for his money and worldly possessions, not to mention breaking his heart."

"Would this be true, doctor?" Lindsey inquired. "Has this been your experience?"

The doctor blushed an even brighter pink and cleared his throat. In an attempt to speak with stoic composure, he replied,

"Ladies, at present I only have occasion to share my ardor of medicine with those in need of healing, however, you do speak the absolute truth. I have known the company of these immoral and unethical women which you refer to, but now my practice leaves little to no time, to share with a woman, yet alone to ever consider falling in love."

I was surprised by his candidness. For a moment, I even felt a sorrow for the doctor as I found myself pondering the vast solitude this man must have experienced over his lifetime, focusing solely on his intense education, his patients and the demanding practice of medicine, but as I considered his statements, I inferred that his words were somehow a convenient manner for him to evade the topic of discussion. I began to wonder if, perhaps, something was being intentionally hidden. I concluded that Dr. Alexis could not devote his time and energy to a relationship with any woman at this stage in his life, primarily because he chose not to give it his attention, for whatever his reasons might be.

I continued to intuit, however, a common bond with this eloquent man, a sadness that he, too, had not found real love, and like me, I understood he must also have tremendous fears to overcome when it came to trusting and loving another soul in this lifetime.

"I have too many distractions and responsibilities in my life," he continued. The doctor told us that it simply could not be, that it was not fair and worthy of him to even consider a committed relationship with a fine woman, however, should his life change, becoming more reasonable and manageable, perhaps he might one day create a place for a woman's passion. Until that day presented itself, he was dedicated to assisting all those who were in need of medical attention and care.

"You must realize that my work brings me so much personal fulfillment and satisfaction, serving to heal others through my diagnoses and surgeries," he said.

"Most definitely," the sisters said, nodding their heads as they listened to his story.

Dr. Alexis paused, "There exists, however, a darker side to my profession as well. Unfortunately, there are so many ill people in the world." He told us that sadly, he was very cognizant of the fact that he could not save all of them, although this did not stop him from attempting to heal as many as possible through his caring and compassionate acts of surgery. He told us that he was often surrounded by so much despair and grief in life. "There are times my world can even become horrifically overwhelming."

I pondered his words, surmising that if an acceptable woman was to ever come into the doctor's life one day, well, let's just say she would have to be extraordinary on every level as a human being and a spiritual being–truly understanding and supportive of his path in this world. Likewise, I sensed he would be accepting and supportive of her path, but somehow I also believed the doctor was not open to permitting love to enter into his heart at this time. He seemed closed, almost one-dimensional regarding this view. Of course, I understood that he was a surgeon, and therefore dealt with an exact science, but I remained puzzled. Why did it have to be one, or the other? Why couldn't an individual have both - true passionate love and a healthy productive career? I could only gather that it must require the insight of a truly enlightened soul to balance a healthy lifestyle of both thriving romance and the demanding digressions of a medical profession.

"Doctor, do you ever share time with women?" Lindsey interrupted again. "Are you ever in their company, other than in the role as a physician? Wouldn't you just adore being with a woman for the sake of satisfying your physical mortal needs? Or, are you strictly this devout monk of medicine?"

"We have quite frankly heard enough," shouted Marcella as she grabbed Lindsey by the arm, abruptly escorting her out of the bedroom suite.

140

"I am so sorry, doctor," said Clara. "I am embarrassed by Lindsey's blatant behavior. Her prying and intrusiveness regarding your personal life is absolutely unacceptable. Please forgive her rudeness."

Over the years the sisters had learned to maintain a low profile, yet their efforts to advise and counsel Lindsey in this regard, remained unsuccessful. Unfortunately, Lindsey chose to ignore their warnings, preferring to live her life on the edge, so to speak. Of course, this was the script she had written for herself. This was her path at this time.

Dr. Alexis looked directly at me and responded, "Ladies, I am very much aware of the harmony and the balance, or rather, the lack of which I need to create in my life. Perhaps, the future holds the answers to all of these questions. I remain hopeful, however, that one day I will be able to have a fuller life, an existence including not only my passion for medicine, but a life involving a fine woman."

His commitment to medicine and his selfless service to others, led all of us to the conclusion, the doctor was truly a compassionate man. His heightened level of spiritual awareness was a clear indication that Dr. Alexis was an evolved individual, a soul who had learned grand lessons while experiencing numerous past lives.

"Doctor, we thank you for your time assisting Grace today," said Marcella "It was most kind of you to journey to the estate in this horrid weather. I know that she is especially grateful for your personal attention and the medical care which you so generously endowed upon her."

"It was the right thing to do," he said, as he smiled looking in my direction. "I am pleased that I was of some assistance to all of you."

"Doctor," I said. "Will I remain in your care, now that I am with child?"

141

"Unfortunately, the logistics of traveling from Boscastle to London and London to Boscastle will prove to be an obstacle for me to care for you as a patient." The doctor hoped that I would understand his reasoning, explaining that his medical practice was currently in London. It was not at all common for him to have ventured west into the region of Cornwall. It was only upon rare occasion as now, when he could create some time to take a short holiday in the seaport of Boscastle. He told me, however, he was leery of the long journey that would endure, that geographically it would make for an undesirable and precarious commute in my physical state. "It will be dangerous for you to travel over several days to London, just to be in my care. In fact, I'll be returning to London by coach this evening," he continued. "I assure you that I'll try to visit when I again set my sights westward toward Boscastle. I wish all of my patients were as kind and compassionate as you." He told us that he shared a great friendship with Dr. Harrington and his gracious wife, Lady Kathleen. He continued, "I'm certain Dr. Harrington will take excellent care of you during these upcoming months."

Unable to contain my seesawing emotions of disappointment and pleasure, I remarked, "Although, I sense that my travels eastward to London will be few, I shall make a point of calling upon your office when I am in the city again."

He smiled at me and replied, "That will be quite fine. I shall look forward to your visit. In fact, Grace, should you again one day return to London to reside, perhaps you may even decide to give birth there. It's just something for you to consider within the upcoming months." The doctor told me that I must now focus on getting more rest and improving my nutrition, instructing that I must make an effort to eat well, to moderately consume more freshly cooked fish, fruits, vegetables, eggs and milk for my personal well-being, and for the health of the child.

142

"Promise me, that you'll eat more than just biscuits and hot tea."

Nodding my head, I said, "Perhaps I shall even consider returning to London sooner than I anticipate."

I told the doctor that Worthington Estate was in Westminster, at the west end of town. In an effort to cut all ties with my past, I had secured the London estate, dismissing the service staff until further notice. I had not forgotten, however, the fact that much unfinished business still loomed with Constable Gordon, all of which could potentially call me back again.

"Please know, doctor, that you're always welcome in my home, whether your travels take you east or west," I continued.

He replied, "Well there you have it! Thank you for the gracious invitation. I shall look forward to that day." The doctor thanked the sisters for their hospitality as he moved in my direction. I repositioned myself, shifting my body in bed and pulling the blanket closer towards my chin.

Then, quite unexpectedly…he embraced me, whispering softly into my ear, "With the magic of time, all will be well. There is nothing to fear when you listen to your heart."

I was melting inside, genuinely touched by his gesture of affection as I thanked him for his compassion and assistance today. Reluctantly, he arose from the bedside, preparing to depart as I continued to observe him gather his belongings within his black medical bag. With his feet stepping unhurriedly towards the doorway, he followed the Lumiere sisters out of the bedroom suite. At last he motioned, turning his head in my direction. He glanced again into the room as his eyes search earnestly for one last, long gaze into the depths of mine. With our vision fixated upon each other, I felt as if his essence approached the threshold of my soul.

Welling tears clouded my eyes as I tried to find the appropriate words to speak. "Thank you again Dr. Alexis. I'll never forget you."

Summoning all the strength in his statuesque body to refrain from returning to my bedside, he paused in the doorway and remarked, "Please remember my words, Grace."

I nodded my head and softly repeated his words to myself, vowing from that day forward to always keep this memory close within my heart.

Descending the massive staircase, the sisters escorted Dr. Alexis to the estate house foyer.

Mr. Abernathy retrieved the doctor's cloak and top hat as the coachmen led him towards the elegant coach in waiting. Rising from my bed, I wrapped my white blanket around my shoulders, and rushed across the room to the westward windows, hopeful of catching one last glimpse of this compassionate man.

Within the light of glowing lanterns, I could see the sleeting rain still falling upon the frigid estate grounds. The combination of the evening's darkening sea mist and precipitation only obstructed my bird's eye view from the vantage point upon an orchid-colored velvet window-seat cushion. I shivered from the chilled, damp air as I snuggled within the blanket, longing for one last glance into the doctor's eyes. With vision focused, my eyes followed the doctor entering the doorway of the horse drawn carriage.

"What a blessed soul!" I murmured, as he looked upwards in my direction. We exchanged smiles, sealing our newly established bond of friendship. I knew from that very moment, there was something very special about Dr. Christophe Alexis.

As I sat by the large western windows, I adhered my sight upon the black carriage, watching it become smaller and smaller, rolling toward the large black estate gates. Blowing a kiss towards the diminishing coach, I whispered, "Until we meet again. I pray my love will kiss you in a while." Gradually the carriage disappeared,

144

vanishing as if engulfed by the darkening horizon. With quill pen in hand, I mindfully scrolled the doctor's words upon a piece of white parchment paper.

With the magic of time, all will be well. There is nothing to fear when you listen to your heart.

Eleven

Love is a feeling, more than just a word
Sometimes spoken, like music to be heard
Love is a feeling, within your heart and soul
It has no limits, a kindness that you show

Love is a feeling, a memory, a kiss
An attraction to another, even more than this
Love is a feeling, a closeness that's Divine
A destiny that calls you, perhaps a past lifetime

A sense of sadness overwhelmed me as I considered all that had unpredictably transpired on this day. Arising from the window seat, I walked towards the beckoning comfort of my featherbed. From the corner of my eye, I found Marcella framed within the chamber doorway. As she approached me with outstretched arms, we embraced each other. I held onto her as if I were holding on for dear life, trembling from what I could only attribute to the combination of chilling sea air and my overwhelming uncertainty.

"More will be presented as time passes," she said. "You must listen and befriend awareness."

I merely wanted this day to end, for my body craved sleep and I longed to curl up like a cat into a cozy ball of fluff, my mind waning into the safety and comfort of another dimension, into my world of dreams. I wanted to believe that I could avoid all the monotony which was now confronting me, yearning to snuff out all of my woe, lulled into a state of nothingness where I could at last shut out the world and re-emerge refreshed and tranquil. I told Marcella about all of the divergent feelings that were running unbridled within me.

Without a doubt, I was becoming more conscious of the awesome changes in my life and clearly this was troublesome. The letter I had received today from Madame Pucelle was just one of many mounting pressures slowly wearing upon me. The strange out-of-body incident that I experienced while lying upon the drawing room floor, was still gnawing at my mind. I explained to Marcella, how my body seemed to leave my physical form, as if I was floating above the world. I told her of the baffling vision with the disfigured and scarred fellow who had an uncanny resemblance to Lord Russell, how he chased me at nightfall within the city of London and then suddenly disappeared when I stumbled upon the isolated coach, only to discover Madame Lela Pucelle seductively poised within the arms of the slave, Elijah.

If this vision spoke of the truth, I was now more befuddled than ever. Was this grotesque, tall light-haired stranger really Russell following me? Did my brother-in-law play a crucial role in Kendall's disappearance? More importantly, was Russell really in pursuit of me? For an instant, I thought that perhaps his presence served a role merely as a compass to direct my hovering essence toward the direction of the coach. As I pondered this situation further, I had begun to intuit that Russell might have solely been the catalyst for my shocking discovery of Elijah's intimacy with Madame Lela Pucelle.

I now could only wonder if Madame Lela Pucelle, Elijah Foster and Lord Russell truly had some direct involvement, some deceptive connection with my missing husband. From the conversation that transpired within the vision, I concluded that all three individuals were now somehow directly involved with Kendall's disappearance. This was all the more unnerving as I shuttered at the thought of having to look over my shoulder, fearful of my own demise. The appallingly scarred face of Russell was etched clearly within my mind; however, it was the presence of Madame Pucelle within this vision that proved of paramount concern. Was this revelation significant? I certainly wanted to believe it as such.

Furthermore, could the future birth of a child to Madame Pucelle actually have been fathered by none other than Elijah? Could Kendall's role be one of merely a pawn for something so grand? As my mind raced in thought, I even began to wonder if there was an actual pending birth in the picture. Could this entire scenario be simply a malicious effort on the part of Lord Russell, Madame Pucelle and Elijah to extort money from my marital estate? If so, then for what purpose? Might this be nothing more than sibling rivalry between Russell and Kendall? Remaining in thought for a few moments, I pondered within the silence and murmured, "If Kendall and I were to both perish, the doorway to our combined financial assets of Thornwood Estate and Worthington Estate, would legally become wide open to Russell, without any interference from the law."

So much had occurred over the course of the past few months, resulting in my feeling rather beleaguered with life. My thoughts were clouded in a haze of contradiction. One moment I was joyful and filled with elation. Then, with the blink of an eye, I was beset with sadness. All the while, I was truly confused, sensing increasing passion for Dr. Alexis. What was happening to me? I barely knew the man, yet my heart was whispering, nudging me to remember, to keep him in my thoughts. Was he just a fantasy? All this was occurring so unexpectedly and I could not help but wonder, if I would be able to keep pace with the changes. Quite honestly, I feared the challenges would soon plow right through me. Could my life become any more complex?

"Believe in yourself and in doing so, you will see the return of all your abilities, most importantly your healing powers," Marcella said, as I continued to listen. "It's not easy to trust the unknown, to have complete faith in the future when you are suffering."

"How will I ever be able to cope with these burdens? I cannot even begin to express my true sentiments for this doctor?" I said, as I stood up. "I don't know which way to turn–right, left, up or down, nor can I make sense of how to live my life. There are just so many complications within the state of my present affairs."

I sat upon the featherbed as Marcella held my hand comfortingly within her grasp. "You must focus on staying centered and balanced, being true to yourself and true to your child. Think about keeping yourself and the baby healthy, rested and nurtured. There is no urgency in addressing the issue of Madame Pucelle's letter. Let time pass. Just let this be. Why should you adhere to her demands and her time schedule?"

"I would like to believe that you're correct. What if she is somehow involved with Kendall's disappearance?" I inquired. "What if the vision actually speaks of the truth? Then, my life would also be in grave jeopardy."

"I sense that Madame Pucelle is playing a charade," she replied. "I shall pray you will beat her at this game of deception. You are too clever to even begin engaging in this matter according to her rules. Let time run its course to unveil all that needs to be revealed. Bathe in the silence of this moment."

"Do you really sense she poses no threat to me?

"Be still," Marcella replied. "Seek the calm of harmony and balance. This tart could have much or very little to do with Kendall's disappearance. We simply must await the passage of time for the appropriate answers."

"I'm besieged at the very thought she may truly be carrying Kendall's child," I seethed. I told Marcella that the news of this mistress soon to bear forth the first Worthington heir, was like a piercing dagger in my heart. I wanted Kendall to die. I wanted Madame Pucelle to die. I wanted Russell and Elijah to die, and now, I even considered my very own death.

"Grace, try to recollect of ever having heard of this woman's name mentioned in passing. Could you have made prior acquaintance with her within your social circle in London?" Marcella told me to remember if I ever had occasion to cross paths with her in the past. "Or, can you recall even exchanging the briefest of conversations with her in years gone by?"

"Unfortunately, I have not the slightest clue as to what this woman may actually look like, other than the image of her from the vision," I replied.

"Although this may come as a surprise to you," Marcella responded, "I do have some insightful knowledge. Let me begin by revealing a few pertinent facts. Perhaps then, you may recall having met her."

I could only brace myself for the news that awaited my ears, as I took a deep breath anticipating her words. Marcella told me that over the years, Madame Pucelle had sowed quite an unruly reputation for herself within London as the proprietor of an upscale brothel. She was a shrewd, manipulative soul, a woman in the business of earning her keep from the pleasures of the flesh. The translation of her French name into English, connoted one who was *virginal*, however, ironically the present conversation was leading me to a new perspective…this was all a far cry from the truth of the matter. Her lusty antics had created a history that reeked of deceit–a reputation that had far preceded her on the streets of London, enough to make even a promiscuous sea-faring pirate turn a brighter shade of pink. The dandies that she lured were in her company for only one reason, not including the sipping of afternoon tea and speaking of the weather. Her intimacies with the upper crust of the opposite sex were far-reaching, and encompassed many more than the likes of Lord Kendall Worthington.

"Keep the faith," Marcella said reassuringly. "Kendall was not her first conquest, nor I fear, will he be her last."

151

"I am hopeful," I said with a puzzled look upon my face.

"You must do more than merely have hope. Pay heed to my words, she said, "Believe in the Higher Powers and believe in yourself. All things are possible, if only you believe."

I nodded my head and said, "How is it that you know so many particulars about this woman?"

"Believe!"

Again, I found her statement to be all the more perplexing, yet I could only surmise the Higher Powers were speaking, enlightening Marcella with information for my benefit. Once again, I found myself grateful for the magic's guidance and intercession.

"Do you mean to say that Madame Pucelle may be carrying the child of another man?" I said. "Perhaps, it's really not Kendall's child?"

"This could very well be the case."

"Why would she claim to be pregnant with Kendall's child, if this is not the truth?" I asked, trying to make some sense of this increasingly bewildering situation.

"Grace, collect your resolve and your thoughts. Why even question as to *why*?"

Although I was open to listening to Marcella's words, I must admit that at times I wondered how she could take the complexity of a scenario, paring it down into what seemed to be a rather simple matter. Truly, this was just one of her many gifts.

She told me that the situation merely was, what it was. Albeit rather remorseful, Marcella requested that I try to imagine myself in this desperate woman's shoes. Life was hopeless for her. From Madame Pucelle's perspective, she had nothing to lose and everything to gain by her actions. Marcella further explained that Madame Pucelle focused her priorities upon attaining material wealth, rather than on accruing the wisdom of the soul. She stooped to the lowest of levels to succeed at her game of extorting financial assets from, not only myself, but from many other

152

affluent members of society. Given the opportunity, Marcella sensed that Madame Pucelle would gladly rob me blind of my rightful inheritance–the combined property and financial assets of both Thornwood and Worthington Estates.

"Opportunity has never presented me with even a remote acquaintance with Madame Pucelle," I insisted.

"Firstly," Marcella snapped, "She is a flesh-sucking whore, a skillful and ruthless opportunist adept in the art of deception and manipulation to acquire whatever, and whomever she sets out to divide and conquer. She chooses to live her life obsessing upon material gain and acquisition. Sadly, she believes with her every breath, this is the path to a life of true happiness and fulfillment. For her, it is all about the physical and material world…the spiritual world is nonexistent."

"Do you actually believe this whore may have some knowledge regarding Kendall's disappearance? Do you actually believe she could have harmed him, or ventured so low to commit a murder?" Marcella told me there could be plausible motive, if Kendall truly was intimate with Madame Lela Pucelle. Perhaps upon hearing of the pregnancy, he may have chosen to deny any responsibility for her in this condition.

"Believe me," Marcella said, "People become desperately manic in dire times such as these." She explained, only the Higher Powers truly knew what Kendall may have initially promised Madame Pucelle while consumed within her passionate embrace. There were so many possibilities. Marcella's gut feeling, however, was that when the reality of this pending birth presented itself, Kendall might have refused to even acknowledge that he was the father of the child, thereby disallowing all financial support to Madame Pucelle.

"Might it even be possible that Madame Pucelle actually entrapped Kendall with the intent to become pregnant, so that she may forever live her desired life of leisure and affluence?" I asked.

I thought how this would be ideal for a whore, the ultimate situation, in as much as she would not have to work the streets another day in her life.

"Yes, Madame Pucelle could have truly cashed-in on this dandy husband of yours, only to use him as a meal ticket to luxury," she said. "Sadly, this is all very plausible. Trust. One day the truth will be revealed. The truth is always more powerful than deception."

"When do you think we'll know more?"

"It is simply a matter of time," Marcella continued. "I pray that you will one day bear all the fruits of your labors and eventually reap a plentiful harvest. I sense that it will be well worth your patient waiting. Now rest, and be mindful of all that I have said. Remember, timing is everything. Timing is of the essence."

I laid my head upon a soft white pillow on my bed, thanking Marcella for her compassion and insight. It had been a long and tiresome day.

Prior to excusing herself from the room, Marcella said, "You have not eaten a mere morsel today, not even a biscuit or a scone. Shall I have the kitchen staff prepare you a meal?"

"Not at this moment, thank you. I seem to have lost all interest in food today. Perhaps later tonight, I may have more of an appetite."

"I do worry about you, Grace. You are so thin and frail, but you remain strong in spirit, determined and accepting of your precarious situation. For now, try to rest, and simply release your worry."

I pondered her words. They posed a huge challenge for my weary soul. Rest, however, did sound absolutely wonderful, yet the word, *conspiracy,* rang loudly throughout my entire being. Something was strongly perplexing and remained foul. Now I was even more determined to make some sense of Kendall's disappearance. I knew that I must silence my mind, to calm the

154

many voices, thoughts and questions softly whispering within my head—all of the *what ifs* that now blurred my clarity.

I prayed that the Higher Powers, the spirit world, would once again speak to me, presenting information, clues and knowledge that I needed to become aware of. I believed the recent lucid vision was possibly blatant confirmation of my worst fears, my most dreaded nightmare that somehow Madame Lela Pucelle and Elijah were intimately involved, and that Lord Russell was also part of the puzzle. Not a moment passed, without the haunting memory that Kendall remained mysteriously missing and quite possibly even dead. However, most disturbingly all accusing fingers still pointed hideously in only my direction.

Twelve

Sometimes we have a lot to say
And, oftentimes we choose not
Words are means to express a thought
Those deepest from the heart

Sometimes we just need to trust
Believe in love, our fate and lust
Vow to seek our highest good
Hearts will answer as they should

In recent days, I had surprisingly found myself arising early, a
rather uncommon behavior for me, which I gathered could
only be attributed to my insomnia. Reading the local journal,
The Royal Cornwall Gazette, became a part of my morning
routine as I sipped a cup of chamomile tea and nibbled upon a
homemade lemon-currant scone, in an effort to alleviate my
morning sickness. Perusing the paper, I sat upon an overstuffed
chaise positioned within a cozy corner of the elegant drawing
room. In fact, at times I even began to feel as if my body was
transforming into an overstuffed piece of furniture, my protruding
belly growing rounder and larger by the week. Much to my
disproval, the entire kitchen staff had been stringently instructed
by Marcella, to feed me morning, noon and night. The estate head
cook, Beatrice, had been a lasting fixture within Thornwood
Estate nearly all of my life. *Eat, drink and be joyful,* were her
infamous words. I could still hear them ringing within my ears, as
she approached me this morning on her mission with another tray
of her succulent baked goods.

Beatrice was a white-haired plump woman of four-and-sixty. I
cannot remember her not ever having a white French apron

encircled tautly about her rotund girth. Each passing year, her largesse seemed to also increase, keeping in pace with the progression of time. Her fleshy abundance was clearly indicative of her outstanding culinary talents.

"Yaw have hardly touched your breakfast, Lady Grace. What's it going to take to convince yaw to eat better. I shan't be wantin' to visit when yaw six feet under. So, yaw had best pay heed to me words…eat, drink and be joyful while the sun's up, my lassie."

"I have no appetite," I sighed, trying not to appear rude with my disinterest in carrying on further conversation as I focused my sight upon the morning paper. Beatrice placed her full tray of assorted sweet rolls and hot Scottish oats upon the small rose-marbled table that rested beside my chair, and reluctantly departed.

In recent days, I seemed to have become obsessed with keeping abreast of all the news in Boscastle Harbor and the regional happenings. The latest reports continued to focus daily upon the tragic sea disaster off shore. As each day passed, I read more and more about the wreckage, collected to determine the identity of the ship and its crew.

But, today's headlines took me off guard as I found my heart coming to a halt. *Ship's Identity Confirmed As The Destiny. Ship And Crew Perish With No Survivors.* Thoughts of Ian ran amuck within my head. I felt the panic rapidly consume me. Nervously, I sat upon the drawing room chaise lounge.

"I knew it," I whispered.

Tears welled within my eyes. All along I had sensed this ship had more significance for me, than what was originally apparent, however, I had prayed throughout the passing days and nights that my instincts would prove false. Was this to be Ian's fate? I wondered how this could be, since I had clearly remembered Ian Cutter to be such a worthy and adept sea captain. For a moment my thoughts rambled, leading me to consider the notion that

158

perhaps the fair-haired Captain was not even aboard, but the idea of a sea captain failing to sail his very own vessel was ludicrous. I was only misleading myself. If there truly were no survivors, then Ian Cutter was surely a departed soul beyond the veil. The news was in black and white before my very eyes. I felt powerless. The irony of Ian's demise at sea seemed twisted, if this was to be his fate—his destiny.

The month of March passed slowly in Boscastle, finding me still lost in limbo with the inability to achieve resolution within my personal matters. During this time, I had become increasingly distraught, more and more apprehensive regarding both my pregnancy and the letter I had received from Madame Pucelle. Disturbed by the monetary demand, I even surprised myself with the bold thought of considering the option of paying an unannounced visit to this whore's residence in London. I wondered if perhaps then, I would be able to evaluate the situation more fully and with the utmost of clarity, but I had become increasingly fatigued each day from my very own pregnancy and emotional unrest. Did I dare to venture eastward to London again, placing myself into still, yet another stressful situation, and directly in her path? I wondered what she was really like, this lowly creature of such questionable character. I wondered what it felt like to arise each morning as Madame Pucelle, to experience life on her terms cunning, deceitful and manipulative.

The month of April awakened to the unveiling of spring's renewal, making its presence felt, in and about the village of Boscastle, greeting me well into my fifth month of pregnancy. The winter snows gradually melted, the sound of icicles dripped from rooftops in watery embrace within the sun's radiant warmth.

Memories of the doctor were still ever present, vividly dancing within my mind. I could not seem to forget him, the memory becoming almost compulsive in my days. I dearly missed him—his voice, his smile, his deep-blue eyes and his nurturing compassion.

However, reality reared its ugly head once again, with the candid fact that I barely knew this man. I could only speculate that perhaps all of the fantasies and the dreaminess I was experiencing were merely a result of my physical condition.

For several days, I pondered the situation. At last, I concluded that with the anticipation of the spring's warmer, more predictable weather, a journey to London in the month of May would suit me all the better. I would be well along into my pregnancy, beginning my sixth month. The roads would be unhampered by the winter's snow and soon the dryer weather would make itself known. I thought about the fact that I might also call upon Dr. Alexis. I sensed, however, that my true intentions deemed this as much more than merely a medical visit to consult with him. I could hear my heart echoing within my chest as I grew increasingly elated with the thought of this visit. In the back of my mind, I held onto a ribbon of desire, the possibility that Dr. Alexis would assist with the delivery of my child in the late summer. The month of May sounded like the perfect time. Surmising that the spring would be most opportune, my mind was made up. I would depart for London after the Festival of Beltane–the first of May.

As the days of April passed, I anxiously made preparations for my journey, and on this particular morning, I knew there was something that still must be tended to, before my arrival in London. I had long procrastinated the announcement of my pregnancy to the Bishop, feeling consumed with increasing uncertainty over the response that my correspondence might elicit.

"Ah, good morning," exclaimed Josephina and Caron, speaking in their native French, as they suddenly appeared in my bedroom suite.

"Good day," I replied. "I must once again thank you for attending to my fire throughout the night. The warmth has enabled me to get some much needed rest. Surprisingly, I even feel refreshed to begin the day." I continued, "There's so much that I must do–so much is necessary to discuss and to review. Josephina, please summon the kitchen staff to prepare my breakfast and Caron, please instruct a housemaid to draw my bath water, for I have much to accomplish today. Hurry! No dawdling. I must draft a letter for immediate delivery to London." Pausing to reflect upon my words, I motioned to my attendants to gather my fine writing papers and ink with quill pen.

"It is of the utmost importance that a message be delivered to Bishop Samuel Bartholomew. I have volumes to tell him, so much to share with him–this news of the coming of our child."

I could feel my tongue fumbling from side-to-side within my mouth as I sounded these words. My faced flushed a bright red with embarrassment as I hesitated, realizing that I had quite unintentionally elicited my clandestine desires aloud. I wanted to kick myself as I bit my tongue. How could I have been so clumsy? Josephina and Caron quickly gazed at one another in sheer and utter amazement. The look of awe splattered upon their faces, announced loud and clear they could not believe what their ears had heard, nor fully comprehend the statement that had just flown out of my mouth. The girls giggled nervously and immediately excused themselves to complete their morning tasks.

"Oh, my," whispered Caron. "Did you hear what she said? I'm in shock."

Josephina quickly replied under her breath, "Hush! Do you realize what's happening? This is scandalous, an enormous discovery."

"What will become of Lady Grace?"

"We must absolutely keep silent," Josephina continued. We must make a promise to never speak another word of this unless we are only within each other's company. Is that perfectly clear?"

"Of course!" exclaimed Caron, nodding her head adamantly.

After completing my bath, the French sisters proceeded to assist with my selection of dressing attire for that morning. As my pregnancy had progressed, I found it was clearly not unusual to casually change my clothes, not to mention to change my mind several times per day, depending upon my activities, the hour and needless to say, my mood.

"Nothing seems to fit. I really need more leeway within the fabric of these garments," I said, frustrated with this fashion dilemma. "Well, ladies, I do believe another wardrobe is in order. Soon, we must make a trip into the village center of Boscastle to have some fabulous clothing tailored. I refuse to sacrifice style for function while in this state of largesse. When this child finally arrives, however, I plan to have an additional chic wardrobe designed. Once again, I shall be the most well dressed woman when returning to London."

Josephina and Caron giggled, continuing to dress me in the many layers of fine French lace undergarments. During the past month, my body had begun to show a substantial change within the pregnancy. My fuller, blossoming breasts and the widening of my midsection proclaimed loud and clear, the coming of a child.

Caron and Josephina completed my dressing with a lovely French silk frock of lapis-blue, accented with a pastel-pink petticoat. It had always been one of my favorites and was recently altered by the local seamstress, Mary Hilgarde, to accommodate the enlargement of my bosom and girth as the pregnancy advanced. I truly loved everything French– the culture, the people, the fashion, the food, the wines, frolic and fun, and I dare not forget to mention, the alluring charisma of the French men.

The promise of the coming of a child had given me so much to rejoice about, so much to at last be thankful and appreciative of. I could feel myself glowing, beaming with sensuality. After the first few months of queasiness, my pregnancy now seemed to agree with me, only further enhancing my physical attributes. As I

162

moved to the side of the room, I paused to observe my changing physique within a full-length mirror.

"How beautiful I feel carrying this child!" I murmured. Motioning to Josephina, I requested again that she bring me a quill pen, ink and some of my finest parchment paper.

Alone I sat in reflection for several moments before transcribing my correspondence, for I could only pray the Bishop would understand my unyielding need to be with him. Now more than ever, it was paramount that I inform him of—the truth. This affair had gone on far too long. At this time, I believed it was vital that we took the necessary steps to reunite once again. If I did not see him soon, I felt as if I might even die from my unbearable heartache. Sitting at my mahogany desk in the western corner of the bedroom chamber, I began to write. The turbulent sea churned and tossed in the distance as I gazed up from my paper. As if mirroring my overbearing fullness of emotion at this time, the sea seemed to understand my fear and anxiety.

Five April, 1811

Dearest Samuel,

I send you blessings on this day, for I have so much news to share with you. Let me commence by expressing that I have truly missed you, since my sudden departure from London in February.

Although, I contemplated telling you all of this in person, I felt it best to prepare you for my upcoming visit during the month of May. I have dearly missed your guidance and counsel. There is much to be revealed. Samuel, the seed of our love grows deep within my womb. I pray you will openly welcome this news of my pregnancy and my return to your embrace.

The child that grows within me is a bond of our love. Now, more than ever, I need you by my side. I must see you. The sooner—the better, my love. I am forever yours,

Grace

Thornwood Estate, Boscastle, England

I reviewed the letter, kissing it for good measure, and held the parchment to my breast. My heart pounded loudly within my chest. For an instant, I had second thoughts about my actions. Should I simply wait and surprise the Bishop in May with my unannounced arrival in London? Surely, one look at my belly would say more than what words could ever express, but my inner voice persisted, prompting me to proceed with sending the correspondence. I could only pray to the Higher Powers that in time, the answers would all appear.

Folding the document neatly into thirds, I inserted the letter into a white rectangular envelope, sealing it with warm beeswax. I closed the envelope and pressed firmly upon the warm wax, imprinting the Thornwood Estate seal, a crucifix entwined within a blossoming rose vine.

"Give this letter to Mr. Abernathy and have him oversee its delivery by courier as soon as possible. Hurry, for I have little time to waste. Listen carefully," I continued, presenting the sealed envelope to my attendants. "Inform Mr. Abernathy that this letter is to be hand delivered only to the Bishop and to none other. Is this understood?" Caron and Josephina nodded their heads, taking the letter from my hands.

"Quickly, ladies. Run along."

The French sisters departed, carrying the thin parcel downstairs

Looking at each other, they could only roll their eyes in dread, anticipating the emotional upheaval that would be eminent in future days.

"What will become of our dear Lady Grace when the Bishop finds out the news of his child?" Caron inquired.

"Hush," Josephina replied. "We must keep quiet. I can only suppose there will be much talk of denial and refusal on the part of the Bishop to accept any responsibility for his role. I can't imagine that the Bishop would risk his calling with the church to openly accept Lady Grace and this child. Don't you agree?"

"Perhaps," said Caron. "However, I would like to consider that the Bishop will come to Lady Grace's bedside with wild abandon, proclaiming his love for her, forever more–until the end of time."

"Oh, Caron! You've always been such a romantic," exclaimed Josephina. "How utterly ridiculous! Surely, you cannot possibly even begin to believe that the Bishop would ever risk his reputation, let alone his prominent standing within the Church of England. Needless to say, this man would be excommunicated from all bonds and affiliations within the church. If this secret should ever get out, let's just say that the Archbishop would more than likely have the Bishop's head on a plate."

Josephina reached the foot of the main staircase, handing the letter over to Mr. Abernathy, and instructed him to carry out the guidelines set forth by Lady Grace. He, in turn took the letter to the coachman, Michael, who carried it by horse into the bustling village center of Boscastle, delivering it to a trustworthy courier. The courier assured Michael that the parcel would be dispatched that very same day.

When Michael returned to the Thornwood Estate house, he approached me, verbally relaying the courier's message, "All is well, Lady Grace. Everything is in order regarding the delivery of your correspondence. It will arrive in four to five days, by mid-April at the very latest, and shall be delivered directly to the Bishop at his residence, Lambeth Palace."

"Thank the Higher Powers this is in the works," I said with great relief etched upon my face. Now I sensed that I must only be patient and busy myself, avoiding any further loss of my peace of mind.

"I believe a visit to see the seamstress, Mary Hilgarde, is in order," I said, now turning towards my two attendants. "Let's be off into the village. Boscastle in the spring will do me a world of good."

Gathering a brilliant pink lace-trimmed satin shawl around my shoulders, Caron, Josephina and I entered the coach. Weather permitting, the ride into the village would be an hour at the very most. My anguish during the past several months had left me a prisoner confined within the estate house. At last, I was delighted to be wearing colorful garb once again, excited at the thought of viewing the sights, hearing the nautical sounds and inhaling the succulent salt air within the active seaport.

As the carriage neared the village, I observed the once familiar gabled slate-covered rooftops. The village cottages clung precariously along the hillside leading into Boscastle Harbor, and as the coach entered onto High Street, I recollected the bustling marketplace. Calling aloud to the coachmen, I instructed them to halt. They commandeered the carriage to the roadside. I was determined to walk the remainder of the distance…two short blocks to Mary Hilgarde's establishment, for I yearned to mingle at last with the townspeople and breathe-in the fresh sea air.

With Josephina and Caron by my side, I strolled amongst the wide assortment of marketplace stalls. The fragrant scent of rosemary, sage, chamomile, frankincense, patchouli and lavender wafted within the air as I strolled by two elderly women, hearing them argue at the adjacent stall with a dark-skinned vendor.

166

"These herbs and spices are of little use to me at these outrageous prices," the one woman yelled.

"Just give us a fair fee," the other chimed in.

"It's all or nothin, me ladies," the muscular, dark-skinned man replied. "What yaw see is what yaw gets."

I could not help, but be amused at the bantering about me as I passed by, my eyes now making contact with the dark-skinned vendor.

"I know thee!" he shouted in my direction, distracted by my presence. I tried to ignore his bold query, for I thought surely there must be some gross error in judgment on his part. I knew the likes of very few in Boscastle, especially that of a tawdry street vendor, but the disheveled, dark-skinned man persisted.

"Hey, I'm talking to yaw. Yaw can be no other than Lady Worthington." His attention was now focused on only one thing, as he casually consented to the two matrons, and moved from behind the stall to approach me.

"I believe you are mistaken," I abruptly said to him. He seemed such a lowly soul, covered with dirt marked upon his dark body. His black African skin, glistened in the sunlight as I observed his weathered clothing, yet I couldn't help but notice his soil-encrusted fingernails as his actions took me off guard, motioning to take my hand. I took a step back, nearly losing my balance upon the slate flagstone as I stepped upon the toes of a woman standing among the encroaching spectators, who had now swiftly gathered about me. A whiff of this man's stench was an overbearing revulsion, sending my lungs gasping as I turned my head to breathe fresher air.

"I don't mean to be frighten yaw. I see yaw with child, me Lady. Per chance, yaw the one mistaken," he continued.

Oddly, an awareness quickly struck me, as if the light of a candle suddenly illuminated a darkened room. This man *was*

167

familiar, none other than, the former head servant at the Worthington Estate house in London.

"Oh, dear God! Is it truly you…Elijah? What brings you to Boscastle?" I queried, embracing him, now unaware of his unsavory odor. A rushing flood of sentiments returned to me, prodding at my heart strings, for the absolute truth of the matter was, in past years Elijah and I had on occasion shared more than merely an employer versus domestic relationship within Worthington Estate in London.

My mind now piqued with questions, of which the most disconcerting was why Elijah had vanished from the estate house on that mysterious night of Kendall's disappearance.

"What happened on the night of fifteen November after I journeyed to the Cathedral?" I inquired looking into his darkened lusty eyes. With my no sooner mentioning these words, he fell to his knees, his body crumbling upon the flagstone. In all honesty, I now found myself in a state of awe, for in my many years of knowing Elijah, I had never seen him succumb to tears. A crowd was quickly gathering about us, as the local townspeople chattered vociferously amongst themselves with growing curiosity.

"It's Lady Worthington," whispered a young man.

"How dare she be wear'n such colorful apparel!" gossiped an elderly woman. "Her husband's body has yet to be found, but I know she's the one."

"She's gone and killed him off," said another.

My heart sank, listening to the unsolicited accusations within the crowd. I knelt beside the now sobbing Elijah, putting my arms around his shoulder, although I was still somewhat puzzled by his overwhelming display of grief. The crowd continued staring, as I listened to the sound of their surrounding voices gasping in horror. They watched me intently, alarmed that I had done the unthinkable as my pink lips…softly kissed Elijah upon his full black lips.

168

Josephina and Caron nudged my arm and whispered, "Come this way Lady Grace. We must move onward, for Mrs. Hilgarde awaits."

"In a moment," I said, ignoring their request, attempting to further bring some comfort to Elijah. I wanted him…again. "Please return to me," I whispered into his ear, pleading with him.

"You may reside with us at the Thornwood Estate in Boscastle. I will see to it that you are fully re-instated with no reprimands, nor punishment."

"I'm not of yaw world, me Lady. I'll only be trouble," he sighed. "I'm not worthy of yaw kindness, for I have done yaw terribly wrong."

"What are you saying?" I demanded, raising my voice as I now looked him directly in the eye. "Speak to me…please."

A shout from a chunky young man in the crowd rang out, "She's a murderer. The village Constable will sort this matter."

My heart sank, as I feared the law encroaching upon me. In a panic I arose, embracing Elijah once again. I felt uncontrollably drawn to him as if I was melting within his firm black arms. Elijah's hand brushed against my thigh, lovingly stroking the dust and dirt that had adhered upon my lapis-blue dress from the slate-flagstone of the marketplace.

"We must speak again, but how may I contact you?" I inquired, reluctantly motioning to my attendants that we had overstayed our welcome. The last thing I desired at this time was another intrusion from the law into my personal affairs. I had already experienced enough harassment from Constable Gordon in London. Although I yearned to remain with Elijah and further discuss personal matters, my better judgment was speaking loud and clear. For all intentions at the present moment, I realized both Elijah and I must part for the time being and maintain a low profile.

"Tis not safe nor wise for an upper crust lady likes yaw self to be found in me company," he whispered. "Yaw needn't come looking for me. Now, I too, must be on me way," he continued, arising abruptly from his knees. "Rest assured. I've got me ways. I'll find yaw again, me lady," he said with his teary eyes gazing upward into the sky.

Within the heavens, the cackling sound of birds rudely penetrated the air, as I observed two large black ravens circling overhead. I gasped, hurrying into the thick of the crowd as I swiftly maneuvered my way towards the awaiting coach. Oddly, I sensed at that very moment a most horrifying thought. These black ravens could be none other than, the two transformed intruders who had stalked me in prior days. I could only wonder if per chance, Elijah had some association with those highwaymen who had descended so ruthlessly upon our coach, disrupting our journey to Boscastle that cold February night. Now, more than ever, the remote possibility of Elijah's involvement with the disappearance of Kendall was fixed within my head, standing boldly at the forefront of my mind. Elijah's participation seemed more than a mere likelihood. My heart was saddened, for something was appallingly wrong.

Thirteen

The mist ahead now clouds my eyes
An ominous gray of shadows thrive
Within my heart and soul tonight
I ponder what's to be my plight

Time passes slowly as we share
The droplets of love's waters here
Caressing moments all too few
Reminding me that I need you

It was now early May and I was well into my sixth month of pregnancy. My original travel plans to return to London were delayed by my continuing uncertainty as I observed the passing of the Beltane Festival, a festive holiday honored not only by the Pagan townspeople, and reflected within their celebratory parades embellishing the village streets. But, in particular, Beltane was recognized by the Wiccan community in Boscastle and throughout England with the partaking in clandestine rituals of divination occurring within the velvet of nightfall – a mystical welcoming of the onset of spring with the hopes of a promising summer.

Three long weeks had elapsed since the letter to the Bishop was dispatched and my encounter with Elijah in the village square. Rather perplexingly, there had been no communication from either party.

Becoming more and more anxious, even paranoid, with anticipation, I found myself pondering all types of hypothetical questions and scenarios to rationalize this inexplicable silence from both parties. What if the Bishop refuses to come and visit me? What if he never really loved me?

What if he denies that I am to give birth to his child, and that he is not the father of this child? And, what if Elijah is somehow responsible for Kendall's disappearance? What shall I do now?

That morning I once again dressed with the assistance of my attendants. Irritable from sleep deprivation, I remained fearful of the unknown. Tears welled within my eyes as I sobbed.

"Why is my life so difficult? When will I ever be at peace?"

Passing by the chamber door, Marcella quietly entered the room and approached me.

"Grace, is there something you need to share with me? You know how I sense your discontent. I have been feeling your sadness ever since your return to Boscastle. The other sisters as well, are concerned for your health and happiness. Please, speak the truth."

Embracing my arms around Marcella's thick waist, I clung to her as if hugging the broad solid trunk of an aged oak tree.

"I don't know how to even begin to tell you what truly needs to be revealed," I said. My voice trembled from the daunting burden of my woe.

"Speak the words and you shall feel an inner peace," she said with encouragement.

I took a deep breath, aware that what must be spoken was not going to be an easy task. I feared there simply was not any manner to prepare Marcella for this news. My body shuttered with hesitation.

"Since I've never been able to conceive during the course of my nine-year marriage, it seems highly unlikely, rather uncanny that the father of my child could ever be Kendall. Wouldn't you agree that the odds are slim to null?"

"Please continue," Marcella said. "What are you saying?"

"Rather, I sense the father to be none other than someone else…Bishop Samuel Bartholomew. What am I to do now?" I blurted aloud, releasing a huge sigh with these very words. At last, my secret was verbalized, and strangely I felt as if the weight of a mountain had been removed from my shoulders.

"Do absolutely nothing," she replied.

"What?" I inquired, observing her in bewilderment.

"Trust. More will be revealed."

"The Bishop is ignoring my pleas. He is blatantly indifferent to my affections. He is so uncompassionate, yet my heart still grieves for him. I must take some action. How can I simply do nothing?"

Marcella motioned toward me, sitting upon the bedside as she held my hand, in an attempt to calm and restore some sensibility to my emotional outburst. "This monotony in your life, this confusion is of your own doing," she said. "Of course I am sympathetic to all that has transpired, but you must firstly understand and face the reality of your situation. There are many choices in life. Now you must live with the choices you have made. It really is that simple."

I attempted to dry my tears, aware that I would not be receiving very much sympathy from Marcella regarding my quandary.

"You are correct, Marcella," I said. "This is what I have chosen. I must absolutely live with my choices and face the consequences of my decision to be involved with the Bishop on more than a spiritual level. Do you think he may still have feelings for me?"

"That, and so much more is still to be determined," she said softly.

"I cannot understand why he persists in ignoring me?"

"He also has choices, Grace. How can you be certain, the Bishop is the actual father? Although I sense you desire him to be the true father, I believe there is still more to be revealed with this story of yours."

A knock upon the bedroom chamber doors startled me as I swiftly turned my head to see who stood within the doorway. Clara entered the room holding a white letter within her hand.

"Please excuse this intrusion. I thought it best, however, to promptly deliver this parcel to Grace. It's addressed in your name and has arrived by personal courier only moments ago." She extended her hand with the thin white envelope. "I hope that it brings forth an answer to some of your concerns. I pray for blessings with this communication, and an easing of your turmoil."

Standing up from the side of the bed, I ran toward the doorway to retrieve the letter from her. "Thank you, Clara. I pray it's an answer to my prayers." Fumbling with the wax seal, my thin fingers pried anxiously at the edges, tearing open the envelope only to discover a folded white letter within. Immediately, I recognized the handwriting. It was indeed, from none other than the Bishop. I took my place at the bedside and silently read his message.

Nine May, 1811

Dearest Grace,

Giving much thought to your recent correspondence, I remain somewhat baffled by its content. It's true that I have always been quite fond of you, and I pray that I have been a comfort to guide and counsel you during those difficult and tumultuous days of your marriage. I am hopeful, however, that I have not misled you.

Your declarations of love for me are rather flattering, but please know that first and foremost, I am devoted to my calling with the Church of England. Of course, I will never forget the special joys that we shared together in prior days.

Regretfully, my schedule at present is so overwhelming that I will be unable to accommodate you in London. I am presently obliged to continue with my spiritual guidance to the many new parishioners, some of whom, like yourself,

need my immediate counsel and care to ease their painfully difficult marital situations. I pray that you understand.
Blessed be God,

Bishop Samuel Bartholomew
Lambeth Palace - London, England

I was stunned, in a stupor of shock and disbelief from his words. The tears flowed from the corners of my eyes, the words still ringing within my head. I read the letter again and again, searching for something that I may have missed, some small sign to give me hope of the Bishop's compassion and love, some tiny clue of his acknowledgment of the pregnancy and his desire to accept my love and this child.

Marcella and Clara enfolded me within their caressing embrace. They had sensed this drama long before it ever came to fruition before my eyes.

"Is there anything that we may do for you, Grace?" asked Clara.

I sat in silence, pausing to wipe my tears. "Well, actually yes. There is one thing that you both could do," I said with reserve. "Cast a spell upon the Bishop to bring him running into my arms again. Can you?"

"Have you completely lost your senses, Grace?" Marcella replied. "Have you forgotten about fate and destiny? A spell at this time will only serve to complicate the issue of your pregnancy."

"I absolutely agree," said Clara. "A spell will certainly interfere, rather than assist with these matters of the heart at this time."

"If the Bishop is to be in your life again, time will put him there," Marcella continued.

"This feels so hopeless," I shouted angrily. "Please leave me alone. I need to think things through."

Marcella and Clara honored my request and departed the room. As I sat alone within my chamber to ponder my plight, I was filled with disbelief, enraged that the Bishop would not receive me upon my return to London. I stood firm with my allegation. The Bishop was the father of this child—our child. At present, I could only pray this news would one day bring him running back to me, and for a moment in my desperation, I even thought about the possibility of seeking Lindsey's assistance to cast a spell. Surely, she could do this without delay.

I continued to read the letter in my state of exhaustion, lying my head upon my pillow. My mind was restless as I tossed and turned within my bed. At last, my thoughts drifted to another time and place. Once again, the spirit world was beckoning me to listen to their words and view the images gesturing forth within my dreams—all for a reason.

As the reverie unfolded, I became fully aware of the image of a very pregnant woman in my presence, observing her walking, waddling towards a door resembling that of a prison gate, or what appeared to be an entryway of a cell. It wasn't long before I realized this soul could be none other than, Madame Lela Pucelle. With breasts as ripe as melons, they were swollen and overflowing from within the confines of her snuggly fitted, low-cut, coral-colored dress. She appeared as if a ripened piece of fruit, its skin stretched to the limit and bursting at the seams — beckoning to be hand-picked and harvested from the vine. Coming into greater focus, she appeared about to give birth at any moment.

Envisioning this underground area similar to a damp clandestine cellar, I could hear the clamor and feel the vibrations of the carriages traversing back-and-forth above me. I sensed that I must be beneath the street level within the bowels of a city, somewhere perhaps in what I could only gather was London. Continuing to observe the scene, Madame Pucelle kicked a squealing rat out of the way as she sluggishly approached the cell door. I observed a glowing lantern within one of her hands and a loaf of green moldy bread clutched in the other. The horrific, dank stench emitted from the darkened enclosure was potent enough to nearly cause me to faint from the potent fumes.

I was repulsed, wondering who, or what, could possibly be held captive within this cell. What poor miserable soul was deserving of such an ill fate, locked behind that gated cell door? My eyes followed her every action as the scene unfolded before me. I felt as if I was a privileged spectator with a front-row seat, viewing this drama upon a stage with the creative direction of the spirit world. Lady Pucelle lifted the lantern and held it closer to the gated cell-window, pressing her fleshy face against the metal bars to peer within the interior of the darkened enclosure. It was a tiny blackened space, infested with rats, rubbish and disease. The thick stench of feces and urine, the vile fragrance of human waste, filled the air. Runoff rainwater from the street above, trickled downward into the cavernous underground, dripping its slime upon the oozing blackened, mildewed stone walls and floors. Again, I took notice of the unbearable odor, the scent of death, as I struggled to cover my nose and mouth with a kerchief.

The putrid aroma was enough to make me gag on my very own tongue as I tried to hold my breath. My lungs were bursting, aching for fresher air.

Holding a torn rag within her hand, I observed Lady Pucelle also covering her nose to block the horrific smelling fumes from further penetration.

"You old goat," she yelled, peering into the cell. "Are you still alive, my love?" Cackling aloud with laughter, she continued, "I have brought your favorite supper—a loaf of my delectable home baked bread, made nearly two weeks ago, and of course it's all for you."

I observed her puffy hands tossing the moldy, stale bread through the iron gated bars, watching intently as the bread fell

177

into a puddle of urine within the cell. At that instant, I could hear a faint sound, stirring from within the enclosure...a moaning, vaguely similar to that of an injured animal whimpering in fear. I wondered if this could possibly be an animal in captivity. Perhaps it truly was an old farm goat?

Although barely audible, there was no doubt in my mind that I was soon aware of a human voice, the strained and parched words of a man. I stood in bewilderment, my body frozen in fear, still puzzled as to his identity.

"Have you agreed to at last sign the contract?" she inquired, staring squarely into the cell. "Or, have you forgotten the terms?" There was only the reply of silence. "Let me refresh your ever failing memory," she ranted.

"Firstly, you must seek a divorce. When you're free and clear of that naïve waif you refer to as Grace, you will consent to matrimony with me. Certainly, you recognize our relationship is true love!" she exclaimed.

"Once you sign the papers, all of your wealth, property and material possessions will become equally mine. This includes both the London Worthington Estate and the lovely country home in Boscastle, Thornwood Estate."

"Lastly," she continued, "As your new wife, we'll live happily as a family–you, me and our soon to be infant child. That is, if you are intelligent enough to choose wisely and survive this ordeal, my dearest. Otherwise, it's just me and the child, but there's no need to worry about us. We shall manage quite fine without you."

I stared at this scene in disbelief. There was now no doubt in my mind, this woman was none other than, Kendall's mistress. Although I wanted to believe this could not possibly be Kendall imprisoned within the cell, it seemed my worst fears were about to be confirmed.

"Which part don't you seem to understand?" she shouted in exasperation.

178

"Never!" the raspy voice replied from within the cell.

"You know I have the upper hand, whether you sign, or not. You will either ink your name on this contract, or I shall simply abandon you to die and rot. Regardless, your wealth still rightfully becomes my property, and your revolting brother, Russell, as God's witness will attest to all that has transpired. I am pregnant with the only heir to the entire Worthington Empire. Or, have you forgotten that passionate evening seven long months ago? You pathetic bastard!"

Madam Lela Pucelle continued to bristle, "Of course, don't let that upset you. You should know by now, there is always a price to pay when I am involved. I will bear you an heir, and you shall make me an affluent woman, showering me with all of your fortune. I don't really need your love. Your money will do fine. It's strictly a business endeavor, a matter of economics. I have been your mistress for simply too long, and it's high time you made me an honorable woman. Now sign on the line, or rot your life away!"

I awakened from the dream, weeping aloud in my bed. As my senses adapted to the familiarity of the surroundings within my chamber once again, I laid awake in awe of the conversation that had transpired. I pondered all that had been presented to me, wondering if this really was my lost husband within this horrid reverie. Could it truly have been Kendall behind cell bars within those dungeon walls? And, what did his brother, Russell have to do with this? Was this to be Kendall's fate? How could he have been so blind, falling prey into this woman's intricate web? How could he have been so deceived, misled and entrapped by her pleasures of the flesh?

If the Higher Powers were revealing this as truth, I sensed that my husband would pay a dear price for his deeds, perhaps even with the loss of his life. Kendall betrayed my love for that of another. Although it was ruthless extortion on the part of Lady

179

Pucelle, I sensed it was just a matter of time before the Divine would ensure his and her accountability for these actions, sealing both their fates.

As I continued to contemplate the dream, the sensation of a gut-wrenching pain shot throughout my pelvic area, as if a sharp knife was cutting deep into my womb. Attempting to arise from the bed, I reached for my black-velvet robe, gasping aloud as I observed my body lying upon the now bloodstained featherbed. A pool of blood, vibrant red in coloration, fully encircled my lower body. Gazing blindly into the roaring fire within the massive marble fireplace, I was clearly in shock, paralyzed as my tongue thickened in fear. My mouth attempted to shriek in sheer horror at the sight of my very own blood as I stuttered, attempting to speak aloud.

"No–No–No! Spare my child! I implore the Higher Powers. Please not this. Save the life of my child."

Josephina and Caron swiftly responded from the adjoining room, entering my chamber and rushing to my bedside.

"Oh! Mon Dieu!" exclaimed Josephina as she held my hand, trying to comfort me.

Caron opened the bedroom chamber doors and shouted aloud within the hallway, "Please come quickly. Hurry! Lady Grace has taken ill."

Marcella and Clara were the first to arrive at the scene, with Mr. Abernathy following thereafter. Immediately, they instructed Mr. Abernathy to dispatch the coachmen. Quickly summon Dr. Harrington from the village."

The house servants carried pails of warm water to my bedside as Clara swathed and sponged my bloodied body, in an attempt, albeit unsuccessful, to keep me from panicking.

"We must save the child," exclaimed Clara.

I continued to lose blood, my body paling to an ashen gray with every agonizing cramp. I shivered within the coldness, remorseful with the thought of what was occurring.

"Why me? Why? Take me, but spare my child's life," I moaned. This torture endured for what seemed like an eternity, until at last, the frail and elderly Dr. Harrington arrived. With compassion, he tried to ease my physical pain and discomfort, however, there was little to nothing that could be done in consoling me.

"Try to relax, Grace. Push, merely push and let us ease this pain for you. Another time perhaps, my dear child– another time."

Hearing his words, I knew deep within my heart and soul that the inevitable was happening. I screamed aloud in pain as I pushed with what little strength remained, releasing the stillborn child from within my womb, now keenly aware of the sisters, gasping aloud in horror.

"This child can be neither Kendall's, nor the Bishop's," murmured Marcella in confusion.

Dr. Harrington held the stillborn fetus within his hands. With a paling look of shock upon his face, he exclaimed, "This child was fathered by none other than, one of black blood–an African!"

Patricia Grace Joyce   *The Magic of Time*

Fourteen

There is more to be said than what meets the eye
It is clear to me now; you're not willing to try
For years this unrest has been torture to my being
I have cried, I have stressed, searching for a meaning

All the while you have promised, only empty words
It is time to be true, understanding the unheard
The secrets and the mysteries will eventually reveal
All of the misgivings that you tried to conceal

D r. Harrington's words sent my thoughts reeling back again to the night of the fifteenth of November. I thought about Kendall's physical abuse within the bedroom chamber, absolutely knowing all along there was another lurking amongst us. I no longer had any doubt. The father of my child was none other than the Worthington Estate head servant, Elijah Foster.

Never in a million years would I have ever initially envisioned myself within the arms of this man. That was, until I began to share more and more time with him. It was most often during the evenings that Elijah and I secretly devoted our time together. Every night on which Kendall abandoned me, departing to play amongst his array of tawdry women, I would clandestinely summon Elijah to join me within my chambers. We had a special code, so to speak…a discrete signal.

At dusk I would deposit a gold coin in the bottom of Elijah's drinking cup, stored inconspicuously atop a kitchen shelf. Each evening, Elijah would check for the coin. Discovering the coin within the cup, indicated that our rendezvous was on, and its absence meant that our evening meeting was not suitable. All the while, I remained cautiously confident that the service staff and in particular, my personal attendants, were unaware of my secretive communication and intimacies, for I made certain of this. Within the solitude of nightfall, Elijah would surreptitiously journey from the confines of his cramped servant's quarters into the luxurious abode of my grand chamber suite, entering through the hidden inner stairwell. With each passing tryst, Elijah and I grew to understand each other. I taught him English, and in turn, he taught me the ways of his country, the rhythm and the magic of Africa.

Over the course of his years at the London estate house, I had become enamored with him, convinced that he, too, cherished me. From the onset of our affair, I imagined that Elijah would never be more than just a passing fancy, yet I was rather surprised that our intimate antics had gone on for so long, more than two years. I guess one could say, Elijah fulfilled a sexual hunger that no man since the sea captain, Ian Cutter, had ever come close to satiating.

That mysterious night of fifteen November, still had much to say. Marcella was absolutely correct. There was plenty to my story than what met the eye—deceit, sex and lustful passion involving not only myself, but Kendall, Russell, the Bishop and Elijah.

I told Marcella and Clara that on the night in question, Elijah and I were drowning in a pulsating sea of raw heated passion, just prior to Kendall's untimely return to Worthington Estate. Startled at Kendall's disturbing entry into the estate house, there was no manner for escape. I instructed Elijah to be silent, no matter what happened, commanding him to quickly seek refuge within the heavy folds of the plush ivory-colored brocade wall draperies as I swiftly pulled the bed linens around my naked body. I could only imagine, Elijah must have watched in horror that night, paralyzed with fear as Kendall placed the elegant silk bed-pillow over my face, nearly suffocating me to death…taking great pleasure with sexually violating me in our marital bed.

I wanted to believe that the absence of Elijah's intervention on that night, could only be accredited to his overwhelming fright. I wanted to believe that he must have been frozen with indecision, fearful that his master, Lord Kendall would discover his unsanctioned whereabouts, cruelly punishing him…should he dare to step forward from the safety of the veiled curtain.

In retrospect, I prayed that Elijah was not liable for Kendall's mysterious disappearance, hopeful that he had not sought revenge, killing Lord Kendall after my departure that night from Worthington Estate. One issue, however, persisted to remain a mystery to me – the question as to why Elijah had also abruptly disappeared on that very same night.

As I continued to reveal my story, I told the sisters that I had taken a personal vow of silence, wanting to only protect Elijah, for I knew he was a gentle soul, incapable of harming even an old dog's flea. I sensed deep within my heart that Kendall's disappearance was the malicious act of another, still to be revealed, but if Constable Gordon ever caught wind of this news, he would most certainly assume that Elijah and I had masterminded a plot to eliminate Kendall. Without knowing the whereabouts of my former Worthington head servant to now attest for my innocence, I could only sense that it would be a matter of time, before I would eventually be summoned to return to London to answer additional questioning. My thoughts wandered, wondering if this was to transpire, the Constable would inevitably imprison me at the horrific Newgate Prison, seeking a public trial with charges of murder.

I knew very well that my worst nightmare could quite possibly, soon become a reality–Kendall would be found dead and for myself, the death penalty with a public hanging in London at the city gallows. More and more, I wanted to believe that Elijah held the clues to the mystery of that night in question, that Elijah was confirmation of my innocence.

The loss of my child, however, also had consumed me at this time and nearly sent me toppling over the emotional edge into a deeply despondent state of depression. Mentally, physically, emotionally and spiritually I was bereaved, filled with despair. For weeks I ate meagerly, sometimes even refusing all nourishment. Turning away any visitors, I refused to elaborate upon my situation. I only wanted to exist within my self-imposed solitary confinement, often believing that I was preparing myself for the inevitable.

The months slowly passed, like the sands of time dwindling through an hour glass. It was late May, and I had no desire to ever return again to London, for I was fearful that the Constable may have been alerted to my miscarriage and the questions revolving around it. The weeks progressed as I found myself pondering more and more unanswered questions. "What was the meaning of life? More specifically, what was the meaning of my life? Sometimes, I wondered if life was even worth living. I had grown weary from all of my misfortune, feeling increasingly diminutive and lost in my world. What would become of me now? What was the reason for all of this suffering? How would I ever be able to determine Elijah's whereabouts?

With all of this ambiguity, my clouded mind was continuously drawn back to that dark night in question, and the bewildering vanishing of Kendall. Still, it seemed as if some powerful energy had an inexplicable influence over me, urging me onward. I had to take into consideration the persistent messages from beyond the veil that continued speaking to me through my dreams and my intuition–Lady Pucelle's involvement with my husband, the possibility that Lord Russell may be connected to some degree, my affair with Bishop Bartholomew, my relationship with Elijah, resulting in my pregnancy, and the recent devastating death of my child. Oddly, my strong feelings of lust and desire for Dr. Christophe Alexis endured, overshadowing all of this woe.

I felt hopeless, only believing that Marcella, Clara and my Thornwood Estate service staff truly cared about me. Oftentimes, my feelings wavered like a ship without a port. Kendall had vanished, the Bishop denied any intimate involvement with me, Elijah remained strangely unreachable, and Dr. Alexis was so busy with his medical practice, he did not have time to pursue a personal relationship, yet alone with a woman who he believed to be pregnant, geographically undesirable and mysteriously abandoned by her very own husband.

The matter regarding Madame Lela Pucelle's extortion note and her pregnancy with Lord Kendall, however, continued to be a nagging burden upon my mind. There seemed no obvious way for me to prove, nor disprove Madame Pucelle's claims that she was truly carrying my husband's child. Still confused as to where, or why Kendall had disappeared, I had remained uninformed and quite removed from what was happening with the investigation in London.

Since my arrival in Boscastle, there had been no word from the Constable. Although I found this odd, I sensed that for the time being, no news was good news. However, as the weeks ensued, I grew progressively more anxious and consumed with paranoia regarding my status within the eyes of the law. My inquisitiveness finally got the better of me. At last, deciding that the best defense would be to take an offensive position, I made preparations to send a query to the Constable. As I sat in reflection, Lindsey made an unexpected appearance at my chamber door.

"Good day, Grace. Would you care to join me to delight in some fresh air? I plan to travel by carriage into the center of Boscastle, a shopping trip to the village market place along the harbor for some beeswax candles, oils and herbs. You really should get out of the house. It would do you a world of good."

"Lindsey, what could possibly have possessed you to request my attendance in the village?" I asked, looking at her in awe.

"I thought this might give us an opportunity to settle our differences with each other—fair and square. Let bygones-be-bygones, so to speak. Together, you and I could stroll along the docks and view the wonderful male scenery that abounds in port. I know for a fact, there are several new schooners in the harbor…filled with a glut of alluring and tempting eye candy for us to peruse, and perhaps even sample."

In all honesty, to say that I was a bit shocked at Lindsey's request, would be a gross understatement. For an instant, I thought about why she would ever, in a million years, entertain the idea of my company, yet I gleefully accepted her invitation. After all, perhaps it would do me well to venture into the village, walking amongst the glorious outdoors again.

"Lindsey, that's a splendid idea," I replied. "How thoughtful of you to invite me! I will ready myself and we shall be on our way shortly. I need to pick up a few items from the market place as well."

The fact of the matter was, I was hopeful that I might actually have the good fortune to stumble upon Elijah selling his various commodities once again at one of the vendor stalls. I could only pray to the Higher Powers that he still remained within the village. "It will be healing to be outdoors again, especially along the Boscastle waterfront on such a beautiful sunny day," I continued.

"However, first, I must pen an urgent letter."

"Can it wait until later?" Lindsey demanded.

"I'm afraid not, for I am anxious to send word as soon as possible to Constable Gordon regarding the status of the investigation."

"I have little time, nor patience for you to correspond with the Constable," she rudely blurted aloud, throwing my senses off guard. "When will you accept the fact that your husband is never returning to you again?"

Quite taken aback with Lindsey's response, I stared at her in horror. "How dare you speak of Kendall in this manner! As you well know the investigation has yet, to determine his fate."

"He has moved on, my dear. He is not with you anymore," she snapped. "Accept this and do not ever speak another word of him. It exhausts me to no end when I hear you discuss him. Kendall is simply where he needs to be, with another woman who can give him all that he lusts. Obviously Grace, you could not!"

My thoughts raced back to the horrid dream, that awful vivid reverie of Kendall in captivity. I paused, taking a deep breath to gather the strength of a response.

"I have had enough of your evil ways, your rudeness and incorrigible attitude!" I raged. "Be off with you! I will do what I feel is necessary from this point forward. There is no longer any need for your input on this matter. Furthermore, should I want, or desire your advice, I will ask for it. Obviously Lindsey, you too, cannot give me what I so dearly need."

Lindsey turned a cold shoulder to me as she moved towards the door.

"I shall gladly be on my way," she retorted. "I trust that you shall need my assistance one day. Remember my words. When that moment arrives in due time, I will be the only one who can provide you with all that you yearn. Fair warning, Grace. Beware of the Constable."

With that said, Lindsey rushed out the door, heading in the direction of the stables. I thought about what had just occurred and wondered what this conversation was really all about, but I could not be bothered with wasting more precious time worrying about Lindsey and her idle threats. It was paramount that I write the letter and concentrate on my situation—my life and what I needed to create peace within my inner being, within my heart and soul.

Fourteen June, 1811

Dear Constable Gordon,

I pray this correspondence finds you in good health. I have been hopeful of receiving news from you. It has been nearly five months since I departed London and still, there is no word. This absence of communication has only led me to believe there has been no change regarding the status of my husband's case—the disappearance of Lord Kendall Worthington from London on fifteen November, 1810.

I remain optimistic, however, to the discovery of his whereabouts. Please note that I fully anticipate the possibility of returning to London in the future with hopes of reopening Worthington Estate. I welcome further discussion of the case and await your prompt reply.

Sincerely,

Lady Grace Worthington
Thornwood Estate, Boscastle, England

With the completion of this correspondence, I once again sought the assistance of my service staff.

"Mr. Abernathy, I shall need to have John and Michael deliver an urgent letter to the village courier. The final destination will be delivery to Constable Nigel Gordon in London. Please see to this immediately. Go swiftly into the village center of Boscastle and contract with the courier. I will await your return with confirmation that all is well."

190

"Of course, Lady Grace. I shall see that all is understood by the coachmen," he replied.

After receiving confirmation later that day from Mr. Abernathy, my thoughts drifted to my most recent dream of Kendall and Lady Pucelle, wondering if it had revealed his true fate–a death in captivity, all for the purpose of extortion. I remained curious. To my surprise, I found myself actually welcoming the day of meeting this woman with the intention of observing the rumored child. I could only pray that someone who knew more information than I did, would eventually come forth with the missing pieces necessary in solving this puzzle. Was Elijah possibly this missing clue?

The June celebration of the summer solstice brought a new awareness to my senses. At last, I had begun to adjust once again, drawing some eye opening conclusions and insights into my own life, as if there was some small sliver of light shining a pathway, penetrating the darkness of my heart and soul. One thing that was quite obvious, my life needed to change. I could not envision enduring a life of despair and misery into an uncertain eternity. Some aspect had to transform. Perhaps, I needed to look at how I was doing things? I began to wonder about what the sisters had been telling me since my return to Boscastle. Did the answers truly exist within me?

As the days elapsed, I was feeling stronger physically, embracing the hope of returning to London to further pursue the disappearance of my husband. The weeks slowly passed and I still had not received a reply from the Constable. Putting my thoughts on paper, I attempted to make some sense as to what had happened in the past, what was happening in the present and what I yearned to occur in the future.

Throughout the upcoming days and weeks, I penned my intuitions on paper. Initiating the writing of a personal journal, I found my daily entries to be even alarming at times, exposing

191

some very inconsistent behaviors and attitudes towards people and the manner in which I was living my life at this time. I had come to the conclusion that my life had been one of nearly that of a whore. Truly, I had hardly been loyal and devout within my marriage to Kendall. I realized that I must choose to live my life differently, with greater integrity, compassion and decency.

Maintaining a journal had become a cathartic release, which I had quite unexpectedly discovered through the written word. Finally, I was able to express my deepest, darkest and dearest personal desires. As time moved along, my words began to bring a sense of renewal into my life, transforming me, and revealing a new path to achieve happiness and more joy…a bliss. For the first time in many years, I now felt a healing, a soothing of my personal wounds through these essays and verse. Little-by-little, the written word was becoming a vehicle for me to explore and discover myself, a pathway to finding inner peace.

As I continued to take daily strolls along the beautiful Cornwall coast, I sensed a spontaneity and an openness to life again. I was committed to this search of my soul's true path.

"At last, perhaps I have found my peace," I whispered. I felt as if I was becoming whole once again. The fragmented, needy woman that had made herself known as Grace Worthington was slowly dissipating. With each passing day, I was learning to simply let go, as I felt the changes consume me. Could it be that I was at last understanding my true purpose, my identity? Who is the real Grace Worthington?

July's hot summer weather brought great warmth to my heart and soul. I felt as if I had reached a turning point in my life. Albeit my choices had been confusing at times, I now chose to live my life differently, and to rid myself of all that was a burden to me, including the stressful persons and situations, and the negative blocks to my happiness on this quest for a personal identity–my true destiny in this lifetime. I resigned myself to move forward on my path, fully aware that I must simplify my life. I could not maintain the monotony of being in this limbo much longer, even though I realized this was going to be difficult. I remained determined, however, vowing to change.

My focus now demanded that which served to be solely for my emotional healing and my personal development as an individual with integrity and wisdom. I yearned for the day when I would be able to trust again, eventually finding my balance and harmony. In doing so, I prayed that I would be able to help others to also learn to discover their balance and harmony–to trust and love again. I wanted to believe that through my writing, I would someday develop into the woman that the Higher Powers intended for me to become.

Gathering my writing pens, ink and paper, I donned a fashionable broad-rimmed bonnet to protect me from the gusting wind and bright sunlight. Off to the garden I discretely strode, feeling as if I might write forever. My thoughts were bursting to get out, like a raging river, ready to overflow its banks. As I sat on a small, white wooden bench within the magnificent rose garden on the Thornwood Estate grounds, I penned my thoughts in verse upon parchment paper.

Without any warning, I suddenly heard a rustling in the lush woods that lay just beyond my vantage point, and I wondered what could be hiding within the surrounding thick brush.

"Who goes there?" I inquired aloud. Listening for a reply, there was only a stillness, interrupted by the distant cries of seagulls and the sound of the wind breezing through the whispers of tall pine trees. The sugary sweet scent of roses danced about me, infiltrating my senses.

Again, I heard the crunching of leaves from within the woods. There was now no doubt in my mind, someone or something was definitely lurking in the brush. This time the interruption was louder and closer as I anxiously listened to the marked approach of footsteps–the crackling sound of leaves and foliage being pressed underfoot. "Is anyone there?" I inquired, my voice now quivering as I swallowed hard.

Still, there was no reply. As each second passed, I wanted to flee, fully aware that I was certainly not fabricating these noises. Nonetheless, I hoped that perhaps it was all a figment of my overactive imagination, trying to reassure myself that it was merely the wind frolicking within the surrounding forest.

Unsuccessfully, I attempted to refocus my attention upon my writing, yet my composure was still somewhat rattled. With every effort to collect my thoughts, I found myself only to be distracted by the unnerving sounds within the brush. This time, however, I detected a voice…the distinct whining of a horse. I cringed at the very thought that perhaps I was being stalked. Abruptly, I arose from the garden bench, tightly clutching my writing papers securely within my arms. "Who is there? Who is it?" I screamed with fear as I anxiously stood watchful, desperately considering my best route of immediate escape.

Fifteen

The blowing winds darling are close to my side
Never too far, yet always astray
I speak your name aloud, with soft whispering lust
Imploring your heart and soul to hear me pray

But, you are not here
And, I am not there

The blowing winds ever so close to my side
Wishing and hopeful one day you will appear

Come to me darling
Perhaps you are near?

Forever wishing and hopeful you will answer my prayer

To my surprise, a dark-haired figure appeared before me, a well-proportioned gentleman boldly emerging from the surrounding thick brush. He was fully clad in hunting attire, muted in coloration–a combination of dark green, chocolate brown and pale sand that softly blended with the surrounding landscape and foliage. Although camouflaged in these colors of nature, I immediately recognized him.

"Oh, Dr. Alexis!" I sighed with relief. "You nearly scared the living daylights out of me. Thank the Higher Powers it is you!"

"My apologies, Lady Grace. My intentions were not to startle you," the doctor replied. "I merely sought to discretely approach the estate house. I needed to confirm that it was truly you. It must have been my horse that gave me away, since I am usually quite light on my feet when traveling alone," he said, smiling while observing me intently as he tied his horse to a nearby pine limb.

He continued, "I am so pleased to have stumbled upon you within the garden."

"Please, let's put all formalities aside, doctor. Call me Grace. And what brings you to Boscastle? How did you find me here?"

Smiling, he replied, "I've journeyed again to the west coast on holiday. Dr. Harrington, his medical associates and I are involved in some marvelous dove hunting today. Remarkably, in the distance, I recognized Thornwood Estate and the large black entry gates. Forgive me, but I realized as I traveled nearer to the property, that indeed, it was you sitting here alone on this rose-crested hillside."

"Well, Dr. Alexis, you not only stumbled upon me, but nearly frightened me to death!"

"Alarming you was the furthest thought from my mind," he said. "Please excuse my intrusion, but it is such a pleasure to again be in your company. I must admit you do look splendid, so fit, elegant and rested for one who has recently given birth. I am in absolute awe of your recuperative powers. The most important thing, however, is that you continue to get your rest. How are you feeling?"

I could sense my cheeks flushing to a bright red, as I tried to avoid looking directly in his eyes. I held my head down, hiding my anguish as tears began to trickle forth. My eyes swelled as I held back my emotion. "Oh, I am as well as can be expected," I murmured.

With a perplexed look upon his face, he continued, "What do you mean *as well as can be expected*? For one who has recently given birth, you look quite fine, in the pink of health and astoundingly remarkable. You are such a woman of modesty, Grace, but obviously it appears that I have arrived much too late to assist in any way with the delivery. I actually expected you to be fully showing–radiant in your last months of pregnancy. Somehow, I must have miscalculated."

I could not bear to speak. With each passing second, I could feel my throat tightening from the anxiety. I stood helpless, listening to his words as his questioning persisted.

"How are things with you, and how is the child?" he continued. "When I did not hear from you, I assumed that you could not journey back to London. How did the pregnancy fare?   Most of all, I look forward to seeing the child. I am certain that this child must be so special. Tell me. Are you the proud mother of a little girl, or a little boy?"

I remained silent. My mouth felt as if it was simply frozen, incapable of speaking…until I burst into tears and blurted aloud, "I lost my child in the sixth month, Dr. Alexis."

By the look upon his distorted face, the doctor was quite stunned, shocked and noticeably flustered by my response. Approaching me, he placed his strong arms firmly around my shoulders, drawing my limp body closer to him.

"Grace, please understand that I had no idea.," he said, continuing to cradle me within his arms. "I am embarrassed, so upset that I have misjudged what has happened. You are going to be fine. As a matter of fact, you *are* fine. There is a time and place for everything. I suppose that you already know this, but nothing in life is an accident. It is all for a reason, and I trust you shall have a healthy child one day. This simply was not the appropriate time. The Universe works in mysterious ways. It was not meant to be for you right now, for whatever the reasons. We may never know why things occur in our lives until much, much later."

Weeping within his arms, again I could not find the words to speak, yet somehow I simultaneously felt as if a great burden had been lifted from upon my tiny shoulders. It was reassuring just knowing that Dr. Christophe Alexis was again by my side.

"Your words are comforting," I murmured, gazing upward into the depths of his large blue eyes.

"Please, dry your tears, Grace. My intentions are not to babble on, but I pray that you and your husband may be blessed with another child one day."

"At the moment, that is highly unlikely, Doctor."

"I do not understand?" he queried, searching my face for an answer.

"My husband's fate remains unresolved. Perhaps you have forgotten? Kendall is still missing and with each day that passes, there seems to be little hope of his ever returning to me again."

"I don't know what to say. Except, that I am saddened to hear this," he said. "Excuse my forgetfulness, but I seem to be making a muddle of our conversation. My objectives are not to pry into your affairs, it's just that I have great concern for your well being."

"You're very kind, doctor," I replied.

"Although this may sound rather odd, I sometimes feel a strong inexplicable connection to you," he said. "These sensations are quite alarming to me, and I must admit that I do not really understand what is occurring. If my behavior is inappropriate, please stop me, but before you do, let me state one matter."

"Go on, doctor."

"Please try to understand," he said with hesitation.

"Oftentimes, I cannot seem to get the thought of you out of my mind."

"Oh, continue," I said with encouragement, "What specifically are you referring to? What are you saying?"

"Grace, this is rather difficult for me to explain, but I sense as if there is some overwhelming attraction between us, that somehow we have a mysterious bond with each other," he said nervously. "On occasion, I even wonder if I have simply lost my mind, since I cannot decipher the rhyme or reason of this. Oh, well, I needn't bore you any longer with my folly. Perhaps it's just my imagination."

"Please tell me more," I said, as I dried my tears.

198

"For instance, why would I be so disposed to depart the company of my dove hunting party to seek you out today? What would ever possess me to do this?"

I remained silent for a moment as I considered the doctor's words. I wanted to show him my affection by softly kissing his lips, and holding him close to me in a long embrace. At that very moment I wanted to make passionate love to him, lost in a sea of undulating emotions, but I was fearful, afraid that my bold actions might serve to only alarm him.

"As you know, my medical practice permits little leisure time for me to socialize. My commitment and focus are solely on my profession, patients and medical practice," he continued. "Thus, I must firstly concentrate on my profession. Only then, may I permit myself to indulge in taking small breaks, in an effort to create some personal time whenever possible, such as this hunting holiday in Boscastle with Dr. Harrington. However, my personal life remains quite unsettled."

"Do you loathe women, doctor?" I inquired, observing the small beads of perspiration collect upon his brow.

"Not at all," he replied uneasily. "But, I am unconvinced that I would be willing to share my life, or exchange marital vows with a woman. I am undecided if I could ever make this commitment to another, since I am such a free spirit, like you, Grace. I sense that you, too, require this freedom to survive, like a lovely white rose blowing in the wind. Am I correct?"

I hesitated before speaking. "It seems we have much in common, doctor. For, I have not been able to find a proper gentleman to become a part of my life. Although my past personal involvements have been numerous, today I am simply not willing, to give my heart and soul to merely anyone. I sense that it will take an extraordinary and unique individual to touch my heart, for me to ever commit to love again."

"What about your husband? Do you love him?"

199

"At one time in my life, I truly loved him, but over the years my marriage grew to be intolerable, and with his disappearance, I sense that Kendall is no longer to be a part of my life, that he has chosen to move on. I often sense that he has crossed-over as a soul beyond the veil."

"What makes you deem this to be so?"

"I have my reasons, doctor. Trust that I simply know. I also believe there is something very special which you and I must do together. There are no accidents in life. The Universe has brought us together for a purpose, of which still remains to be seen."

"I am not so certain," he remarked. "I know this thought may resonate as somewhat peculiar to you, but oftentimes I believe, that I will never be able to trust a woman again. My work seems to be the only means to fill my time and to satisfy my passions at this point. I am thankful to the Higher Powers that I have my profession."

"I sense that you have been hurt by another," I continued. "I too, know this pain, but I ask that you consider an important aspect of this matter. Perhaps you were simply involved with the wrong woman, Dr. Alexis?"

"I suppose that is somewhat possible."

"Every day I pray that the Higher Powers will send the love of my life to me," I said, looking into his eyes. "I can only trust, and continue to have faith. For now, I am learning to let go, and to bless these energies, inviting all that needs to be. Although it's difficult at times, I try not to focus upon my past trials and tribulations. I remain hopeful that happier days will emerge in my future."

"Quite possibly, this is what I too, must instate within my life. I sense, however, this is much easier said than done, Grace."

I told the doctor that I knew how complicated this was, for I, too, had great misery with another in my life. I explained to him that it was paramount he moved forward with his life, in an effort

200

to release the past, and to stand tall with an open mind in acceptance of the present and the future.

"Your words inspire me, Grace. I shall pray that one day, the love of my life will be sent to me," he said, placing a soft and gentle kiss upon my forehead.

My face was flushed with warmth as I found myself surprised at his spontaneous gesture of affection, yet I was simultaneously pleased that he was able to express some sentiment for me. Again, I thought about taking this much further. But, did I dare?

Although I was reluctant to listen, my better judgment was telling me that I must refrain, to take smaller steps and savor our association. Over the passing months I had become aware that it was necessary for me to handle my personal relationships, a great deal differently. The past behavior of throwing myself at a love interest had certainly not gotten me very far. Now I needed to reflect within my heart. The seeds of this friendship with Dr. Alexis had already been planted, and I prayed they would grow to blossom.

The doctor motioned toward his horse, continuing to hold me in his arms. "I must return to my hunting party," he said softly. "For, I know they will be distressed to see that I've misread the trails and strayed from the group. However, I do hope that you and I may stay in contact. Please write, and let me know what you are doing. Of course, most definitely, do let me know if your travels shall bring you to London again. As I have said in the past, you are always welcome."

"I shall correspond with you, Christophe," I said, noticing a smile on his face upon hearing me speak aloud his first name again.

"Farewell, Grace. Let's try to stay in touch," he said, releasing me from his embrace. As the doctor moved forward to untie his horse, I observed him turn around to give me a smile and a wink of his eye. Taking his mount, he continued, "Oh, and Grace…if

201

you should write, please understand that it may take a while for my reply. I sometimes take several weeks-to-months, before I may respond to even my closest friends. It's just that I'm so busy with my work." With that said, his handsome horse swiftly galloped away into the distance.

I thought about all that had just transpired. Dr. Alexis's request for my staying in touch with him was colored by an aura of genuine flattery, a lovely gesture on his part; albeit I found it rather strange that he could not respond for weeks to perhaps even months. Something was not making sense. Pondering the situation further, I wanted to give him the benefit of my increasing doubt, but I wondered if a doctor's life was truly so harried and short of leisure time, that it was out of the question to correspond in a timely manner. In the same breath, I couldn't help but speculate, that if he considered me a friend, he would not behave in such a manner. Then again, could it actually be possible with all of Dr. Alexis's patients, surgeries and evaluations, so little time remained to write a note?

Although I was puzzled, deep within I knew there was still a persistent unexplainable attraction to this man, a charisma that I could not resist, deny, nor fully understand at this time. I too, had absolutely felt this sensation of a connection from the initial moment I had set eyes upon Dr. Christophe Alexis. At the moment, I only wanted to believe that fate had initially brought us together on that stormy winter's day in February, locked in his embrace within my chamber suite. My emotions overwhelmed me as I softly blew a kiss in his direction, observing him vanish on horseback into the horizon.

"Christophe," I whispered. "I only pray that you honor those unforgettable words which you spoke to me in February."

With the magic of time, all will be well.
There is nothing to fear when you listen to your heart.

As I continued to sit in the garden, my thoughts were lost. "Might it actually be possible that the doctor truly cares for me?" I whispered.

Only the Higher Powers knew the answer to this question. Time would tell. I wanted to stay in contact with him and decided that I would now focus my energies in his direction, upon the essence of Dr. Christophe Alexis.

As my imagination waxed, I speculated if perhaps one day, we might be reunited. Sitting amongst the glorious sea of multicolored roses, I prayed to the Higher Powers, wishing this bond would grow to become more than a magnificent friendship —more than I could ever possibly envision at this time.

Patricia Grace Joyce   *The Magic of Time*

Sixteen

Are you just a fantasy?
Some illusion teasing me?
Praying love is meant to be
Could you be my destiny?

I awaken from my dreams
You have disappeared it seems
Wondering if you might return?
Will fate send the love I yearn?

With each passing summer's day in the month of July, I grew even more excited anticipating my eventual return to reopen the Worthington Estate house. Although I adored the sea and the Western coast of Boscastle, England, I continued to feel a tremendous magnetism pulling me back to London. Of course, this overriding attraction was my anticipation of meeting with Dr. Alexis again. In weeks prior, I had written a letter of correspondence to him, however, I had yet to receive a response. My recent encounter with the doctor, perplexing as it was, would continue to become a part of my daily thoughts–an obsession.

"Today, I shall write again to him," I murmured, for I had this insatiable longing to simply communicate, wanting him to know every detail of my pending plans.

Fifteen July, 1811

Dearest Christophe,

How delightful it was to meet with you in the rose gardens atop Thornwood Estate! I pray that your dove hunting proved to be worthy of all efforts involved.

Anticipating my return to London in the month of September, it would be marvelous to visit with you again, should time permit with your busy schedule. Perhaps you may even be available for afternoon tea?   Do take care of yourself, and know that I keep you in my thoughts and prayers.   I look forward to your reply.

Warmest Regards,

Grace Worthington
Thornwood Estate - Boscastle, England

I placed the document within the parchment envelope, lovingly waxing the seal with the impression of the Thornwood Estate coat of arms which bore the cross, entwined within a blossoming rose vine. After giving explicit instructions to Mr. Abernathy, he followed through with the precise specifications for the coachmen to have the letter delivered promptly via messenger at Dr. Alexis's residence in London.

On that same afternoon, I considered measures to take a walk, but feeling rather fatigued, I decided to get some rest before venturing outdoors. As I lay upon my bed, Clara tapped lightly upon the open chamber door, summoning my attention.

"Am I disturbing you, Grace?"

"You are always welcome. Please come in."

"I have been thinking about you all day," she continued. "Are you aware, there will be a full moon this evening?" Immediately my attention switched from the notion of rest, to Clara's words. I sensed something was on her mind, something mystical.

"I gather you have come to bring me some insight, Clara?"

"Take a moment and read this verse," she said handing me a large, chocolate-brown, leather-bound book. I believe it is a wonderful spell when cast under the auspices of the full moon. It may provide an answer to at least one of your questions."

"A spell? What kind of spell?" I queried, sitting upright as I took the unique volume from her extended hand.

"It's a love spell, dating back to many centuries ago, but it only works under the glowing radiance of a full moon. Thus, it is absolutely crucial that you cast the spell tonight."

"Tonight?" I inquired, glossing over the yellowed pages.

"If you miss this opportunity, you will have to wait until the next month's full moon," she sighed.

"Tell me more," I pleaded enthusiastically, sitting upright upon my featherbed.

"This is how it works," she continued. "If something is truly destined to be, the spell will only assist to make your wish transpire more swiftly. What do you think? Will you give it a try?"

"Are you sure that it's safe, and that the timing is right for this?"

"It's absolutely foolproof," Clara replied. "Have I ever led you astray? Read what it says… *This spell is to be cast when seeking to clarify and solidify a romantic bond with a love interest.*"

"This does seem appropriate, as if it might work for me. What do I need to do?" I asked.

"Listen carefully," she replied, inserting her hand deep within the pocket of her silk heather-colored frock. "Take this small red candle and carve into the wax, the name of the one you desire. However, you must never reveal the identity of this individual. It must be kept a secret. Only you, need to know the identity of this soul. Carve the first name of this person using something dear to you."

Clara told me to use my gold crucifix that hung on a chain around my neck. It had a sharp enough edge, and would cut nicely into the wax. I took the red candle from her, and I removed the cross and chain from around my neck. Carefully, I followed her instructions, inscribing the name of my heart's desire into the soft wax.

"All right. What's next?" I eagerly inquired.

"Take this piece of red paper, and tear it into the shape of a heart."

Again, I followed Clara's instructions step-by-step, anxious to move on to the next task.

"What shall I do now?"

"Write your heart's desire's name onto the red paper," she replied.

I took my quill pen and ink in hand, as I intently wrote the name of my love interest onto the red-paper heart.

"Are you ready to hear more?" Clara inquired.

"Yes," I replied, anxiously nodding my head like a porous sea sponge awaiting to absorb her every word.

"Carefully, you must now prick your finger. Your blood must merge onto the paper with your love's name. Use this sewing needle. Can you do this?"

"Completely," I replied, hesitating before I pressed the needle-point into the flesh of my finger tip. I winced from the pain. Releasing the needle, I squeezed the pink tissue, paying particular attention to the flow of crimson-colored blood.

"Is that it?"

"That's perfect. Your blood upon the red-paper heart with your beloved's name will create a love bond between both of you," she said, gazing at the piece of blood-stained paper. "Now you must

take this red rose. Place it into the small vase next to the candle. Position the blood-stained red-paper heart underneath the vase."
I listened to Clara, my ears keen to her every word.

"Light the candle and make your love wish," she continued.

"When the candle has totally burned, take the remaining candle-wax, the rose petals, the red heart-shaped paper and place them all in a small box. Do you understand?"

"In a box? What shall I do with these things in a box?"

"Take them down to the water's edge tonight. You must bury the contents of the box in the sand."

"But, where?" I inquired, staring at her with bewilderment.

"Somewhere, anywhere that feels right. A place that you sense is correct. It must be near the shoreline, however, so that the waves will eventually take the contents out to sea."

"All right."

"Oh," she continued, "It is very important that you do one final thing."

"What is it?" I asked, concerned if I was going to be able to remember all of these various steps, and in the order in which she had outlined for the spell to be cast properly.

"As you remove each of the various items from the box, place them into the sand…under the light of the full moon. You must pray to the Higher Powers. Ask the spirit world to assist in bringing your heart's desire to you, to bring your love's desire into the light—into the light of life, so that this soul may one day reach for you. Do you have any questions?"

"I hope that I remember everything."

"Focus on your heart's desire. Light the candle and let it begin to burn. When the flame has consumed the candle in its entirety, you must depart tonight, journeying alone under the light of the full moon to fulfill the love spell. All will be well."

"Alone?" I said, with much reservation. I told Clara that it would be dark and I dreaded the thought of traveling by myself down to the water's edge. "I shall be frightened. Couldn't you come with me?" I pleaded.

"The spell will not work if I am with you. You must go alone and proclaim your love under the magical full moon. Are you brave enough, my dear?"

"Well, of course," I insisted. I felt an overbearing hesitation within my bones as I continued to speak. "I will do this tonight and declare my love," I said. I prayed that through the act of focusing all of my attention on my heart's desire, all would truly be well tonight.

Several hours passed as the candle burned, welcoming the nightfall. I gathered the contents into a small wooden silver-colored box. In solitude, I set out for my destination, journeying down the coastal path which led to the majestic coastline. The light of the full moon was brilliant as it lit the way. While walking, I pondered much of what still needed to become resolved in my life, determined to find my balance and harmony - the inner peace I craved to assist me with following my true destined path in this lifetime.

As I arrived at the beach, I observed the radiant full moon hanging in the sky on this sultry summer's night. I removed my shoes and silk stockings to enable more ease in walking upon the sand. Sensing that I had found a place close enough to the water's edge, I remembered Clara's words. If it felt *right*, place the contents of the box there.

Quickly, I dug a hole in the sand using my hands as a shovel to scoop the waterlogged earth. I buried the rose petals, the candle-wax and the red-paper heart inscribed with my beloved's name. Looking upward at the abundant full moon, I spoke aloud seeking the blessings of the spirits.

I implore the Higher Powers to bring to me my heart's desire. Please bring his love into the light, so that one day he may reach for me.

210

With the spell now cast, I stood upright and proceeded to walk along the coast under the magical light of this full moon. I contemplated the love spell and all that I hoped would one day manifest in my life, all the while, keeping in mind the image of my heart's desire.

Gazing into the distance towards the Boscastle lighthouse, I observed its brilliant guiding beacon of light, dusting its rays upon the churning sea, but oddly I sighted a glowing light approaching me along the shoreline. It appeared to be a lit lantern, carried in hand by a rather tall gentleman.

The memory of the February night of my return to Thornwood Estate filled my head. For an instant, I even thought that perhaps this was the very same fellow combing the beachfront, who I had observed from my chamber window.

As the man moved closer, he appeared to be fair-haired. I paused in reflection and continued to observe him walking slowly in my direction. Peculiarly, he too, was alone on this night as I viewed him with curiosity from afar. The distance and the darkness hindered my vision, making it complicated for me to put together any form of recognition.

Cautiously, I resumed my walk along the shore, carrying my lit lantern and moving my bare feet in a playful dance, synchronized with the rushing motion of the surf. The waves crashed powerfully upon the shoreline as my steps led me nearer, and nearer to the approaching figure. All the while, I could only wonder who this person could be. I found myself inexplicably drawn to him. My sense of fear, however, had uncannily diminished to the point where I now found myself boldly pacing in his direction. Perhaps my curiosity had once again taken over, getting the better of me.

The gentleman was statuesque, a rather large man, but slim. I considered why he was outdoors walking the beach alone on this night. Perhaps he was simply contemplating his life as I was in this

211

moment? For an instant, I wanted to believe that perhaps, he too, was casting a love spell under the gaze of this full moon. The night was warm and calm, yet a formidable coastal wind gusted from the west. At last, I found myself within a suitable range of vision to focus more upon the figure approaching before my eyes. Quite remarkably, the gentleman appeared to be engrossed with focus upon me.

I thought about the notion that we might have met before. How strange, if indeed this was true, for I actually had very few acquaintances in this part of the country. I had been living my recent days in Boscastle, as more of a recluse during these past months. My disinterest in climbing the social ladder had certainly inhibited the creation of any new and significant liaisons within my life.

As I neared the stranger, he seemed to be smiling at me, and rather shockingly, his form even took on an eerie resemblance to that of a thinner version of Kendall. I stopped in my footsteps and caught my breath, now staring at the stranger with a perplexed look upon my face. In my confusion I prayed to the Higher Powers.

"Please tell me this is not he," I murmured. I wondered, might it be that Kendall truly had returned? Now it was imperative that I met this gentleman face-to-face, but how could this be my husband?

With mixed emotions, I found myself continuing to move forward in his direction. There was no turning back. I knew that I must discover his identity by studying his face, hearing his voice and looking him squarely in the eye. I needed absolute proof. Only then, would I be convinced that it truly was, or was not Kendall.

"Do I know you sir?" I said, looking in his direction. "Have we ever had an occasion to make acquaintance with each other in the past?"

212

"Are you speaking to me?" he replied rather aloofly.

I thought about his arrogant response. Well, who else was here in our presence? Of course, I was speaking to him. As I struggled to withhold my curtness, I responded, "Most certainly, sir. Yet, perhaps we may know one another?" The stranger did not reply, but continued to approach until he was standing directly before me.

"No, that would be quite impossible," he finally replied. "I am not from these parts, but from distant shores."

Eyeing him intently, I surveyed his physical characteristics with greater scrutiny. His appearance was easy on the eyes, a rather attractive fellow with locks of blond hair that blew carefree with the wind, leading me into the penetrating gaze of his sparkling green eyes.

I stared at him with intensity, and with much relief concluded this was most definitely not my husband. Quite obviously, he was far too handsome a man to ever be Kendall Worthington. However, physically he did bear some resemblance as a leaner, yet muscular version of him, similar in coloration and stature as well. As I observed him further, the gentleman seemed to even take on some of Kendall's mannerisms.

I persisted with an ardent examination, now sensing more and more, an uncanny similarity between this fellow and Lord Russell. For a brief instant, I believed that I might be hallucinating, but I knew better, surmising that it was just my over active imagination at work again. In my wildest dreams this could never be Lord Russell, since this gentleman had a nearly perfect complexion, a gorgeous porcelain face. There were no telltale signs of the dreadful scars that marred Russell's face.

I reflected, continuing to scrutinize this man, realizing that something was very peculiar about this stranger as I looked upon his hands with greater detail. He was wearing white gloves. How odd, to be wearing gloves on a warm summer's night. I found this all becoming increasingly surreal.

Although he appeared to be a stranger, his voice had a familiarity, sounding a bit like, none other than...Kendall. This man, however, had more of a nasal quality. Could he possibly be Kendall, or possibly Lord Russell? Clearly, I was in a quandary. Who was this eccentric fellow?

"May I be so forward as to ask which port is your origin, sir?" I inquired. My curiosity had been entirely aroused.

"Ah yes, my fair one. You may ask, but I may not give you the answer that you seek."

I discovered myself becoming increasingly uncomfortable with this last comment as I pondered his words. What was he hiding? He spoke in rhymes and riddles, and seemed like such an illusive soul.

"You are a man of few words," I said, now determined to exit this scene. "I must be on my way. Good night."

Turning around to face the cliffs, I motioned forward to retreat from him, but in my attempt to do so, the stranger suddenly lunged towards me, grabbing hold of my arm.

"Wait!" he pleaded. "I only wish to shield you from any further grief and misfortune. I know of your despair and misery. You deserve so much better and one day you shall have it all. You shall find true love. With the magic of time, all will be well."

"Let me go," I retorted, attempting to pull away from him, but my legs grew numb and my feet were frozen in my tracks. An eerie chill tingled over my skin. "Those are Dr. Alexis's words," I shouted. "Who are you?" There was an uncomfortable silence as the stranger stared defiantly into my eyes.

There was no doubt in my mind that I was absolutely convinced of one matter...I preferred not to be in the presence of this soul any longer. Goose bumps appeared upon my skin as I observed his gaze continuing to cut through me; his eyes adhered

214

upon my face. There was something unnerving and evasive about the gentleman, not only in his mannerisms, speech and physical appearance, but his statements were misleading–extremely elusive, as if he was intentionally hiding behind a veil.

I thought about how he could possibly know of my angst. My privacy had always been paramount to me. I knew that I had never shared these thoughts with him, nor had I ever discussed my yearnings for an absolute love. Who was he? Who had he spoken to? I could only determine this man was up to no good. My intuition was prodding me to move onward and to do so swiftly, or else endure the uncertain consequences.

"Farewell," I said, as I became more and more uncomfortable with every second that I remained in his company. "I really must be on my way." I wanted to run in the opposite direction. I knew, however, this would only serve to alarm him to my overwhelming fear. Smiling nervously, I engaged this opportunity to take one last look at his face, before fading into the darkness. He was definitely odd, strange, unique or perhaps just different as I continued to question again and again the facts–something was not quite valid with his appearance, or with his comments. I attempted to maintain my composure, walking onward along the coast as swiftly as possible. I prayed to the Higher Powers that he would not follow.

Again, I thought about how his face was foreign, but at the same time it puzzled me that his essence was so familiar. His skin had appeared to be atypical, although I knew how preposterous this all sounded. It had a softness, a refined quality as if not belonging to him, or on the face of any man for that matter. It was similar to the flesh of a baby, a child's complexion…pure as cream.

Pondering this, I only became increasingly confused by his demeanor. His face gave me the distinct impression, that somehow it had been miraculously transformed. I wondered how someone could have perfect facial features and such a flawless complexion? In spite of his attractiveness, something still remained questionable and uneasy regarding his refined features– something familiar, yet odd. What if we really had met before?

Glancing discretely over my shoulder, I moved with quickness and determination in the direction of the coastal path as I continued to observe the light-haired stranger standing by the water's edge. His lantern hung by his side. The full moon illuminated his tall statuesque physique, creating a haunting elongated shadow upon the sand. Still apprehensive that he would follow, I watched intently. He stood poised before the crashing waves, and as I stared at him, I felt mesmerized within a trance.

If I could just get far enough away from him, I knew that I would be safe. I moved steadfastly in the opposite direction, all the while, praying that he would remain stationary, so as to enable me enough time to make my escape. Finally, I reached the coastal path. Watchful of his figure in the distance, I sat upon the ground, putting on my stockings and shoes. Arising, my body tingled all over as I suddenly felt as if I could soar effortlessly like a seagull. I climbed the hillside with agility, swiftness and skill, as if floating…my feet barely touching the cobblestone path. As I reached the doors of the estate house, I shouted in praise, "Thank the Higher Powers!"

I was grateful for my safe return to Thornwood Estate, but as I entered into the marble foyer, I was distracted by a faint noise, startled by the unexpected presence of, none other than Lindsey. There she stood, looming before me in silence. Her dark penetrating gaze cut through me like a surgeon's scalpel.

"Avoiding someone?" she cackled.

Before I could reply, I sensed there would be trouble. For certain, Lindsey would welcome this opportunity to draw my blood, if I did not escape her ruthless interrogation.

216

Seventeen

Life is never what it seems
Sometimes lost in hazy dreams
Then one day the sun does shine
Suddenly you're not so blind

There are bumps along the way
Curves and turns that cause delay
True emotions that you feel
Leading to a love that's real

Rise above the dark and gray
Knowing love will guide the way
Shining light on one Divine
A true lover worth your time

"Where have you been?" Lindsey continued. "Could it truly be her Royal Highness, Lady Grace Worthington–The Queen of illicit love and obsession? Or, are you the Princess of fantasy tonight?"

"Who gave you permission to enter into the estate house?" I inquired, attempting to ignore her comments as I felt myself drawn closer into her gaze. Swiftly, I brushed past her, venturing earnestly into the drawing room in search of Marcella and Clara, as an austere feeling of desperation settled upon me.

Lindsey followed me like a faithful hunting dog, all the while continuing with her banter.

"Stop your childish behavior! I am here with the sisters' blessings."

"Where are they? I must speak with them," I persisted, all the while trying to evade Lindsey.

"The only one you really need to speak with is me," she replied. "I'll tell you everything that you yearn to know on this night. I dare you. Ask me your questions."

"Leave me be," I said, feeling my body cringe as I tried to walk away from her. "You are the last person that I would ever want to speak with at this time," I shouted, growing angrier by the second. "You cannot fool me! I realize your intent is truly self-serving and not of any sincerity to assist me. I know this all too well. If you believe that I would ever begin to confide in you…well, you are gravely mistaken, Lindsey. Now get out of my way and let me be."

"How dare you talk to me in that tone of voice," she retorted.

"You have such arrogance. You really don't have any inkling as to what is truly going on. Do you? You are such a nonsensical woman."

"What are you speaking of?" I inquired, somewhat perplexed by her condescension and elusive commentary.

"Wake up, Grace," she shouted. "You are blind to so much, only because you choose not to deal with life in terms of reality. If you took the time to open your eyes wide enough, you might see what is actually happening all around you."

With my curiosity and ire simultaneously provoked, I acquiesced, "Very well, Lindsey. Tell me all that you have to say."

"That's more like it," she replied, her head held erect with self-importance.

"Firstly, men manipulate and abuse you, only because you enable them to do so. I know all about the Bishop Bartholomew and Lord Russell. Even your womanizing husband knew how to work your puppet strings, and let's not forget that pathetic slave, Elijah Foster. Now you are even obsessing about this socially deprived medical man. Grace, you can do better than this!"

218

"Christophe is a talented surgeon," I interjected.

"Doctor, or surgeon…whatever you want to call him—*this monk of medicine*. My advice to you is to stay away from Dr. Christophe Alexis. He does not have eyes for you, nor will he ever. Rather, his interests yearn to be within the arms of other women - many others."

"How would you know?"

"Again, you have apparently forgotten much of the magic, dear one. My mystical powers are finely tuned. When I simply need information, all this requires is for me to look deeply within your eyes. The eyes tell me everything," she continued. "Leave the doctor alone. Let someone, like myself, show him the ropes and give him what he truly needs."

"How can I be certain this is the truth?" I shouted as tears welled within my eyes.

"Trust my observations. The doctor is indeed, a needy soul when it comes to lust and physical desire. He merely deserves a good woman, like me, to help him express his passion," she remarked, staring defiantly at me.

At that moment, Marcella unexpectedly entered the room, intently observing the two of us engaged in heated confrontation. "Ladies," she interrupted. "You know that I disapprove when you quarrel. Please, attempt to at least find some thread of peace with one another. Life is too short, to continue living in this manner. I could hear both of you carrying on, all the way down the hallway and into my bedroom chamber."

"Oh, I am so sorry Marcella," I said. "I hope that our voices did not disturb you from resting. I only wanted to find you and Clara. However, since you are here, perhaps I could speak with you now, that is, if you should feel up to talking?"

"Go ahead, she replied, smiling at me with compassion in her eyes. "What seems to be so bothersome?"

"I would prefer to speak with you alone, if possible, my glance directed towards Lindsey.

"Lindsey," Marcella commanded, "Please, we would like some privacy at this time. Return to your quarters. If you so choose, you may join us later this night."

"It's obvious that Grace does not want to know the truth," Lindsey roared, shrugging her shoulders as she marched abruptly out of the room.

"Thank you, Marcella, for your intervention," I said.

"One day, you must learn to deal with Lindsey on your own terms, Grace. Try to focus on the magic and use it to protect yourself from her wrath," she continued. "Otherwise, I fear you may eventually succumb to one of her contemptuous ploys. Now tell me, what is on your mind?"

I relayed to Marcella that I had much concern over the puzzling incident that occurred this night while I journeyed along the coast. "I met an unusual man, a very strange and peculiar fellow, yet I do not know his name, nor could I even begin to really understand what he had to say. I only sensed that something was not proper with him."

"What were you doing walking alone on the coast this night?"

"It seemed like such a beautiful night to take a walk under the light of the magnificent full moon, a lovely occasion to walk along the shore, and hmmm," I said, hesitating as I realized that Marcella was not finding much credence in my words. "Actually, I wanted to cast a love spell."

"So, you cast a love spell under the light of the full moon?"

"Yes, Clara advised me to do so," I replied with concern. "Have I acted too swiftly?"

"Although this is truly a wise occasion to do so, do not reveal to me the name of your beloved," she continued. "For the spell to work, you must carry this secret close to your heart."

220

"It is an absolutely brilliant night," I continued. "The moon tonight is certainly larger, fuller and much brighter than I can ever remember."

"Tell me more," Marcella insisted. "Did you recognize this man? Had you ever seen him before?"

"No, but he seemed familiar in some vague manner."

I told her that I could not make heads, or tails out of this situation. He had blond, beautiful hair, brilliant green eyes and a physique that could persuade even the most satisfied woman to turn her head and stare boldly with desire. However, it was his skin, the complexion of his delicate and refined face that had me the most puzzled. He had the most gorgeous and radiant skin that I have ever seen, especially for a gentleman. It was like cream and even glistened in the light of the full moon. I wondered if once again my imagination was playing games with me, for this did not seem truly possible.

"Calm down, and try to recall more details," Marcella said. "What else was there about this man leading to your inferences?"

"Oddly, it was as if I somehow knew him, and he somehow knew me, but I could not place the time or circumstances that we had actually met. Furthermore, he wore white gloves. Why would someone wear white gloves while walking along the coast on a warm summer's night? Do you find this strange? Am I making any sense, Marcella?"

"On the contrary, you are making perfect sense. Your intuition, the inner voice, is telling you one thing and your mind and reasoning are telling you another. If I were you, my dear, I would go with your very first feeling, your gut instinct about your encounter with this stranger. Now what might that be?"

"My first feeling was, I sensed an immense physical attraction to him. But, there was innately something evil or foreboding about him, something dark, mysterious and hidden."

221

I told Marcella, I could not receive a clear response from this fellow when I asked him elementary questions. He seemed to purposely avoid my queries. Rather, he spoke to me in rhymes. I wanted to get as far away from him as possible. I even felt as if he may have actually been Lord Russell who appeared in my past vision, chasing me in the city streets along the River Thames. But, his face was not morbidly scarred like that of Lord Russell.

"I am so confused," I said with a sigh of desperation.

"Are you all right?" she inquired with concern. "I hope that he did not try to harm you, or follow you back to the estate house?"

"I'm fine now, but I must admit, my encounter with him was unnerving, and as foolish as this may sound, he actually reminded me in some absurd manner of Kendall, or even his brother, Lord Russell." I told Marcella that it was really ludicrous for me to think like this, but that is exactly what I sensed. Somehow, I could only believe that I had not seen the last of this fellow. More would be revealed, all within due time.

"Yes," she said. "Give this time. Trust and have faith. You know there is a reason for all that occurs within our lives. Nothing in life is an accident or coincidental. Destiny will ultimately always have the final word in life."

"Thank you, Marcella. By the way, where has Clara disappeared to?"

"She journeyed into the village to purchase some fabric, herbs, candles and oils. It has been quite awhile now. Perhaps when Clara returns, we shall all convene and partake in a glass of claret. Would you be open to conversing about this further?" Marcella asked.

"It would be comforting to speak with Clara as well. I'm not sure, however, that I would welcome Lindsey's presence. I simply do not trust her, nor have I for a long time."

222

"The two of you must learn to get over your disagreements from the past once and for all. Lindsey really can be a very lovely and sensitive soul when she makes an effort to do so."

"Maybe she just chooses not to be a sensitive soul around the likes of me," I said.

I told Marcella that I had made countless attempts to bury the hatchet, extending my kindness to Lindsey, but every time I did, she took full advantage of me, once again betraying my trust and confidence.

"I really should set some boundaries," I continued. "I need to be more aware of how I interact with her. Although I will attempt to give more effort to be peaceful with Lindsey, do not expect me, however, to open my soul to her this evening. My life is not an open book when it comes to confiding in Lindsey."

"Very well," Marcella said, reluctantly. "When Clara returns from the village, we shall all get together. Maybe you will feel differently then, about Lindsey?"

"A glass of wine would be splendid," I replied, but do not get your hopes up about me changing my mind," I insisted, even more adamantly. "Until Clara returns, I'll be in the drawing room, playing my piano."

Sitting in solitude upon my piano bench, I contemplated my feelings regarding Kendall, Lord Russell, Dr. Alexis, Bishop Bartholomew and Elijah Foster. Everything inexplicably seemed to constantly return to only one...the doctor. I pondered why I could not get this man out of my head. It was as if I found myself constantly yearning and craving him - morning, noon and night. Was this an obsession or could it really be love? One thing was for certain; my heart could no longer deny that I felt his essence every day.

Would Dr. Alexis promptly answer my correspondence? I longed to hear from him. All I understood at this time was the presence of a compelling force between us. I felt as if a silver cord linked us wherever we might be and I sensed that we would always be joined in some way, shape or form.

Although this was a comfort to me, it was so very confusing, for I truly believed that a bond with Kendall, Lord Russell, Elijah and the Bishop had also existed in the past. Here too, was attraction that I could not deny, nor ignore. Even though I sensed that my intimacy with them was all for a reason, I wanted to believe they, too, must have felt more than merely friendship towards me. Had my pregnancy gone well, I wondered about the reality that Elijah would have been the father of my child.

I continued to juggle the idea that perhaps I should make contact with the Bishop to absolve him of any responsibility for my pregnancy. I wondered if perhaps by doing so, his feelings for me might alter in a positive way. I concluded that I should write…"I pray to the Higher Powers for clarity," I murmured, as I departed to the privacy of my chambers and drafted a letter with quill pen and sepia ink.

Seventeen July, 1811

Dearest Samuel,

Although it has been quite some time since we last communicated, I received your correspondence dated 11 April, 1811, and I pray my letter today finds you in good health and spirits.
Of course, I am most understanding of your busy schedule with public appearances, counseling, aiding and assisting the many lost souls who are beckoning for your Divine words and blessings. I understand the comfort that you can give to a woman.

Please know, that I plan on returning to London sometime within the month of September. I will be residing at Worthington Estate once again and welcome you to join me for tea, should you be agreeable to sharing an afternoon

*together. I have important matters to discuss. One, of which you urgently
need to be informed, is…my pregnancy terminated abruptly with the passing of
my child. Only now, have I been able to determine that you played no role, for
the father of this child was distinctly that of another…a man of African
blood.*

With Warmest Regards,

Grace Worthington

*Thornwood Estate
Boscastle, England*

I sealed the envelope, stamping it with the beeswax and the
Thornwood Estate seal. On this occasion, I personally welcomed
the task of taking the letter in hand. Quickly, I ran to the stables in
search of the coachmen. It was paramount that I find them before
the return of Clara from the village, in order to insure the
confidentiality of my actions. At last, locating Michael alone at the
stables, I observed him grooming one of his horses.

"Thank the Higher Powers that you are here," I said with relief.
"But, where is John?"

"He's gone…left for Boscastle with Madam Clara and dis
matter of delivery of yaw letter to Dr. Alexis. The courier will be
takin care of all dis."

"That's excellent, but it's vital that we keep this amongst
ourselves. I hope that I need not remind you, how private I am
concerning my personal life. The last thing I need, is for Lindsey
to catch wind of any of my correspondences."

Michael nodded his head, implying his full understanding of the
situation. "I have important business for you again," I continued.
"It will be necessary for you to deliver, yet still another letter to
the courier with explicit instructions."

I told Michael to instruct the courier that no one was to accept this document other than the Bishop himself, encouraging him to swiftly make his departure before any of the sisters discovered his whereabouts. "Clara will be returning from the village very shortly," I insisted. "Please hurry. May the Higher Powers protect all of us, if Lindsey should catch wind of this."

"Yeah, me lady," he replied nodding his head.

"It is absolutely imperative this letter be delivered to only the Bishop Samuel Bartholomew,," I said again, reinforcing the urgency of my words. "Do I make myself perfectly clear?"

"Indeed, me lady," Michael said, taking the letter from my extended hand. "And dis here courier shall kill both birds at twonce with delivery of dese letters for both the doctor and the Bishop."

Of course, I was well aware of the fact that not all those within Thornwood Estate were presently encouraging me to pursue a personal involvement with Dr. Christophe Alexis, nor the Bishop Samuel Bartholomew. I had my reasons, however, for wishing at this point to have all communication with both men kept to my discretion. I also realized that I was placing tremendous trust in Josephina, Caron, Mr. Abernathy, as well as my coachmen. In the past they had all sworn to secrecy regarding these intimate matters of the heart. I knew they were worthy, for never had they given me any reason to doubt their loyalty.

Michael immediately departed on horse for the village of Boscastle, taking a clandestine route through the forest. A tan leather shoulder-pouch strapped tightly about him, concealed the letter to Bishop Bartholomew. No sooner had I entered into the estate house, I could hear the thundering of the horses in the distance. The black carriage was approaching, winding its return towards Thornwood Estate.

Within minutes, the coach had reached the massive black gates. As I waited outside, Mr. Abernathy had also heard the distant rumbling, joining me to welcome Clara back from her journey.

"Where has Lindsey run off to? Or, is she lurking closely in the garden?" I inquired.

"I believe she is at her quarters," Mr. Abernathy replied.
"That's absolutely perfect," I said. "I pray that Marcella, Clara and I, may meet for an aperitif as soon as possible. Please summon the house servants to have both port and claret brought to us in the drawing room, preferably without Lindsey's knowledge."

I was worried, anxiously anticipating the upcoming evening discussion with the sisters. Lindsey had already voiced her malicious unsolicited opinion regarding Bishop Bartholomew, Lord Russell, Elijah, Kendall and Dr. Alexis. Furthermore, I could only sense that Marcella and Clara would not be in agreement with my rekindled interest in pursuing more than a friendship with the doctor. Additionally, I knew my past affairs with both Elijah and the Bishop would be points of major contention. I breathed deeply, trying to relax before the discussion commenced.

Pacing within the drawing room, I speculated for a brief moment as to why I was even placing myself in this soul-baring situation? Was I deceiving myself? Indeed, I already knew the answer to my query. I needed to find my balance and harmony. I ached within, yearning to heal and regain my equilibrium, so that I could at last view my life with more clarity. I believed that the mystical sisters would speak the truth to me. I pondered, however, if I would be strong enough to accept all that was about to be revealed. Would the Higher Powers at last enlighten me, shining a ray of brilliant white light upon my many unanswered questions? Even with these uplifting thoughts, reality found me still standing within the shadow of uncertainty. What was to be my destiny?

Patricia Grace Joyce   *The Magic of Time*

Eighteen

There are three women by the sea
Who live a life of mystery
A life they chose before this time
Assisting those who seek to find
Their destiny in this lifetime

Beyond the veil, another place
The energy of spirit space
The images of choices made
Revealing all that's meant to be
These Mystic Women by the sea

For several agonizing moments, I paced back-and-forth, awaiting the sisters' arrival within the drawing room. As Marcella and Clara entered the room, we each took our respective seats about the ebony-colored round table. The port and claret were most welcome, the finest from Paris and were displayed elegantly in crystal decanters with a selection of delectable French petit fours and sweet chocolate truffles.

The house servants poured and served the libations in French crystal stemware, as Clara prepared to speak.

"Marcella tells me that you have something on your mind, that you need to discuss some issues? I was wondering when you would grow to this point, Grace. I must say, I'm pleased you desire to share your concerns with us for more clarification."

"Tell me what I must do," I anxiously blurted aloud.

"Keep in mind that we may only advise you," she continued. "We know, ultimately you are going to do things as you choose, yet hopefully you will take into consideration what we convey as well. We shall reveal that which we see for you at this point in time. This is all we can do. Your free will and the power of prayer, however, may alter, influence, highlight and even transform the fates and the destinies to some degree. Anything is possible in life, but remember that timing is of the essence. There is an aura of time that surrounds each, any every one of us in this lifetime. Everything that is fated and destined will truly happen within its own time. However, depending upon our choices in life, a matter may be colored as a slightly different variation of what is to be. Do you understand?"

"I recognize there are many choices in life," I remarked impatiently. "Now please tell me what the future holds."

Marcella presented to me, a deck of two-and-fifty playing cards as Clara arose to light the white candles about the room. Taking a sprig of sage within her hand, Clara held it to the flame. As she walked within the room, waving the lighted sprig within the air, she dispersed the fragrant aroma in an effort to ward-off any incarnate spirits who might be lurking to interfere with what was about to transpire on this night.

"Firstly, shuffle the playing cards," Marcella said in her raspy voice. "When you're ready, cut the deck into three stacks." She told me that she would lay the cards accordingly, in a face-up position from each of the three piles. The individual cards and their placement would determine all to be seen into the future–my destiny.

"Do you have any questions?" Marcella inquired.

"Not at this time. Please let's continue," I said anxiously, taking the deck of cards from her hands and eagerly following her instructions. After shuffling the cards, I cut the deck into three separate piles. Watching her with keenness, I observed Marcella place each card into a designated position...turning the cards over, one-by-one, until they were openly laid before me in a symmetrical grid-pattern upon the tabletop. Closing her eyes,

230

Marcella sat in silence for several seconds, pausing before she began to speak.

"Let's begin this reading," she continued, looking into my alert eyes. "Presently, you are represented by the center card–the Queen of Hearts. The major vibration that we see in your reading involves one of healing to instill a new path to the heart, to create a path of love in your life. We see that it's necessary for you to embrace the present time for healing and renewal."

"Pardon me," I said, interrupting her. "What do you mean by stating, *we?*"

"I am referring to those spirits beyond the veil who are in attendance for your reading tonight. They bring insightful messages for you."

"Is there anything I should do or say?" I asked.

"The only thing required at this time is for you to be still and listen. Trust that whatever I say is absolutely necessary to be shown to you at this time in your life."

I nodded my head as Marcella smiled and continued speaking.

"We also must urge you to only focus upon yourself and your creative interests at this time. There is a very high vibration regarding words that are coming through to me, something related to writing in this lifetime."

Marcella told me that I had been through tremendous emotional pain. She advised me to remain grounded and to seek the discovery of my balance and harmony through the use of language…healing through the written word.

"Before you become involved again with any man in the future, we believe you must heal and discover who you really are, your true purpose within this lifetime. You have not chosen, however, an easy life," she continued. "Your task is to develop only *you* at this time, then to share your wealth of knowledge and lessons by healing others emotionally, physically, mentally and spiritually with your energies."

"Do you see a man in my future? A doctor?" I inquired, longing for confirmation of my heart's desire.

"We do see Dr. Christophe Alexis," she continued. "However, you really know relatively very little about him. He has not divulged much about himself, other than the matter of stating he works to such a degree that he is incapable of creating time in his life for a fine woman. We remember very well his conversation in your bedroom suite after he examined you, and that hanky-panky embrace when he returned to your chambers."

"But, Marcella," I interrupted as my face blushed to a bright pink. "You cannot deny that he is a good person, a fine and compassionate soul."

"This is all true," she said. "He has many lovely qualities. The doctor is an outstanding human being and well respected in the field of medicine. We believe that you have known this man from a prior life. In fact, we would even go as far as stating, that the two of you have been husband and wife many times in past lives. There is a deep soul connection, a silver cord of radiant light connecting you to him. We sense that your role in this lifetime, however, remains to be seen. Your present life may run its course fairly similar to a role in the past, but your relationship with the doctor is, yet to be. There is a deep sadness within him, a gut-wrenching emotional pain and turmoil, and it appears there is something of significance that he is not telling you."

"What could this be?" I inquired.

"For whatever the reasons may be, he chooses to hide behind his work. There is an issue within his heart that he is withholding from you. Something is not quite clear. We sense, his choice to hide is really a device serving to protect his heart, so that he may continue to ignore what really needs to be dealt with in this lifetime. This picture, however, is not completely lucid. More will show itself over time."

"Why is he hiding something from me?" I insisted.

"It is not for you to ask *why* at this point," she replied. "Let the matter reveal itself when the timing is appropriate. We know that you care about the doctor.

"What shall I do?"

"Continue to let him know that you are a friend, that you truly care about him. This is all that is necessary. Although the doctor is your heart's desire at this time, rest assure he is not the only gentleman who will play a role in your life. We see several lovely male entities who will attempt to come into your life. Have you even heard from Dr. Alexis since that day in February?"

"Looking at Marcella with excitement, I answered, "Actually, yes." I explained to the sisters, the manner in which the doctor had briefly stopped by Thornwood Estate quite unexpectedly, not too long ago, to visit with me in the rose gardens. I told them that I believed it to be purely coincidental. Although I thought at the time, his visit was somewhat odd, it truly was a lovely encounter.

"Nothing in life is merely coincidental," Marcella said. "There is a reason for everything. How do you honestly feel about this unexpected visit from him? I sense more hanky-panky."

"Well, it was all quite puzzling," I said awkwardly to the sisters. "He was dove hunting and claimed to observe me from the outskirts of the woods. He said that he was drawn to me like a magnet, that he had this overwhelming attraction to come see me. He told me that he wanted to try to stay in touch."

"Has Dr. Alexis stayed in contact with you? Has he communicated and corresponded with you?"

"I have not heard from him, not even a peep, yet I know he wants me to remain in communication with him," I continued.

"Grace, these matters of the heart must be navigated slowly, Marcella said. "We have seen that romance must begin as a mutual friendship, to truly grow and blossom. Love takes time, and love takes two individuals that willingly want to give and share with each other. Love must be nurtured and cared for like a precious rose."

"I can explain all of this," I interrupted.

"Please, do so," Marcella continued.

"The doctor told me that it would be very difficult for him to reply to my letters for weeks, to even months, due to his busy schedule in London. He has so many patients, surgeries and a tremendous case load. I understand how weary he must be."

"I pray, one day you will learn that for a relationship to thrive and grow, it must have a balance–a give and a take. For a friendship to grow and become love, there must be a mutual ebb and flow, like a river that meanders and hugs its graceful banks, a harmony of two souls appreciating the true essence of each other. It cannot be one person giving and the other person taking, nor can one person be acknowledging and the other person choosing not to deal with life."

I sat in silence, continuing to listen intently as Marcella spoke.

"You say he cannot respond to your letters any sooner than weeks, to even months at the very earliest?" she inquired.

"Yes," I replied, with confusion.

"This is something we simply do not understand," Marcella continued. "Quite possibly, this is a clear sign that the doctor is either not interested in developing a friendship, or shall I go even further in stating he is not interested in creating an honorable relationship with you. Perhaps, however, this is merely a picture of fear that we see on his part."

Marcella told me that two of the greatest powers in life were love and fear. "We would like to say that he is merely frightened at this time. We sense that he fears making contact with you," she said. "We do see, however, much personal conflict going on within him. But, he is an intelligent man. Yes, we sense it is more a picture of fear than a disinterest regarding this matter of the heart. He is not ignoring you intentionally. We believe that he thinks about you every day. Trust and continue to pray to the Higher Powers that all will be well."

"I too, think of him each day," I said as I prayed in silence that all would be well.

Clara suddenly stood up and walked around the table to sit next to me. "Like the doctor, you also have many fears to overcome," she said. "We see you surrounded by tremendous anxiety, concerned there may never be another trustworthy soul in your life again."

I nodded my head, acknowledging her statement.

"This makes perfect sense to us, since your trust has been gravely violated in the past." She continued, "We encourage you to keep the faith and to understand that in doing so, one day you will be able to regain your confidence in life."

Clara told me to give this matter some time, and to simply let life present all that needed to manifest forth. "Believe in what we say," she continued. "If a man wants you to become part of the inner circle of his life, he will absolutely put you there. Dr. Alexis's behavior at the present time is unacceptable to us. We question that he would wait this long to respond. If a man wants to get a woman's attention, he knows how and most definitely will."

Sitting motionless, I listened intently and with awe to all that she was saying. Clara continued, "Dr. Alexis claims that he has some sense of energy, or a connection with you. We know that you felt this *spark* as well, but we must caution you, the doctor may not be able to move forward with his emotions. We strongly feel that you must keep your heart open." Clara also told me there would be other fine, nurturing, respectable gentlemen who might sweep me off of my feet. "You are a cherished soul," she continued. "Do not underestimate your appeal to men. They adore you beyond a doubt, primarily because you are fair, honest, kind, feminine, elegant, pleasant, understanding, open-minded, intelligent and compassionate."

235

This was all so overwhelming for me as I listened, trying to absorb the pieces of information that the sisters were revealing.

Clara continued, "We highly believe that the doctor may play a significant role in your life one day. However, this is a matter that still needs to evolve and be played out. It will present itself in due time."

Clara told me that by actively trying to pursue this man, however, I would only delay what was to be revealed. "Everything happens within its own time," she continued. "You must let time reveal all to you, when it is the appropriate occasion."

"Is their nothing that I can do?" I exclaimed.

She replied, "You do not want to create a relationship with Dr. Alexis within an inappropriate time frame, simply for the reason that if you do, the spirit world is stating that the bond will not be fulfilled. You must live your life and let the doctor live his. Then, perhaps one day when you least likely expect to hear from him, the two of you may be reunited."

As I sat at the table, my mind was totally focused upon Clara's words. "Although we see this strong attraction between you and the doctor, we also see the image of another handsome fair-haired man with light eyes. He is extremely drawn to you, but there is something rather unusual about him. Hmmm," she continued, pausing to reflect. "I do not know exactly what this is. Initially you will be curious about him, that is…until you discover the truth. In fact, you may be quite astounded as to what is revealed."

"Could this be the gentleman who I met this evening while walking along the coast?"

"Possibly," she replied. "The spirit world, however, is still showing me that you are, and will continue to attract an assortment of gentlemen into your life. Of course, we must observe and consider the type of individual, someone is attracting. Sometimes a person may draw undesirable and lowly entities into

236

their life. In your particular situation we see a mixture of people–some are fine, honorable and evolved, but we must caution you to beware of the negative entities that will try to enter you life."

Clara further explained that she saw me having to think about making decisions–picking and choosing from some of these men in the months to come. She prayed that I would make the right choices in my personal life and have clarity. Fortunately, the spirit world was showing her that I would have the presence of lucidity about me.

"Oh, Clara, I am so enamored with this doctor!" I insisted. "I can no longer deny that I have developed feelings of affection for him. I have reached a point, where my inner voice, my heart is telling me to listen and to follow my truths. I must admit, at times I remain confused, and I find my feelings shifting, since I am still attracted to the Bishop, and sometimes I even desire to be with Elijah."

"Although there is this great desire where the doctor is concerned, we do see the Bishop as well. However, this is not something that the spirit world is encouraging. We see the doctor, the Bishop and Elijah playing very different roles in your life. More needs to be revealed in order for you to make a clear decision about these men. The spirit world is also showing me a picture of what looks to be Lord Russell Worthington. This is perplexing to us. Are you still involved with him?"

"You must be mistaken. I have absolutely no interest in Russell," I insisted, gazing in awe at each of the sisters.
"It seems as if he remains to have a rather keen interest in you," Clara said. "Quite obviously, you are unaware of his love."

"Love?" I inquired. "Russell and I are only of the past, something that was at one time in my life," I maintained. "Our affair is over. He and I were only briefly intimate prior to my relationship with Kendall."

"For you, it may be a relationship of the past, but I am seeing that this man has never forgotten you. We definitely feel as if he will try to make contact with you again. Yes, he has an overwhelming desire, an all-consuming interest in you. We would even go so far as to state, that Lord Russell is obsessed with you.

"What should I do?"

"Clara continued, "Until that time presents itself, the spirit world is saying you must be patient and remain mindful that everything happens in its own time. Timing has a destiny of its own."

Marcella interrupted, "We really think this issue of your attraction to the doctor and the various gentlemen that are connected to you, is something that will transpire to be a secondary matter. What is clearly paramount at this time, is the subject of you continuing to grow and to develop yourself."

Putting it rather bluntly, Clara told me that the spirit world really did not care what happened within the lives of the gentlemen who could potentially enter into my life. The sisters were only concerned at this time about me and all that kept me healthy. "You must remain balanced and in harmony, fulfilling yourself, so you may assume the healing role that the Universe has intended."

As I listened to Marcella and Clara speak that night, I became increasingly motivated to move forward with my life. They stressed it was imperative that I strive to remain optimistic and to consider my needs with benevolence—to nurture myself with love, dignity, honor and respect. For, if I do not first honor and love myself, then who will?

They told me that I must consider myself worthy—truly deserving of having a happy, fulfilling, loving life with someone special. The sisters insisted that if I believe all of this deep within my heart and soul, then it will one day be possible to attract a wonderful soul who is as worthy of me, as I am indeed deserving of him.

They encouraged me to live my life–to trust and keep my heart open to Dr. Alexis, confirming there was a strong spiritual bond and physical connection between us.

"Let the doctor live his life, as you uphold the belief that perhaps one day he might awaken from this slumber of fears, and reach for you. He will realize that you have truly been a friend to him–a kind, trustworthy, compassionate, loyal and loving soul. The sisters continued to further explain, that the spirit world was well aware of my feelings for Dr. Alexis. They understood that I loved this man, but it was necessary for the doctor to awaken to his personal feelings within his own time. At present, the consensus seemed to be, for me to merely *bless and release* this man, to remain detached from him.

"This will pose quite a challenge," I said.

I told the sisters, although I wanted the doctor in my world, I was quite cognizant of the fact there was little-to-nothing that I could do, or say to make this a reality at this time. His choice to ignore me, avoiding any communication and interaction was of his world, not mine. I simply did not exist in his realm. If all of these prophecies were true, I could only surmise that it was not the appropriate time for a relationship with Dr. Alexis. However, I knew that I must now take on the onerous task of trying to convince myself *to bless and release* him.

The sisters informed me that I possessed tremendous creativity, that it was just bursting to pour forth from within me. They believed that I would share this creativity with the world one day through my healing energies. And they urged me to remain focused upon myself for now–to nurture and develop all of my creative abilities and talents, so that one day I may give my work to the world.

"Write, play your music, paint and work your magic. In doing so, you will heal yourself and grow to understand why all of this is occurring in your life. Trust and have faith that the doctor does care about you. He is simply not ready to become involved with you, nor any other woman at this point. He has much growing of his own to do. If you are truly a friend, you will give Dr. Alexis the time and space to develop and grow spiritually as well. Keep repeating, *I bless and release you.* This will get easier with each new day."

"Am I to live as if a nun in a convent for my remaining days and nights, just waiting for all of this to transpire?" I inquired. "Is this to be my fate?"

"There are many possibilities," Marcella said. "By *blessing and releasing* this man from your thoughts, you will open the door for other male admirers to enter your world. There will be lessons to gain from all of them, more opportunity for personal growth."

The sisters revealed they sensed these potential men in my life would appear to teach me more about myself, each playing various roles. I, in turn, would have something to also offer and teach each, and every one of them. The spirit world viewed this as being positive.

"There are lessons to be learned by all of us along the path that we choose to walk," Marcella continued. The sisters told me, however, that I must not merely sit and wait for anything, nor anyone, especially in relation to my personal life.

"Enough of this grieving over the past!" Clara declared.

"Enough of this waiting for the Bishop, Elijah and the doctor to reach for you! It's time you finally took control of your life. *Bless and release* all of them and move forward. If something is meant to be, know in due time that it will truly present itself."

I thought about what the sisters had said on this night. Although it was all fine in theory, I seemed to be having great difficulty with fully understanding this concept of *blessing and*

240

releasing. Even though I understood that I must move forward with my life, at the same time I was emotionally torn, yearning to be with my heart's desire.

"We know that the mind, the body, the heart and the soul all have their hungers," Marcella said. "But you must ask yourself if this is correct. Is this person that you desire, truly appropriate?" She told me to give these gentlemen some time, and most importantly, to give myself time to fully appreciate why I felt as if certain individuals should be in my life. As time passed, I would begin to understand who was the most significant and deserving individual to share a loving and fulfilling bond.

"All of your emotional turmoil and indecision will one day fade away," she said. "As time passes you will be able to clearly hear the whispers of your heart."

"Is it true that my husband may now only be someone of my past?" I inquired.

"In all honesty, we do not see Kendall playing a continuing role in your life," she replied, "This is primarily because he never has been truly connected to you—spiritually, physically, emotionally or mentally, however, he has not crossed over at this time. Kendall is still a presence within the physical world."

"I feel relieved in one sense," I said. "But, on the other hand, do you see me remaining a suspect in this case?"

"Let things be, and stop searching for an answer to this puzzling situation with Kendall," Clara replied. "Live your life, Grace. Merely trust. This is where the power of faith enters. All of your questions will be answered when the appropriate time is presented.

"There are great lessons to be learned from suffering and challenges. You are growing spiritually, learning many lessons as the time passes," continued Clara. "During the past months, I have seen that you have grown to have more patience in your life, to focus on what really matters for you to develop yourself and your varied creative abilities. You are learning to become the woman that you are destined to be in this life - the real Grace Worthington. One day you will come to the realization that love and compassion begin with honoring and respecting yourself. Only when you have embraced your personal value, will you be able to truly share your creative gifts with the world. It is at that moment, when your healing energy will radiantly disperse to nurture and guide those who surround you. Trust and continue to have faith, the light of life shines brightly within your heart and soul. All the answers are within you, waiting to be discovered."

I vowed to the sisters that I would keep the faith, especially during those very difficult times of striving to stay centered and focused on developing myself. I wanted to believe that my life experiences, both the benevolent and the bad, had truly served me many learned lessons and would continue to show me where I must venture into uncharted waters.

Clara said, "You have journeyed now to a place in your soul where you have never been before. You are moving beyond pain through your healing, and you shall continue to learn within all of your relationships. Hopefully, there will never be a need to repeat these lessons again."

"Do you see that I may one day determine my destiny?"

"Life must be lived in balance and harmony with compassion and respect for the self as well as for others, for one to truly fulfill their own destiny," she replied. "We all have a destiny on this good earth to fulfill, but there are many challenges and choices to make in creating what we are fated to manifest in this lifetime." She told me, life is an extraordinary and unique journey for each and every one of us.

My life was the path that I had chosen to write as my destiny, before I entered into this world. This was merely what I had chosen for myself. Now it was mandatory that I faced the many challenges and surmount the obstacles with courage and poise.

"Listen to the inner voice deep within you," Clara continued. "This is the heart of your soul. The whispers of the soul will always lead you to the truth."

Nineteen

My feelings rush, I dream at times
Anticipating your sweet eyes
I think of you with lust and sigh
Now just a memory dancing by

Trust in your heart, time will surely tell
A flow and rhythm that all is well
Patience and practice, teach us to accept
Time is a process worthy of respect

The warmth of August, passed slower than the dripping of viscous sap from a majestic spruce tree. I found myself still anxiously awaiting correspondence from Constable Gordon, Bishop Bartholomew and Dr. Alexis. Each day seemed like an endless struggle, with not so much as a solitary word from London. Life had become increasingly confounding, and I was reluctant to focus upon my writing. Oftentimes, I found myself daydreaming, fantasizing in an imaginary world that involved solely me, and my various love interests. This matter of *blessing and releasing* was certainly posing an overwhelming test for me, more than I could have ever envisioned. Needless to say, Dr. Alexis continued to remain my heart's primary desire. Nearly a month had passed since my last unanswered correspondence to him. I continued to try to *bless and release* the doctor from my thoughts. Some days, however, proved to be more taxing than others. Creating a distraction, I busied myself with the preparations for my much anticipated journey.

Though matters were in a constant state of disarray, I looked forward to embarking…hopeful that the month of September would return me to the grand city of London. Yet, uncertainty prevailed as to determining an exact date of departure.

"Josephina and Caron," I said. "I think it best that we begin to pack." Within my indecisiveness, I told my attendants that I might even want to depart earlier than I had originally intended. I could not bear to be kept in this state of limbo any longer, waiting in eagerness each day for a message from afar or any indication as to what was happening with Kendall's disappearance.

An overbearing sense of stagnation consumed me. I felt unproductive and dismal. As I thought about what to do, to ease this emotional torture, I only knew one thing for certain. It now became necessary for me to take control and end this situation. Josephina responded, "We are happy to assist."

Caron nodded her head and spoke, "We are looking forward to returning to London with you."

Without my attendants' assistance, I realized that I would be even more scattered than I already was at the present time, however, with the preliminary stages of my packing well underway, I paused, requesting Josephina and Caron to depart from my chambers.

"Ladies, I truly need a moment to collect myself this evening." Josephina and Caron promptly dismissed themselves, returning to the servants' quarters as I prepared to pen my thoughts upon paper. I considered that if I were to write a verse, it might serve to help me *bless and release* Dr. Alexis, Bishop Bartholomew and even Elijah from my thoughts.

I bless and release you
From my presence of mind
This stress to appease you
Is obsessing me blind…

246

Nightfall softly surrounded the Thornwood estate house, like a baby cuddled within a woolen blanket. The thundering gallop of a horse's hoofs could be heard approaching swiftly as I labored within the bedroom chamber, organizing and repacking my assortment of clothing that would accompany me to London. I arose swiftly from my chaise. Peering out from my chamber window, I observed a courier on horseback standing before the entrance to the estate house.

"Thank the Higher Powers," I murmured. "I pray this is word from Christophe, or possibly from Samuel." Rattled with confusion, I anticipated the notion that it might in reality be a response from the Constable.

I ran from my chamber, descending the massive spiral staircase to meet the courier. Before I had arrived, however, I found Mr. Abernathy standing in the foyer to accept a white parcel in hand. As I came onto the scene, I leaped in earnest from the last stair, firmly planting myself in front of him within the center of the marble foyer.

"Mr. Abernathy, please tell me this is a message from London," I pleaded, hopeful there would be benevolent news awaiting.

With a look of puzzlement upon his face, he responded, "I believe that it might actually be from out of the country." Mr. Abernathy told me that the courier had mentioned this was a parcel from Paris, France.

Surprised, I continued to interrogate him for information. "Is it for me?"

"It appears to be addressed in the name of Madam Lindsey," he said, pausing to clear his throat.

"Lindsey?" I remarked with disappointment. "Who is it from?" Mr. Abernathy hesitated, "Lord Russell Worthington."

Stunned, I instantly grasped the envelope from Mr. Abernathy's hands and read the elegant writing for myself. I absolutely

247

believed that unquestionably he must have been mistaken. Surely, the letter was for me. Although a well-spoken man, Mr. Abernathy was not highly educated in matters of reading, nor writing, but upon examining the parcel I could not fathom my very own eyes. The writing was as plain as the sepia ink upon the white parchment. In fact, the sender was truly, none other than, my despicable brother-in-law, Lord Russell.

"What could this be?" I murmured. I thought about the notion why Russell would have ever been in contact with Lindsey. What would possess him to journey to Paris? Reluctant to return the letter to Mr. Abernathy, my mind drifted in a hundred directions. I suddenly became more than eager to find Lindsey, hopeful of discovering the answers to some of my questions.

"Mr. Abernathy," I persisted. "Find Lindsey. She must open and read this letter immediately."

Taking the correspondence from my clenched hand, Mr. Abernathy sent two of the house servants on a mission to determine the whereabouts of Madam Lindsey that evening. Somehow, I sensed that locating her would be more of a chore, than I would be up for. Lindsey never made her whereabouts common knowledge, and she could be just about anywhere—in her quarters, in the village, or even, I dare say, strolling within the St. Symphorian Church cemetery. All I knew was, I must possess that correspondence. I prayed that Lindsey was at home this evening. I simply had to know what was going on. It was imperative that I found some answers soon, or I felt as if I would lose my mind. Mr. Abernathy exited the Thornwood Estate house as I followed closely at his side, like a bee hovering about a sweetly scented blossom of clover. We were on a mission to find Lindsey.

Within several minutes of frenzied exploration at the cemetery and the barn, at last we observed the distant glow of candlelight within her residence. We approached the main entry doors.

"Madam Lindsey," Mr. Abernathy said, tapping upon the entry doors. Only silence prevailed as we anxiously awaited a reply. He continued, "I have an envelope that was delivered in your name."

I listened intently, hopeful that she would hear his plea and come forward to answer the door. Within seconds, the unlocking sound of the heavy metal bolt rang true as the massive oak door barely opened. Only the width of a small crack welcomed our presence. Lindsey peered outward, looking upon us with disgust.

"Speak, for I have no time for your folly," she commanded.

"Pardon my intrusion, Madam Lindsey," Mr. Abernathy continued with reverence. "I come with urgent business, a delivery of a parcel in your name."

Slowly opening the door a smidge wider, Lindsey awaited the document. At that moment, clutched within her hand, I observed what was doubtless one of her many clandestine spell casting manuals. This one in particular was entitled *The Season of the Moon.* Looking out from the darkened entry, she spoke with feigned intrigue, "For me? Who could this be from?"

"It's from Lord Russell," I rudely blurted aloud, interrupting the conversation. Staring upon me with odd curiosity, Lindsey snatched the envelope from within Mr. Abernathy's extended hand. I observed her face glowing, brighter than the radiance of twenty candles as she perused the handwriting upon the envelope. In doing so, she looked up, continuing to keenly observe me, all the while focused upon my increasingly paling face.

"I'm curious as to why my brother-in-law would have reason to correspond with you?" I persisted. Throughout my nine years of marriage to Kendall, the elusive Lord Russell had barely made an effort to even communicate with me, yet alone, with any family members in Boscastle.

Lindsey remained silent, intently shifting the envelope, turning it over-and-over within her hands. "I find this all very unusual," I continued. "Don't you?"

"Absolutely," she replied. "It's very peculiar. I cannot imagine why he would want to be in touch with me, but needless to say, he truly has written. How dear of him! Now if you don't mind, I prefer to read this document within the privacy of my chambers."

This was most definitely, not the response I desired to hear from her. I sensed there was more to this document than she was revealing. I even wondered if quite possibly, Lindsey had been anticipating its arrival. Trying to think quickly, I suggested an alternative.

"Why not read the letter to me as well? Perhaps Russell might even make mention of Kendall? I have been on pins-and-needles, awaiting some word regarding his disappearance. It has been weeks since my correspondence to Constable Gordon, and still there is no reply."

"Oh, Grace," she responded. "You have been waiting months to hear about developments in your husband's case. What difference does a few more weeks make? Relax and know that eventually the Constable will get around to replying to your letter. I have told you in the past that you must stop being so hopeful of Kendall ever being found. Hasn't it dawned upon you yet?"

"What?" I inquired, as I felt my face flush with warmth like the sudden fire in a burning field.

"It's quite obvious this dreadful case is not of paramount importance to the Constable."

I stared at her, trying to absorb her words…but wanting in reality to flee. "What are you saying?" I mumbled defensively as I grew angrier by the second.

She snapped at me, "Constable Gordon has written you off–just like your husband and so many others have done. Good night, my dear."

Clutching the letter securely within her hand, Lindsey slammed the door shut, leaving Mr. Abernathy and I standing baffled upon

250

the porch stoop. I now feared the impossible - never knowing the meaning of this puzzling correspondence.

As Lindsey bolted the entry door, I could only envision the pleasure that she would take sitting upon her bed, opening the letter ever so carefully so as not to tear any of the contents.

I was indeed, a desperate woman as I stared at Mr. Abernathy, hopeful of somehow gaining entry, hopeful of hearing anything— some clue or word from her regarding the letter's contents.

"It appears that she has spoken," Mr. Abernathy said, encouraging me to depart with him. "Come this way, Lady Grace. Madam Lindsey is definitely not what you need at this time." I could only imagine at this point that Lindsey dared not, to let me view this correspondence, and at the same time, I sensed that I would nearly die from the shock of its news.

Mr. Abernathy departed as I bid him farewell. I, however, insisted upon remaining at Lindsey's residence along the cliff side, hiding within the overgrown thicket of lush evergreen bushes beneath her bedroom chamber window. Discovering her window pane ajar, I sensed that good fortune was upon me, but I wondered if perhaps I had truly gone too far, willing to risk possible confrontation with her once again.

As I lay in waiting like a fox stalking its prey, I observed Lindsey opening the parcel, exhibiting great precision not to damage the document.

"Ah," she said, excitedly. It has been far too long since I have tasted the sweet nectar of love. I pray Russell will assist me with my plan at last."

I was thankful to the Higher Powers. At least I could hear Lindsey well enough within the room, to interpret most of her words. Through the veiled sheer-curtained window, I studied her sitting in silence as she began reading the letter with undivided attention. Lindsey appeared to read the letter a second time, as if to fully grasp all that was being conveyed to her.

251

She sighed and spoke, "I only wish my heart's desire, Dr. Alexis, was resting by my side. I must reprimand Russell," she continued. "He is taking too great a risk by sending correspondence to me at Thornwood Estate."

I thought it rather odd that Lindsey would be conversing with only herself inside the bedroom chamber. No doubt, she was oftentimes bizarre, yet I had never known her to engage in lengthy discussion alone. Was she losing her mind? Then the notion struck me, perchance she really was not alone. I attempted to get a clearer look within Lindsey's chamber space, all the while, careful not to draw attention and alert her to my presence.

My eyes searched within the dimly lit chamber, suddenly distracted by the vague outline of an elderly man, sipping a glass of what appeared to be red wine. He sat comfortably within the shadows. I gasped, catching myself just short of shouting aloud as I contemplated who this soul might possibly be. Staring in disbelief, at last I confirmed that the figure was none other than, Dr. Perry Harrington.

Although I had always questioned Lindsey's mental health, I absolutely knew that she was not physically ill. Now I pondered the matter of what business Dr. Harrington could possibly have involving Lindsey that necessitated his visit. Again, I wanted to flee, but at the same time, I remained stunned, my body frozen as a result of this unexpected discovery.

"Russell is such a naughty boy," Lindsey scolded. "His words speak volumes. It's quite obvious that he is consumed with overwhelming passion, but dear Russell must learn to handle his obsession for Grace in another manner," she continued, giving the letter to the doctor so that he might read the correspondence.

"Sending a letter by courier is far too perilous, should it land into the wrong hands!" she snapped. "Grace has already had her curiosity aroused, far too much. Now I must partake in the

252

onerous task of having to downplay all of this, as just some remote nonsensical letter."

"Try to have patience. It is only a matter of time," Dr. Harrington replied. "Do not worry yourself with the details. I assure you, I have taken care of everything. Grace will not be obstructing our way much longer. Lindsey, you know that we are all counting on your assistance with this matter."

I could not believe my ears. From the gist of this conversation, it was more than apparent that they were plotting against me. I sensed that my demise was inevitable if Dr. Harrington, Russell and Lindsey had anything further to say about it. I could only pray to the Higher Powers that the ensuing conversation would divulge additional detailed revelation.

Unfortunately, with these very thoughts, I observed Lindsey and Dr. Harrington exiting her private chambers to relocate within the interior of the drawing room. Although I tried to attune my hearing to what was being said, I was at a loss. I simply was not privileged to hear the remainder of the conversation that night. For well over what I had estimated to be at least an hour, Dr. Harrington lingered within the cottage.

At last, I observed the elderly doctor departing shortly thereafter, returning to his coach which stood clandestinely within the dense surrounding forest. As I remained in hiding, there was no indication, however, Lindsey might ever budge from within her cozy abode that evening.

My desire to learn of the letter's contents had now progressed well beyond a casual inquisitiveness. My only wish was to attempt to read the letter at some point, the sooner, the better, and hopefully it contained important clues. Firstly, I needed an explanation of Dr. Harrington's presence in Lindsey's room on this night. Secondly, what was Russell's motivation for writing the document? Lastly, quite possibly, the letter contained explicit evidence as to Kendall's fate.

Reluctantly, I surrendered, returning to the Thornwood Estate house. Pacing within my bedroom chamber, I thought about the likelihood of how I would ever be able to access the information I sought. Of course, Lindsey had no intention of voluntarily sharing the contents of a letter from Lord Russell with me, for I sensed, she was already quite envious of my past association with him. Furthermore, from the conversation that I had overheard, it became more and more obvious: Lindsey had a personal interest at this time in Dr. Christophe Alexis as well.

It is no secret that Lindsey had always been resentful of me and the men I entertained. As a matter of fact, she was envious of any man who looked at another woman. I wondered why she couldn't just let bygones-be-bygones and move on with her life? I no longer had any romantic interest regarding my brother-in-law. As far as I was concerned, Lindsey could have this loathsome man, yet my interest in Dr. Alexis was altogether another story. At this time, I was most certain that Lindsey, Russell and Dr. Harrington were up to something, and I did not sense that it was benign. This situation was becoming increasing burdensome.

Pondering the thought that Clara might be willing to assist me with some insight regarding this matter, I departed from my room in search of her, hopeful of summoning a guiding message from the spirit world. As I ambled down the long darkened hallway, my erratic path crossed with that of Caron and Josephina. In an instant, something seemed to possess me as I felt a tingling sensation all over my body. I swiftly motioned to my attendants to follow me.

"I require your assistance with a terribly urgent matter," I anxiously blurted aloud. "I know that I can trust you both and have full confidence that you will be able to aid me. Listen carefully. Here is what I am proposing."

"Of course. We are always at your service," Josephina replied.

"Wonderful. Please listen to my every word," I said. "I shall require one of you, to locate the letter that is within Lindsey's possession."

"What letter?" the attendants queried in harmony.

"I don't have much time to explain. I fear that Lindsey may destroy it." Hastily, I told Caron and Josephina my concerns regarding the situation of Lindsey's letter from Lord Russell Worthington. "I sense that it may very well reveal something pertinent to the investigation and the disappearance of Kendall. Which one of you is up for this task? Will it be you, Josephina or you, Caron?"

Both girls looked at each other with tremendous trepidation, pointing blindly at the other. Shrugging my shoulders, I shook my head in disapproval. "I know this is not going to be easy," I sighed. "But, I must have one of you slip quietly into Lindsey's residence this night and search her bedroom chamber. It may even have to be done while she is asleep. You know, she does sleep soundly, and this will only act to our advantage. Of course, there is some risk involved. I pray to the Higher Powers Lindsey will not awaken while you are venturing within her abode. Do you understand what I am requesting? I must get to the bottom of this. I need answers, for I have grown desperate for the clues to Kendall's fate."

Caron and Josephina looked at one another, mortified with the very thought of encountering Madam Lindsey within her private bedroom chambers.

"Lady Grace, surely, you of all people, realize that Madam Lindsey has tremendous powers to perform unspeakable acts of malice," Caron said with dread in her voice. "Do you remember the horrid spell she cast upon a long lost lover, the elegant Mr. Barnaby Radcliff?"

255

Josephina interrupted, "He was the most sought after bachelor in Boscastle, at least until Madam Lindsey got her evil hands on him."

"How could I ever forget?" I remarked. "However, that was then…and this is now. I will protect you. I'll help you. Together we will outsmart Lindsey."

"With all due respect, my lady…unfortunately your powers at this time are nil compared to those of Madam Lindsey," Josephina said, meekly.

I told Caron and Josephina that although my powers had waned over the years, I would invoke the aid of the spirit world to protect us. "I will beseech the blessings beyond the veil."

"It was a horrendous spell," Josephina continued, still not convinced of my assurances. "I remember Mr. Radcliff's dark-brown hair, turned completely white overnight as he swiftly aged into a feeble old man. Eventually in days to follow, it was even rumored that he mysteriously passed on. No sign of him remained, ever since that appalling night with Madam Lindsey."

I told Caron and Josephina that things were different now, explaining that my powers–the magic I had lost in years past–was slowly returning to me. I felt stronger and more confident that I would continue to nurture my own magical powers of the craft. I sensed that the essence of who I was becoming, was at last emerging from the depths of my lost past.

"Lady Grace, since you will not be intruding on Madam Lindsey, it's so much easier for you to speak positively of this situation. What if Madam Lindsey awakens, and I am standing squarely in front of her?" said Caron. "How am I to explain myself? I have absolutely no business in the privacy of her home, yet alone within the seclusion of her chamber suite."

Josephina interrupted, "I too, am fearful of Madam Lindsey, should she find me scavenging amongst her personal belongings. We all realize, she is the epitome of darkness. This is most dangerous for all of us. Oh, so terrible! Madam Lindsey will surely seek revenge on me and Caron, and then on you, Lady Grace. No one is immune to her wrath. This being the situation, I believe we shall need a few days to ponder your request. May we consider this for a while? I beg of you," Caron pleaded. "Permit us to give you our answer in a week's time."

"That is not acceptable. I require your help this evening," I insisted. "This matter is urgent and simply cannot wait until the end of the week. Timing is of the essence. You both have never let me down in the past. I know this can be done, and I will expect your answer within the hour."

Exasperated, I departed into the rose gardens, leaving Caron and Josephina alone to deliberate my pressing request.

"Josephina, I would feel better about this, if we both could act together," Caron said. "Might we both go into Madam Lindsey's bedroom chambers to locate the letter? You know, it could be anywhere, and I am fearful she may have already destroyed it."

Josephina replied, "This could be true, but what I dread the most is Madam Lindsey's wrath. If she should ever discover that you or I were involved with giving the letter to Lady Grace–well, I think you already understand the consequences. Our lives would be miserable from this day forward, truly a living hell. Madam Lindsey would make a point of wreaking havoc in our lives and ultimately would seek revenge even on Lady Grace."

"She is outrageously evil with no remorse for her victims," Caron said. "I absolutely believe that she is capable of casting a spell upon us. What if she had us injured or destroyed? What if we were to die? Moreover, what if Lady Grace was to perish?"

With great excitement Josephina interrupted, "I have an idea! Listen carefully. For this letter to be retrieved, we merely need to distract Madam Lindsey. Only then, will it be possible to safely rummage about her room. For certain, I will not venture into her suite during the night if she is physically present. Surely, she could

257

awaken and find us. I as well, would rather die, if this should happen. Arranging for her absence from the cottage would be the safest way. Don't you agree?"

"That's wonderful!" Caron replied. "But, I still have my reservations. Although Lady Grace wants this letter found this evening, and truly seems to believe the document contains some enlightening news, I have never known her to be so desperate and determined to do anything as devious as this."

"You and I both know that when Lady Grace has a sense about something, it usually transpires to be true. Though her powers have waned, she continues to radiate an aura of white light," Josephina said. "Thank the Higher Powers that she is a positive healing force in our world. For our sake, I pray to the Higher Powers that the magic has truly returned to Lady Grace."

"I dare not even think about what could happen, when the lightness of Lady Grace meets the darkness of Madam Lindsey," Caron said. "Furthermore, if Madam Lindsey remains within her chambers, I certainly do not wish to be the one who disturbs her. She could stay there throughout the duration of the entire night. You know, she has always been discreet about her activities. Perhaps, even as we speak, she is concocting strange potions and casting spells."

"I have another idea," Josephina said. "Listen carefully. Mr. Abernathy may be able to help us. Of all people, he unquestionably, would be able to distract Madam Lindsey. If we put our heads together, we could devise a foolproof plan."

"Brilliant! Let's find him," Caron shouted, grabbing Josephina by the arm. Immediately, Caron and Josephina departed on a hunt for Mr. Abernathy. Entering the marble foyer of the estate house, he approached them through the large entry doorway.

Josephina rushed forward and said, "Mr. Abernathy, you have to swear that you will not tell a soul. Promise this. Please. Please say you will."

258

"What?" he inquired with a look of clouded confusion within his eyes.

"Swear first and then we shall continue," she replied.

"Ladies, is this another one of your escapades? I do love your humorous antics, but what is this all about?"

"We shall tell you, only if you swear first to never utter a word of this to anyone," Caron replied. "Do you swear?

"Absolutely. Now what is it? What are you fussing about?"

"It's the letter."

"A letter?" he inquired.

"The parcel that was sent by Lord Russell to Madam Lindsey," Caron continued. "It's as if Lady Grace is on fire, just burning with curiosity to read its contents. She thinks that Lindsey is up to no good–something evil, and we believe this too."

"We all know that Madam Lindsey has a way of creating ill will, even from the most innocent of circumstances. What are you asking me to do?" he inquired, pausing as he stared at Caron and Josephina. "Do you expect me to retrieve the letter from Madam Lindsey? Because if you do, you both must be sick in the head."

"Mr. Abernathy, you are the only one we can trust," Josephina pleaded. "In all honesty, we are frightened to do this alone. Perhaps, you could merely distract her? Caron and I will then search her bedroom chambers. Could you do this for us?"

Mr. Abernathy stood before them, his face perplexed with the situation presented by Josephina and Caron.

Josephina continued, "More importantly, could you do this for Lady Grace? That is all we ask of you."

"Yes," said Caron. "This is all we request. It should be simple to distract Madam Lindsey since she likes you; rather, she lusts after you like her desire of any man donning a pair of well-hung pantaloons. Maybe you could go so far as to flirt a bit with her, or even a good deal more?

259

"Oh, yes," Josephina said, giggling uncontrollably. "That would be absolutely perfect. You could tease her! You know that she absolutely adores you. I can almost hear her voice in my head, *Oh, Bradford, observing you is always such pleasant scenery.*"

Mr. Abernathy blushed as he listened to Caron and Josephina carrying on in jest.

"Well," he sighed. "Firstly, I want you to understand that if I agree to this, it is only because I am doing so on behalf of Lady Grace. She is beautiful and kind. If I should ever be able to kiss Lady Grace's soft full lips one day, that would truly be a dream!"

"Mr. Abernathy, that *is* truly a dream," Josephina said. "And it's never going to happen. Lady Grace is too busy lusting after the Bishop, Dr. Alexis and even Elijah Foster to ever notice the likes of you."

"Hush, Josephina, stop your cruelty," Caron interrupted. "Of course, Mr. Abernathy is entitled to his fantasies, but for the time being, Mr. Abernathy, you are just going to have to settle for a piece of Madam Lindsey's derriere!"

With a broad smile upon his face, Mr. Abernathy egotistically replied, "Very well, ladies. I shall take great pleasure in luring Madam Lindsey into the night air with me. It's quite possible she may want to stroll with me this evening on the estate grounds. So, listen carefully. Here's my plan."

Mr. Abernathy told Caron and Josephina that he would deliver a note to Madam Lindsey's residence, clandestinely slipping an invitation under her door to meet by the St. Symphorian Church cemetery gates on the northwest side of Thornwood Estate. He reminded the French sisters that Madam Lindsey was a needy soul, ready to jump on anything, or anyone who showed her the smallest inkling of attention.

"We shall see how far this goes," he said. "If all fairs according to plan, I believe that I shall receive even more than I bargained for. I am up for this challenge!"

260

Caron and Josephina sighed with relief. "Excellent!" replied Josephina. "We shall see how this all plays out. Let's all agree that you, Mr. Abernathy, must have Lindsey out of her residence by the eight o'clock hour tonight. Is this acceptable to all?"

"It shall be a simple task, merely child's play," he boasted. "Just watch me. Now let's write a note to secretly lure Madam Lindsey into my arms. I will need your assistance with this."

Josephina and Caron quickly departed from the foyer to locate a piece of Lady Grace's writing parchment, a quill pen, ink and an envelope. Upon their return, they joined Mr. Abernathy within the drawing room, drafting a brief note to set the plan in motion.

Five September, 1811

Dearest Madam Lindsey,

From afar, I have watched you in silence for much too long. Your beauty and eloquence have left me paralyzed with lust for only one. I beg of you. Please put an end to my misery.
Meet me this evening at eight o'clock at the north cemetery gates. With anticipation, I shall await your passionate lips. I assure you that our rendezvous will be mutually satisfying, and you have my word, this encounter will be nothing short of unforgettable. I do believe you are that special soul, I so dearly need to fulfill my burning lust. I will discreetly await your arrival.

Forever Yours,

A Secret Admirer

"Perfect!" Caron exclaimed. "Madam Lindsey will not be able to resist."

"Everything is falling into place," Josephina continued. "Lady Grace will be so pleased to hear of our plan."

"When Madam Lindsey departs to be with Mr. Abernathy, we shall explore her cottage. I feel certain that we will have plenty of time to find the letter," Caron said. Looking at Mr. Abernathy she continued, "Be sure you do not return to the cottage in Madam Lindsey's arms. We shall need at least an hour, perhaps even two, to successfully rummage through her chambers. Can you do this?"

"Of course," he replied. "I'm already quite excited."

"Tell me, Mr. Abernathy…I'm curious as to why you seem so anxious to carry out this escapade?" Caron inquired. "Surely you realize, dealing with Madam Lindsey is like playing with fire, and if you don't mind me saying so, she is not exactly your type."

"Dealing with any woman is like playing with fire," he chuckled.

"But, with this one, I do not plan on getting my fingers singed. It will give me great pleasure to be able to assist Lady Grace in some manner. We have all observed Lindsey's ruthlessness with not only Lady Grace, but with many others. Let's just say, I shall be most delighted to engage myself with this task and will relish the encounter, knowing that ultimately, I am assisting Lady Grace through my activities with Madam Lindsey. From the first kiss, to the stroke of my fingers along Lindsey's quivering thighs, I shall merely fantasize that I am actually with none other than, Lady Grace. What a fantasy that shall be! I will give Madam Lindsey a night to remember. Perhaps I might even surprise myself and enjoy this tumble in the grass. Trust me. By the time I get done with Madam Lindsey, she will be begging for more." He continued, "Ladies, you have absolutely nothing to fear. I don't expect to return early, for I shall look forward to taking my time with this wanton harlot."

Twenty

I always thought this was to be
Yet, somehow sensed you doubted me
And, questions lingered endlessly
Not knowing if you cared for me

What once was cloudy, now appears
The fog has lifted my past fears
Sun shining through the mist, my dear
And, all I know is - I still care

I was lost in thought, disturbed by the notion that Dr. Perry Harrington and Lord Russell were involved in some deceitful scheme with Lindsey. What made matters worse, I was not sensing a very good feeling about this at all. I wondered what could possibly be the connection between them. Even though the Higher Powers were telling me to tread carefully, my curiosity about this mysterious letter had now turned into an obsession. I was determined to discover the content of this correspondence, and was willing to even consider taking the risk of searching her residence myself, should I not be able to receive the assistance from Caron and Josephina.

The sudden sound of approaching footsteps brought Mr. Abernathy into view as I sat in the estate gardens upon a slate-stone bench, surrounded by the many vibrantly colored flowers. The roses were at their prime, growing abundantly in every direction that my sights ventured. However, I sensed by the solemn, determined look upon Mr. Abernathy's face that he had something of grave importance on his mind, more than a frivolous discussion of garden flora.

"Please excuse my interruption," he said. "I have news."

"News?"

"A clever means to locate the letter from Lord Russell," he replied, smiling proudly as he stood before me.

"Mr. Abernathy, how did you catch word of this clandestine matter?" I inquired, quite taken by surprise. We both exchanged broad smiles, as if we could read each other's minds. "Oh, yes," I continued. "Let me guess. Could it be that my two little French bon-bons enlisted your assistance? Have they put you up to something underhanded, sir?"

"As usual, you have come to the correct conclusion, Lady Grace," he said. "Josephina, Caron and myself have devised, what we believe to be a foolproof plan to locate the letter, and with entirely no reflection of your involvement whatsoever."

"Tell me more," I said, encouraging him to sit beside me. "It's important, however, that my participation be cloaked in secrecy," I continued, "I fear if Lindsey were to determine the extent of my intrigue, there would surely be vengeful wrath on her part, to say the least."

I listened attentively as Mr. Abernathy explained the plan to me in great depth. On all accounts, I was touched by his efforts to assist me in this precarious endeavor. The fact of the matter was, I was so moved by his support that I leaned towards him, planting a kiss upon his cheek.

"I will never forget this act of kindness, Bradford. You are a darling man to assist me. I will forever be grateful for your loyalty." Mr. Abernathy blushed a bright shade of pink. I sensed he appeared to be truly enthused by my gesture of affection, as I realized that my merely speaking his first-name aloud, made an unforgettable impression upon him.

264

"Be very careful," I continued, all the while encouraging him to move forward to enact the plan. I reminded him to be on his guard at all times as he carried out the logistics of this endeavor to distract Lindsey.

"Don't forget," I said. "She is a cunning witch and has her devious ways to compel you to say, and do more than you could, or would ever imagine. You must be as shrewd as she. In fact, you must outwit her by being even more adept than her trickery." I told Mr. Abernathy that I would anxiously await his return. At last, I sensed some relief, certain that Josephina and Caron would now locate the letter within Lindsey's residence.

"I will be quite fine, Lady Grace," Mr. Abernathy said. "There is no need to worry. Rest assuredly, I will not jeopardize you with my compromising acts. I do hope that you also understand, this is purely a ploy on my part to bargain for some time, so as to enable the discovery of the document. I have never been enamored with Madam Lindsey, nor is there a smidgen of anything personal or romantic between she and I. Rather, I abhor her and her cruelty to others. Do trust, Lady Grace, I will give Madam Lindsey all that she truly deserves, and even then some!"

"I understand," I replied, nodding my head. "I will await your return within the safety of my bedroom chambers tonight. Simply tap lightly upon the private hidden stairwell door that leads to my room. Our code will be two distinct knocks upon the back door to my chamber. When I hear you, I'll grant you access into my suite. Once we are in the privacy of my boudoir, we will discuss this matter in much greater detail," I continued, emphasizing that it would be a precarious venture.

"I absolutely understand," he replied.

"Do you have a trinket to place around your neck for protection?

"What?" he queried, looking at me, at a loss for the meaning of my question.

265

"A charm for good fortune, such as a cross that you could wear to ward off Lindsey's evil powers?" I persisted.

"I'll be fine."

"Listen to me," I insisted, "You must wear a cross. Do you have one?"

"I have a gold cross on a chain that belonged to my father. It's in the servant's quarters," he replied.

"That's perfect," I continued. "Be certain to secure it about your neck before departing tonight. Oh, and there's one last thing."

"That would be?" he inquired with a bewildered look upon his face.

"Pray to the Higher Powers that all will be well."

"You have my word, Lady Grace."

Mr. Abernathy assured me that I had nothing to fear, yet as I thought about the prior warnings from the Higher Powers, I insisted further that he pay heed to my words.

"Tread cautiously, and do take care in your affairs this evening with Madam Lindsey."

"Indeed, I shall look forward to returning to celebrate our good fortune," he replied.

I sent Mr. Abernathy on his way, bidding him farewell and wishing him good luck as I smiled, observing his muscular physique as he retreated into the lush gardens. I could not help, but admire how devoted and kind he had been to me throughout the past "My dear Bradford," I murmured. "I may have to reward your loyalty and bravado when you return to my chambers. You too, may receive your just desserts, and even then some."

My confusing yearnings of intimacy, increasingly bombarded my thoughts, leaving me in a state of bewilderment. What was the true source of my passion? Why was I obsessed with thoughts of love, lust and desire? Though, there was no doubt in my mind on this night, these overwhelming sensations were winning the war,

266

so to speak, I continued to have difficulty merely *blessing and releasing* my lustful thoughts, and the men who were attached.

Whatever would occur tonight between Mr. Abernathy and Lindsey, I knew that it was deceptive and not proper, and although I recognized in my heart that it would be scandalous for me to act on my passions, my mind drifted…amused with entertaining the fantasy of Bradford Abernathy.

The plan to recover the letter had been set into place. Now there was no turning back. Mr. Abernathy exited Thornwood Estate to lay in waiting at the cemetery gates, bordering on the outskirts of St Symphorian's Church. Filled with anticipation, I waited within my chambers for Lindsey's departure. Assembled in silence with Josephina and Caron at my side, together we huddled within the darkness, our eyes adhered to the window, in search of Lindsey's figure leaving her residence. If all went according to plan, we were hopeful that she would be lured effortlessly into the arms of her *secret admirer.*

The clock was soon to strike the eight o'clock hour and still, there was no sign of Madam Lindsey stirring from within her residence. I contemplated the manner in which she would choose to make her exit on this night, since there was more than one mode of departure. A side gate also permitted access to the cottage through the adjacent gardens. I had surmised correctly, suddenly observing a diffused silhouetted figure moving swiftly along the path.

"At last," I said, gleeful that Lindsey had taken the bait–hook, line and sinker. "There she is with candle in hand, scurrying into the woods." Of course, I had no doubt that Lindsey was dressed in her very finest, most likely wearing the best of French lingerie under one of her many pretentious ball gowns.

"All right, ladies," I yelled aloud, instructing Caron and Josephina to begin their search. "Get going and bring the document to me. Timing is of the essence!"

"Farewell," said Caron, her eyes filled with fear. "We pray this all goes smoothly and without incident."

"The real surprise would be, if the letter is nowhere to be found," I said, hopeful that Lindsey had not resorted to drastic measures of already destroying it. If this is to be the situation, Lindsey may have burned it as some sort of offering."

"My greatest fear is that she may have even cast a spell," Josephina said with a stressed look upon her paling face.

"And hopefully this spell is not directed at any of us!" Caron said.

"Move on!" I insisted. "No more of this dilly dallying. You have work to do."

Josephina and Caron were obviously quite nervous with the task ahead as they scampered down the hillside to begin the hunt. Now I could only wait for the French sisters to return.

As the night passed, my patience began to wear thin. I heard the clock in the drawing room chime, ringing in the nine o'clock hour. I wondered what could be taking them so long. What seemed to be the delay?

At half past the nine o'clock hour, Josephina and Caron finally returned to the safety of Thornwood Estate. Arising from my chaise lounge, I heard them tap upon the chamber door, and I nearly stumbled from my excitement running to greet them.

"Well? Give it me! Where is it?"

"Something is terribly wrong," replied Caron.

"We cannot seem to locate the letter. We have looked all throughout Madam Lindsey's private chamber, even within each of the rooms," continued Josephina. "We searched high and low, amongst the furnishings and within the crevices of the fireplace stone. It appears, this letter simply does not exist."

"I saw it with my very eyes! It must exist!" I shouted in frustration.

"We even rummaged within her dressing table, under her mattress, the bedding and within her personal belongings," continued Caron. "You must believe us when we tell you, it clearly is not within her quarters."

"That's impossible!" I cried aloud, as I felt panic settle into every bone and muscle within my body. This letter seemed far too important, for Lindsey to merely destroy it, especially since she had shared its contents with Dr. Harrington. At this point, I still did not understand what Lindsey was up to with Dr. Harrington and Lord Russell, but I planned to make it my business to further unravel this mystery.

"This is exactly what I feared," I continued. However, since Lindsey has not yet returned, I beg that you both depart and investigate her quarters again. I absolutely must have that letter."

"Of course, Lady Grace," the French sisters replied, hesitating to move toward the door. "But, what if she returns this time and finds us? She will certainly invoke her wrath."

"Do not fret," I replied, assuring them they would only need to inform Lindsey that I had sent them into her residence to borrow some French perfume that I so enjoy—the one that smells like one hundred freshly cut roses."

"She will wonder how we got into the house," sighed Josephina. "How do I explain that we used your spare key?"

"Merely tell her that you found the side doorway unlocked. Madam Lindsey will believe you, especially since she departed in such haste to meet her mysterious beau. Take a deep breath and stay calm. Use this as your alibi should you have the misfortune of crossing paths with her. Is this understood?"

Josephina and Caron nodded their heads, reluctantly departing my chambers to continue the search once again.

"A perfume that smells like one hundred roses!" exclaimed Caron with a smirk on her face. "How can Lady Grace ever believe that Madam Lindsey would accept this as truth?"

"Hush'" Josephina said, as they made their way again down the hillside. "We can only pray that Madam Lindsey is more gullible, than we would ever believe her to be."

As the night continued to pass slowly, once again I heard the clock chime. It was now half past the eleventh hour, and still I sat alone within my chambers...until, at last a knocking upon my chamber doors delivered the return of my two French attendants, but instantaneously my face turned from joy to gloom. Caron and Josephina were empty-handed once again. Weary from the frustration of the night, I reluctantly dismissed my attendants to retire to the servants' quarters.

The sound of the clock chimed one o'clock in the morning, awakening me from my slumber. I had dozed off into sleep, reclined upon the window seat. My restlessness was obvious as I found myself mumbling once again, "Where could he be? What could possibly be happening with Mr. Abernathy? Why has he not returned to my chambers? What could be his reasoning to stay with Lindsey for such a lengthy rendezvous?"

I realized there could be more than one scenario to this matter, but my mind led me to the most obvious conclusion–Lindsey and Mr. Abernathy must be consumed in the throes of passion. He was evidently in no immediate rush to return to the estate house.

I found myself becoming all the time more aggravated, sitting and waiting with no clues, and no signs that this venture would ever resolve itself. I reflected and fantasized about what might be happening as I heard the clock chime again, announcing the two o'clock hour. My fantasies persisted as I moved from the window seat, reclining my tired body upon the bed until drifting into sleep. Entering into a dream, I discovered myself in the presence of Dr. Christophe Alexis. His arms encircled my waist, his full lips kissing me with passion. Gently, I could feel the touch of his warm and nimble fingers, caressing the nape of my neck as he unbuttoned my dress with great care. One button at a time, he slowly disrobed

270

my clothing until I stood naked before him as pure as a white rose without thorns. Kissing my breasts, he whispered into my ear.

"My lovely Grace, I have always wanted you. I have always hoped this glorious evening would finally arrive, where we may at last share ourselves and unite as one."

I was paralyzed with rapture by his actions and his words, powerless to resist his affections within the dream. My hand slowly stroked his brunette locks as he gazed into my blue-green eyes and kissed my lips again—a kiss so sweet and wet, like succulent honey dripping from a beehive. I unbuttoned his silk chemise, removing his vest, unbuckling his belt, as I fell to my knees and caressed him with my lips. He passionately moaned, pulling me closer as our bodies softly fell together upon the floor, like rag dolls playing in the brilliant glow of candlelight. I observed our shadows on the distant wall, dancing a dance of passion and desire. The rhythm of his body moved me to tears as I sighed with pleasure. I yearned for more as he kissed my skin, softly parting my wet lips. I felt a brilliant flash of warmth. His firm body gyrated to a rhythm I had never experienced before, as his lips played deliciously upon my breasts. Our bodies were entwined in ecstasy.

"I have never known a love like this before," he whispered into my ear. "I shall lust for you every day, my lovely Grace. Promise me that you shall always be mine."

There was a faint sound at the chamber door as I awakened, disoriented to find myself alone once again within the darkened room. I wondered who could be knocking at my main chamber door at such an early hour. My attendants had been dismissed, and surely, it was not Mr. Abernathy. He had explicit instructions to do otherwise.

With a look of disillusion and confusion upon my face, I quickly arose and ran to the main entry doors of the chamber, wrapping a woolen shawl around my shoulders as I maneuvered my tired body. I shivered with pleasure, recalling my delightful reverie as I approached the door, for there was no longer any doubt in my mind that I truly missed Christophe, and now my empty heart only echoed my longing to be comforted again within his embrace. However, arriving at the chamber suite doors, my lustful thoughts swiftly adapted to the immediate matter at hand.

"Who is there?" I whispered through the crack in the door jam. Pausing to pay heed for a response, I was taken aback by the absence of a reply. I thought, at last, perhaps Mr. Abernathy had finally returned, and was unquestionably playing some prank on me. He always did have a wonderful sense of humor. But, why would he be tapping upon these doors? I explicitly told him to return via the hidden stairwell entrance of my private chambers.

Unbolting the secured door, I slowly swung it forward to rest ajar, only to find myself staring at what I wanted to believe was some grotesque illusion, a gross figment of my imagination. I stood aghast, my tongue tied in knots–speechless.

"My God! Bradford, what has happened?" I screamed, forcing the words from within. "Who is responsible for this odious act?"

Mr. Abernathy was unable to answer, as I observed a horrific display of crimson blood spurting from the deeply slashed wound about his neck. Staggering, he fell into my arms. His white-lace shirt was torn and covered with broad brush strokes of brilliant red, like a canvas anticipating its grandiose creation.

"I'll help you," I said reassuringly, perplexed as to how this could have ever occurred. Fear consumed me as thoughts flashed haphazardly throughout my mind. What would become of this poor soul? All of a sudden, I noticed the absence of the cross around Mr. Abernathy's neck.

"The gold cross!" I exclaimed. "Did you forget it?
There was no reply from him as his face grew ashen in color. "How could you have forgotten?" I continued. "You promised!"

272

In the confusion of this moment, I managed to drag his body, gently lying Mr. Abernathy upon my chamber floor. Placing my hands over his wound, I focused my energies.

"Be still. I must heal you," I whispered into his ear.

Instantaneously, Mr. Abernathy motioned with his left hand as if wanting to give me something. Reaching for my arm, he groped at my side, trying to summon my full attention. I could see the excruciating pain within his eyes as I continued to ignore his distracting movements.

"Do not move!" I persisted, determined and focused only upon invoking the magic. I spoke aloud, chanting a verse to summon the Higher Powers, channeling my healing energies with those of nature in an effort to merge with his weakened life force.

Full moon dancing on the sea
Light of life return to me
Heal this wound for all to see
Bless his soul eternally

Hearing the voices of the sisters approaching from the hallway, I continued to heal Mr. Abernathy with my powers. With outstretched hand, he again attempted to invoke my attention, tugging adamantly at my frock.

"What is it?" I sighed, whispering into his ear. Speak to me!"

His clutched hand opened before my eyes, revealing a crumpled piece of white parchment.

"Thank the Higher Powers," I murmured as tears welled within my eyes. Immediately I recognized that indeed, it was the letter. I could not believe my eyes, yet I deduced that Lindsey must have had the correspondence in her possession when she met with him at the cemetery.

As the sisters approached the chamber suite, I hastily concealed the parchment within a pocket in my sleeping gown, for I feared that Lindsey might be brazen enough to actually make an appearance. My assumptions were once again proven correct, as Lindsey accompanied Marcella and Clara, entering the room with a rehearsed look of horror upon her face.

"Grace, what have you done?" Lindsey shouted. "What has happened?" We must summon Dr. Harrington," she continued, observing me with disdain.

"I sense that will not be necessary," commanded Marcella with compassion in her voice. It appears that Grace's powers have returned to her. Mr. Abernathy is living proof. I believe that Grace has indeed, saved this man's life."

As we gazed upon our butler, his face had amazingly transformed from a paling gray, returning to a warm peach tone. The blood that flowed profusely from his neck, had now ceased, the wound miraculously rejuvenating new flesh, and sealing the gash. All that remained was a thin pink line, barely marking the site of initial incision.

I was ecstatic, filled with glee as I embraced Mr. Abernathy. Although he was still in a weakened state, he stirred and attempted to sit upright.

In a state of shock, I ignored all of the questions being thrown about the room. Something truly wonderful was happening. Bradford Abernathy had been given another opportunity to live.

"It's a hoax," yelled Lindsey, flailing her arms into the air. In her rage, I could not help but notice something shiny, a brilliant ornament swinging from her neck. It was without a doubt, a gold cross…none other than Mr. Abernathy's.

"Surely, you are not making sense, my dear," said Clara, as she gazed upon Lindsey. "This can only be the magic returning to Grace."

"I don't believe a word of this. We must contact the authorities in Boscastle," Lindsey ranted. "I gather that once again, we have another mystery to be solved. It is imperative the village Constable

274

be notified to evaluate all that has transpired here this evening. This is absolutely a matter for the law."

Looking at Lindsey with scrutiny, I declared, "Most certainly, we do have another mystery to be solved, one that revolves around you this time!"

"You have utterly lost your mind, Grace!" Lindsey swiftly retorted. "An injured man is lying upon *your* bedroom chamber floor at three o'clock in the morning. How dare you point a finger in my direction! I think not, my dear!" she exclaimed, departing the room in a raging flurry.

In the distance, I could hear her shrill voice as she blurted a verse aloud.

Flame of candle
Cast this spell
Turn the handle
Fare thee well

Carry Christophe
To my side
Forever more
Our love abides

Lindsey's voice grew fainter with her every step as she marched along the hallway, descending the main staircase and exiting the estate house in the direction to journey down the hillside to her private residence. Her sudden disappearance from the scene and her lack of compassion, only further aroused my suspicions that Lindsey was ultimately responsible for this heinous act.

I sat next to Mr. Abernathy, observing him as he slowly became more alert. Although I was able to activate his life force energies, impeding the flow of blood and healing the gashing physical wound that had traversed his throat, his vocal chords had not responded. He remained powerless to speak.

I told the sisters everything about the plan that Mr. Abernathy had devised with Caron and Josephina. I surmised that Bradford Abernathy must have incurred Lindsey's rage at some point during the night and had desperately sought out my intervention, only to awaken me by tapping upon the main chamber doors. I now understood, it was impossible for him to have ever made his way up the hidden stairwell to the clandestine entrance of my chambers. Mr. Abernathy must have used every ounce of strength and determination, just to climb the main staircase, struggling to alert me of his dismal plight.

"The coachmen will summon Dr. Harrington at daybreak," said Marcella, as she and Clara assisted to move Mr. Abernathy into a private bedroom chamber. "I sense that he will be fine. Perhaps with the doctor's examination, we will be able to diagnose more concerning Mr. Abernathy's inability to speak."

She continued, "Grace, be certain not to utter a word of this to any of the service staff. I will inform them with a meeting in the morning at the ten o'clock hour in the drawing room. Now let us try to get some rest. I sense this will be a long and demanding day for all of us."

As the monotony of the early morning hours subsided, I knew that I would not return to my bed, sleeping restfully. Although I had healed Mr. Abernathy, my powers were still not fine-tuned enough to fully return his speech. I wondered how I would determine the truth of all that had occurred on this night at the cemetery, if Mr. Abernathy were to remain incapable of speaking, and I knew better, than to expect him to convey his ordeal through the written word. Although I had attempted in past years, to teach Mr. Abernathy to read and write beyond his less than adequate primary level, he had never been eager to learn to read, nor write little more than his name.

276

With all of the excitement of this night, I remained wide awake, lying motionless upon my featherbed within my chamber suite. In an instant, my thoughts flashed brilliantly as I sat upright. Remembering the crumpled letter, stashed clandestinely within the pocket of my sleeping gown, my eyes filled with tears of joy. Unfolding the parchment in anticipation of reading the contents, I whispered, "Deception is a ghastly game, yet played by many just the same. I shall beat Lindsey at her ruse. Thank the Higher Powers…the magic has returned to me!"

Patricia Grace Joyce   *The Magic of Time*

Twenty-One

Life is not always what it seems
Our trust in others sometimes deems
A different ending than we had hoped
We dangle by a cord and grope
Not understanding, we barely cope

Deception is a ghastly game
Yet, played by many all the same
Our eyes were blind to their intent
But, trust one day they will lament
Have faith a true love will be sent

In the dimming candlelight, I sat anxiously upon the side of my bed and focused on the correspondence. Squinting my eyes, I drew the letter closely into the light, observing the sepia-colored lettering which laced the elegant white parchment.

Twenty-Two August, 1811

Dearest Lindsey,

I send you greetings from Paris this day. My visit to the Cornwall region earlier in the month was divine – a much needed recuperation. I am most appreciative of your past efforts to rendezvous for some quiet time together, but as always, it was much too short. Soon, my dear, things will be different due to your intercession.

All is going according to plan in Paris, and London as well. My goal is to return to London at the time of next month's full moon, when I shall update you with my ongoing transformation.

We seem to have, however, a predicament involving the matter of timing. It is paramount that you intercept Grace, delaying her arrival to London until my recuperation in Paris is fully completed. It will be necessary that specific details regarding the relocation of the operating theatre, be fully enacted at Worthington Estate in London. Grace must never be made aware of any of the medical procedures that have transpired within the underground cellars of the Worthington Estate house.

I should hope we might be able to detain her arrival indefinitely, so that Dr. Harrington and his associates may continue to do their medical research and carry out the necessary surgical procedures. This would be the most ideal situation. Please see what you can do, my dear. I am confident that you will use your mystical powers to the fullest!

As you know, the surgical procedures in London have not been without difficulty. All seems to be going as best as can be expected at this point. I feel confident that it will only be a matter of time, before we have won over Dr. Christophe Alexis's total support with this project. I assure you when this occurs, we shall see even more significant physical results than what has been accomplished thus far, by Dr. Harrington.

Dr. Harrington believes I may require additional surgeries until we see the much anticipated transformation with my face. I anxiously await a consultation with Dr. Alexis, for he will make the final decision on what needs to be further enacted.

Time is required to convince Dr. Alexis in becoming a part of our plan. He holds the key to this experimental surgery, ultimately becoming a successful reality. I know of none other, who has the doctor's knowledge in this revolutionary medical procedure. He is truly a gifted surgeon and an extraordinary man.

Since Dr. Alexis's surgical skills are renowned internationally, it would be a tremendous coup for us to have him as part of the team. At present, he remains uninformed as to the monetary benefits regarding this medical venture. With the much anticipated vow of his commitment to the project, we will ultimately notify him of the fiscal rewards. These financial benefits continue to increase well beyond the stretch of the imagination, as long as there is a steady supply of cadavers to harvest for human flesh. As of yet, this has not posed a problem, since we have always had a continuous supply of bodies, thanks to the assistance of Elijah Foster.

As Kendall's health is now fairing quite poorly, we shall make the best use of his cadaver in transferring his flesh to my face. Observing the situation at this time, I am making steady progress with my recovery. In fact, I was in awe that Grace was not able to even recognize me when by mere chance; I crossed paths with her while walking along the beach in Boscastle last month. In due time, I pray that with the final surgeries and my physical transformation, she will finally become mine, to love and adore. Grace has always been in my heart.

At long last, with the anticipation of my brother, Kendall, out of the picture, my goal is to become so physically desirable that Grace shall never refuse me again. I am excited merely writing about this possibility.

I will remain here in Paris for the next two weeks before returning to London. Lindsey, please know that with all of your assistance and efforts, you have nothing to fear. I will guarantee and personally see to it that Dr. Christophe Alexis will become yours.

Lastly, Madame Pucelle seems to be improving; however, there were complications with the birth of her child. Unfortunately, the boy did not survive.

Sincerely,

Russell Worthington
Hôtel de La Rêve - Paris, France

I laid my head upon my pillow and stared at the ceiling in a daze. I could not believe what I had just read. Once again, I slowly read the letter, my head feeling fainter with each passing moment. My stomach nauseously twisted into a tight knot. If this correspondence spoke the truth, Kendall's soul was actually approaching the point of departure on this earth, soon to cross-over to the other side beyond the veil.

"Could he truly be near death?" I whispered. I thought about how and when this would all occur. I remembered within the sisters' prophetic reading, they had seen visions of him still being alive only a few weeks ago. I feared Kendall's health must have swiftly taken a turn for the worse, and I thought about the possibility that perhaps he was verifiably held captive in the cellar of Worthington Estate. I wondered if this could have been confirmation of the dream that I envisioned several months ago, viewing him confined behind bars in a tawdry, dank cellar. At this very moment, I vividly recalled how a very pregnant, Madame Lela Pucelle taunted him with manipulative self-serving demands. If this was the truth, Kendall may truly have been confined against his will.

As my mind wandered, I even thought about the notion that perhaps Kendall had been plotting all along with the others in deceiving me during these many past months. Remaining confused as to what role his disappearance may have truly played, I could only wonder about what he had hoped to accomplish by vanishing. However, perhaps Elijah had always been a key part of this scheme, deceiving me through his intimacies to await the opportune moment with assisting to kidnap Kendall, thereby providing the primary donor for this surgical project. If this was the fact, I believed now, more than ever that Elijah Foster played a major role with Russell, Lindsey, Madame Pucelle and Dr. Harrington. Somehow, they were all linked together in this deceptive muddle, and I feared that Kendall's demise was progressively more eminent.

Sitting in silence, I continued to reflect about the past months of strife and stress. Many questions still remained, yet finally there were at last some answers manifesting.

If Lindsey had intentionally played a part in this, I now believed that she was less than a wretched soul. How I despised her! Yet, I also felt a great sorrow in my heart, for she had indisputably, misused her powerful mystical abilities from the very start. I could only pray to the Higher Powers, one day Lindsey would pay for her abuses to me and to so many others.

My thoughts now returned to Madame Lela Pucelle. I had no pity whatsoever for this miserable soul, concluding that her existence had only served to reap misery and despair in my life. How could I ever forget that she attempted so cunningly to deceive me with her bribery and extortion, her personal affairs with my husband? I now realized there would always be a price to be paid in life for every choice we had chosen to make. Madame Pucelle had sowed her own garden of misery. The innocent child that she carried for nine months within her womb did not deserve to be born into such a deceitful world, and rightfully so, this tiny soul was now at peace, choosing to return to the other side – the glorious realm beyond the veil.

I wondered what motivated the elderly Dr. Harrington to play his role in this. He certainly was not a skillful surgeon, by any means. I could only construe that perhaps this was why the situation deemed necessary, Dr. Alexis's participation in this venture.

Pausing in thought, I attempted to quiet my mind and make some sense of it all, yet so many puzzling questions persisted. Furthermore, I deliberated the idea that Lord Russell had committed the ultimate betrayal. Why was he in Paris, and what could possibly have been his involvement with the medical world? I had never known him to be concerned with humanitarian causes, nor in the study of medicine. Additionally, his statement that *he was recuperating*, left me clueless. I wondered what truly motivated Russell to submit to a surgeon's knife? I thought about what he could possibly be recuperating from, finally assuming that quite likely, this recuperation must have had everything to do with the reconstruction of his grotesque facial scar and the replacement of his thumbs…a transformation utilizing Kendall's flesh.

My mind was hurriedly racing, wondering what type of medical venture this could be. How morose that the mention of cadavers to harvest flesh was part of this entire mystery, and a plentiful supply of corpses at that! Lastly, I thought about how Russell could even remotely believe that I would ever become a love interest in his life again. As far as I was concerned, my relationship with him was over and done with—dead as a doornail.

Within all of this uncertainty, I knew in my heart that I must move forward, insuring that my friend, Dr. Christophe Alexis was not deceived and manipulated as I had been. I was determined not to permit him to suffer a wound like mine. At this point in time, all signs indicated that Dr. Alexis might need to be rescued from falling as prey into the evil hands of Madam Lindsey.

If I had anything further to say and do about this matter, I wanted Russell and Lindsey to suffer, to pay an awesome price for all this heartache. Although I did not fully understand this letter of correspondence, I did sense that whatever they were involved with, could not be for the benefit of humanity.

"Surely, Lindsey and Russell plotted to profit financially in some way, shape or form," I mumbled. Though, I seemed to have become a renewed object of Russell's affection, I vowed that he would never have me again, nor would Lindsey ever have Dr. Christophe Alexis.

The other area of greatest confusion was the matter of the acquisition of cadavers for this clandestine surgical project. I was fully aware that it was common practice for the cemeteries to be foraged by rogues for fresh bodies sold for profit, but I was in shock that Elijah Foster would have ventured to go down this corrupt path. If this was verifiably the case, I knew he must be punished. It was such a horrid crime, yet if Elijah could rob a grave, I believed he could certainly be capable of abetting a murder – cold blooded murder, perhaps even Kendall's. I could only infer that Elijah was the informant, the eyes and ears to keep abreast of my whereabouts, and the force to offer the plentiful supply of fresh cadavers for Dr. Harrington to perform this so called, experimental surgery.

Continuing to stare at the letter in utter amazement, I could not remain silent any longer. It became increasingly paramount, that I warn Dr. Alexis of the evil lurking so near to him. I was determined to thwart all efforts, to insure that Lindsey, Madame Pucelle, Russell and Elijah would never have their way, and if Dr. Harrington had truly deceived me as well, his actions incriminated him, as much as the others.

Now it was becoming apparent that I had to immediately secure some assistance. Constable Gordon must be made aware of all these recent developments. Lindsey must be held accountable for her ugly deeds. The truth must be revealed. And, with my thoughts directed to writing Dr. Alexis, I hoped to depart for London as soon as possible. My entire being resonated with the essence and belief that I must now put an end to this heartache.

I was perplexed as to how the sisters could possibly get any rest, after the excitement of what had transpired earlier this night. Needless to say, my efforts to sleep soundly remained futile. My eyes were wide open. I was awake and eager to get this matter resolved with discretion and in no uncertain terms, with the utmost of secrecy. Understanding that I must exercise great caution, I was also aware that I needed the aid of another to carry this out successfully. I thought about who could be trusted. Who would be the best candidate for me to confide in? I could only trust my dearest friends to assist me in London. However, I realized there were very few that I would ever still consider as friends. I debated if perhaps I should once again invoke the confidence of the Bishop. My heart was speaking once again. I had to see him, and I trusted that he would provide a safe haven for me in London. Certainly, he would protect me from Lindsey.

Hurriedly, I wrote a letter to the Bishop, becoming increasingly alert of perhaps even knowing too much, for my own safety at this point in time. I had knowledge of privileged information, and I could not afford to have Lindsey become aware of this, for I feared a dismal fate by her hands.

Six September, 1811

Dearest Samuel,

I pray this letter finds you well on this autumn day as I write with great urgency for your assistance. My arrival in London will be within the week. I will not be staying, however, at the Worthington Estate house. Your trust, guidance and insight are necessary once again, to provide a safe haven for me. No one must know of my whereabouts.

Of course, I would never impose upon you, but I am a desperate woman and have none other, that I may trust with this matter. A courier will notify you of my arrival in the city. At that time, I will reveal more details to you. With blessings,

Grace Worthington
Thornwood Estate, Boscastle, England

Again, I read the letter to the Bishop, then approvingly waxed and sealed it carefully within an ivory envelope. "Very well," I whispered. "But, I must also warn the doctor of these matters, and I pray that I am not too late."

Six September, 1811

Dear Christophe,

286

I have not heard from you in quite some time and continue to pray all is well with you. This letter is sent with great urgency, for there is much for you to be forewarned of. I will be arriving in London within the week and must absolutely meet with you. There is a matter that needs to be brought to your attention. I say this with the utmost reservation and discretion. You have my assurance that I will go into detail when we meet again. Perhaps we could rendezvous at Westminster Abbey? I sense this would be the only location we may be safe to converse.

Upon my arrival, I will send for you via messenger. Please take care and until then, be well, my friend.

With Love,

Grace

Thornwood Estate, Boscastle, England

With the completion of the letter to the doctor, I also waxed and sealed the envelope. Taking both envelopes in hand, I made my way by candlelight into the cool early morning air. I could see the stables in the distance, darkened with no evidence of light glowing within. Searching for the coachmen, I spoke aloud as I made my way through the overgrown brush that surrounded the barn.

"Michael? John? Are you here? I realize that it's early, but I must invoke your assistance," I whispered.

As I listened for a reply, the sound of silence rang clear and loud. Entering the stable from a side door that stood slightly ajar, I timidly moved within. I could hear the horses stirring, acknowledging my presence. The smell of raw hay infiltrated my senses, as I stood with hesitation within the darkened and damp enclosure. I was fraught with anxiety, anxious to have the two

287

parcels delivered by courier as soon as possible. Oddly, I suddenly heard the noise of what sounded like a deep, raspy voice.

"What on earth are you doing here?" I shrieked, abruptly turning around, only to find Lindsey standing before me. I wondered how she managed to find me, however, before I could move, Lindsey disappeared just as quickly as she had manifested before my eyes. I attempted to regain my composure, chuckling at myself with relief, wanting to believe this was all just my overactive imagination at work. Nervously, I advanced, as my hands groped along the roughly textured surface of the wooden stable walls to sense my whereabouts within the barn. With every step forward, I tightly clutched the thin white candle. Again, there was a voice, but this time it sounded much louder. I turned swiftly with the candle held in outstretched hand, only to discover there was no one.

A sudden wind gusted into the stables sending a chill, through what seemed like, every bone within me. Madam Lindsey appeared once again. This could only be her black magic, I surmised. My mind was spinning, creating outrageous rationalizations of Lindsey's intent. Dreadfully, I could only imagine that she was casting a despicable spell upon me as I struggled to keep my wits about me, yet with this very thought I instantaneously tripped, losing my balance.

Stumbling, I fell upon the crisp hay which covered the stable floor. At that moment, the candle immediately disengaged from my grasp as I felt myself tumbling towards the ground as if in slow motion. I could now only watch in vain. Within seconds, the straw and hay atop the stable floor began to burn uncontrollably, crackling alive in leaps and bounds. The fire was wild, raging…taking on a life essence of its own, and now dancing all around me. Quickly, I stood up.

"Help me! Help!" I screamed.

Although I was in shock, my thoughts immediately turned to rescuing the horses. "I must set you free," I cried aloud. As I moved further away from the heat of the angry orange-red flames, I could hear the familiar voices of Michael and John.

"Lady Grace, where are yaw? You must get yawself out! Hurry! Hurry! We'll release dem horses. Jest get out!"

In the midst of the thickening smoke, I faltered in my tracks, brushing up against what I could only believe to be the ethereal entity of Lindsey. I gasped as chills of ice ran up-and-down my spine. Michael lunged forward and embraced me within his arms, guiding me safely through a side exit to the outdoors. Nearly breathless, I scrambled to the top of the hillside.

The smoke-filled stable rapidly transformed into a relentless inferno as I watched safely from a distance. The coachmen were able to free all, but one of the horses as the fire raged and burned frenziedly. It seemed as if there would be no redemption to salvage the stables. The structure was a total loss.

"Thank you for your help, and thank the Higher Powers you were not harmed," I said to Michael and John, as they joined me upon the grassy knoll.

"We was fast asleep on dis here side, behind dis stables, Lady Grace," Michael said. "We dared not sleep in dere. We heard what be strange voices about us. I guess dis be a lucky thing we was too scared to be asleep inside."

"Too spooked," John said as he shook his head in agreement. As the fire continued to rage, illuminating the night air, I thought about the coachmen's words. I knew deep within my heart and soul that the spirit world had spoken again at Thornwood Estate.

Soon after, the Lumiere sisters arrived with the entire service staff, observing the fire burning its course. Subconsciously, I began to prepare myself for the series of dreaded questions that would inevitably be posed. Marcella looked in my direction and without saying a word, drew me into her embracing arms, whispering softly into my ear. "Grace, trust, all will be well."

"Will my life ever be well?" I inquired.

"The spirit world has spoken again, urging me to warn you. There is something of great importance you need to be aware of."

"What? I don't understand." I insisted.

"You must not go to London." For the time being, remain within Boscastle."

"But, why? What's the problem?"

"There is more to your situation than what meets the eye," Marcella commanded. "It's too dangerous for you to travel with the knowledge that you now possess. I fear that your journey will not be safe. Remain here, and answers will present themselves. Stay focused and centered. You cannot possibly solve this mystery on your own. Please promise me that you will stay. Please, I beg you to listen and pay heed to my words."

I was confused by Marcella's plea, but for whatever the reason may have truly been, I wanted to believe her words, trusting the realm beyond the veil had communicated all this to protect me from whatever, and whomever. Reluctantly, I acquiesced. "I promise. However, must I remain at Thornwood Estate forever?"

"Forever is a state of mind. Destiny will return you to London," she said. "Timing is everything. Trust that all will be well."

I thought about her words. Timing once again, appeared to be the determining factor. I found myself awakening to the truth that timing was, and always would be, of the essence. It truly was a matter of time.

"Lindsey's letter must be destroyed," Marcella continued. "I assure you that matter will take care of itself. Let the law resolve this situation at Worthington Estate in London. You have done enough. Simply let things be. Whatever is going to occur in London shall transpire as it should, and in its own time…not in your time, nor mine, yet uncertainty shrouds the face of whether

290

this will be good or evil. The final outcome remains to be seen. The veil will one day be lifted for all to be revealed."

"But, I must warn Dr. Alexis. I fear that he may be in grave danger with Lindsey."

"You are not to interfere with this," she demanded. "The spirit world is telling me that justice will be served, if you do not intervene. You will only delay and make matters worse by your efforts in an attempt to take control. Let go, and permit the Higher Powers to intercede. Trust that those involved will reap what they have sown, a bountiful harvest of both good and evil."
Hugging Marcella, I squeezed her with great relief, holding her tight as if there were no tomorrow.

"Did you truly believe me when I told you that Lindsey had something to do with maiming Mr. Abernathy tonight?"

"Absolutely," Marcella replied. "You are stronger than you know at this time. Saving his life is more evidence that your magic is returning to you. Even though death is only in our physical world as we know it here on this earth, there is never death of the spirit. The soul lives forever. The soul is eternal. The spirits of your mother and father, the elegant Duchess Sarah and the charming Duke Jonathan will always protect and guide you throughout this lifetime, always. You are a healer, and must carry on, walking this new path, aiding those in need by invoking the magic of your gift."

"Thank the Higher Powers," I sighed aloud. "But, who will protect Dr. Alexis?"

Marcella smiled and replied whispering again into my ear. "I sense that he will be fine. He is an honorable, compassionate man. The doctor is well aware that something is not acceptable with this medical venture. Trust, Dr. Alexis will be guided to a higher level of understanding. Let this matter rest. You absolutely must not interfere." She continued, "He will be warned, but it shall not be

291

by you, nor me. Let the spirits take care of this, for they do not need your intervention."

Although puzzled, again I acquiesced, nodding my head as I reluctantly handed-over Lindsey's letter to Marcella. "I will continue to *bless and release*, praying that one day with the magic of time, all will be well."

Marcella replied, "We sense you feel as if this may be impossible. Rest assuredly, if you continue to use your powers in a benevolent manner to heal others, and also focus on developing yourself, you shall have nothing to fear."

"Why is this happening?"

"One day you will clearly understand."

"I believe with my entire being, that Lindsey was responsible for the fire. She must be held accountable for her dreadful deeds," I insisted.

"Give this time. Lindsey will reap what she has sown. We are all eventually held accountable to the Higher Powers."

Over a period of hours the flames had eventually subsided, until only a sea of smoldering darkened embers remained. The stables had been completely destroyed in the inferno. "The horses will still need to have shelter from the unpredictable weather," I insisted. "Do you think, however, we could have another barn built as soon as possible, Marcella?"

"It's imperative," she replied. "Tomorrow, Michael and John will go into Boscastle to secure the necessary materials. With many hands, it will be constructed in a matter of days. Permit time to take care of all that is necessary. Let the world beyond the veil work its magic through you."

Slowly, I felt as if I was beginning to understand that even though some matters were fated, and destined to occur – I still retained the power of free will. I realized that my choices in these

292

matters were directly linked, enough to affect the outcome of situations and could very well transform my fate – for the benefit and even the detriment of my life and the lives of others.

"I must speak with you further regarding Kendall," I insisted. "I believe that I have possible confirmation of Kendall's demise. In Lindsey's letter, Russell refers to Kendall as fairing poorly and that his death is likely to follow. If he speaks words of truth, at last I may finally experience a sense of closure to this crisis."

Marcella replied, "Be patient and move forward with your life. Embrace the future with your eyes wide-open and your heart filled with the anticipation of happiness and love. You must leave the past behind, to become fully aware of the present."

"Thank you for sharing your wisdom," I said. "Again, your words inspire me, bringing such comfort."

Marcella was truly a blessing, and I sensed that something was changing within me, inside every minute particle of my very being. Call it my attitude, or maybe even my disposition. Somehow, I was transforming. From the memory of myself as a frightened, needy woman, I was now different, yet I would never forget that dismal day in February when I had initially returned to Boscastle.

As I ascended the grassy hill leading to the estate house, I reached into my pocket. Removing the letters that I had written to Dr. Alexis and Bishop Bartholomew, I tore them into tiny pieces, and tossed the white parchment into the air, watching the flurry of paper-rain disappear into the gusting coastal wind.

"I shall continue to bless and release Bishop Bartholomew and the Dr. Alexis," I whispered. "I trust and have faith that in doing so, the Higher Powers will permit all to be revealed within its own time." With these words spoken, my eyes welled with tears. Again the winds gusted, swooping upwards, scattering the remaining particles of paper, like confetti, into the early morning sky.

Patricia Grace Joyce   *The Magic of Time*

Twenty-two

The pains we experience as we travel through life
Make us numb sometimes when recalling our strife
Through learning life lessons we each find release
A place deep inside us, bringing forth inner peace
And finally realize we can heal this disease

Create time daily to smell the fragrant roses
Never take for granted the challenges life poses
In acceptance of our pain, the heart is truly healing
Expressing a balance and harmony by revealing
The soul embracing love with compassion and true feeling

That evening, Marcella had ordered another coven meeting. As the grandfather clock struck the nine o'clock hour, I viewed the Lumiere sisters assembling in their seats at the round table. I couldn't help but notice, however, that Lindsey was not amongst us as I entered the drawing room.

"Where is Lindsey?"

Madam Clara responded, "Please join us, Grace. We were wondering where you had gone off to."

"I was napping within my chambers," I muttered, but my thoughts were still focused on Madam Lindsey.

"I hope you feel more rested?" she inquired, as she sat upon her chaise, smoothing the wrinkles in the folds of her crimson-colored silk dress.

"Indeed," I replied. "But, please answer my question. Where is she?"

"I was hoping that you might be able to inform us of Lindsey's whereabouts," Marcella interrupted.

Marcella told me that she thought Lindsey was in the village, or had returned to her residence. She had even gone as far as imagining that Lindsey and I might have reconciled our differences, hoping that she was with me.

"Not at all," I insisted adamantly. "I have intentionally kept my distance from Lindsey, especially since I believe she attempted to nearly destroy Bradford Abernathy. Although he cannot speak to relay the details of his ordeal, my senses point only to Lindsey as the force behind this atrocity. I simply will not ever trust her as openly as I once did in the past, and still I sense she is up to something morose, on a quest too eerie for me to even envision."

"I fear that your senses are accurate," Marcella said. "Time shall determine what she is plotting."

"I thought you were all aware of Lindsey's urgent departure this morning," Clara interrupted, hesitating nervously with a paling look of worry upon her face.

"Lindsey has left the estate?" Marcella inquired with alarm in her voice. "Where has she run off to this time?"

"I too, was quite concerned when I saw Lindsey with two horses hitched to a carriage at her quarters," Clara replied. "I believe she was instructing Michael to assist her with a journey."

"What are you speaking of? What journey?" Marcella yelled aloud, arising from her cushioned chaise. "Did Lindsey say where she would be traveling?"

"She only mentioned that a gentleman in London needed her assistance, something about a dear friend whose heart was broken and required her immediate intervention."

"This does not appear positive," Marcella continued. "I sense, however, that Lindsey may be involved in more than she might be able to handle. Regretfully, this could somehow play-out to unleash the doom of our dear sister."

I was certainly surprised at the exchange of conversation carrying-on within the room. "What shall we do?" I blurted aloud, feeling more and more uneasy by the minute. "How shall we stop her?" The sisters looked in my direction and spoke at once in harmony, "Stop her?"

"You, of all people, must surely recognize the fact, there is no stopping Lindsey when she makes up her mind to move forward with a plan," said Marcella. "I believe, however, that her antics involve none other than Dr. Christophe Alexis, but this ploy of hers may quite possibly backfire in her face." Marcella looked at me and continued, "Do you remember what Dr. Christophe Alexis told you?"

I could only think of the very first, and quite obvious, notion that came into my mind. "Of course," I replied, speaking aloud the doctor's compassionate words.

With the magic of time, all will be well.
There is nothing to fear when you listen to your heart.

"Our advice to you at this time is to do just that. Again, we must caution you to keep your distance from Lindsey. Listen to your heart. Move forward with your self-development to discover your true identity, your true path, and in doing so, continue to pray to the Higher Powers that all will be well."

"How can you actually believe Lindsey's plan may involve Dr. Christophe Alexis?" I inquired.

The sisters sat in silence, tensely eyeing one another. I was now even more concerned as I sensed the corner of my mouth twitching uncontrollably from my nervousness.

"Tell me this is not to be," I pleaded with them.

"We would like to indicate differently," Clara said. "But, Lindsey has her sights set upon none other than, Dr. Alexis." Clara told me, she had sensed this from the very first day Lindsey had laid eyes upon the handsome physician. She recounted the conversation that Lindsey had with Dr. Alexis at the time when I had fainted in the drawing room, hitting my head upon the table leg. "Do you remember how Lindsey relentlessly questioned the doctor in our presence, and beyond respectability?"

"How could I ever forget?" I replied. "I recall that she was incorrigibly rude, to the point where you had to physically escort her out of the chamber suite." Through my infatuation with the doctor, I had in a sense become blind, unaware of the true intentions of Lindsey's manipulative behavior.

"The doctor can take care of himself," Marcella continued. "I only pray that he knows right, from wrong. Although Lindsey will most definitely impose her affections upon him, time will tell whether he responds with open arms. I believe that she may pursue this matter much, much further than the doctor may ever imagine, and you know that Lindsey always gets what she desires."

"Let's see what comes to light this time," Clara said, with encouragement in her voice. "This shall be quite interesting."
Although I was reluctant at this point to discuss anything, other than Lindsey's plans to enamor Dr. Alexis, I asked the sisters to give me any insight and guidance they could possibly offer at this time. My head was swirling with fantasies, imagining Lindsey lying in bed, and embraced within Christophe's arms. Though, I tried my best to regain my composure, and to the surprise of the sisters, I even poured myself a stiff glass of bourbon with hopes of softening the edge of this news.

"The spirit world is showing us that you hold the key to this dilemma," Marcella said, "You already have the answers to your questions. Nothing has changed regarding the solution. The truth still remains hidden within your heart and soul." She continued, "Albeit rather disturbing at this time, please understand that with your growing awareness, we have faith the truth will prevail, manifesting the answers to your many questions."

"However, we must inform you that sometimes matters may appear to become more severe, before evolving to bring about the

298

good in a situation," said Clara. "With the blink of an eye, your life can transform for better, or for worse."

"As time passes, you shall instinctively go to the sea and walk along the shore," said Marcella. "You have always had an affinity for the sea, the healing waters of life. Take your pen, ink and writing papers with you. Gaze upon the majestic ocean waters from atop the Cornish cliffs. Then, journey down to the surging water's edge, and sit upon the sands to write all you discover has been hiding in your heart and soul. You will find the answers. Listen to your heart."

I embraced Clara and Marcella, wishing them a restful night before retiring that evening into the solitude of my chambers.
With the days that followed, I continued to reflect upon my past dreams as I walked amongst the thriving estate rose gardens. I sat and pondered awhile, taking my pen in hand, jotting my thoughts in verse as I inhaled the scent of roses surrounding me in a flowing sea of endless color.

A Rose Without Thorns

A Rose without thorns
That blows in the wind
A dance that is learned
Caressing the sun

Nurture your heart
In lightness and dark
Your passions and loves
Trusting angels above

Envision your life
Less hardship and strife
With purpose and growth
Express love like prose

Be kind to your soul
It smiles through you
Risk living a dream
Your destiny beams

Soft petals of white
The blooms of delight
The scent of perfume
And, shine like the moon

Reach high for the stars
Trust all will transpire
Search near and look far
Become who you are

I gathered my papers, pen and ink, excited once again with the notion of journeying onward, strolling down the coastal path to the water's edge of the beautiful Cornwall coast. Along the Cornish cliffs, the glorious Atlantic sea had always called to me, comforting me with the sound and motion of the water's surging ebb and flow.

Sitting upon the warming sands, I further contemplated my current situation and all that had transpired over the course of a year in my life since the disappearance of my husband. Deep within, I tried to listen to what my heart was telling me. I thought about the many questions that were still unanswered, and wondered how I would uncover the answers that lay discreetly inside me. What was I truly feeling at this very moment? What was my purpose in this lifetime? What were the many lessons from these matters that had been presented in my life? What was I really feeling within my heart and soul? Who was the true Grace Worthington, and what was my soul's destiny?

Looking upward into the afternoon sky, I began to formulate my thoughts, observing the graceful swooping motion of a solitary seagull, gliding within the brilliant turquoise-blue sky.

There Is A Seagull

There is a seagull in the sky
I can see it flying high
With its wings spread east and west
Leading me to the water's edge
On an ocean ever so blue
I still only think of you.

There is a seagull in the sky
Soaring mighty as I sigh
Walk along the sandy shore
Hoping one day you'll be more
Trusting that the future holds
A place together for us to behold

There is a seagull in the sky
Observing me as time goes by
Our eyes meet to clearly show
All my desires will soon be so
Let the wind blow, feel the gusts
Your love for me I dearly trust

There is a seagull in the sky
This I know, still deep inside
We cherish love within our hearts
Two souls unite, each play a part
Creating a bond for all to see
Fulfilling fate and destiny

At last, I had come to the conclusion there was really only one direction for me to now proceed. I believed that my true path was about sharing the powers of my healing energy with others, through my actions and my words, to renew and revitalize their spirit, and to soothe their weary hearts and souls. Ultimately, I sensed this healing energy would bring forth the magic. My destiny would be revealed through love, compassion and tolerance for others. This healing would be multifaceted, however, bringing comfort physically, emotionally, mentally and spiritually to those in search of an authentic life. I sensed that my path was to honor and celebrate my magical powers in a healing capacity, this light of life that I had found once again within my heart and soul. I could only pray to the Higher Powers, that all of this would one day transpire in some manner with my heart's desire.

Although I remained focused upon the transitioning uncertainty in my life, I believed my real path was at last unfolding. I wanted to accept as truth, that it was possible to heal myself through my actions and words, and in doing so, that I could also heal others. All the while, my inner voice continued to urge me to return to London.

"I must strive to inspire others to never give up, to always move forward, choosing to seek living life in the lightness of love, rather than in the darkness of fear," I murmured. "And, I must absolutely speak with Christophe again."

Hurriedly gathering my papers, pen and ink, my footsteps climbed the coastal path, leading me home to Thornwood Estate. I felt a nimble lightness in my stride, as I sensed the energy of excitement radiating from within me. Entering the estate house, I returned to my private chambers, only to be surprised at the discovery of a white parchment envelope that laid propped against my pillow cushion. I could only wonder who could have sent the correspondence.

Anxiously, my eyes perused the envelope as I smiled. It was at last, a letter from none other than, Christophe. Having grown remiss over the passing months about ever hearing from him again, I anxiously tore open the envelope and read its contents.

Twenty-Three September, 1811

Dearest Grace,

I pray this letter finds you healthy and happy. At last, I have finally created some time to share a few words with you. Having been incredibly busy with my medical practice, I continue to be drained physically, mentally, emotionally and spiritually.

Please know that I truly appreciate your efforts, your many attempts to stay in touch with me throughout these passing months. You have been a bright light in my otherwise wearisome and exhausting days and nights.

The autumn weather is absolutely splendid. Should you consider a journey to London, I welcome the thought of seeing you again. I am anticipating plans to attend the Prince Regent's Harvest Ball in late November. If you enjoy dancing as much as I do, perhaps you might consider the notion of attending as my guest? It would truly be an honor to have you in my company. Until we meet again, I shall anxiously await your reply.

Fondly,

Christophe
444 Park Place
Mayfair, London, England

I closed my eyes, holding the crisp white parchment paper closely to my breast as I silently made a wish. "At last, his heart speaks the truth," I whispered. "The path to love is through listening to the whispers of the inner voice." My heart would lead me on my soul's life journey. I could no longer deny, nor ignore its calling. "I must absolutely travel to London and attend the Prince Regent's Harvest Ball," I murmured as I gazed upon my reflection within a large chamber mirror.

Joyously dancing about the room, I felt exuberant and repeated those unforgettable words of compassion that Dr. Alexis had lovingly whispered into my ear.

With the magic of time, all will be well.
There is nothing to fear when you listen to your heart.

I rushed to the corner of my chamber and sat upon the chaise at my writing desk, as I searched within my heart, finding the words to compose a letter of reply.

Twenty-Nine September, 1811

Dearest Christophe,

I pray this note finds you in splendid health and frame of mind. I am writing to graciously accept your flattering invitation to attend the Prince Regent's Harvest Ball.

May our paths meet in London. Until then, with the magic of time, all will be well. There is nothing to fear when we listen to our hearts. Enclosed is a verse that best expresses my sentiments at this time.

With Love, Light and Blessings,

Grace
Thornwood Estate, Boscastle, England

The Dance of Hearts

If you reach for me
I will reach for you
But, for this to be
We must dance as two

Put your hand in mine
Walk me through the steps
Let me take my time
As I catch my breath

Draw me close to you
Whisper in my ear
Say that you are true
Someone who will care

I can hear my heart
As it beats aloud
And the music starts
Playing for us now

Then, you look at me
With your deep blue eyes
Dancing gracefully
And, your brilliant smile

Since the day we met
I have yearned for you
Never will forget
You embraced me too

My heart skips a beat
As you glide and dip
And, you taste so sweet
As I kiss your lips

I look in your eyes
As you kiss my breast
Feeling passion rise
Love does all the rest

From that day forward, I vowed to become the woman that I was destined to be, and I prayed to the Higher Powers that I would grow more aware, hopeful one day of discovering my true identity. For only then, would I be able to openly share and express my true love for others. I now believed, this was when all would at last be well in my life. With every passing day, I would have nothing to fear if I listened to my heart.

Within the privacy of my chamber, I sat at my desk and wrote for several hours, composing poetry that was abundant with emotion, hopeful of creating verses that would convey my true feelings at this time.

As I closed my eyes, however, weary from all of the revelation on this day, I was suddenly alerted by the distant galloping of horses approaching the estate house. Descending the main staircase, I rushed into the foyer, meeting the sisters as they eagerly approached the marble-floored entryway. Before any of us could barely utter a word, a loud pounding sounded upon the solid double doors, echoing like boisterous thunder throughout Thornwood Estate.

My curiosity was fully aroused, my imagination spinning fantasies of Dr. Alexis returning to passionately greet me, embracing me within his arms as he softly kissed my lips. Reality, however, was soon to take its rightful place. Standing before me was none other than, Constable Nigel Gordon, his hands clutching a thick leather-bound bundle of documents, while his Deputy dangled a pair of handcuffs within his outstretched hands. "By the power of His Majesty, The Prince Regent of England, I herby declare you under arrest, Lady Grace Worthington—charged with the murder of your husband, Lord Kendall Worthington and with the practice of sorcery!"

Patricia Grace Joyce   *The Magic of Time*

Twenty-three

I want the days of yesterday to vanish with the wind
To journey on the waves of joy, to start my life again
I want the days of yesterday to welcome love anew
Begin a new reality, that breathes so free and true

For many years believing you were needed in my space
A missing part, a love gone bad, I never could replace
But, now I understand that what I missed was only me
Somehow I lost my heart and soul, my true identity

A sliver of sunlight cut through the cell bars, as I awakened from a restless night. I lay upon my wooden cot, staring at the four dingy graying walls closing in on me. The haunting cries of prisoners wailing aloud had filled the night air and continued into the early hours of daybreak. I was frightened, fearful of everyone, and everything about this horrid place. "Is there no end to this woe?" I muttered aloud. The smell of feces and urine surrounded me – the calling of death.

My heart sank, now realizing that destiny had indeed, returned me to London, yet far from the manner of elegance that I had grown accustomed to. My fate now seemed to be none other than, to rot within this barren, God forsaken place – Newgate Prison.

I, however, was immensely grateful to have bought my passage into a solitary cell by crossing several palms with silver and gold coins upon my arrival last evening. Additionally, I was fully aware that so long as I had my wealth to fall back upon, I could at least soften the blow of the horrors that awaited me in this chamber of tortures. However, I feared that all the precious metal in the world would never be able to earn me a pardon. With King George III officially declared insane, my fate was at the mercy of his pompous, self-indulgent son, the Prince Regent. I was fully aware that the charge of murder was not one to be considered lightly, especially when involving the death of a spouse. Kendall's blood was on my hands; at least that's what the law was asserting.

Oddly, I seemed, however, to be receiving standoffish treatment. The guards were more fearful of me, than I was of them, afraid of something that I could only conclude was the apparent fallout of the second charge against me, witchcraft…the practice of sorcery.

Although I had been placed into solitary confinement, by what I had considered at the time to be an omen of my ability to procure my way, the prison guards exhibited no favoritism. In fact, they seemed to go out of their way to make my stay miserable. My clothes were removed and confiscated, only to be replaced by a soiled graying frock. I was permitted no visitors at this time. A paltry meal of dried bread, a porridge of cornmeal and a cup of water was slipped through the cell bars, enabling me to partake in some nourishment. However, who would even consider the notion of eating under these conditions? I spat the moldy bread out of my mouth, and drowned its putrid aftertaste with a gulp of tainted water. It smelled and tasted worse than the rancid runoff water from a drainage gulley along the Thames. I had forgone chancing a mouthful of the gruel, observing the fruit flies that had drowned within its pasty slurry.

Attempting to focus and concentrate on my plight, I invoked the Higher Powers, pleading for revelation of what I needed to be aware of. Strangely, the message I was receiving at this time was that I must keep my wits about me. If I were to ever get out of this death hole, it would be paramount that I employ my energy to stay alert and aware of my senses. I wanted to trust that the power of my magic would one day free me from this horrific nightmare.

Quite peculiarly, I heard the clinging of metal, which I could only determine as the familiar sound of the guard's keys, jingling within his hands. There was a knocking at my prison cell door as I heard the gruff coughing of the guard. How bizarre, I thought, as I cautiously moved from the corner of my darkened cell and approached the pounding. Why would he be knocking? He had the keys. I was the helpless victim behind gated bars. I thought about the absurdity that the guards might at last, have consented to granting me access to the outdoors, sanctioning a departure from my enclosure for a brief walk in the warming sunlight of the exterior courtyard.

"Who is there?" I timidly inquired.

The prison guard replied, yelling rudely into the cell enclosure, "You have your first guest, Lady Witch."

I shuddered at his words, now dreadfully cognizant that the charges of witchcraft had, in fact, contributed to the reticent treatment I was experiencing within the prison. I wondered, if perhaps, in addition to the charge of murder, that somehow a report detailing the return of my magical powers had been maliciously divulged to the authorities. The malevolent image of Madam Lindsey suddenly swirled within my consciousness. Would she have stooped so low as to insure my demise through this revelation to the authorities? My instincts were telling me, this was absolutely the scenario. Madam Lindsey had committed the ultimate betrayal – a fellow witch deceiving another. I was not only facing death at the gallows, but burning at the stake.

The guard's words had echoed my fears of impending doom as he chuckled loudly while unlocking the cell door, yet the thought of having a visitor, momentarily filled my soul with elation when a barely audible voice, whispered my name.

"Grace. It's me, Lady Kathleen—Lady Kathleen Harrington."

Slowly, the weathered rusty cell door creaked open, revealing the startled presence of a very elderly, white-haired and fragile looking Lady Kathleen Harrington, standing before my eyes.

"Thank the Higher Powers, it is truly you, Lady Kathleen. How wonderful it is once again to see you. It has been far too long, since we last crossed paths," I blurted aloud, rushing forward to greet her in embrace. "How did you manage to finagle your entry into the prison without alerting the suspicions of the guards? They tell me that I am in solitary confinement; at least until a magistrate is willing to hear my case, and I fear that could be many months from now."

"I'm desperate to speak with you, Grace," she said anxiously. "I took a bold chance that I would be able to pay off at least one of the guards, praying that I would not be physically removed from the prison, or even charged myself for abetting a witch."

"What?"

"This is why Clara and Marcella have remained at a distance, for they too, without a doubt, would be imprisoned along with you. Unfortunately, this case is more complex than any of us could have ever imagined. Lindsey has really made a mess of things."

I told Lady Kathleen that I also had the eerie suspicion; there was something more to my situation than what met the eye. Now I knew…my instincts were absolutely proving to be on target.

"I had heard the dismal news in Boscastle village of Bradford Abernathy's maiming," Lady Kathleen continued. "How horrible for him to have endured such a dreadful encounter in the woods with Lindsey! Who would have ever expected the extent of his injuries? The sisters tell me that, had it not been for your healing intervention, this man would surely have passed on."

With a confused look upon my face, I said, "And, this is why you have come to see me? To discuss the matter of our butler, Mr. Abernathy?"

"Not exactly. Not *that* matter, Grace. Firstly, I have come to give you my prayers. I've been praying for the safe return of your husband, Lord Kendall Worthington. Have you any further news?"

312

"I actually do have some information, but I believe that it's mostly hearsay. I have yet, to receive any confirmation of physical evidence of his death," I said. "Thereby, I really do not understand the charges that have been brought upon me. I sense, however, I cannot believe anything or anyone until I get absolute verification. I am still awaiting final word from Constable Nigel Gordon. He assures me that he has proof of Kendall's death, although I have yet, to hear of it."

"This does not sound positive," Lady Kathleen remarked. "But, what news have you actually heard, my dear?"

"I would rather not say at this point," I replied. "All I can tell you is that it does not look optimistic that Kendall will ever be found alive. I can only continue to pray to the Higher Powers."

"How terrible!" she gasped aloud, holding the palm of her hand over her mouth as she attempted to cover the twisted expression of awe reflected upon her bewildered wrinkled face.

"In my wildest dreams, I simply cannot imagine that you had anything to do with your husband's disappearance. Has the Constable lost his mind?"

"It seems so," I concurred. "It's reassuring and comforting to at least have your support. I feel that as time passes, I will be vindicated. I want to believe, and trust that all will be presented at the appropriate time."

Nodding her head, Lady Kathleen continued, "Yes, yes, my dear. I, too, have faith that all will be well. Now let me take this opportunity to elaborate further as to why I have come to visit you on this September morning. I have some difficult affairs to discuss, but the time has come for you to know of these matters."

"Of what are you speaking?" I inquired, gesturing with my hand for Lady Kathleen to rest her fragile, thin frame upon my wooden cot. Sensing this was going to be a rather lengthy and distressing conversation, I suggested we make ourselves as comfortable as possible within my austere cell.

Lady Kathleen told me, that before we discussed anything further, she thought it best to bribe one of the guards for some libations. "Fortunately, I have brought plenty of silver and gold coinage,"she said, looking toward me as she shifted her body uncomfortably upon the hard wooden surface of the cot.

"Guard!" she shouted through the small gated window on my door. "I have a proposition for you."
I could hear the guard rouse and the sound of his heavy footsteps as he neared the cell.

"Proposition?" he inquired, as he peered lustfully at me, licking his slobbering lips as if I were to be his next meal.

"There is a generous payment for you sir, should you be able to bring us a bottle of whiskey, and only the very finest will suffice."

"Whiskey?" I inquired, gazing upon Lady Kathleen. "I thought, rather, that perhaps we might partake in a spot of tea."

"Ha! You won't be find'n a spot a tea in these parts, me ladies," the guard rambled. "I'll fetch yaw the good stuff, but yaw had best make it worth me while now. Or, I shall leave yaw be."

"I fear that I am well beyond the moment of sipping tea, Grace," she continued, reaching into the bodice of her orange-colored silk dress. Two gold guineas instantly appeared before the guard's eyes. She slipped one through the cell window into the guard's fleshy grubby hand. "The other will be yours when you return with the bottle."

There was nothing civil concerning my life situation anymore. Actually, the very thought of drinking a cup of tea simply seemed ludicrous. Considering the circumstances, tea would never be adequate. From now on, it was whiskey – the tonic of the devil. I feared that I had at last succumbed, seduced by the dance of Satan's evil. However, I knew it was all an effort to mask my heart and soul from my hopeless quandary.

"Let's get down to business," I urged Lady Kathleen. "What are you speaking of? Please tell me what matter is troubling you."

314

"I have actually come to discuss an issue involving my very own husband, Dr. Perry Harrington and his associates, here in London," she replied. "I am fearful that something has gone horribly astray. Something is just not precise."

"Continue," I said, urging her to avoid needless interruption, for all I could think of at this time was the increasing fear rising within me. I shuddered with the thought that perhaps there was more vile news on the way.

"Tell me what concerns you," I insisted. "Who are these *associates* that you are referring to?"

"I want you to understand that I come to you for other reasons as well," she said coyly. Firstly, I need your absolution. From the depths of my heart and soul, I beg for your pity. Can you ever forgive me?"

"Why do you plea for my forgiveness?"

I paused, hearing the approaching footsteps of the guard returning. The door to my cell swung open as this large deplorable man stood gruffly before us with the whiskey bottle grasped tightly within his hand. Lady Kathleen handed him the second guinea as promised, observing him snatch the coin and place it within his torn pant pocket.

"Catch it and it's yours," he yelled, as he quite unexpectedly, tossed the glass bottle of whiskey in my direction. Swiftly retreating, he slammed the cell door.

I could hear his laughter echoing in the distance as I lunged forward. Fortunately, I intercepted the bottle's fall using both of my hands, grasping it in mid-air before the precious contents tumbled to the floor, splattering in all directions about the cell.

I handed the bottle to Lady Kathleen, as she sighed with relief, "We are blessed!"

In an attempt to remove the cork, I observed Lady Kathleen place her brittle yellowed teeth around the bottle's neck, pulling until she was able to loosen the seal. At last, it popped. She spit the dry cork from within her mouth as I gawked in astonishment. Then Lady Kathleen took a swig of the fragrant caramel-colored liquid and passed the bottle to me. Memories of Captain Ian Cutter quickly passed within my mind, just as swiftly as they departed. He had taught me many skills.

"Go ahead," she said. "Drink. I assure you, it gets easier and tastier with every swallow."

With absolutely no reservation, I put the bottle to my lips and took a huge gulp.

"It's to die for!" I mused.

"Grace, this is not going to be easy for me," Lady Kathleen continued. "Finding the right words is never simple, but I feel as if the time has come where you must be informed of the truth. I have grown wearisome in my old age to consider hiding this any longer. You need to know what has occurred in the past and how it all relates to the present, and most importantly to your future. This matter has simply gotten too large, out of control for me to hide any longer. The days of yesterday are gone. It's time for all to be revealed to you."

I was quite keen on listening, as I took another swig from the whiskey bottle, encouraging Lady Kathleen to speak. "Please go on. I realize that you are stressed over this issue, but I beg you to tell me more. What is it? Who is involved? And how does it affect me?"

Lady Kathleen took another large gulp of whiskey. "Of course, you are aware that your dear mother, Duchess Sarah and I were extremely close friends, prior to her untimely death nearly one-and-twenty years ago."

"Certainly," I said, giving her my full attention.

"Your mother and I were like sisters," she continued. "We did everything together and shared even our darkest secrets, matters that we would never dare utter to Duke Jonathan, nor Perry."

316

"I was just a young girl at that time," I said, nodding my head. "I do, however, remember hearing that you were close friends, and I recollect that in prior years, the Lumiere sisters mentioned you were like another mother to me as well. You and my mother were indeed, the best of friends. Please Lady Kathleen, continue."

Observing her taking, yet another swallow of the whiskey, I sensed that Lady Kathleen was uncharacteristically unsure of herself. I found her demeanor to be rather peculiar and wondered if she would ever continue with this bewildering conversation. My patience was wearing thin. Finally, she took a deep breath and spoke.

"So many years have passed, and I have become such an old, feeble woman, nearly four-and-eighty years of age. My husband, Dr. Harrington, has shared much information with me throughout our many years together; but, Grace, there is one thing that I have always promised never to reveal. Both my husband and your mother demanded my unconditional silence."

Lady Kathleen told me that she felt, however, at the present time, it was absolutely necessary for her to finally divulge the truth. My curiosity was more than aroused. I was anxious and wanted to physically pull the words out of her mouth.

Again, I pleaded with Lady Kathleen, "Please, just say what it is! I cannot stand to endure this anticipation much longer. What is so important? What is it that I have been unaware of all these years?" Lady Kathleen sighed, "Grace, your husband, Lord Kendall Worthington is actually your brother, a half-brother to be precise."

"That's ludicrous!" I said, gasping with an incredulous expression of awe smeared upon my face.

"Please hear me out," she insisted. I told you this was going to be difficult."

"Have you lost *your* mind, Lady Kathleen?"

"Believe me. I speak the truth. I can explain everything."

317

"Go on."

She blurted aloud, "Your mother, Duchess Sarah had kept this a secret for many years from Duke Jonathan and from you as well. Sarah was a shrewd and clever woman, and I always alleged that her treacherous death...her falling from the Cornish cliffs, had much to do with the Duke discovering a secret – discovering your mother's deceit."

I was mystified as my ears listened intently to Lady Kathleen's story. Interrupting once again, I said, "Please speak slowly and explain the circumstances from the very beginning. When was this? And how did this happen?"

"Very well," she replied. "It seems that I have unintentionally gotten ahead of myself. I will journey back to the days of yesterday, to the time when this all occurred. Let's begin when your mother, Duchess Sarah gave birth to triplet sons, many years prior to your birth, my dear."

"Triplets? I have three brothers?"

"Yes, but I must go on," she insisted, and continued to tell the story. "Deep in her heart, Sarah knew that these children were not fathered by Duke Jonathan. Additionally, the pregnancy was an arduous one for your mother. Of course, Sarah sensed that she was having twins, but who could have ever envisioned the arrival of triplets?"

Lady Kathleen told me that my mother had been ill, nauseated throughout the entire duration of the pregnancy.

"She was a miserable soul...tormented mentally, physically, spiritually and emotionally. I can recall there were times when her spirit descended to such a low point, regretfully your mother even considered taking her own life. Duchess Sarah was truly consumed with her own deceit, guilt and infidelity. Thus, when the children were finally born, your mother clandestinely made arrangements to have them vanish – to appear as if the children had been kidnapped.

318

"My mother would never stoop to such a despicable act," I retorted.

"Listen to my words," Lady Kathleen continued. "This occurred shortly after their birth, when the infants were only just a few days old. One morning they were fine, and by that very same night, the three cradles were discovered empty. Somehow, the triplets mysteriously disappeared from Thornwood Estate during the night."

She told me that throughout the passing years, the public assumed the three boys had merely died a few days after the difficult birth, at least that was the story Duchess Sarah was pushing. It was all very clandestine...a cover-up for what actually occurred.

I could feel my face flush with horror. "How could this be? Who would kidnap these poor defenseless souls? Could it have been a servant? This is all so dreadful," I said with a look of dismay upon my face. "You must be mistaken. This surely was not my mother," I shouted in a rage.

"You have every right to be angry," she said. "This is a horrendous matter."

I wondered what kind of woman would plot to have her very own children taken from her embracing arms, but before Lady Kathleen could speak, I interrupted again.

"Why did my mother choose not to raise these children? Why would she ever consent to have the children disappear? Surely, you must be mistaken? Duke Jonathan is the father of these children. I know my mother adored him. She would never stray and give her love to another man – never!"

"Try to remain calm," Lady Kathleen replied. "All of these questions that you raise are precisely what I thought as well, at that time. To my surprise it was later revealed, however, your mother had furtively taken a lover."

"What? Have you gone mad?

319

"I speak only of the truth."

"If not Duke Jonathan, who was the true father of these children? Who was my mother involved with? Please, you must tell me," I begged.

Lady Kathleen divulged that my mother was involved with a wealthy businessman who frequented the Cornish cliffs. This gentleman was connected with the affluent maritime shipping industry, and dealt with the ship captains within London and Boscastle harbors.

"His name was Duke Garrett Worthington," she continued. "Duke Garrett had an extremely profitable import and export business, among a variety of other investments and enterprises throughout Europe." She further explained that he was well traveled, intelligent, powerful, eccentric, worldly and attractive. "A handsome specimen of a man, if I might say so myself," she continued. "Most women swooned as he walked by, most women, except your mother, that is."

"How is this so?"

"Your mother was an incredible challenge for this man. He was accustomed to attaining whatever, and whomever he wanted in life, but Sarah resisted his every flirtatious effort. Although it's true she was adoring and in love with Duke Jonathan, one evening lust and desire came knocking loudly at her door, so to speak."

Pausing to take another sip of whiskey, Lady Kathleen pressed the bottle to her thin quivering lips. The caramel-colored fluid swirled and splashed within the interior of the bottle, coating the glass walls with a syrupy film. In contrast, I felt such an emptiness within myself, discovering my soul once again yearning. I longed to find something – anything, or anyone to fill this voided space as I repositioned myself upon the wooden cot, listening to all that Lady Kathleen was revealing.

"Continue, Lady Kathleen,"

She nodded her head. "As I was saying, your mother was such a challenge for him. The Duchess Sarah Thornwood was all that Duke Garrett Worthington could talk about. He had to have her. He was obsessed with her and promised a menagerie of material wealth and monetary benefits. Still, your mother was loyal within her marital commitment. She would not budge. She was not interested in Duke Garrett's worldly possessions. Your mother was wealthy in her own right. She had her health, and a wonderful husband, Duke Jonathan. Duchess Sarah lived a comfortable and affluent lifestyle, knowing better, than to ever imagine that money and material wealth could bring true happiness."

"So, why would she ever consider an affair?" I inquired. "Ah! There was one thing that your mother could not have within her very own marriage to Jonathan."

"And what might that be?"

"A child, my dear. Sarah was never able to conceive with Duke Jonathan. Oh, believe me they tried. The years passed and still, they remained a childless couple. Your mother finally confided in me one day, expressing her true feelings. She was happy within her marriage to Jonathan in every way, shape and form except one."

"In every way except, that she could not have a child?" I queried.

"Sadly, this is the truth," Lady Kathleen replied. "After many years of marriage, Sarah was truly desperate to conceive with Duke Jonathan. In her every waking hour, it seemed that she was obsessed with the very thought. She yearned to be a mother. It was even rumored that Duke Jonathan and Duchess Sarah had been nicknamed the *lovebirds*."

"Why?" I inquired, looking at Lady Kathleen with bewilderment.

321

"They seemed to share so much time in the throes of passion – always together within their bedroom chamber," she said. "And then, one day a *miracle* occurred."

"What?"

"Duchess Sarah realized she was at last pregnant—very pregnant indeed," Lady Kathleen said, clearing her dry, raspy throat. "Would you care for more whiskey?" she inquired, passing the bottle in my direction.

I nodded my head as I reached for the bottle. Placing the container to my lips, I abruptly took another long swig of the potent tonic, before handing it over to Lady Kathleen, encouraging her to do the same. "So, Duchess Sarah had another child?" I inquired. "Was that child, me? Is this what happened next?"

"Not exactly. The pregnancy I am referring to, occurred many years prior to your birth. I shall get to the particulars of your birth later on," she said. "It appears that in a moment of weakness, your mother gave into Duke Garrett Worthington's passion. Her lust and zeal finally got the better of her."

"What happened?"

"It all transpired one evening in London," Lady Kathleen replied. "Your mother and I were among some of the most prominent guests in London, attending a Grand Regal Ball at the Royal Palace. Duchess Sarah had initially journeyed to London to have some new clothes made, including a spectacular sapphire-blue ball gown. Unfortunately, your father was in Paris on business. As fate would have it, they would not be together at this elegant soiree."

Pausing once again to clear her throat, she said, "I know from this point forward, you will have many questions. Please feel free to stop me, should I not fully explain myself." I nodded my head as she continued, "Surprisingly, Duke Garrett Worthington and his wife Duchess Martha had also received an invitation to this

Grand Regal Ball. When Garrett set his sights upon your mother, unescorted by Duke Jonathan that night, he planned to take full advantage of the opportunity. Of course, he had to be discreet, since his lovely wife was in attendance, standing dutifully by his side."

"This seems highly unlikely," I said. I thought about how Duke Garrett could possibly flirt and pursue my mother while his wife, Duchess Martha was attached to his arm at this event?"

"Well, as I mentioned earlier, Duke Garrett was accustomed to always getting his way. It seems that he had one of the servants accidentally spill a tray of red-fruited punch upon Duchess Martha. The poor dear. Her lovely saffron-yellow ball gown was hideously stained with the vivid red concoction. Justifiably, Martha was mortified and insisted upon immediately returning home. Needless to say, she left promptly in a carriage - without Duke Garrett."

I nodded, shaking my head in amazement as Lady Kathleen continued her story. "You see, the plot now thickens. The Duke and his wife, Duchess Martha were apparently not getting on very well in their marriage, and the Duchess Martha also desperately wanted a child. However, like your mother, she remained unable to conceive. Duke Garrett also yearned to be a father. He desperately wanted a child – a Worthington heir. Let's just say that in the past, Duke Garrett was willing to have that child with almost any woman who walked the face of this earth, but ever since the day his eyes stumbled upon your mother, it was a very different scenario."

"Different in which way?"

"When he first laid eyes upon your mother, Duke Garrett, swiftly fell in love with her. He only desired for Duchess Sarah to become his bride one day, to be the mother of his children. He was obsessed, and his attraction to your mother was the only thing he could even think about at times."

I remained motionless, paralyzed with shock as I listened to Lady Kathleen's conversation. She paused again, and inquired of me, "Are you sure that I am being clear about all of this? Am I making sense to you?"

"Yes," I murmured.

"Because your mother's desire to desperately conceive had also become an overwhelming passionate quest, the obvious occurred. Inevitably one thing led to another that night."

"How could you possibly know all of this?"

"I was there, attending the ball with Dr. Harrington. I clearly remember cautioning your mother to be wary of Duke Garrett. I warned her to stay as far away from him as possible."

"Did my mother fall in love with Duke Garrett?"

"Far from it. Your mother *never* loved this man."

"I don't understand."

"Hear me out," she demanded. "After the ball, your mother was nowhere to be found. I assumed she returned alone to her London residence at that time. Apparently she did. She was, however, not alone. Garrett and Sarah became intimate strangers from that night forward."

"Am I to believe that my mother conceived triplet boys with another man who she did not love? Duke Garrett Worthington?"

"Sadly, this is the truth. Your mother conceived these boys with none other than, Duke Worthington. This is a fact."

"Where are these triplets? They would be men today."

Lady Kathleen continued speaking, "It was a dreadful pregnancy for your mother. She loved her husband, Jonathan, but was carrying the children of another man. You must be mindful of the fact…before, during and after the pregnancy, Duchess Sarah never loved Duke Garrett. Your mother was beside herself, knowing she had succumbed to her own selfish yearnings and to Duke Garrett's lust and affection. Sarah knew that she acted wrongfully, and she could never tell Jonathan about this

324

rendezvous. You must believe me. Your mother truly loved Duke Jonathan to her death!"

"Who are these triplets? Do I know them today?"

Lady Kathleen could not look me squarely in the eye. She nodded her head as if to say, yes, and then spoke with hesitation, "I believe you know two of them. The third child, however, was rumored to have been so sickly, that he eventually died."

"Tell me their names," I demanded as I abruptly arose from the wooden cot.

Again there was a long pause. Lady Kathleen took a deep breath and sighed aloud, "Lord Kendall and Lord Russell are your brothers."

Patricia Grace Joyce   *The Magic of Time*

Twenty-four

The secrets of a heart and soul
When taking time to hide a truth
And, wound another to the core
Creating anguish and despair
Upon a loved one unaware

I pray for healing deep within
A salve that soothes, a life destined
That I may grow to understand
This meaning of my strife and pain
Becoming whole to love again

Taking the bottle of whiskey to my lips, I swallowed even harder. My mind spun wildly within a haze, as I haphazardly placed the glass vessel upon the cell floor. With my senses increasingly numbed, I felt more prepared to hear almost anything at this point in our conversation.

"This is absurd and absolutely unfounded," I said with belligerence. "Do you really expect me to believe what you are telling me is the absolute truth?" I thought about the lunacy of how I could have ever married my half-brother, Kendall, and to make matters worse, if this was factual, I even had an intimate relationship with my other half-brother, Lord Russell.

"Why was this information concealed from me?" I inquired, growing more humiliated by the second.

"Unfortunately, this is precisely what I have been trying to tell you, but you fail to comprehend the magnitude of this information in full," Lady Kathleen said.

"Are Kendall and Russell aware that I am their half-sister?"

"Absolutely not. They have no idea whatsoever. Listen carefully," she continued. "Your half-brothers are heirs of Duchess Sarah Thornwood and Duke Garrett Worthington, and herein resides the genuine irony. Although the brothers remain unaware, their birthright, rightfully entitles them to both inheritances - Thornwood and Worthington Estates"

"My God! But, what happened to the third child?"

"Dr. Harrington delivered the triplet boys, yet unfortunately, the whereabouts of the third child has never been confirmed," Lady Kathleen replied.

She told me that after the triplets were transferred into the custody of the Worthingtons in London, the third boy was found to be quite ill. Duke Garrett and Duchess Martha were said to have reluctantly surrendered the frail boy into the care of a small convent, located somewhere within the city of London. At some point, the boy was then taken to France, presumably to another convent. "All I can confirm is that the child was terribly ill," she continued. "The London doctors gave little hope of his survival past the first month. Unable to manage this situation, the Worthingtons were hopeful that the nuns at a convent in the remote village of Lourdes, France would be able to intervene and care for the ailing boy, nurturing him back to health. From that day forward, however, no word of the boy has ever been acknowledged." Lady Kathleen further explained, since the child was never heard of again, everyone simply presumed he had passed on.

"Was there ever an official documentation of his death?" I inquired.

"Not to my understanding," she replied. "There is no existing Certificate of Death, and this makes the matter of him still being alive, a very plausible likelihood."

"He's alive?"

"Marcella and Clara absolutely believe this third brother is thriving and even living in London today, yet many probabilities remain. The child may have been given to another family and even undergone a name change as well. We simply have no way of knowing, that is, unless this individual today may have knowledge of the unusual circumstances that surrounded his birth and the days which immediately followed." Lady Kathleen told me that she was always hopeful this third brother might one day, step forward to claim his rightful place within the world as an heir to both Thornwood and Worthington Estates.

"How did this kidnapping actually transpire? Can you give me any more details?"

"Unfortunately, I know everything," she replied. Lady Kathleen revealed to me, that my mother and Dr. Harrington had drafted specific instructions for the disappearance of the three infants, outlining undercover arrangements for the three children to mysteriously vanish. The boys were kidnapped only two days after their birth. Of course, in reality, it was a hoax abduction. Under the light of a full moon, the three infants were taken from the warmth of their cradles at Thornwood Estate and secretly transported eastward to London, arriving within days to the Worthington Estate home. The plan was that they would be adopted by the Worthington family in London. Duke Garrett Worthington was fully aware of these prior arrangements. Dr. Harrington had revealed to Lady Kathleen that all of these plans were premeditated.

"Duke Garrett Worthington openly welcomed these children into his home, for after all, they were his very own flesh and blood," Lady Kathleen continued.

She told me that all of the adoption arrangements were made with Duke Garrett's full knowledge, and Lady Kathleen again assured me this matter was prearranged with both Dr. Harrington's and my mother's consent.

"Did Duchess Martha Worthington have any knowledge of the affair between my mother and Duke Garrett?" I asked.

"Not that I could ever deduce," she replied. "Duchess Martha was never aware of her husband's intimacy with your mother, nor was she cognizant of the clandestine circumstances that transpired with the acquisition of the children."

Lady Kathleen informed me, Martha Worthington was merely overjoyed that Duke Garrett was able to make the arrangements to obtain, not only one newborn child, but triplet boys. And Duchess Martha was always of the understanding that the children were born to one of the royal servants at the palace–a fabrication to conceal the truth. Furthermore, Lady Kathleen explained the prominence and power that Duke Garrett Worthington wielded throughout England. As a prestigious businessman, his wealth commanded great attention and authority.

"Please," I begged. "Tell me more about this tale at the Royal Palace."

"The story emerged that a beautiful servant girl died while giving birth, since it was just too much of a physical stress for her to have endured the birth of the triplets."

"Could there actually have been a palace servant who gave birth to these children?"

"Not in this particular circumstance," Lady Kathleen said. "Grace, I understand that you must be in shock, and that you do not want to believe my words, but I know for a fact, my husband, Dr. Perry Harrington, delivered these three boys at Thornwood Estate. They were birthed from your mother's womb, not by some royal servant."

She told me that the only similarity with Duchess Sarah and this fictitious servant, was that my mother had such tremendous pain and physical distress during the birth, she nearly died.

I sat back, cradling the sides of my head within my hands, as I reflected upon this absurd scenario laid out before me. Looking at

330

Lady Kathleen, I searched her eyes for some clue, or a sign of some other option. She was absolutely right. I really wanted to believe this story could not possibly be the truth. Observing me, Lady Kathleen could only sadly hang her head.

"Let me clarify all that you have spoken," I said to her. "I need to make certain, I am hearing this in the correct vein."

"Go on," Lady Kathleen remarked.

"Duke Garrett Worthington deceived his wife, Duchess Martha Worthington in a covert extramarital affair with my mother, Duchess Sarah Thornwood. My mother gave birth to triplet boys, of which she had actually conceived with Duke Garrett, and not with my father, Duke Jonathan. After the birth of the triplets, Duke Garrett Worthington involved your husband, Dr. Perry Harrington in a secret plot to kidnap the children, thereby enabling Duke Garrett and Duchess Martha to adopt the boys."

"Absolutely!" she exclaimed. "Now you are beginning to see the real picture. It was all rather complicated, not to underestimate the manipulation and gross deceitfulness involved, yet simultaneously this was really quite extraordinary."

She told me there were unforeseen repercussions that no one, would have ever imagined at that time. No one had taken the time, to contemplate any further than the clandestine adoption of the children. The ramifications of this plot far exceeded anyone's conception. What seemed like a foolproof plan to all of those involved, slowly detonated explosions along a wild and furious timeline into the future. She explained, the loss of the three boys actually proved to be quite catastrophic for Duchess Sarah, not to mention, the anxiety and emotional grief that Duke Jonathan experienced.

Lady Kathleen revealed that throughout the passing years, Duke Jonathan truly believed he was the rightful father of the triplets, for he had no reason to ever doubt this. The tragedy of the boys' disappearance was so devastating, that Duke Jonathan was compelled to construct a memorial in their honor, a three-sided room built within Thornwood Estate, that being the drawing room. It served as a place of solace for him to grieve the loss, a destination where he would often retreat to lose himself in his piano music.

"I always thought it rather unique that this room existed," I said. Now I was beginning to understand its real purpose and the deeper meaning behind its construction.

"Your mother, however, was plagued by her ongoing tremendous guilt and remorse."

Lady Kathleen explained that Duchess Sarah, in contrast, found absolutely no comfort within this three-sided room. To her, this room was simply an irritating, abominable reminder of her betrayal and deceit, for she could not bear the fact that she violated her marriage vows.

"It's true, your mother was always shrewd and manipulative, but now she would have to face living her life, carrying the cross of her illicit deeds."

"How horrible!" I gasped.

"Yes," she replied. "And I have lived a long and tumultuous life married to Dr. Perry Harrington, all the while, trying to keep this matter a secret for many, many years. My husband and I did what we had to do at the time."

Lady Kathleen told me, not all physicians had good morals, and some were certainly not good businessmen, that even some had no idea or knowledge as to how to invest their earnings. While numerous medical doctors had no sense for business, others had excellent business heads, surrounding themselves with good investors to assist in making financial choices. Unfortunately, Dr. Harrington was among the prior sector. Lady Kathleen explained to me that she and Dr. Harrington urgently needed financial assistance.

"Duke Garrett Worthington made us an offer that we simply could not refuse at that time. We were desperate for additional income to pay off the many gambling debts that Perry had amassed, and the money that Duke Garrett paid to us was truly a handsome fee – nearly 150,000 pounds."

Lady Kathleen continued, "In exchange for this sizable payment we agreed to enact the plan, discreetly arranging for the disappearance of the three infant boys from Thornwood Estate, yet we were sworn to secrecy, forced to keep quiet to protect this enigma and many other mysteries as well." She told me that Duke Garrett was adamant about them upholding a vow of silence to insure the protection of Duchess Sarah.

"Poor Duchess Sarah," Lady Kathleen continued. She was quite literally having a breakdown from all of the stress and strain in her pregnancy, in addition to the guilt, remorse and deceit she experienced with this overwhelming betrayal."

Lastly, Lady Kathleen revealed that my mother's inability to accept and love the triplets was the icing on the cake, so to speak. In what should have been a very joyous and happy time for most parents, Duchess Sarah was depressed, despondent and overwhelmed with grief when the triplets arrived into this world. After the birth of the triplets, it became increasingly apparent to Duke Jonathan, with the passing days turning to weeks, then into months and eventually years, Sarah was clearly losing her mind—rapidly approaching insanity.

"So, you did it for money?"

"Though, I cannot erase what I have done, I am certainly not proud of my actions, and it appears there is even more that I have grown remorseful of," she replied.

"This is your conscience speaking, Lady Kathleen." I said.

"Yes. You see, I have continuously lived my life in fear, keeping so much hidden from you and all the others."

She persisted by telling me that nearly six-and-twenty years after the birth of the three boys, Duchess Sarah had progressed to a point of debilitating mental illness. She was not of sound mind, and had also become quite physically ill. Lady Kathleen further explained that on one particular occasion, my eternally devoted father, Duke Jonathan sent a coachman into the village of Boscastle to find Dr. Harrington. There seemed to be some difficulty, however, in locating the doctor's whereabouts. Several hours later, when the doctor finally did arrive at Thornwood Estate, Duke Jonathan was livid, engaging in heated conversation with him.

Lady Kathleen told me that Duke Jonathan was more than mildly upset with Dr. Harrington. He repeatedly questioned the doctor regarding his tardiness and delay in responding to his urgent request for a physician.

"What happened next? Was mother all right?"

"As was typical behavior for Dr. Harrington, he was in a state of inebriation and made light of the Duke's cross words." She told me that Dr. Harrington was unfazed by the Duke and proceeded into the privacy of my mother's bedroom chamber, to examine and take care of her, yet while the doctor was within the solitude of the private chambers, something quite unexpected and unforeseen occurred.

"What?" I inquired, anxious to know the fate of my mother.

"Dr. Harrington seduced Sarah."

"My God!" I gasped, grappling with the whiskey bottle. Again, I took a long swig of the mind-altering fluid.

"Your mother had always pleaded she was a victim, totally unaware or accepting of the doctor's advances." Lady Kathleen told me there was a passionate exchange of intimacy between the two of them, and she further elaborated, this was the story according to my mother.

"Duchess Sarah always claimed it was a forced intimacy," she said. "Your mother was well beyond a subtle state of insanity at this point. Who would ever believe her now? I, however, have always had my doubts, knowing the shrewdness that your mother had always possessed and used to her advantage."

"She actually told this to you?" I inquired, with a look of shock upon my face. "How could this occur between my mother and your husband?"

"I still ask myself that very question almost every day. It became apparent, the truth of the matter was, in addition to again destroying her own loving bond with Duke Jonathan, your incoherent mother could not resist destroying my marriage as well. She chose to involve herself passionately with my very own husband, Dr. Perry Harrington. Although I realize that she was not acting as a sole participant, her actions were reprehensible, yet she is not to blame in total. It takes two to create this dance. Today I understand more than I would ever like to admit. My husband played a major role as well – fully taking advantage of a feeble-minded woman."

"But Lady Kathleen, you and my mother were the best of friends," I said.

"So much for friendship," she replied with sadness. "Obviously, your mother had other motives, an agenda that I was unaware of. And for many years prior to her mental illness, she understood that Perry and I were miserably unhappy. It was quite noticeable that our childless marriage was not a blissful one. Your mother fully knew this because I made a point of confiding in her, naïve to her underhanded exploitation. I trusted her. I would tell her everything—all of my joys and sorrows."

"I am so sorry to hear this, Lady Kathleen. If you would prefer, you do not have to say another word. I sense how painful this must be for you."

"Let's just say that throughout the many passing years I have had to learn to move beyond the pain. However, I often wondered why I ever stayed with my husband I now believe that I was merely a frightened soul, drifting through life—lost in the relationship, lost in our marriage and lost within myself. I never had my own identity. I was always Lady Kathleen Harrington, the doctor's wife, and today I truly regret that I did not do more with my life. This is another reason why I have come to see you. You must not follow in my ways, Grace. Too many people live their lives looking for answers on the exterior, rather than looking within themselves to find their personal truths."

Lady Kathleen told me, most people fail to understand that without an identity and purpose in life, no other man or woman will ever suffice to make them happy.

"Happiness comes from within. It is an essence created within the depths of the heart and soul," she said. "One must develop as a whole person before venturing into an intimate romance with another. One must have an identity. When this occurs, then two individuals may successfully come together as independents and unite as a whole, a true partnership with each other - a blissful union."

I listened intently. Even though my situation seemed bleak at Newgate Prison, for an instant I could actually feel myself finding hope within these words that I was hearing.

"Otherwise," she continued. "The union will fail at some point, should an individual not have a true sense of who they really are. Both individuals must come into the relationship as independents, equally whole and healthy individuals, for this union to ever truly flourish and thrive. In doing so, they compliment each other with intellectual interests, their passions and most importantly with tremendous love for each other."

"True love?"

336

"Yes, true love, my dear. When two souls yield to one another, there is mutual respect, a sharing and a giving to each other with open hearts."

I thanked Lady Kathleen for these words of wisdom. I told her that I was still learning with every new day, and although at times it could be frightening, I strove to discover the truth – to develop my own identity, trusting that one day, I would become a part of a loving union - a true partnership.

"You are a gifted woman and have learned your lessons well," Lady Kathleen said.

"I am grateful for the guiding insight of the Higher Powers. But where was Duke Jonathan when my mother was seduced by Dr. Harrington?"

"To complicate matters," she continued. "Duke Jonathan walked into the private bedroom chambers and found both your mother and Dr. Harrington heavily involved in the heated throes of passion. Then low-and-behold, nine months later your mother gave birth to a baby girl."

"Do you mean that I have a sister, too?" Lady Kathleen paused, sitting in silence.

"Continue, Lady Kathleen. Who was this child?"

"This beautiful infant girl was none other than, *you.*

Patricia Grace Joyce   *The Magic of Time*

338

Twenty-five

Deceit, despair and agony
Three words befitting only thee.
And I deserve to know the truth
That yours was all a cunning ruse.

The days of yesterday are gone
And nothing now can right this wrong
But deep within my heart and soul
A second chance shall tell me so

As I stared at her wrinkled face with disbelief, Lady Kathleen continued her story.

"Your mother could not bear to have you disappear from her life, as did the infant triplets. Although she was never able to prove whether you were Duke Jonathan Thornwood's child or the child of my husband, Dr. Perry Harrington, Duchess Sarah always sensed the identity of the true father. After your birth, and in spite of her denials of infidelity, your mother's conscience finally got the better of her. Your mother finally openly confided in me. She knew all along that deep in her heart and soul, you were truly a Harrington and not a Thornwood. Regretfully, since that day of her confession, your mother and I terminated our friendship."

"You are not well," I said, observing Lady Kathleen's paling face and trembling lips.

With tears welling within her eyes, Lady Kathleen replied, "I must continue. You must know the absolute truth. Your mother betrayed me when she chose to become intimate with my husband. She begged for my forgiveness. Yet, at that time I could not find the compassion, nor any reason in my heart to grant her wish."

Lady Kathleen told me, she wanted my mother to feel the pain, the emotional anguish that she, herself, was experiencing at that time. She desired for my mother to take her agony to the grave, telling her, that she could never forgive such an injustice. At that time, Lady Kathleen was consumed with rage for both Duchess Sarah and Dr. Harrington, and explained to me that she carried her fury within her, for far too many years.

"I am sorry this misfortune occurred in your life," I said. "But I feel as if you are somehow blaming me for my mother's gratuitous and self serving actions?"

"Pardon me. That is not my intention, Grace. I only want you to know that I have finally absolved your mother, and I have even forgiven my husband. I believe, one day Dr. Harrington will reap all of the heartache that he has sown, all of the injustices and evil that he has bestowed upon so many. One day, his lust for women, sex and material wealth, shall catch-up with him. My husband is a weary, old man now. With each passing day, I can see that his conscience is getting the better of him. There is nothing more that I can do for him. In my heart, I understand that he suffers from his past misdeeds and infidelities. He does not sleep well at night."

I was speechless and stared at Lady Kathleen in absolute amazement as I searched to find the words...

"Why are you telling me this now? I am baffled as to why you have chosen to come forward and reveal so much to me as I sit awaiting my death. I fear that if you indeed, speak the truth, then my marriage to Kendall was suspect, since we are actually brother and sister. I unknowingly exchanged wedding vows with my very own half-brother!"

"In time, I believe the Higher Powers will confirm my revelations," she said. "I have come forward only for your highest good, to protect you and bring awareness. I am an old woman, Grace. Look at me and see within my eyes, I am speaking the truth."

340

Lady Kathleen told me that she never had motive, or intent to inflict harm upon me, nor to give me false hope. Rather, as time passed over the years, Lady Kathleen was constantly reminded of her duty to come forth—most especially now that her days were numbered. Lady Kathleen encouraged me to share today's disclosures with those individuals who needed to know as well. She believed that one day, Dr. Harrington would be stopped from inflicting any more harm than he had already done.

"I cannot stress enough, the importance of paying heed to my words," she persisted.

I sat in silence and continued to pause, pondering these revelations, Lady Kathleen had brought to me today.

"Do you really think I am so naïve to believe that my mother deceived Duke Jonathan and gave birth to a total of four children with two different men?"

"It is your choice whether to believe, or not," Lady Kathleen replied. "I have laid the truth before your eyes – Lord Kendall, Lord Russell, the missing triplet and yourself are the four children birthed by your mother, the two fathers being Duke Garrett Worthington and none other than my husband, Dr. Perry Harrington."

I could only pray to the Higher Powers that the missing triplet had truly passed on, and was now at peace, for I sensed that any news of his present day whereabouts, would truly serve as another blow to me. Lastly, I was flabbergasted at the possibility that Dr. Harrington could very well be my father.

Nodding her head, Lady Kathleen continued, "You have been kept in the darkness for far too long. Now you need to see the light and understand, all is being revealed for your benefit, for your highest good."

"Do you feel up to hearing more?" she inquired.

I could sense the blood drain from my already paling face. "It is paramount that I hear every word. I must know the entire story."

"I always had suspicions and fears that eventually Duke Jonathan would discover the many deceptions and lies that existed in his marriage with your mother," she continued. "I even thought, like so many of the other villagers, that Duke Jonathan actually was responsible for Duchess Sarah's death – believing that he chose to ruthlessly do away with your mother, throwing her, and himself from the Cornish cliffs, in what had always been rumored to be a murder-suicide. Now I know better, than to have made such an assumption. Throughout the years, I have carried privileged information regarding the true motive of this incident."

"What do you mean?" I could feel my body shivering, my face turning even paler with the sound of these words.

"I know for a fact, it was my husband - your real father, Dr. Perry Harrington who pushed Duke Jonathan from that treacherous cliff during an altercation along the coastal path."

"How could you know this?" I insisted.

"Perry's conscience finally got the better of him, and he admitted this all to me," she said.

I could almost not believe my ears, but I had to embrace the fact that all of which Lady Kathleen spoke of on this day, was the truth. I sensed, the spirit world had sent her to intercede on my behalf during my darkest hours, so that she might bring me the awareness that I had so dearly prayed for.

"Unfortunately, when your mother tried to intervene in the scuffle between Duke Jonathan and my husband, she was accidentally pushed as well. Such a tragedy!" Lady Kathleen continued, arising from the cot as she paced to-and-fro within the cell.

She further elaborated, telling me that Dr. Harrington had never been able to forgive himself for his despicable actions on

342

that day. He was overcome with despair, for it was unlike him to ever let his temper garner the better of himself. To this day, he regretted that he was confrontational and argumentative with the Duke. Dr. Harrington only wished that he could have turned back time and relived that dreadful day, changing fate and destiny.

"Tell me all that you can remember," I said, encouraging her to go on. Lady Kathleen recalled the incident, divulging there was pushing and shoving along the coastal path when Duchess Sarah tried to intervene during this altercation between Dr. Harrington and Duke Jonathan.

"Then, suddenly the Duke stumbled!" she exclaimed.

"Oh, my God!" I said, hanging my head as I prepared for the worst.

"Falling from atop the jagged Cornish cliffs to his death, his body plunged into the raging Atlantic, yet Duchess Sarah also lost her balance. Tragically, her footing slipped from atop the rocky cliffs, thereby, condemning her, as well, to a certain death." I sat in silence and cried as Lady Kathleen rushed to my side, embracing me within her arms.

"This has been such a horrid burden for me to bear over these many years," Lady Kathleen said. "And I can only imagine it has been outrageously unsettling for you to hear all of this revelation this day. The time has finally come for the law to know the truth. I must involve the authorities," she continued. "Constable Nigel Gordon must be made aware of the facts."

"Do you think, perhaps this was all an unfortunate accident?" I inquired.

"I have always wanted to believe that it was purely a mishap, but throughout the years, my heart has been telling me, it may have been premeditated—a death plot against Duke Jonathan so that my husband could freely devote himself to your mother. Today I have reason to believe that Dr. Harrington has become involved with yet, even more deception in London."

343

"What are you saying?"

"I can only construe that Dr. Harrington, Lord Russell, Madame Pucelle, Madam Lindsey and even Elijah Foster have all plotted against you and Lord Kendall, to acquire the Thornwood fortune." Lady Kathleen told me, however, that she perceived with every bone within her frail body that Dr. Harrington and Lord Russell were the masterminds behind Kendall's disappearance.

"Now I fear they have come, implicating you with false evidence in Kendall's death and incriminating you with your magical powers of the craft. You are a strong woman, however, and have resisted their demands and challenges of the past. I feel certain they can only have been surprised that you endured this ordeal so well, and for so long."

Lady Kathleen further explained, she feared something had grown much too large to keep secret in London, and those individuals involved in this plot had intentionally misled the innocent.

"The almighty and endless quest for power, fame, riches and material gain must cease," Lady Kathleen vowed, taking the empty whiskey bottle within her thin hands. With every ounce of her ninety-pound frame, she threw it against the cell door. "At last, it is time for this to finally come to an end."

I shook my head in disbelief, staring at Lady Kathleen, before taking her frail hand within mine. Whispering into her ear, I said, "But Lady Kathleen, with all the woe that has transpired, there is something quite wonderful that still remains for us."

Lady Kathleen stared at me with a peculiar look of bewilderment in her eyes.

"You are actually my stepmother," I blurted aloud.

"Yes, my dear," she replied, kissing me upon my cheek as a tear trickled from the corner of her eye. "However, I am embarrassed to say, I have not been a very good mother to you. For the sake of concealing the many secrets, I have lived in fear for so many years, concerned that Dr. Harrington would do something hurtful to you." She told me that she had forced herself to keep a very low profile, as she could only standby and watch the Lumiere sisters raise me into the beautiful woman that I had now become.

"Before I depart today, you must know one thing - my primary goal shall be to secure your freedom. The time has arrived where I must sacrifice my safety so that you are not injured," she continued, arising from the cot. "This is the least that I can do for you. Regretfully, I shall never be able to make up the lost time to you." Lady Kathleen explained, she was ashamed of the wasted years that she chose to ignore me out of regard for her own personal comfort, and her resentment for my mother's actions.
"Grace," she continued. "Do you think that you could ever find it, within your heart and soul to forgive me?"

I felt as if my head was spinning in a whirlwind as I arose, and hugged Lady Kathleen. "I love you now, as if you have always been my very own mother," I replied. "Of course, you are forgiven," I insisted. "Let us both try to move-on, from this day forward."

I told Lady Kathleen I could not thank her enough for revealing all of this information to me today, that she had finally brought me clarity, peace of mind and knowledge to better understand myself and my life journey.

The days of yesterday were now in the past, and I no longer wanted to waste time focusing my energies upon what once was. I vowed to awaken and appreciate every day as a blessing, cherishing each moment, and continuing to heal my pains through developing myself as an individual.

"I remain hopeful of someday fully loving another soul…unconditionally with compassion and joy. From this day forward, I shall strive to choose love over fear!" I said.

I could see by her drowsy eyes, Lady Kathleen had become increasingly intoxicated as well, consumed not only with whiskey, but with exhaustion as each revelation had been disclosed. Reluctantly, I realized that it was time for her to return to Boscastle, journeying westward again to the tiny village by the sea.

"Before I leave," she said, "I want you to be aware that I am prepared to assist you in any way, shape or form with the charges that have been handed down upon you. Whatever you do, please do not give up hope. Your life may change in an instant. Remember, Clara and Marcella must linger at a distance until it is safe for them to approach the prison. At this time, the likelihood is that they are working from afar to free you. Trust that the risk of the sisters' presence in London is much too great a chance for them to take under the current unstable circumstances, for I feel certain the Constable would surely throw them behind bars as well."

Although I had initially sensed the sisters' inexplicable absence at Newgate prison to be rather puzzling, I had grown to understand the complexity of my situation through Lady Kathleen's revelations.

"But I must ask one thing of you," I said, my eyes tearing as I strained to speak.

"What is it?" she inquired, peering at me with curiosity.

"Believe in my innocence."

Lady Kathleen hugged me, placing a kiss upon my forehead, and said, "Trust in the magic of time."

Twenty-six

If, per chance we have this dance
Could it be more than just per chance?
A meeting of our hearts and souls
A love that bonds to make us whole
Perhaps a vision of romance?
If, per chance...

If it's truly meant to be
Our lives will flourish...you and me
Two souls united in this world
A magical blessing of love unfurled
Perhaps a vision of romance?
If, per chance...

Standing upon the wooden cot, I peered from the tiny cell window into the blazing sunshine, hopeful of one last glimpse of the elegant carriage pulling away from the prison. With a tear in my eye, I sadly waved farewell to Lady Kathleen and returned to pacing the interior of my dingy enclosure. Lady Kathleen had been my first visitor. I prayed, however, that she would not be my last.

With every day that I remained in confinement, I tried to stay focused upon the passing of time within this horrid place, carving a notch in the wood upon my cot by using a sharp stone that had quite fortuitously crumbled from one of the interior walls. It had now been three-and-thirty days, just over a month since that haunting night of my arrival at Newgate Prison. I realized this was negligible for prison time, since many others before me had endured years of dismal waiting, in anticipation of a trial date.

In the recent passing days, I had overheard the guards' ironic referrals to the prison as *The Castle*. I, however, was still locked in solitary confinement, high atop this *Castle*, unable to mingle, nor interact with any of the others who had been accused of similar criminal acts, or dare I say, even worse. In some strange way, I felt my solitary confinement, ironically served to protect me at times from the masses within this hell. The guards had also spoken of the many cells containing well over twenty to thirty women, crowded within a small enclosure. The likes of all kinds, including rogues, and even those despondent souls who had pleaded   innocent   were   amassed   together—murderers, philanderers, debtors, thieves and the oddity of a common displaced housewife.

Each day, it seemed that my reality was increasingly oppressive. Not only was I accused of the murder of my husband, but I had been officially charged with the practice of sorcery. A lady of well means, such as me, was said to be a rare encounter within Newgate, and the likelihood that I could double as a murderer, and a witch, was even more exceptional.

I strived to remain optimistic as the days drifted by, but with no encouraging news and no additional visitors, my thoughts slowly wafted in-and-out of my reality. At times of weakness, I only envisioned my doom, recreating within my mind an image of my body being slowly drawn to the gallows, my neck cuffed with a solid iron necklace, held firmly in place as I stood atop a removable wooden staircase. Under the direction of the Executioner, those stairs would be slid away from beneath my feet, allowing my body to fall freely to my demise. Then with a blink of an eye, my neck would snap, cracking aloud for all of the attending public to hear. My eyes would roll backwards within my head as my limp body dangled for what seemed an eternity, until the last breath and drop of life energy would slowly dissipate from each and every cell of my weary, fragile self. I would be declared

348

dead, yet in actuality, I would only be unconscious …barely breathing.

However, this would not be the end of my torture, for the Executioner would then prepare my body to face the second charge - a witch's death of burning at the stake. My wilted body would hang until the Executioner skillfully secured it to a wooden stake. Piles of faggots would be stacked about me, layer-by-layer. With any compassion, the flames would be so high, the viewing public would be unable to observe my sufferings, granting a *dead* woman some degree of privacy. I shuttered as my imagination swiftly returned me, to the security of my cell.

With each new day, I could only hope that evidence would come to light, awakening the Constable, and thereby enable my freedom from within the clutches of this nightmare. My hair had begun to fall out, and I could only gather this was a result of a combination of factors – lice, malnutrition and the stress of my ordeal. By now, I could feel every bone in my body as I moved my thin fingers along the contours of my rib cage.

Like the sea, my sleep was restless each night as I found myself tossing and turning upon the barren hardwood cot. I had managed to payoff another guard to secure a thin blanket, rumored to have been left behind by a female prisoner who had recently hung at the gallows outside my very window. Once again, the winds billowed to-and-fro within my small cell, announcing the radiance of the full moon, dancing across the skies. I drifted in-and-out of sleep, anxiously awaiting the dawn's morning light, in search of the answers deep within my heart.

This particular night seemed to pass even more slowly than those previously as I entered into a dream state once again. Within this reverie, I observed a team of medical doctors huddled within a bright, candlelit room. Quite bewildered, I found myself standing within the operating theatre of what appeared to be a medical facility.

I observed a surgeon, focusing his attention with great skill, mental concentration and visual acuity over the pale body of a gentleman. Cautiously, I moved closer, nearing towards the operating table, only to realize that this surgeon was none other than, Dr. Christophe Alexis. He was meticulously performing a surgical procedure, carefully cutting upon the gentleman's body with detailed precision. Instantly, pooling brilliant-red blood poured forth from the torso and streamed uncontrollably onto the surrounding white-marble floor.

Without delay, I fetched a large, natural sea sponge and a bucket of warm water that rested within the corner of the room. Crouching upon my hands and knees, I attempted to swath the oozing red fluid, absorbing the crimson blood as it rapidly collected all around me. Dr. Alexis kneeled down upon the floor next to me and placed his hand upon my shoulder as I observed the glimmer of a tear falling from his eye. I could feel his overwhelming pain as I positioned my arm around his shoulder, embracing him as I softly spoke in an effort to soothe his soul.

"You did the best that you could, Christophe."
Taking me within his arms, we kneeled together in silence, positioned upon the floor of the operating theatre.

"This was Kendall's time to cross over," I continued, still caressing the doctor's slumped body within my arms. We are truly spiritual beings, merely trying to live a human existence on this earth. When it is our time, we are called forth by the Higher Powers to cross over. We must move forward and answer that call. There is nothing to fear, for we return once again to our spiritual form and journey homeward. There is no death. The soul lives forever. The soul is eternal."

"Such calming words of consolation, Grace," he said. "You, of all people, have always been here for me with compassion, truth and encouragement. Your healing energy and love have been a radiant beacon of light in my darkest hours, a tremendous support for me. I so often see such pain, grief and despair in life. You have helped me to view my life differently, becoming more aware of the light of life, this healing energy that exists within every one of us, within each and every soul."

The darkness of nightfall opened to the lightness of a new day as I awakened from my dream.

"This can only be more revelation," I murmured, as I stared upward, towards the shadowed ceiling within my cell. Recollecting the dream, there was so much blood, and it was none other than, Kendall's blood upon Dr. Alexis's hands, dripping upon the operating table and onto the marble floor. I thought about the overwhelming grief, anxiety, emotion and turmoil that resonated from within the doctor's voice. Now I understood more of what needed to occur in my life. The magic of the Higher Powers once again was bringing forth disclosure. I discerned that Dr. Alexis must have attempted to assist Kendall in his darkest hour.

"He tried to save my husband's life," I mumbled aloud.

The dream guided me to understand that Dr. Alexis's profession as a surgeon and physician had a multitude of challenges, and the suffering of others was an emotional darkness of which I believe haunted the doctor. Furthermore, Dr. Alexis was a caring, compassionate soul and fully recognized this despair deep within his heart and soul.

I too, had felt his compassion and empathy. Now more than ever, I viewed a clearer image of the role that I must play in conjunction with Dr. Christophe Alexis within this lifetime. His passion for medicine and his desire to selflessly assist others in their time of need was absolute confirmation—we were both healers in our own right.

Quite unexpectedly, my attention was distracted as I heard the familiar pounding of heavy footsteps, approaching in the direction of my cell. As I listened to the recognizable jingling of the guard's keys, I grew anxious, hearing a set of additional footsteps echoing in the distance. I wondered who was there, and what business this person might have had to draw them within the bowels of Newgate Prison. With these very thoughts, I could hear the footsteps continuing to increase in volume. As they grew noticeably louder, I sat upright, repositioning my body upon the cot.

"Who could this be?" I murmured, fearfully. "And what has fate planned for me on this occasion?"

Within moments, I heard the guard shuffling his feet outside my cell door. The sound of the key within the metal lock scraped the interior keyhole as he motioned to insert it. With a twist of his wrist, the key screeched, unlocking my cell. I stood upright, frozen with fright, cowering within the cobwebbed corner, for I could only imagine more dismal news, though, my heart longed for a ray of hope. The cell door suddenly swung open with a loud creaking noise as my eyes watered, preparing for my doom.

But my entire face lit up with excitement and I could hear my heart racing with anticipation. Before me stood the massive guard, and a handsome youth, not more than thirteen years of age. I could only wonder of his identity and the purpose of this visit, that is, until I viewed a parcel within his hand.

"It seems yaw have gotcha self a visitor, Lady Witch," the guard said, as he stood boldly within the frame of the cell doorway.

"Are yaw Lady Grace Worthington?" the handsome youth inquired meekly, gazing in awe upon me as I crouched disheveled within the darkened shadows.

"Who wants to know?" I inquired, leery of the boy's intentions.

"Well, madam. Yaw see, I can't but read much. All I know is dat this here lot tis from the law. The Constable, his self, has sent it from the Old Bailey to be delivered to yaw. I have come thru this God awful place, jus ta find yaw. So, here it tis, and if yaw tis truly Lady Grace Worthington, then me job tis over."

352

"Indeed," I said, now standing upright to approach the courier. "And who might you be, my dear child?" I inquired, extending my hand from a distance, still untrusting of his purpose as I reached for the securely wrapped packet of papers.

"Hanley Pennifeather, madam. If yaw look here on the envelope, maybe yaw can figure out who could be send'n it. Here yaw go, madam. I must be on me way now. I haft another delivery to make within the city before nightfall. Then I be off for me mum's place in Brighton."

I smiled, gently taking the bundle from the young court messenger, thanking him as I heard the guard jingle his keys impatiently.

"Before you depart, may I request a small favor of you, Hanley?"

"I suppose, madam. What tis it?"

"I desire for you to deliver one last message to a dear friend in the city," I gently pleaded as my eyes welled with tears.

"Yaw needn't cry, madam. Go on," he continued.

"Please tell the surgeon, Dr. Christophe Alexis…that I love him."

"Yaw wish tis granted. I shall carry yaw words to him."

"Thank you," I said as my emotions overwhelmed me. I hugged dear Hanley and whispered into his ear. "With the magic of time, all will be well. There is nothing to fear, when you listen to your heart."

Suddenly, the guard briskly intervened, separating the child from my embrace. Firmly grabbing the boy by the arm, he approached the cell door. However, before exiting, I could not help but notice, Hanley quickly gazed over his shoulder, and looked into my eyes with a smile beaming upon his face, and a glimmer of hope in his eye. Gruffly, the guard shuffled the boy out of the cell, taking great pleasure in slamming the door, and shouting, "Farewell, Lady Witch."

353

My eyes searched the envelope, front-and-back for a return address. In what seemed like the passing of merely seconds, I could hear the young courier outside my window, mounting his horse and vanishing from the main entry of the prison as the sound of the horse's gallop grew faint until disappearing into nothingness.

Studying the parcel, I thought that it was odd; there was no return address on the exterior of the bundle. I cringed, pausing before opening it. As I removed the outer leather wrapping, the parcel revealed several legal documents and enclosures with evidence of an official seal. Additionally, there was a letter written on elegant white parchment. It clearly was addressed in my name.

Sitting upon my wooden cot, I took a deep breath and sighed aloud as I prepared myself for everything, and anything. At last, I determined from the signature that it was correspondence from none other than, Constable Nigel Gordon. Could he possibly have more information concerning Kendall and the investigation? If so, what if this was substantiation to further implicate me? I wasted no time in reading the document.

Ten November, 1811

Dear Lady Grace,

Since the disappearance of your husband, Lord Kendall Worthington nearly a year ago, I must declare, this case has always been in the forefront of my mind. Your husband's sudden and mysterious disappearance was an odd situation, quite strange, yet not uncommon when I considered the unhappy marital life you both shared. I must also admit, I had always suspected that you played a key role in this case.

In light of the evidence and information I recently received, however, I am writing to you with sincere apologies and regret. I only hope you may find it in your heart to forgive me for my inaccurate assumptions.

354

Firstly, I must remorsefully inform you of the death of your husband, Lord Kendall Worthington. Enclosed is the death certificate officially confirming and validating his passing.

Additionally, there seems to have been an unusual situation regarding your husband's death, involving a clandestine medical venture in London. The court has secured a sworn statement from an informant who appears to be a blood relation to Lord Kendall and Lord Russell – a third brother. His knowledge of a plot to kill Lord Kendall was paramount for a breakthrough in this case. Although this news may be somewhat of a shock to you, this informant is none other than, Dr. Christophe Alexis. Additionally, we have offered the doctor protection, fearing any reprisals against him from the alleged suspects.

Apparently Lord Russell Worthington played a major role in what we have now determined to be an extortion plan to attain your monies and also a new identity through a bizarre physical transformation involving a series of surgical procedures.

The true motive for Lord Kendall Worthington's disappearance, involved greed, lust, vanity and deception at any cost. It appears, there had been an ensuing rivalry over the many passing years between your husband and his brother, Lord Russell. They both challenged each other for status, prestige, physical beauty, wealth and even the love of the same woman - that being you, Lady Grace.

Furthermore, there is evidence to implicate Dr. Perry Harrington, a local brothel madam known as Madame Lela Pucelle, Madam Lindsey Lumiere and an African man who goes by the name of Elijah Foster. Unfortunately, all five suspects are nowhere to be found within the city at this time. Word on the streets, however, substantiates they have departed London to relocate in Paris. Although England is actively involved in war with France at this time, I assure you that we shall conduct a search in Paris, developing further clues to locate and apprehend these offenders.

There is no longer any doubt in my mind that you are an innocent victim in this case. I hereby grant you a Pardon by Clergy, with the blessing of Bishop Samuel Bartholomew.

It would be my pleasure to convey the facts of this case further to you. Your release from Newgate Prison is to take place at sunrise. For the time being, please know that I will await your instructions regarding the details of your husband's funeral and burial arrangements.

May God be with you,

Constable Nigel Gordon
London, England

I could not believe the words that had been inked boldly upon the parchment as I continued to read the letter again, and again. I was in awe as I stared into space, lost in thought. A third brother was indeed, truly alive.

"What good fortune!" I screamed aloud, elated by the news. I was absolutely shocked. Dr. Christophe Alexis was the missing triplet, and now a half-brother to me. It was paramount that I showed my appreciation for all of his efforts in coming forward to present evidence with Kendall's case. There was so much to still discuss, yet it was my primary focus to meet with Dr. Alexis again upon my release, for his intervention and the Bishop's pardon had truly saved me from the unspeakable horrors of the gallows and burning at the stake.

This letter was beyond my wildest expectations; however, it confirmed many of my ongoing suspicions. Although questions remained concerning Elijah and what role he could have possibly have played in all of this, I surmised that he must have been responsible for kidnapping Kendall. All along, I had wanted to believe in Elijah's innocence, that his disappearance was an action, fearful of the repercussions from his master on that night in question. Regretfully, this letter revealed that Elijah Foster was far from above suspicion.

The experiences of the past harrowing year had brought me full circle to a new awareness in my life—beginning with my intimacies with Bishop Samuel Bartholomew and Elijah Foster, Kendall's disappearance, the letter announcing Madame Pucelle's pregnancy and her self-proclamation as Kendall's mistress, the encounter with Dr. Christophe Alexis after my fall, the news of my pregnancy and the unexpected death of my unborn child, the maiming of Mr. Abernathy by Lindsey, my healing abilities manifesting forth in saving his life, Lady Kathleen's revelations with the news of my parents' true demise, the love triangles that had transpired, the knowledge of my blood relation to the Worthington brothers as a half-sister and my relation to Dr. Harrington as his daughter, my ongoing prophetic dreams – most importantly, the reverie which revealed Dr. Alexis's efforts to save my husband's life, Kendall's eventual passing, and now the efforts of Bishop Samuel Bartholomew assisting the law to free me. Lastly, this shocking declaration of the identity of the missing third Worthington brother as Christophe, found me overjoyed, and in a state of elation within my tiny cell.

Through my many dreams, so many revelations had manifested forth from the spirit world, urging me onward from beyond the veil. So much of what the Lumiere sisters had spoken of, appeared to have truly occurred within its own time – both the benevolent and the evil.

I was released from Newgate Prison at sunrise on the morning of eleven November, 1811, nearly a year after that haunting night of fifteen November, 1810. The night in question had initially unraveled my life, turning me inside out, only to bring forth what I now recognized were magnificent blessings of awareness, enabling my personal transformation. I had become fully cognizant that my identity as Grace Worthington departing Newgate Prison on this morning was quite different from the woman I was, nearly a year ago. Looking back towards the

357

daunting prison tower, I gazed long and hard at what had been a period of captivity that I would not soon forget.

Moving towards the exterior prison gates, I observed in the distance a tremendous gathering, a crowd of onlookers who had convened outside the prison, yet my thoughts were quickly distracted, melting into a state of euphoria as I turned around. My eyes were fixated upon the unforeseen, for I could only yell out in joy at the vision set before me.

"Thank the Higher Powers it is truly you, my dear friend!"

Dr. Christophe Alexis extended his elegant hand, pulling my frail body closely to enfold me within his arms. With tears in our eyes we walked together in the direction of his awaiting black coach.

The approving roar of the crowd grew deafening as they chanted aloud, "Queen of Hearts, Queen of Hearts…Queen of Hearts!"

We paused, staring upward into the distant eastern sky. Vibrant colored ribbons of safflower, aqua and lavender clouds streamed across the horizon and reflected within our enamored eyes. The autumn sunrise announced the awakening of a new day and our stirring unbridled passion. We were not merely two individuals drifting aimlessly through time on this earth. Destiny had at last, brought our souls together for a distinct purpose. We both had grown to understand that when we learn through the experience of actually feeling our pain and suffering, we may only then begin to truly value the meaning of love. I believed Christophe and I were destined to heal, not only each other, but to touch the lives of many others on life's journey into the future.

Christophe's lips softly caressed mine as he pulled me closer into his embrace. He sighed and whispered softly into my ear, "I love you, Grace."

"And I love you," I said, taking his hand into mine.

As the crowd continued to celebrate my release, Christophe's penetrating gaze peered deeply into my eyes. I succumbed to tears of joy, feeling a tingling sensation of exhilaration dancing throughout my entire being. The gentle essence of his compassionate adoration fully enveloped me. At last, our souls had been reunited as he took pause and whispered softly into my ear.

"With the magic of time, all will be well. There is nothing to fear when we listen to our hearts." Locked in tender embrace, I gazed upward into the radiant morning sky...when all of a sudden, the clouds darkened, and the winds wisped furiously as two large black ravens appeared, circling ominously overhead. I could hear Christophe's heart pounding as he held me closely within his arms, as I am certain he could also hear mine.

I clung to him as we swiftly advanced towards the safety of the carriage. Without any warning, however, the sound of gunfire cut through the excitement of the crowd. Instantly their bellowing grew silent. I was confused, disoriented as to what was occurring, as Christophe's body slumped forward, falling clumsily into me. "Christophe! No!"

I struggled to support his weight, holding him within my arms, until he collapsed upon the earthen ground. As I knelt down beside his lifeless body, I cradled his bloodied head within my aching arms...rocking my body to-and-fro in a state of shock.

"Speak to me...please, Christophe"

At last, an onlooker approached as I desperately gazed upward, only to be startled by the presence of a woman wearing what appeared to be a masquerade costume...a long black gown with a mask of brightly colored ornamental feathers surrounding her face.

"Help me...please." I cried out desperately.

The masked woman stood frozen, barely budging an inch in response to my pleading, until suddenly her right hand revealed a smoking single-shot pistol. As she dropped the weapon to the ground, her left hand suddenly revealed a second single-shot pistol from the pocket within the deep folds of her elegant dress.

"If I cannot have him, no one will…"

"Who are you?" I screamed, until suddenly the shrill tone of her voice brought forth total recollection to my consciousness. I wondered how this could be happening, as I panicked, sprawled upon the ground beneath her feet.

"Stop Lindsey! I beg for your mercy!"

"You must be destroyed!" she screamed at me.

In a jealous rage, Lindsey stared blindly within my eyes. Steadying her aim, she fixated the gun upon me. I heard the sound of the pistol, cock backwards in preparation for firing…when to my utter amazement, the trigger suddenly jammed. I swiftly stood upright, taking this opportunity to invoke my magic, casting a powerful incantation as I raised my hands upright and twirled my numb body round-and-round about her.

Beyond the veil…beyond the veil
The Higher Powers weave this tale
Declaring all that's meant to be,
I hereby set your spirit free…

Within seconds, Lindsey re-cocked the gun, this time taking aim, but holding the gun to her very own head. The blast of gunfire deafened my ears, as I suddenly fell faint to the ground. The darkness of swirling shadows immediately filled my eyes as I felt my soul drifting through a voided space until reaching the familiarity of brilliant rapidly whirling colors…a journey through time.

"On the count of three, you will fully awaken as Graziella Fortuna, departing the past to fully return into the present lifetime with total recall of the experience. One...two...three."

My heavy eye lids slowly opened as I peered upward into the pristine face of Dr. Alexander. The sound of his soft, soothing voice was music to my ears, surrounding me once again in a blanket of compassion.

"Welcome back!" he exclaimed as tears welled within his eyes.

"What tremendous words of revelation you have spoken on this night!"

With my gaze still fixated upon Dr. Christopher Alexander's eyes, I sat upright upon the couch as he simultaneously repositioned himself comfortably beside me. My emotion consumed me as I wept uncontrollably.

"Christopher, hold me," I said, taking his hand within mine.

"You are back where you belong, Graziella...right here with me."

As the tape recorder continued to record the sounds and conversation of the night, I suddenly realized this experience had truly been a turning point not only for me, but for the doctor as well.

Embraced within his arms, I felt as if I had known this man my entire life, or perhaps, even forever. Together we reclined upon the couch as his elegant fingers played with the zipper upon the bodice of my black cocktail dress. Swiftly, he pulled in a downward motion, revealing my bare shoulders, until exposing my breasts. I could feel his warm, soft lips gently kiss my flesh as I, in turn, unbuttoned his starched white shirt and unbuckled his black leather belt until motioning with my fingers to unzip his blue jeans.

"I feel as if I have known you a million years," he said, caressing my body within his firm arms. But I need to tell you something," he said as he paused to look into my eyes.

361

"Please…don't talk. Just kiss me." As he pulled me closer, I could feel his arousal, and I knew he too, could sense every bit of mine.

"I have always loved you," he moaned. "So much that, I almost feel guilty saying this." He took my hand within his.

"What is it?" I asked, curiously peering into his eyes.

"I don't know how to tell you, but the envelope on your car tonight…well, I'm embarrassed to say that I actually…" he said with pause, then seductively kissed my breast.

All of a sudden, the increasing arousal within the room was suddenly cut by the interruption of the ringing of a doorbell.

"Damn it! He sighed. "Stay here, I'll be right back."

"Wait! I need you to tell me…to explain."

Swiftly tearing himself from my embrace, he arose from the couch and zipped-up his jeans.

"Who could be here at this ungodly hour of the night?" he mumbled.

"But…"

"I love you, Graziella," he replied seductively as he turned around. As he exited the room, I could feel my body tingling from head-to-foot. I rolled my head back upon the soft white-leather cushion as I wondered about his statement, but my fantasies took hold of me. I wanted this man now, more than ever, and I knew he would have me tonight. In the background, I could hear him unlock and open the front door. A woman's loud voice broke the silence.

"I have come to finish what you started!" she shouted as rage exploded from her within her being. Suddenly the passion and serenity of this night was transformed into an angry monster.

"Rachel! No! Stop! I can explain," the doctor screamed.
What seemed only a split-second brought forth the penetrating sound of a gunshot filling the warm night air.

362

I was stunned, dazed as I yelled aloud, "Christopher!" Then, another loud shot rang out, and only an eerie silence remained as I stumbled, making my way to the front porch. I could never have envisioned what was soon to present itself on this night. Not only was Christopher lying lifeless in a crimson pool of his very own blood, but an unfamiliar blonde-haired woman was sprawled upon the sidewalk, with a gaping orifice upon her forehead releasing a bloodied river.

In a surreal state of mind, I collapsed to the ground, groping at the doctor's listless body as my hands cradled his bloodied head within my lap. Rocking to-and-fro, I sobbed in disbelief as the radiant glow of the full moon beamed downward upon my hands. Dripping in Christopher's blood, I suddenly realized that something strange, odd, something quite extraordinary was transpiring as my eyes quickly discerned…a physical change. Six fingers now extended from each of my hands.

"My God! The magic!"

Swiftly, I raised my bloodied hands, reaching upward into the night sky, each finger now fully bathed within the incandescent glow of the brilliant full moon as I smiled upon one luminous star. I understood, my life would never be the same from this moment forward…that I must bring Christopher back to life. My fingers appeared iridescent as I placed my hands with care upon his forehead, covering the gashing wound, and I chanted aloud.

Surround our souls in truth tonight
As darkness fades to morning light
And, never more to fear what's right
Our love does yearn to reunite

Instantly, Christopher stirred, miraculously awakening from death's hold as he gazed lovingly into my eyes. I caressed him in my arms, sobbing joyfully. No words could express my

363

ecstasy…no words, until the sound of his melodic voice softly transformed the hanging silence, whispering to my soul as my heart felt his compassion fully embrace me once again.

"With the magic of time, all will be well. There is nothing to fear when we listen to our hearts. For, it is in choosing to love, that we learn to confront our greatest fears."

The End